Jean Patrick sauntered over to her . . .

"You handled him very well," he told Michaella with admiration. "A persistent cuss, wasn't he?"

Gripping her reticule tightly in order to keep from striking him with it, Michaella flashed him an angry glance. The rude gambler hadn't bothered her nearly as much as seeing Jean Patrick merely sit back and watch from a safe distance.

"Well, I was certain you weren't going to offer any help on my behalf," Michaella said, her voice shaking. "Why did you decide to come over here now—because it's all clear?"

Jean Patrick smiled. "Yes, it is safer," he admitted with a teasing light in his eyes. "But not from you."

Startled by the caress in his tone, Michaella jerked her head back up to look at him. In the gauzy light afforded by river mist and twilight, Jean Patrick was even more handsome than ever—a most dangerous fact, she decided . . .

SAVAGE RIVER

D0424487

Other books in the Women of the West series

BLUE FIRE
by Emma Harrington

SILVER EYES
by Laurel Collins

Published by
PAGEANT BOOKS

E.P. MURRAY

PAGEANT BOOKS

Publisher's Note: This is a work of fiction. The characters, incidents, and dialogues are products of the author's imagination and are not to be construed as real. Any resemblance to actual events or persons, living or dead, is entirely coincidental.

PAGEANT BOOKS
225 Park Avenue South
New York, New York 10003

Cover artwork by Franco Accornero

Printed in the U.S.A.

First Pageant Books printing: January, 1989

10 9 8 7 6 5 4 3 2 1

Here's a sigh to those who love me,
And a smile to those who hate;
And, whatever sky's above me,
Here's a heart for any fate.

To Thomas Moore
—Lord Byron

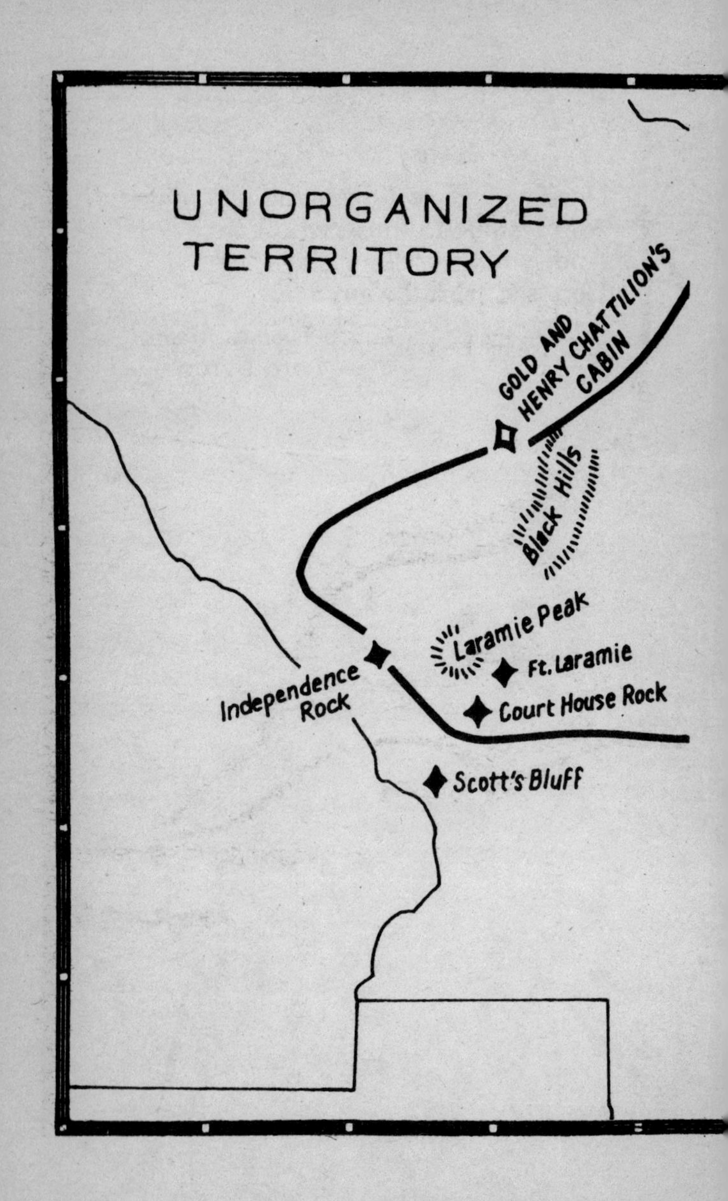
UNORGANIZED
TERRITORY
GOLD AND
HENRY CHATTILION'S
CABIN
Black Hills
Laramie Peak
Ft. Laramie
Court House Rock
Independence
Rock
Scott's Bluff

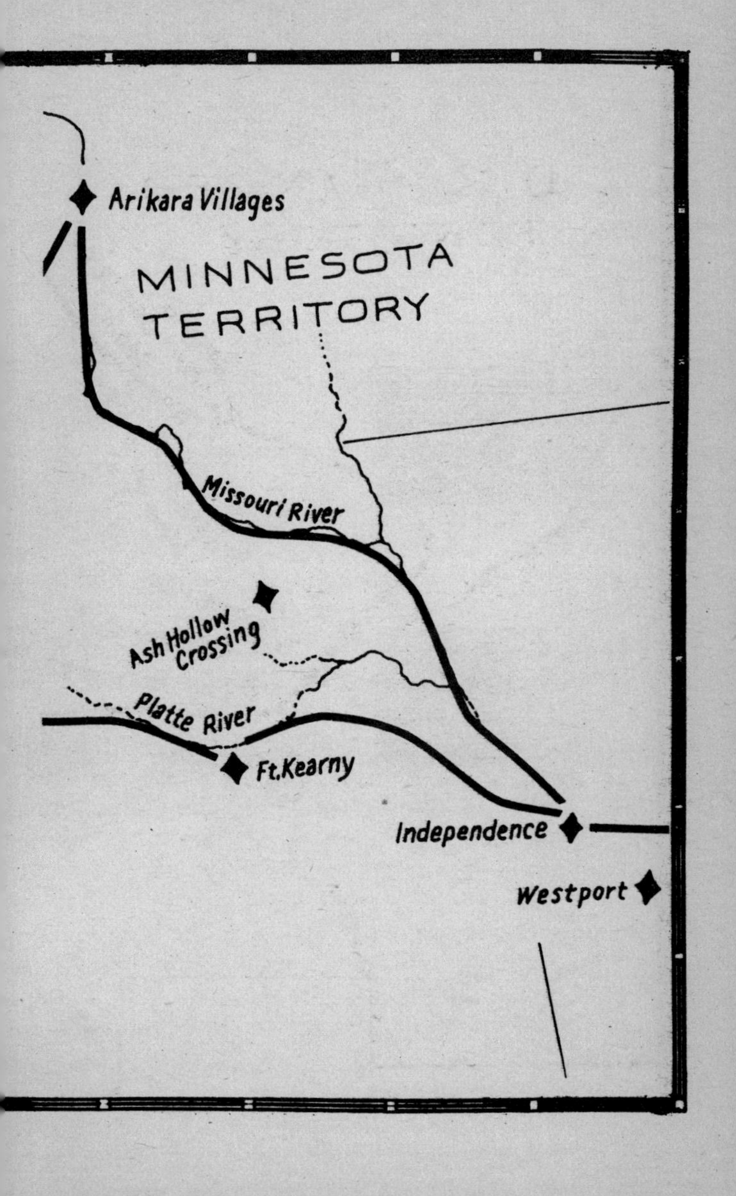
Arikara Villages
MINNESOTA
TERRITORY
Missouri River
Ash Hollow
Crossing
Platte River
Ft. Kearny
Independence
Westport

SAVAGE RIVER

Chapter One

✦✦✦✦✦

Manchester, England
October 1848

IN THE STUDY of Crestmore Manor, the brass carriage clock on the mantel struck twelve noon. On the cliffs below, the wind shrieked and waves crashed against the rocks in turbulent foam. Elizabeth Wright, the respected widow of Captain Jonathan Wright, was struggling with emotions as turbulent as the weather outside, and she paced the floor in great agitation. It was almost time.

Her austere features were set in a grim mask under the wisps of graying hair as she waited with mounting trepidation. Her bony hands were knotted together, twisting a lace handkerchief into an unrecognizable rag. The source of her agitation was the upcoming visit of her nephew, Nolan Ketchman. She had no wish to see him, but she had no choice in the matter.

How had it come to this? How could her late

husband's reputation and fortune now rely on a man such as Nolan Ketchman? But it did. Nolan had made it quite clear that if she refused to give him an interview, she would suffer the probable loss of her fortune as well as the good name of her husband and a sizable interest in the Intermountain Fur Company. That would never do. Jonathan had worked hard, cofounding the company and compiling a fortune by supplying Britain with beaver and other types of pelts from the vast region of uncharted territory west of the Mississippi in the new America.

Now that the fur trade was nearly finished and the company was changing, becoming involved in new wealth-producing ventures, Elizabeth feared that her nephew would use her inexperience to take her share of the profits.

Pausing in her pacing, Elizabeth gripped the back of a chair with white-knuckled fingers and stared blindly out the huge windows overlooking the sea. Years before, Captain Wright had removed his nephew from the fur company partnership when he'd discovered that the young man was attempting to embezzle funds. Now that the captain was gone, Ketchman was determined to grasp his late uncle's fortune. He had sent his aunt a terse letter assuring her that he was privy to secrets that would cause the Wright name considerable grief; hence she had no choice but to meet with him.

Turning away from the window, Mrs. Wright thoughtfully regarded the small locked teakwood box resting on her study table. After keeping its contents secret for nearly ten years, she was certain that somehow her nephew had obtained a copy of the map held inside. If this was true, the entire tale would be revealed, disclosing Elizabeth Wright's breach of trust in the matter of the two young women entrusted to her care after their mother's death.

Straightening her bent shoulders, Elizabeth turned at the sound of carriage wheels in the drive. He was here. She stepped to the front window and peered out as Ketchman descended from the landau. He was tall, with a loose frock coat that hung awkwardly from his thin frame and dangled about spindly legs as he turned toward the door. Elizabeth narrowed her eyes, watching Ketchman purse his lips in a tuneless whistle and adjust his beaver top hat over thinning dark hair. A gold-studded cane tapped against the cobblestone path as he sauntered to the front door. Elizabeth snorted derisively. Such an affectation for a man of only thirty years! Did he think it lent him dignity?

"Fool," she muttered, moving away from the window so that she could face Ketchman when he entered.

"And a pleasant good day to you, Aunt," Ketchman greeted, as he swept his top hat from his head and walked into the study.

"Please, Nolan," was the abrupt answer, "spare me your contrived courtesies. Let us attend to the matter at hand, shall we?"

"Aren't you going to offer me a refreshment, Aunt?"

Elizabeth turned her head. "Help yourself to whatever you can find. You always do."

A sneer curled his mouth as Ketchman poured

himself a glass of wine from the decanter atop a sideboard. After gulping the first glass, he poured a second, then twirled the glass stem between his fingers as he contemplated his aunt's averted face. She was staring out the window, her arms folded across her chest and her narrow frame held close, as if to protect herself against a strong wind. Nolan sipped his wine, dark eyes darting from Elizabeth to inspect the room. His eyebrows held fast in two lines that seemed to crush down upon his lids. Strands of thinning hair fell over his forehead, and he had a nervous habit of running his fingers through it to smooth it down. This only served to make it more unruly, so that he was constantly alternating between smoothing his hair and sipping his wine.

Irritated by his delay, Elizabeth let out a heavy sigh of impatience designed to attract Ketchman's notice. He finally withdrew a fragment of map from the voluminous pocket of his frock coat, then studied it carefully as if he had not seen it for some time. The paper was crisscrossed with lines designating wilderness trails in the lands west of the Mississippi. These lines appeared to break off raggedly at one end of the map. Finally, he looked up from the paper.

"Did you ever find the other half of the map, Aunt? I desperately need the remaining segment."

Elizabeth's lips pinched in disapproval, and her brows lifted. "I have told you before, there was never any second half to the map. It arrived with one edge torn thus. I believe it is possible that the scribe who sent the accompanying letter made off with the remaining piece himself."

"Do you? Odd that the missing piece is quite likely the portion in which the location of the gold is shown. . . ."

"My, but you have a sharp intellect, Nolan," Elizabeth observed tartly. Her sarcasm did not miss its mark, and she almost smiled with pleasure when Ketchman's thin cheeks flushed with anger.

"Open the box!" he ordered brusquely.

"Why? It appears you've seen the contents before."

"I want you to open it again—or shall I take it upon myself to do so?"

Sending a harsh stare at her nephew, Mrs. Wright walked to the desk and unlocked the lid of the teakwood box. Replacing the key in the cuff of her mutton-sleeve dress, she merely watched as Ketchman sorted through the contents. Nothing had changed. The letter and the original segment of map from which she was certain he had made his copy were all that the box contained.

A tiny smile tugged at the corners of her mouth as her nephew gave the box an angry shake. He set it down and stared into it as if he could force the piece he sought to magically appear. Elizabeth's disdain grew as she watched her foppish nephew's frantic search. Finally she could contain herself no longer.

"Have your eyes failed you, Nolan? Is there no way for you to understand that what's there is there, and nothing more?"

The lid slammed down with an angry snap, but Ketchman refused to rise to the bait.

"Could you tell me, Nolan," she purred, "now that the secret is out, how you managed to secure entry into that box?"

Ignoring her question, Ketchman turned to stare at his aunt with blazing eyes. "You're certain you don't have something hidden elsewhere?"

She spread her hands in a deprecating gesture, almost laughing aloud with secret glee at his frustration. "There is nothing else to hide."

A derisive smile curled his lips for a moment. "I suppose it doesn't really matter, not under the circumstances."

She stiffened. "I suppose it doesn't."

Ketchman's smile remained fixed. He had grown accustomed to his aunt's aversion of him years ago, but the concerns of a spindly old woman did not bother him in the least. He was on his way to a fortune—her fortune—and there was nothing she could do to stop him. A small moment of bitterness was allowable under those circumstances, he supposed, if that was how she wished to play it.

Privately, Nolan Ketchman was forced to recognize that not everything was entirely into place yet. All the little details still remained untidy, and he must take care of them if things were to go as planned. In fact, this was only the beginning—much more needed to come his way if he was to succeed in recovering that fortune. The last remaining piece of his plan, the most important piece by far, lay in the hands of the two young women who resided with his aunt. It was their father who had drawn the map and who knew the whereabouts of the gold—that is, if he was still alive.

Ketchman cleared his throat. "Do you think Michaella and Mary Catherine would enjoy an ocean crossing if they believed their father was still alive?"

Shrugging, Elizabeth Wright gave him a hard glance. "I have no doubt that Michaella would wish to sail immediately. It would be difficult for Mary Catherine to break her ties here, however. But in the end, I am certain she would elect to accompany her sister."

A small smile pressed at the corners of his mouth as Ketchman regarded his aunt closely. "Do you suppose old Henry Chattilion is still wandering about in those rugged American mountains?" he asked in an idle tone that didn't fool the woman for a moment.

"That is impossible to say. The letter and part of the map are all one has to go by, and they are a number of years old."

The point of Ketchman's gold-studded cane twirled in a small circle, then he snapped, "You know more than you are telling me!" He stepped closer, the cane thumping to the floor as he leaned on the engraved head and narrowed his eyes. "You know that old Henry is indeed still alive! Am I correct?"

"Nonsense!" Elizabeth Wright drew herself into an indignant knot, but there was a faint gleam of triumph in her eyes as she said, "I lay claim to no such knowledge. You are a fool, Nolan, an incomparable fool. You have as much as I do to go on. Why don't you just travel over the ocean and go into the mountains yourself? *Why* do you need Henry Chattilion's daughters?"

Lifting one dark brow, Ketchman inquired icily, "And why should I wander aimlessly about the wilderness when the Chattilion girls can lead me directly to their father? If he is alive, they will surely find him. And then, my dear aunt, I will have the gold. . . ."

The triumphant gleam in Elizabeth's eyes began to fade, and there was a crack in her composure as she stared hard at her nephew. He was determined to rob her of what was rightfully hers, and she felt helpless to stop him. If it were not for Nolan Ketchman, Henry Chattilion's daughters would never learn whether their father was still alive somewhere in those distant mountains. Nor would they have reason to suspect that he had discovered gold, gold that might otherwise go to *her* estate. And now her smug, impudent nephew stood there gloating, thinking he was going to force her to atone for her past treatment of him! Well, the pompous wretch had better think again if he thought he would easily best her! No, he would have to work much harder at it than he'd planned.

"Nolan, I have just decided to thwart your plan," she rapped out suddenly. "I refuse to tell Michaella and Mary Catherine a single thing you wish me to say! And you, my dear nephew, may go to the bloody devil!"

Recoiling from the abruptness of her refusal, Nolan nonetheless found her defiance faintly amusing. Adversity made victory all the sweeter.

"May I, Aunt? My, aren't we working ourselves into a dither?"

"Leave my house at once!"

Ketchman's thin lips stretched into an unpleasant smirk, and he did not move. "Very well. I will, however, be going directly to the land office with documents that will prove the good captain overcharged the English government *twofold* for the goods he provided them."

The old lady's chin lifted in a challenge. "You cannot prove any such claim!"

"Can't I? Can you be entirely certain of that?"

Nothing was said for several moments. The only sounds in the parlor were the rattle of the wind against the glass panes and the faint, somber ticking of the carriage clock. Elizabeth Wright's erect posture slowly slumped in defeat, and her shoulders sagged.

Noting her changed stature, Nolan continued, "Now that we have *that* settled, I will await your announcement that the Chattilion girls are bound for America. Oh, and be certain their departure is a hasty one, if you please."

The gold-studded cane tapped against the floor as he moved toward the door, only turning back when Elizabeth Wright snapped out his name.

"Nolan! Nolan, I sincerely hope you meet your demise over there."

Hearty laughter revealed long yellow teeth that were much too large for his small mouth. "Do not fear for me, my generous, loving aunt! Let us both pray that I find the gold and never have to return to this gloomy house!"

Bright sunlight reflected off the ebony hide of the mare tethered outside the stable. A slender girl brushed industriously at the horse's already gleaming coat, then stood back to inspect her efforts. The color of the mare almost matched the deep blue-black shine of the girl's hair as she tossed it back from her perspiring forehead.

"What do you think, Mary Catherine?" she asked her younger sister, who turned to gaze critically at the horse.

Resting her hands on her hips, Mary Catherine nodded approvingly. "Though why we are going to so much trouble just for another one of those dreadful *meetings* with Elizabeth Wright, I cannot fathom!" she added.

Michaella sighed. "You know very well why we must look our best, Mary Catherine. That goes for the care of our horses, too. Mrs. Wright is responsible for our welfare, and . . ."

"And is paid quite handsomely for it!" the younger girl put in sourly. "It is certainly not from any charity or affection for either of us that she sees to our needs."

"Perhaps not, but there is little sense in tweaking her nose and giving her cause to withhold a single shilling just because she takes offense at something we have done." Michaella ran her hand over the rippling hide of the mare. "Don't you recall how she threatened to sell our horses if our riding continued to interfere with our music lessons?" she reminded her sister.

Mary Catherine made a face. "Yes, the old harridan! If she knew how much we truly enjoy riding, she would make a point of selling them. I think she dislikes any sort of enjoyment in life, and is determined that we shall have none ourselves."

"Oh, perhaps she's not that bad."

"No? Then why do you suppose we got that dreadful-sounding message from her? To command our presence at dinner tonight! I mean, she suggests the most *dire* consequences are about to befall us! Does that sound like a note a pleasant person would write?"

Michaella had to laugh, and she gazed fondly at the indignant face of her younger sister. Chestnut hair framed Mary Catherine's heart-shaped face and large blue eyes shone above an impudently upturned nose. A faint spray of freckles dusted her nose and cheeks, and her short frame was generously endowed with curves. Michaella, on the other hand, was the total opposite. She was exceedingly slender, and her tall frame almost vibrated with suppressed energy, where Mary Catherine's curves suggested a tendency to indolence. It was Michaella who had inherited the dark hair and eyes of their French father. French and Irish—a combustible combination!

"And I don't even feel like eating in that gloomy old house," Mary Catherine was saying, her full lips pursed in a pout. "We have to endure her company until after the evening meal, and I just know it will be those dried-out parsnips and a huge portion of tough, stringy lamb again! Ugh!"

"Courage, sister," Michaella teased.

"Courage indeed!" Blue eyes flashed with irritation as Mary Catherine warmed to her subject, and she shook a short finger in Michaella's face as she said, "I don't understand her anyway! She has always been so odd, so . . . so *secretive* with us!"

"Perhaps she has always considered us too young to confide in," Michaella pointed out reasonably. "After all, I am just turning twenty, and you are two years younger than I."

Mary Catherine dug the toe of her worn boot into the dirt of the stable yard and leaned against her horse. "I cannot help but wonder what it would be like if . . . if Mama had not died and Papa had not disappeared in America."

"But they did, and we must not fret over matters we cannot change," Michaella said quietly. Her thoughts drifted back to happier times, times when her French father had been in business with Captain Wright in a fur trade venture that had gleaned a fortune in America. America. It had been a wonderful country, and St. Louis had been a true home to them. Neither girl had wanted to leave, but no one had consulted them as to their wishes when their Irish mother, Catherine, had finally left Henry Chattilion. There had been one too many trips into the wilderness to hunt for beaver pelts, one too many winters spent away from home. Catherine had carried out her threat to leave her wandering husband, and had taken their young daughters with her.

"I still think Mama never really meant to stay gone so long, that she thought Papa would come after us," Mary Catherine said.

Michaella shook her head. "To England? She should have known better. Papa loved the mountains far too much ever to leave them behind."

"He loved them more than he did us," Mary Catherine said bitterly.

"Perhaps. Or perhaps he thought Mama would come back when she tired of being a poor relation to her distant cousin." Michaella stroked the mare absently, recalling Catherine Chattilion's disinterest in the grand life-style depicted in her cousin's letters to America. It had been a grand life-style, but not for the poor Irish nobody from America. Catherine had been shunned, relegated to the position of a live-in maid, fetching and carrying for her cousin and hating every moment of it.

"Why do you suppose Mama never went back to St. Louis?" Mary Catherine wondered aloud.

"Probably because of her pride. Although I do think that if Cousin Martha had not contracted a fatal dose of the fever, then given it to Mama, Mama might have eventually swallowed her pride and gone back." Michaella drew in a long breath, then shook loose the cobwebs of the gloomy memories. "But that is only conjecture now, Mary Catherine. After all, that was over ten years ago, and we don't even know if Papa is still alive. Now here we are in Manchester and finally on the threshold of a new life!"

Flashing her older sister a wry glance, Mary Catherine muttered that it was more likely they would be doomed to a life of drudgery as scullery maids to "Lady" Elizabeth! "If you will only realize, we have been under her care for ten years with no hope of relief!"

Michaella slanted her sister a reproving glance. "There are certain legalities and provisions in our guardianship papers that must be fulfilled. I am certain this meeting with Mrs. Wright this evening will answer many of our questions. Perhaps she intends to allow me to handle our trust funds since I am almost of age."

"Or she needs the parlor dusted," Mary Catherine put in with a grimace, making her sister laugh.

"Don't even suggest that in jest!" she begged. "All those horrid little statues squatting about like grim gargoyles! And those wretched vases that look like chamber pots!"

Holding their sides, the two girls went into gales of merriment. "I just hope that I can keep from laughing when I see Mrs. Wright tonight," Mary Catherine gasped between gurgles of laughter.

That did not prove to be a problem, however. The entire evening meal was eaten in virtual silence. Sitting primly in high-backed chairs, Mary Catherine and Michaella dared do little more than nod politely when a footman ladled portions of food onto their plates. Elizabeth Wright sat in strained silence at the head of the table, her brooding gaze casting a pall on the table.

It was only after the soup had been eaten and the dry portion of lamb picked over that Michaella dared speak. Clearing her throat, she looked up at Mrs. Wright's grave face and said, "Excuse me, please, but Mary Catherine and I have been discussing our residence here with you. Not that your hospitality isn't quite generous," she added hastily when Mrs. Wright's thin brows lifted and she fixed Michaella with a glacial stare, "but . . . but we have decided that we would much prefer having a residence of our own. I'm certain you can understand how it is. . . ."

Her voice trailed off as Mrs. Wright continued to stare at her, and Michaella exchanged glances with her sister. It seemed as if Mrs. Wright was lost in a daze, for she did not reply to Michaella's comments for several minutes.

Then, rising abruptly from her chair, she said, "Follow me into the study, please."

Carefully placing her silver eating utensils on the

edge of her plate, Michaella took a deep, steadying breath before rising. She deliberately did not look at her sister, knowing Mary Catherine would be wearing a wide-eyed look of fright on her expressive face. Michaella smoothed the skirts of her drab gray serge gown and followed Mrs. Wright from the dining room into the study, wondering what had caused the older woman to be so grim.

Elizabeth Wright crossed the study and paused beside a table, her hand resting near a small teakwood box. She said nothing for a moment, but gazed down at the little coffer with an enigmatic expression.,Finally she lifted her head and gazed at Michaella.

"I am about to allow you to read a letter that concerns your father and his possible whereabouts in the mountains of America," she said in a colorless tone. Her austere features remained composed, and she reached out to tap lightly on the lid of the box. "It is unlocked, Michaella."

Taking the cue, Michaella stepped forward and lifted the lid. A tattered sheaf of paper lay folded on the velvet lining at the bottom of the box. Lifting it out, Michaella glanced curiously at Mrs. Wright. It was not a letter she held, but a torn map.

"Is this . . . ?"

"No. That is obviously a map. This is the letter." Mrs. Wright held out an envelope. "Read it."

There was the crackling rustle of paper as Michaella removed the letter, and a faint feeling of irritation pricked her at Mrs. Wright's mysterious attitude. She spread the letter out, smoothing the wrinkles. Mary Catherine edged closer to read over her sister's shoulder.

Bents Fort—17 April, 1839. This correspondence addressed to Captain Jonathan Wright in the matter of Henry Chattilion skin trapper and Booshway of this expedition this winter past Mssr. Chattilion fell ill with brain fever as did one Antonne Cardelle. Mssr. Chattilion was saved by root brews made by a Mssr. Lehman who knew of native cures. However Mssr. Cardelle did not survive but related to Mssr. Chattilion before his passing that he had a large piece of gold on his person. This found to be true Mssr. Cardelle then drew a map of the region where gold piece was found and it is Mssr. Chattilion's wish to pursue the gold source on behalf of the Intermountain Fur Company providing the company continue at all expense to care for his family. A map drawn as the same in the possession of Mssr. Chattilion is enclosed.

There was an illegible signature scrawled across the bottom, almost obscured by old grease or tallow stains. Michaella looked up at Mrs. Wright with a frown.

"It has been nine years since your late husband received this letter. What is the meaning of all this now?"

Pursing her lips, Mrs. Wright did not look at the girl for a moment, staring instead at her hands. They trembled in front of her, and she clasped them together and looked up.

"It would not have been fair to you two girls to open up old wounds. I saw no point in giving you hope that your father might still be alive when it has now been almost ten years since he was heard from."

"Fair?" Michaella echoed. "Fair?" Her dark eyes flashed with anger, and her mouth tightened. "How can you decide what is *fair* for another human being in something like this? And what is the point of bringing it to our attention now, when he is probably dead?"

Waving a weary hand, Mrs. Wright turned away and crossed the study to sink into a cushioned chair. She stared into the fire burning in the grate, then heaved a long sigh. "Don't be angry with me," she said so softly Michaella had to draw close to hear. "I was only doing what I thought best for everyone. It seemed so unlikely that he would still be alive, with all those harsh conditions in America and brutal savages running amok and killing everyone in sight. How could I guess that he might still be alive?"

"And what gives you cause to think so now?" Michaella pressed.

A faint smile trembled briefly on Mrs. Wright's lips. "I don't, but someone I know very well does. And if *he* believes it, then it is quite likely to be true."

Michaella shook her head in confusion. "I don't understand what you are saying," she began, but Mrs. Wright flapped a hand at her impatiently.

"Oh, you silly child! You are not supposed to understand anything! You are only supposed to do what is necessary and go to America and find your father. . . ."

Reeling with the shock of those words, Michaella slid a startled glance at her sister. Mary Catherine's normally smooth brow was furrowed in thought, and her blue eyes were narrowed. Then she smiled delightedly.

"America!" she cried, clapping her hands together. "How wonderful!"

"No, it isn't!" Michaella snapped, destroying her sister's euphoria.

"Why, what do you mean, Michaella?"

"Yes!" Mrs. Wright demanded. "What do you mean?"

"I mean I have no intention of going to America to look for my father. It is an utterly ridiculous notion and can afford us no earthly good at all."

Elizabeth Wright surged to her feet. "No," she said, suddenly changing her mind as a new idea struck her, "I think it is an excellent solution to all our problems."

Michaella gave her an assessing gaze. "I fail to see . . ."

"That's exactly it! You fail to see the grand scope, the complete picture! Only think—you will not only find your father—if he is, indeed, still alive—but you will assure your inheritance."

"We already have an inheritance," Michaella began, but Mrs. Wright cut her short.

"No, no, a mere pittance! If what I have heard is true, and believe me, my nephew is rarely wrong when it comes to finding new schemes for money, then there will be enough money for all of us!" A faint glitter shone briefly in her eyes, and an avaricious smile curved her mouth. "Don't you see? You cannot lose! On the one hand you find your father, and on the other, you gain a fortune in gold!"

"And if our father is dead?" Michaella asked in a scathing tone. "What then?"

"Then you don't have to wait to inherit your fortune," Mrs. Wright purred softly.

"And what is your interest in this? I am certain that you don't have just our futures at heart."

"Why, Michaella, how cynical you can be for such a young girl," Mrs. Wright observed. "And how shrewd." She tapped one finger thoughtfully against her chin, raking Michaella's slender frame and oval face with a hard gaze. "I will finance your journey, for payment plus interest. In return, I will be able to squelch some very nasty plans of someone I know and loathe."

"How much interest?" Michaella asked bluntly.

Mrs. Wright smiled. "Ten percent of whatever you may inherit."

"And if it is only handfuls of dust?"

"Then you may forgo my share."

Quickly assessing the situation, Michaella realized that it would afford them the opportunity to escape the stifling atmosphere at Crestmore Manor and the depressing room they shared behind the servants' quarters. She held out no foolish hopes that Henry Chattilion would still be alive, for she had long ago surrendered any of those notions. If he had been alive, he would have searched for his family. But still, he might have left behind a legacy for them, a means of compensation for abandoning them so many years before. A journey to America to look for her father? Why not!

"Very well," she said briskly, "but I will require your terms in writing if you please."

"You, my dear, shall make an astute businesswoman," Mrs. Wright observed caustically.

Chapter Two

St. Louis, Missouri
May 1849

AN EARLY MORNING mist rose in lacy wisps across the river, reminding Michaella of an old bridal veil as it wafted gracefully over wooden docks and slim-lined ships. In contrast to the peaceful air, stone quays teeming with life jutted into the muddy waters of the Mississippi River. She took a deep breath. Her quest had only begun.

After the winter had ended and she and Mary Catherine had boarded the English ship bound for America, there had been another three and a half weeks of ocean travel ahead of them. She had not minded it so much, but Mary Catherine had remained in their tiny cabin almost the entire voyage. Her face had been green, her stomach heaving, and Michaella had nursed her sister through the long voyage.

Finally, that, too, had ended. Then there had been the trip by steamboat down the Ohio to where it met the Mississippi for the final leg to St. Louis. Despite its slow pace, that trip had held a certain excitement, for the steamboat had run aground and the passengers had transferred to a flatboat. There had been nights of sleeping on the boat's hard-planked bottom, and on the times that they had tied up for the evening, the passengers had slept on the ground. By now, Michaella felt that she was tough enough to endure any primitive rigors that might lie ahead of them in this rough, sprawling country.

Leaning against the flat wooden railing that circled the steamboat, Michaella gazed toward the city thrusting up from the steep, muddy banks of the Mississippi River. *St. Louis*. It had been so long, so many years, so many memories ago. Exploding with life, the city's cobblestoned streets and teeming quays lay before her, and somehow it was as if she was home. Her fingers tightened on the railing, not from the sudden jolt as the boat bumped against the dock, but against the jolt of overwhelming emotions washing over her.

How could she have forgotten? How could she have submerged those intense feelings of loss when she had left St. Louis behind? She had left more than a city, more than a childhood home. She had left behind a father, a father she had loved dearly and who had abandoned them. Even now she wondered why Henry Chattilion had never searched for his wife and daughters. If he was dead, she could accept it. But if he was alive . . .

Turning abruptly away from the railing, Michaella gazed at her sister's eager face. She knew Mary Catherine did not feel the same sense of bitter loss, the same harbored resentments that she felt. No, Mary Catherine simply accepted their father's abandonment, which Michaella had never understood. Well, she had been both mother and father to her younger sister, and she would protect her as long as she was able.

"Oh, Michaella!" Mary Catherine cried out, pointing to the waterfront. "Just look! I remember that, don't you?"

Without bothering to turn around, Michaella

nodded. "Yes, of course I do. Only everything is much larger, much busier than I recalled."

Burnished curls bobbed at each temple as Mary Catherine nodded her head, bright blue eyes gazing past Michaella to the docks. "It's almost as if we were home again," the girl murmured, echoing her sister's earlier thoughts.

"Yes, but we're not really. Not yet. We have a lot to do before we can make any permanent decisions," Michaella warned with a slight frown. She pushed impatiently at a loose strand of ebony hair hanging in her eyes, tucking it back beneath the brim of her fashionable bonnet as she watched her sister with worried eyes. Too much could happen. Too many matters were unsettled for her to pin any hopes on a new life yet. She could deal with disappointment better than her sister, and she did not want her to be crushed.

"Oh, pooh!" Mary Catherine was saying with a laugh. "You're always so gloomy, Michaella! We are here in a new land with new clothes and a new life ahead of us! I refuse to let you darken my day!"

A burst of steam from the stacks atop the boat drowned out any tart reply Michaella would have made, and then they were swept along in a crush of people. It was impossible to point out facts to her carefree sister, but Michaella firmly decided to speak to her later.

Swept across the decks and down the wide gangplank that stretched from boat to dock, Michaella and Mary Catherine waited with the throng of other passengers while their baggage was being unloaded. Stone quays were crowded with cargo and animals and vendors and people from all walks of life. Rough seamen rubbed elbows with elegantly clad men in silk hose and velvet cloaks, and the noise was incredible.

"Isn't this exciting?" Mary Catherine shouted at Michaella.

Wrinkling her nose, Michaella nodded slowly. The sour smell of rotting vegetation and animal matter wafted on the river breezes, mingling with the sharp odor of cotton bales and stacks of beaver, wolf, fox, and bear pelts. The levee teemed with people from all walks of life. Many were French voyageurs—the river boatmen—clad in their buckskins and soiled cotton garments. Frontier drifters just in from the mountains were everywhere, conspicuous in their dark, greasy buckskins and fur hats. Men spilled down the hill from the many grog shops lining the narrow streets, foaming tankards in hand as they came to watch the steamships dock.

Michaella glanced around her, noting that she and her sister were the only unescorted young women on the dock. Most of the passengers were male with only a sprinkling of a few dowdy matrons. She began to feel too noticeable and between the catcalls from the rough crowd and the loud whistles and yells, the shell of quiet confidence she had tried to erect around herself disappeared.

"Stand close to me," she muttered to Mary Catherine, who was busily drinking in all the sights, oblivious to the sensation they were creating.

"Why? Oh, I won't get lost," the girl promised. "I'm just so excited, Michaella! Can you believe we are finally here in St. Louis?"

"No. Yes. Here. Put your arm through mine,"

Michaella ordered briskly. "And pull your bonnet down over your face. We don't need to advertise our wares any more than we are doing just by being here."

"Whatever do you mean?" Mary Catherine asked in pretty confusion. She blinked rapidly as her sister tugged at the brim of her bonnet, pulling it low over her face to hide it from view.

"And pull your shawl more closely around you. There. Now stay close," Michaella repeated. She felt like a chicken ripe for plucking, aware of the stares, both curious and lewd, boring into her, and began to wish they could forget about their baggage until later. Taking several steps to the right, she edged closer to the side of the dock, where it was less crowded. She pulled Mary Catherine with her and stood in the shadow of a towering stack of wooden barrels.

Brownish-green river water lapped at the muddy banks only a few feet away, and Michaella gazed out over the river. The morning sun had not yet burned away all the mist, and it clung in tattered strands to the curving shoreline. Swirls of current carried foreign objects past the banks—driftwood, logs, tree limbs, and even an occasional barrel or box lost from some ship. She leaned against the barrels behind her, staring at the opposite bank as if she could see beyond it to the distant mountain ridges in the west.

There was a blur of movement on the water, a vague shape that appeared then was lost in the mist, and Michaella blinked, uncertain if she had imagined it. But no, it was real, for it emerged from the shrouds of mist again. Long shadows swam behind it, and her dark eyes narrowed as she squinted at the form. What was it? A boat? A huge creature of some sort? Then she realized that it was a man in a canoe, one of the shallow-bottomed boats that maneuvered the swift waters of the Mississippi as easily as a huge steamboat.

Relaxing back against the barrel, Michaella watched as the canoe grew larger, steering directly toward the banks where she stood. As it drew near she could see the man inside flanked by a huge bale of furs. Obviously a trapper.

"Another trapper come to town to sell his furs and drink up all his profits," she murmured derisively.

"What? Where?" Mary Catherine asked, turning to look in the direction her sister was staring. "I don't see . . . oh! Now I see him!"

"He just came out of the mist along the riverbank," Michaella said. A stiff breeze tugged her hair free of the bonnet's confines and whipped it about her face in stinging tendrils. Tucking it back inside the wide ribbon tied under her chin, she said, "I thought he was an apparition at first."

"Maybe you were right," Mary Catherine said with a laugh. One hand held her straw bonnet to her head and the other kept her skirt from blowing up to reveal neat, trim ankles and shiny new kid boots. "See how well he handles his boat in this awful current?"

The man worked his paddle deftly from one side to the other, while the canoe skimmed along the current. It glided as effortlessly as a giant fish through the choppy waters, and Michaella could not help a surge of admiration for the man's skill.

When the canoe edged along the banks below them, Michaella saw that the man was young, maybe in his early twenties. Fringed buckskins hugged his lean, muscular frame, and he wore a cap of black and brown fur on his dark head. Long black hair streamed from beneath the edges of the cap, framing a tanned, square-jawed face. As he passed below them he glanced up, and Michaella noted with a start the brilliant blue eyes set beneath a dark swoop of brows. Then he slowed the canoe and turned it abruptly toward the landing.

Jean Patrick Malloy gazed up at the two women above him with great appreciation. He had been alone in the mountains for a long time, but not so long he couldn't admire the sight of two finely dressed young women of exceptional beauty. Obviously just off a boat from the east, they gazed back at him as if he were a demon with a forked tail and horns. Jean Patrick grinned. Maybe he was. After all, he'd been trapping in the mountains for the better part of four years, and must look a sight.

Sticking out his paddle, Jean Patrick felt the slow drag as he bumped against the shore. He was traveling just ahead of a keelboat heavily loaded with furs bound for the St. Louis warehouses. He was the trouble-scout, always paddling ahead of his men to detect any danger to his boat and cargo.

Danger kept his senses finely honed, and he freely admitted to enjoying it. There was a certain element of walking the edge that appealed to him, that made him even sharper for it. He'd lived on the edge of danger since he'd been orphaned at twelve. When his parents had been killed in a steamboat crash, he had been taken into the mountains and brought up by his uncle.

Now the mountains were in his blood. He loved them, explored them, feared them. Jean Patrick had learned the ways of the Indian as well as the white man, and had learned to survive in both worlds. Well-acquainted with harsh winters and burning summer suns, by the time he was eighteen Jean Patrick was a cunning mountain man. By twenty-five he had become a legend.

In a skirmish with the Blackfeet, who killed his uncle in a raid on their homestead, Jean Patrick had distinguished himself by slaying three warriors in hand-to-hand combat. It had been a fierce, bloody fight, but one that had earned him respect from Indian and white man alike. His French-English heritage had lent him the capability of conversing fluently in those languages, and years spent with the Indians left him fluent in four dialects. More than one man had tested his strength, and any who did resolved never to do so again. Jean Patrick walked a narrow path of his own making.

Now, pulling his wet paddle across his legs, he rose to his full height in the rocking canoe and stepped out. Water surged around his knees as he dragged the canoe ashore and tossed the paddle into the bottom. Then he turned to look up at the women who had attracted him.

Placing one hand over his heart, he grinned. "I must say that I never imagined the city would welcome me with such outstanding beauty."

Michaella felt Mary Catherine tremble, and her lips tightened with grim amusement at the man's comment. "You are very forward, sir!"

"Am I? Good. I believe in being direct," was his easy reply. "It saves so much time."

Stilling her sister's step forward with a restraining hand, Michaella snapped, "Not in this instance, sir! We are not accustomed to being accosted by strangers!"

His dark brows rose in mock dismay. "How distressing for you! Then you must never meet fascinating strangers."

"Assuming that you are including yourself in that group, I agree. Now, if you will excuse us." Michaella drew her sister with her, stepping away from the bank and turning her back on the man with the compelling blue eyes and charming grin. For some odd reason her heart was thudding and her throat was dry, and she had the strongest desire to turn around and see if he was watching them. Beside her, Mary Catherine was pouting, as she muttered that she just couldn't see why Michaella had to be rude to the first presentable man they had seen in St. Louis.

Michaella jerked her head around to stare at her sister in astonishment. "You call a man in buckskins and shaggy hair *presentable*?"

"But they were clean buckskins, and he was quite handsome and nice."

"Mary Catherine. . . ."

"And besides, maybe he knows where Papa is, since he is obviously a fur trapper himself."

There was a certain logic to this, but Michaella resisted it. There had to be many fur trappers in St. Louis, and she saw no point in asking every one of them if he knew her father.

"Ah," a deep voice behind them interrupted, "I

take it you young ladies are searching for some-one?"

Whirling around to face the impudent man with the laughing blue eyes, Michaella found it difficult to keep an answering smile from her own lips. Now that he removed his hat, Michaella could clearly see that he *was* handsome, and he had a certain charm to his forward manners, but she had no intention of allowing herself to be drawn into his obviously practiced enticement.

"No," she said at the same time as Mary Catherine said, "Yes."

He looked from one to the other, raking a hand through his thick, dark hair and lifting his brows. "Well? Which is it? Perhaps just one of you is looking for someone."

"Actually," Michaella began, overriding her sister's explanation, "we have just arrived in St. Louis. Once we are situated in our hotel we shall have no problem finding who we seek."

"Oh, Michaella!" Mary Catherine burst out. "Don't be so cautious. He seems nice enough." She turned toward Jean Patrick with a wide smile. "We are looking for our papa, who is said to be in the mountains somewhere. Perhaps you could help us, or even know of him?"

"Well," Jean Patrick began with a laugh, "there are a lot of mountains in America! Do you know which ones he prefers?"

"No, but we once lived in St. Louis, so I thought maybe he hunted in the ones close by."

Another burst of laughter rippled from Jean Patrick's throat at the girl's naiveté. "And what is your papa's name?" he asked.

"Henry Chattilion."

Jean Patrick gave a noticeable start. "As unlikely as it seems, I believe that I have heard of him. It has been some years since, but he once worked for the Intermountain Fur Company, did he not?"

"Yes," Michaella said skeptically, gazing at him with narrowed eyes. "And you are correct, sir—it is a farfetched coincidence that you would know him."

"Farfetched but not impossible," he shot back with an irrepressible grin.

Bridling, Michaella could not stop the sudden lurch in her chest when he looked at her like that, with those thick-lashed blue eyes set in such a handsome face. There was something infinitely appealing about this man, though her every nerve screamed a warning to stay away from him. Charming men were never as charming as they appeared. Hadn't her own father been proof of that?

But as this man was obviously familiar enough with her father to know that he had once worked for the Intermountain Fur Company, she ventured, "Do you know him? Or do you know where he may be found?" she added.

Shaking his shaggy head, Jean Patrick stomped the muddy water from his knee-high moccasins as he said, "No, I can't say that I do. Sorry. I hunted in the central and northern Rockies. Maybe he is somewhere in the southwestern ridges."

"Do you know someone else who might know?" Michaella asked.

Another regretful shake of his head, then: "But I

might be able to find out for you. If you would like to tell me where you will be staying . . ."

"Oh, I am certain we will be able to find someone else to tell us what we want to know," Michaella said quickly, before Mary Catherine could offer the information. "But thank you anyway."

His blue eyes crinkled in amused appreciation. Water squelched from his deerskin moccasins as he gave another stamp of his feet. "Glad I could help," he commented with another laughing glance at Michaella. "Oh, and if you are dissatisfied with your hotel, try the Mansion House. It's the best in St. Louis for rates and accommodations."

"Our thanks for your assistance," Michaella said after a moment of awkward silence. How had he known where they were staying? She exchanged a startled glance with her sister. Then, clearing her throat, she was about to bid him farewell, but he was already gone, sliding down the muddy banks and leaping into his canoe.

They watched in silence as he pushed away from the landing and into the swift river currents. He worked the canoe alongside a keelboat in the middle of the river. Even beneath his coat, his arms flexing with brawny muscle were obvious as he pulled against the powerful surge of water.

As the canoe and man disappeared from sight along the levee, Mary Catherine remarked, "I can almost imagine Papa looking like that when he was young. No wonder Mama fell in love with him!"

Giving her a sharp glance, Michaella snapped, "And I imagine he is just as dependable as our father, too!"

"Probably," Mary Catherine admitted with a sigh, "but he is so terribly handsome. I do hope we see him again."

"Well, *I* certainly don't! I will be quite satisfied if we do not have to see him ever again! A man like that can only mean trouble."

Nolan Ketchman leaned on his gold-studded cane and watched Jean Patrick supervise the unloading of fur bales into the company warehouse. The young man worked alongside his men, directing them in the placing of the bundles before he went into the company offices. He barely glanced in Ketchman's direction as he shuffled through the papers he held.

"Excuse me," Ketchman finally asked, "but I would like a word with you, young man."

Jean Patrick slanted him a polite glance. "Yes?"

"I don't believe we have been introduced . . ."

"I am Jean Patrick. And you?"

Taken aback by the young man's abruptness, Ketchman forced a yellow smile. "Nolan Ketchman. I am with the company . . . an official of high ranking, you know."

Jean Patrick raked him quizzically, then obviously dismissed him as someone of little importance to him. "No, I didn't."

The flat statement brought a flicker of irritation to Ketchman's eyes, but he let it pass. "I noticed that you brought in some extraordinarily fine furs. They are hard to come by these days, I understand."

With a sigh of impatience, Jean Patrick turned to

face Ketchman. He did not trust many men, and there was something about this man that he disliked, a cunning slyness that reeked of evil. "What did you wish to speak to me about?"

Leaning on the head of his cane again, an affectation that Jean Patrick found irritating, Ketchman said, "Allow me to give you some background, as I am certain you do not recall me all that well."

"I do not know you at all," was the blunt reply.

Ketchman held up one hand. "Please, allow me to continue, sir."

Jean Patrick listened with narrowed eyes as Ketchman spoke of his position with the company's home offices in England. He stated that he had traveled to America from England several years before, and that he had been in the mountains during the height of the beaver trade—a foolish boast Jean Patrick immediately discounted. Ketchman was thirty at the most, much too young to have hunted as extensively as he claimed. And Ketchman further embellished this unlikely tale with claims that he was primarily responsible for the company's success in the entire Rocky Mountain region, owing to his great knowledge of where to concentrate on trapping.

Jean Patrick listened with mounting impatience and disgust, and was about to cut off this pompous idiot's recital when Ketchman mentioned a familiar name.

"Who did you say?" he asked Ketchman sharply.

"Henry Chattilion. Do you know him?"

Shrugging, Jean Patrick answered carefully, "I met him once. He was one of the first trappers in the Rockies."

Nodding excitedly, Ketchman blurted, "Yes! Yes, that is him! Do you know where he is now?"

Lounging back against the office desk, Jean Patrick's thoughts flashed to the two women on the riverbank. How odd that he should encounter another person looking for this elusive Henry Chattilion! There must be a very important reason behind this search. . . .

"Do you know?" Ketchman was pressing, his eyes glittering with hope.

"You must be a good friend of this Henry Chattilion," Jean Patrick stalled.

"Oh, very! We have known one another for a great number of years. Henry was like a father to me. He showed me the ways of the mountains and how to trap only the best furs. I would like to see him again after all this time."

As Jean Patrick stared at the thin Englishman, his mouth twisted in a cynical smile. "So, it has been a long time since you have seen that big redheaded Frenchman, heh? That is the Henry you speak of? Red hair and a bushy beard?"

"Yes, yes, that's him!" Ketchman snapped impatiently. "Now where is he?"

Straightening his lean frame, Jean Patrick gazed at Ketchman with grave contempt. "You are a very bad liar, Mr. Nolan Ketchman. The man I described is a big Frenchman they call Sorrel."

Ketchman's cane slammed against the stone floor. "I do not like to be thought a fool!" he grated, his thin brows drawing down in a scowl over his eyes.

"Neither do I," Jean Patrick shot back. "And

may I suggest that the next time you try this stupid trick, you know what your good friend looks like."

Drawing himself up to the extent of his slight stature, Ketchman met Jean Patrick's steady gaze. "My good man, I am well established in this company and *I* suggest that you remember that. If you are not careful, you will not be working for this company much longer."

A loud burst of laughter filled the office, and Jean Patrick's bright blue eyes danced with mirth. "It seems that you know very little about your own business, Mr. Ketchman! I am a free trapper. I take my furs to whoever pays the highest prices. And I am beginning to think a company that would hire an official such as yourself is lacking in good business strategy. Maybe I should take my furs elsewhere, heh?"

Ketchman's pale face took on a grayish pallor. "I would reconsider that decision. The Intermountain Fur Company is among the strongest on this entire continent. You may not be able to sell elsewhere."

Shaking his head, Jean Patrick gave him a pitying look. "There is little danger of that. But I think that I shall mention your warning to one of the senior officers of this firm. Perhaps we will see how much power you *do* wield."

Impotent fury filled Ketchman as he watched Jean Patrick walk away with a loose, easy stride. He would not be beaten! No, he would triumph over all odds and be a man of wealth, a power with which to be reckoned, and then he would see to this Jean Patrick who had dared mock him!

Chapter Three

✦✦✦✦✦

THE HIRED CARRIAGE rocked along the narrow St. Louis streets that dropped down through gentle hills lined with oak and maple trees. Michaella and Mary Catherine pressed eager faces to the dusty windows, peering out at the city. Early morning sunlight still gilded the horizon, yet the city was alive with action. St. Louis—it was a study in contradictions, a city of mixed stench and perfume, of wood shanties and grandiose stone mansions. Carriages decorated in gold leaf rolled through muddy streets lined with oxen and freight carts. Tilting rows of shabby windows framed frowsy women who blew kisses to salvation-selling preachers, while small children played marbles in the gutters.

This city at the edge of the frontier was the meeting place for those who took their living from the wild lands stretching beyond. Here mingled people of every imaginable type and description. Grog shops and streetside taverns bustled with the long tails of French topcoats as well as the soiled cotton and buckskin of the rivermen and frontier drifters.

Sitting back against the frayed cushions of the carriage, Michaella sighed. "It will be impossible to find Papa in this city."

Mary Catherine barely glanced at her. "I don't think so, Michaella. I mean, with all these people, someone is certain to know of him!"

"Perhaps," was the unconvinced reply. "But I hardly think Papa would be here. After all, he always preferred the mountains to the city."

"But he still has to sell his furs," her sister pointed out, and Michaella nodded in agreement.

"That is true. Since we spoke with that fur trapper, I've been thinking. It seems that the best way to find Papa would be to search for him ourselves. I mean, we should travel to the last place he was seen and ask his acquaintances about him."

Clapping her hands together, Mary Catherine's eyes shone with delight. "Yes! Oh, I would like going off on a great adventure, Michaella."

Michaella's lips twisted. It was just like her younger sister to think only of adventure instead of the practicalities of such a plan. She never paused to consider that there might be dangers or hardships. "Well, we shall see," Michaella said after a long moment. "We shall rest for a few days and make our decision after weighing the facts."

The hired carriage lurched to a stop in front of the Mansion House at last, and the two dusty and tired girls stepped down in relief. It had been a harrowing ride through the narrow streets.

"Why, the hotel is quite lovely," Mary Catherine remarked in surprise, gazing up at the stone edifice with wide eyes as Michaella paid the carriage driver. "St. Louis is more civilized than I had remembered."

Lifting her skirts so they wouldn't drag against the dirty walkway, Mary Catherine ascended the steps into the hotel lobby, leaving Michaella to arrange for a porter to bring their trunks into the hotel.

When she rejoined her sister, Michaella snapped, "You could have helped me!" But her sharpness had no effect. Mary Catherine was too busy looking around at the spacious lobby teeming with people. The lobby was furnished with imports from France and England, and stained glass gleamed in the high windows with shades of blue and red. Mary Catherine drew in a long sigh of happiness as the two walked toward the hotel clerk.

Stepping up to the glossy walnut counter that served as the front desk, Michaella drew off her gloves and fixed the clerk with a polite smile.

"A room for two, please."

The clerk's frosty gaze slid from Michaella to Mary Catherine, and his brow lifted haughtily. "Two unescorted women?" he inquired in a doubtful tone.

Michaella's gaze never wavered, and when Mary Catherine turned around she dug an unobtrusive elbow into her sister's side to command her silence. "Yes," she told the clerk. "I am Mrs. Michaella White, and this is my widowed sister, Mrs. Mary Catherine Morgan. We will require a room at once, sir."

The clerk paused, then inclined his head. "Of course. I have a very nice room on the second floor that should suit two ladies quite nicely."

"What did you tell him those last names for?" Mary Catherine whispered when they had crossed the lobby to the wide staircase.

"Unmarried females alone in St. Louis are subject to intense scrutiny," Michaella replied calmly. "I do not intend to feel as if I am an insect under glass, thank you very much!"

"Oh," Mary Catherine replied, slightly mollified.

Their hotel room was luxurious compared to their room at Mrs. Wright's home. And after the several months of travel under much less comfortable circumstances, Michaella shared her sister's delight in the twin featherbeds and china bathtub. Dark blue carpet covered the floors, and a black lacquer dresser with a large oval mirror dominated one wall while their trunks had been placed along another. The china bathtub had been hand-painted with huge blossoms of red and lavender, and the twin beds were canopied, with the coverlets turned down to reveal satin sheets. Luxury, indeed!

Stepping to the long window overlooking the street, Michaella gazed down at the bustle below. They had come so far, and had so far yet to go. Behind her, Mary Catherine was blithely unpacking her things from her trunk, and Michaella envied her sister's uncomplicated nature. If only she could be so carefree and lighthearted, thinking of just the moment instead of the future. Perhaps then she would not feel this weight of responsibility on her shoulders, this constant pricking worry that was always with her.

Tilting back her head, Michaella pressed the pads of her fingers on the nape of her neck and rubbed to ease the tension. Well, it was her lot to be the steady, dependable worker bee, and her sister's lot to be a beautiful, careless butterfly. After all, hadn't men always been drawn to Mary Catherine's wit and gaiety, her bubbling charm? Few had lingered to search behind Michaella's quiet reserve and dark eyes for a spark of warmth. Had they bothered, perhaps they would have discovered a surprising capacity for passion slumbering behind Michaella's heavy-lidded eyes, dormant, waiting for the right man to come along and awaken it.

But no, her dark hair and eyes were unfashionable, and there were so many round, petite women with pale skin and china-blue eyes. Michaella's tall, slender frame was passed by for the others, and her quick wit and intelligence had gone unremarked by any but the local vicar at Crestmore Manor. But then, the majority of men were unimpressed with a female who could do more than play the harpsichord or sing a pretty tune and flirt with a fan.

Michaella turned away from the window with a jerk. She strode to her unopened trunk and struggled with the lock for several moments before she got it open. Lifting the heavy lid, she pawed through the jumble of clothes. Tucked into the pocket of a velvet mantle was an envelope, and she drew it out. The map and letter. The key to the future was contained in the yellowed pages and almost illegible scrawl.

Sighing, Michaella sat down in a tapestry rocking chair and opened the envelope. After reading the letter, she frowned down at the map. It detailed only the eastern half of the trails leading out into the western frontier. While Mary Catherine sang a lighthearted song and shook out the wrinkles in her clothes, Michaella traced a finger along an inked line that went out from St. Louis along the Missouri River, past two outposts called Independence and Westport, then along an overland trail that stretched across the rest of the map, ending abruptly in a jagged, torn edge.

Tapping her finger against the paper, Michaella decided that the places indicated on the map must be landmarks along the trail. It must be. The trail crossed a number of streams and rivers with names such as Big Blue and Platte River.

"And this is Courthouse Rock toward the far end of our piece," she observed aloud, rocking and thinking. "I don't see how we can ever complete our search successfully unless we have the other piece."

"Other piece of what?" Mary Catherine asked absently. Then seeing Michaella glance up with an exasperated frown, she added, "Oh. The map."

"Yes, the map. This silly thing haunts my sleep at night! I do not see how . . ."

"Oh, you worry so much! Don't think about it," her sister said offhandedly. "I don't. I just have faith that we are meant to find Papa. Otherwise, why would things have worked out as they have? I mean, look—Mrs. Wright financed our journey when she certainly didn't have to do so, and now here we are and already we've met someone who has heard of Papa. See what I mean?"

"I see that someone is certainly pulling strings," Michaella said wryly. "What I don't see is the reason behind it. *That* is what spurs me on, not just the hope of finding a father who abandoned us years ago, or even the thought of the gold. It's the knowledge that there is something so important, someone has gone to a great deal of trouble to scheme up this entire situation."

Mary Catherine stared at her blankly. "You don't want to find Papa?" she asked after a moment. "Or the gold?"

"Oh, it's not that, Mary Catherine. Don't sound so dismayed." Sitting on the edge of the rocker, Michaella stared earnestly at her sister. "Don't you see what's happening? There is someone behind all this, someone who is after the gold certainly, but also something else. I don't know who or what! I feel as if it must be important, or they would not be taking so much effort to keep hidden."

"But Mrs. Wright . . ."

"Is just a pawn. No, there is someone else." Michaella glanced down at the map again. "I do not like being thought a fool just because I am female, Mary Catherine. And I do not like being used. I intend to find all the answers to my questions."

Briskly folding the letter and map again, Michaella placed them back in the envelope and rehid it in her trunk. "We shall begin our search with an inquiry at the fur company headquarters here," she stated. "As Papa is a part owner in the company, we should be privy to any information they may have."

"But what if they won't allow us access to the records?"

"Why shouldn't they?"

"Oh . . . I don't know. They've been so secretive until now, keeping the letter and map from us and not informing us that Papa may still be alive. If Mrs. Wright hadn't told us at last, we still wouldn't know!"

"And don't you find that strange?" Michaella asked. "I certainly do. It can only mean that somehow, Mrs. Wright is involved in some sort of scheme concerning Papa."

Mary Catherine's eyes widened. "Mrs. *Wright*?"

"Yes, I am sure of it. Directly or indirectly, she is involved. And in any event, I believe that we should proceed as quickly as possible with a plan. We must take the shortest route we can find and go to where Papa was last seen. We can proceed from there."

Mary Catherine looked doubtful. "Alone?"

"I thought you wanted adventure!"

"Yes, but *safe* adventure!" was the laughing reply. "Perhaps we could hire a guide in St. Louis?"

"Very clever of you," Michaella approved. "I had, indeed, already toyed with the notion. Do you recall Papa talking about a friendly rival of his, a man by the name of Sorrel? I think Papa once said he looked like a giant red horse."

"Oh, yes!" Mary Catherine said. "I do remember! Papa would speak of him and curse, then laugh in almost the same breath. And I remember a big man who would laugh very loud and carry us about on his back, pretending all the time he was a bear!"

"That is the man," Michaella said. "He worked for the fur company also. If he is still there, I am willing to wager that he will tell us all we need to know. And he might even take us to our father."

It was late that afternoon before Michaella and Mary Catherine made their way back down along the levee. The wind was still blowing briskly, whipping at their skirts, hair, and bonnet strings. They had taken a carriage to the top of the hill overlooking the waterfront, then decided to walk the rest of the way. It was only a short distance to the fur company, the driver had assured them, but now Michaella suspected that he had been mistaken. She saw no sign of warehouses bearing the name of the Intermountain Fur Company.

"Do you think we are lost?" Mary Catherine asked uneasily, noting the curious stares they were receiving from the rough, unkempt men who wandered the narrow streets.

"No, of course not. It will be a simple matter to flag down another hired hack and return to the hotel," Michaella lied. Since the driver had put them out at the top of the hill, she had seen no carriages for hire. Just a coincidence, she assured herself. Drawing her shawl more tightly around her shoulders as if it would ward off trouble, she stared directly ahead, refusing to allow her gaze to wander in case she should accidentally meet the eyes of one of those rough men. She ordered her sister to do the same.

"Don't worry!" Mary Catherine whispered back, keeping her eyes trained on the ground ahead of her.

The sisters turned a corner, and sprawling before them were row upon row of warehouses bustling with activity. Wagons rumbled and draymen shouted loudly, swearing at the top of their lungs at mules and oxen. Michaella realized with a sense of dismay that finding the Intermountain Fur Company without proper directions might well be fruitless. Pausing, she surveyed the area and considered her options.

"What shall we do?" Mary Catherine fretted, her blue eyes anxious.

Spotting an old man garbed in buckskin slumped against a post on the edge of the landing, Michaella stepped forward. He seemed harmless enough, with his tufts of white hair and rheumy eyes. A stone jug was perched within easy arm's reach beside him, and he was staring out across the river.

"Excuse me, sir," Michaella said boldly. "We are looking for the Intermountain Fur Company. Could you direct us?"

His gaze slid sideways, brightening as the old man saw the two pretty women. Pulling himself to his feet, he cackled through a tangle of white beard, "Fur company? They's plenny of 'em round here!" He waved an expansive hand to indicate the rows of warehouses, and Michaella shook her head.

"No, the *Intermountain* Fur Company. Have you heard of it?"

"We're looking for a man by the name of Sorrel," Mary Catherine put in, and the old man gave a start of surprise.

"Sorrel? I'd hate to think you're fixin' to take up with the likes of him," the old buckskinner said. A gnarled hand reached up to adjust the otter skin cap that sat lopsidedly on his tufts of white hair, and he grinned, showing gaps in his broken teeth. "He a friend of your'n?"

"Oh, no," Michaella hastened to explain, "he is a friend of our father's. Then you know him?"

"Sorrel?" Another cackle erupted from his age-stitched mouth. "That tall Frenchy can be seen comin' a month away! Maybe a couple of months if'n he's standin' straight up. Yessiree, few are the men who can match that big hoss. Only one other I ever knowed of held his own agin Sorrel."

"Was that man's name Henry Chattilion?" Michaella guessed.

Surprise bracketed the old man's eyes with a burst of wrinkles. "By damn, in all that's holy, how'd ya know that?"

"Never mind," Michaella replied. "I am discovering that he is more well known than I had anticipated. Tell me, do you know where he is?"

"Chattilion? Naw, cain't rightly say that I do."

"Is he alive?"

The old man snorted. "I'd reckon he'd be too mean and ornery to die! Ain' nothin' but Sorrel or a buff'ler stampede could put a hitch in that man's plans."

Bending, the buckskinner scooped up his stone jug, and with a peculiarly graceful motion, positioned it on his left shoulder. "D'ya mind? I've gotten powerful dry."

Michaella shook her head, not caring whether the old man drank from his jug or not. She had learned more about her father in the past minute than she had in the past ten years.

"Do you think Chattilion is in St. Louis or out in the mountains?" Mary Catherine asked when he lowered his jug.

"Well, he sure ain't here, that I do know," the old buckskinner replied with a wink. He dragged a dirty shirtsleeve across his mouth, then added, "He ain't one fer the white diggin's at all. Last I heard, he was somewhere out in Sioux country, up in the Sacred Hills or thereabouts."

Michaella's fingers curled into her heavy velvet reticule as she stared hard at the old man. There was the solid ring of truth to his words, and she wondered why it had been so easy to acquire this information. The buckskinner's next comment dashed her burgeoning hopes.

"Course, that was six, seven years ago." His leathery features furrowed in thought, then he added, "Maybe eight."

Bright tears blurred Mary Catherine's eyes as she turned blindly to her sister. "Then how will we ever find Papa?" she wailed. "It's been so long!"

Looking from one to the other, the old man asked, "You two thinkin' 'bout goin' to look fer him yerselves?"

"We contemplated that course, yes," Michaella answered shortly.

He shook his grizzled head. "Best ta take along a good guide."

Michaella stared at him. "Like Sorrel?"

"Yeah, he'd be a good 'un, I reckon. But he ain't much on travelin' these days." Scratching his jaw, he slanted Michaella an assessing gaze. She stared back at him, and something in her face must have impressed the old buckskinner. Grinning, he said, "Ya just might find old Sorrel here in town instead of up ta his cabin, if'n ya know where to look and ain't afraid ta go."

"And where is that?" Michaella asked crisply.

"Walk on up Second Street and you'll find a grog shop with a flat stone front. If'n Sorrel is in town gamblin', he'll likely be in there drinkin' the place dry."

Fumbling in her reticule for a coin, Michaella offered to pay the old man for his information, but he refused.

"A man's got his dignity," he said. "And if you'll

take some advice from an old codger who knows, keep that money of yours hid good while you're down here."

Pulling the reticule strings tight, Michaella nodded. "I can't thank you enough. You have been very helpful."

His head bobbed, and he cradled the stone jug between his shoulder and cheek as he grinned at her. "And if you two ladies decide to go wanderin' off out in Sioux country lookin' fer Chattilion, 'member ta stick close to other folks. I'd hate ta hear 'bout some buck capturin' hisself some white women!"

"What did he mean by that?" Mary Catherine worried as she followed her sister back up the hill.

"Don't worry about it," Michaella replied smoothly. "It's not likely it will come to pass."

When they paused in front of the flat stone grog shop, Michaella hesitated. Rowdy laughter and crude voices floated through the open door, and she knew it was no place for a woman. A decent woman, she amended silently when she heard loud, shrill laughter mixing with the deep baritones.

"Michaella, you cannot mean for us to go in there!" Mary Catherine gasped in horror. "Why, it's not proper!"

"And since when did propriety get us anywhere?" her sister demanded firmly, pushing the scarred wooden door wider and peering inside. Hazy smoke lay in thick clouds, obscuring shadowy figures seated at crowded tables. Taking a deep breath, Michaella stepped inside, pulling Mary Catherine with her.

At first no one noticed them. They worked their way to the middle of the front room, holding tightly to each other as they skirted tables and lurching men. A number of roughly clad frontiersmen were gathered in a huge circle watching a game in progress. Bottles tilted and mugs were swung high as the men yelled out wagers to one another.

Her eyes finally adjusting to the thick haze that stung her eyes and nose, Michaella saw a massive man seated in the center of the circle. Flaming red hair crowned his head, and he had a red beard streaked with snips of gray. Sorrel. It had to be him. No other man could so closely fit her childhood memories or the recent descriptions. Would Papa be gray now? she wondered suddenly, then thrust the thought from her mind.

Garbed entirely in worn buckskins, Sorrel had a thick red and black fur cap of undeterminable origin perched atop his head. He wore leggings and a blue breechcloth, making him resemble a huge redheaded Indian.

Sorrel and a companion, who looked like a French voyageur, were sitting cross-legged on the floor in the midst of scattered bottles and refuse. They were playing with a set of notched bones, one tossing them deftly from hand to hand while the opponent attempted to guess which hand hid a certain bone. Michaella exchanged a glance with her sister.

"What are they doing?" Mary Catherine whispered loudly, and a man close by overheard.

Laughing, he leaned forward to explain in a thick French accent, "They play the hand game, *petites femmes*! You have nevair seen thees, no?"

"No," Mary Catherine admitted with a shake of her head. "Is it gambling?"

Another raucous burst of laughter erupted from the hawk-faced man, and he edged closer. "*Oui!* The beeg man, he ees winning, winning all the time. LaTrelle, he has nevair been beaten before. But the beeg man, Sorrel, he ees beating him now! *Oui*, I think there weel be trouble ovair thees!"

Barely able to follow his words over the blare of talk and laughter, Mary Catherine slid a questioning look at her sister. Michaella was watching the game intently, her gaze riveted on the players. Sorrel tossed two bones from hand to hand, his mouth split in an easy grin, but his eyes sharp and wary. His meaty hands moved swiftly despite their size, and it was hard for Michaella to follow his quick motions. His opponent's eyes never left Sorrel's hands, and when the red-haired giant finally paused and held out his closed fists, the voyageur hesitated. Finally, he flicked a finger toward the left fist.

"This one," he proclaimed.

Sorrel slowly opened his left fist, revealing a bone with no notches on it. Then the fingers on his right hand uncurled to show a bone carved with deep notches. The voyageur had picked the wrong hand.

As the crowd roared, the voyageur slammed a fist against the planked floor. Tilting back his huge head, Sorrel boomed with laughter, then scooped a large handful of money from the floor between them. Coins spilled from between his thick fingers and rolled across the floor. As he reached out for them, Michaella saw the metallic glint of a knife and Sorrel heaving his bulky form to one side.

The crowd scattered in all directions, men bumping into Michaella and Mary Catherine as they scrambled to get out of the way. The voyageur surged toward Sorrel, but the big man caught his upheld arm before the knife could slash down to his unprotected stomach. Roaring in rage, Sorrel lunged to his knees in a lithe motion, and punched the man in the jaw. The lethal blade clattered to the floor, spinning, as the voyageur landed with a thud.

Two other men came out of the crowd, to assist their fallen companion, as Sorrel headed toward the door. As he moved past, the big man spied Mary Catherine cowering against an overturned table.

Standing with feet apart and arms akimbo, the huge man shook with laughter, earning startled glances from Michaella and Mary Catherine. His big belly heaved as he rumbled loudly, "In all my years, I have never seen *femmes* such as you! Where do you hail from?"

Michaella recovered first. She straightened and met the big man's gaze. "We are Henry Chattilion's daughters," she said, boldly extending her hand. "I am Michaella, and this is my younger sister, Mary Catherine."

Stunned by this revelation, the big man just shook his head in amazement. Finally a huge grin cracked across his face and he boomed with laughter. "I should have guessed! What don't come into this town can't be found on God's own earth! What brings Chattilion's daughters here?"

"Him," Michaella answered. "We are searching for him. He used to talk of you, Sorrel. Do you remember coming to our home many years ago?"

"Of course I do! And I remember two little girls, one so thin and dark, the other round and fair, and they used to pull my beard and ride my back!" Laughter welled again, and Sorrel guided them toward an empty table, setting it upright with one hand and clearing it of empty bottles with the other. "Sit!" he ordered, then stroked his beard as he studied the two sisters. "So you look for your papa, heh? And how do you expect to find him in this big country?"

Again it was Michaella who answered. "We thought you might find him for us," she stated. "Can you?"

"Ah, I can, if he is still in this world, yes. But . . . I do not know if I will."

"Why not? I would pay well."

Chuckling, Sorrel shook his shaggy head. "Ah, you are direct enough, little one! All right—I will tell you." Pulling up a chair and sitting across from them, he locked his big fingers together. "I decided not to go out into that wild country again. I make my living here now, playing the hand game or cards or dice—whatever pays well. There is little risk here, you know? And out there . . . well, out there are enemies, many Indians who yearn to take my red hair and put it on their lodgepoles. I say no, Sorrel, you do not want your hair to leave your head, you know?"

"I can understand your feelings," Michaella began, "but we are most anxious to find our father. Will you not reconsider?"

"Ah, *mes pauvres petites,* I am tempted, truly I am. But I will not, no." Resting his chin in his cupped palm, Sorrel regarded Michaella's crestfallen face for a long moment, then said, "But I do have a little idea. There is a wagon train leaving soon for the west country. If you two head up to Independence, where the trail starts just past the juncture of the Missouri and Kansas rivers, you will find them. My advice is to go with them. Forget about me or any one guide. There is more safety in numbers. There will be a lot of people like yourselves headed into Oregon country, and on into California where there are big tales of gold."

Mary Catherine's head snapped up and her eyes widened. "Gold?" she echoed.

"*Oui*. But there are many stories, and not all can be believed. Many people run out there, risking their lives to hunt for a dream. Pah! I would want more than just rumors before I went that way again."

Michaella was silent. It must be true: there was a fortune to be found out west. Gold. It motivated greed, moved entire cities, and she held a key to it hidden in her trunk. It had been gold which had enabled them to travel to America in search of their father, for if not for the bright promise of stolen gold, Mrs. Wright would have never allowed them to come. And what were her own motives? Did she want the gold or did she want to find her father? Right now she still wasn't certain. At this time she wanted both, wanted to know why her father had abandoned her, wanted to know if he was still alive. If he was not, then one question would never be answered. His part ownership of the Intermountain Fur Company would be passed down to his daughters, and anything else he had accumulated in his lifetime would be theirs also. He owed it to them. He had not given them his time, and Michaella was determined that he would at least give them a future. He owed them that much.

Standing, she said, "Thank you for your time and your advice, Sorrel."

"And do you go on to California?"

"Perhaps. Perhaps not. After all, our father could be anywhere. We do not know his location, and there are many mountain ranges in America," she answered carefully.

Mary Catherine slanted her sister a curious glance. Her cheeks flushed even rosier than usual. Her lower lip trembled, then she blurted, "But we do! What about the . . . ouch!"

A faint smile curved Michaella's mouth as she removed her foot from her sister's instep. "We can only hazard a guess, and that could be dangerous. No, there are no guarantees about what lies ahead of us."

Sorrel's eyes narrowed shrewdly, and he met Michaella's steady gaze. "I understand, *ma petite*. You are a very wise woman, and would be a formidable opponent in the game of hands, I think."

"Yes, I think I might," she agreed smoothly.

The big Frenchman nodded slowly, recognizing the slight gleam in the girl's dark eyes. She was no fool, this one, and he admired that.

"Until we meet again," he said, inclining his head and rising from the table.

"Good-bye, Sorrel," Michaella said, turning and pushing Mary Catherine ahead of her out of the shop.

•

Chapter Four

✦✦✦✦✦

THE HOTEL NOW seemed a haven of safety and security to Michaella. She stood at the window of the room overlooking the street and mulled over the previous day's events. So much had happened, and there were still no answers. She crossed her slender arms over her chest as she regarded the hustle and bustle of St. Louis. Mary Catherine still lay asleep in the comfortable featherbed—having loudly declared that she had no intentions of rising before noon—yet Michaella was wide awake.

Convinced that Sorrel knew a great deal more about their father and the gold than he was willing to divulge, she also acknowledged the fact that there was little she could do if he chose not to help them. Her mouth thinned into a determined line. No matter. She and Mary Catherine would continue the search on their own.

Bright fingers of sunlight slanted through the thick glass of the window to gild Michaella's face a peachy shade of gold, prickling at her eyes and making her squint. She turned away from the window and regarded her sleeping sister with a thoughtful gaze. Shrugging away any lingering doubts, she strode purposefully across the room.

"Mary Catherine. Get up." She nudged her sister with the heel of her hand. "Get up, Mary Catherine."

"Hmm? No, no, it's too early," a mumbled protest drifted from beneath the rose-patterned quilt.

Mercilessly, Michaella reached down to fling

back the covers. "You need to book passage on a steamboat," she said firmly.

Mary Catherine sat up, glaring at her from beneath tousled strands of chestnut hair. "This early? Don't be ridiculous! *No one* rises this early . . ."

"And while you are doing that," Michaella went on, ignoring her protests, "I shall see how much information I can get from the fur company. Perhaps we can begin our overland journey with *some* notion of the proper direction."

Pushing back the hair from her eyes, Mary Catherine gave her sister a glance of alarm. "But . . . but I don't see how we can do such a thing! There are so many different trails, so many side trails that lead from the main road—don't you recall that?"

"Of course I do. That is why I intend to gather as much information as possible from the fur company before we leave. Wear your plainest, most modest gown, Mary Catherine. We do *not* need to attract undue attention!"

An hour later found Michaella—garbed in a plain gray gown with a high neck and long, tight sleeves, a large-brimmed hat, and cotton gloves—standing before the Intermountain Fur Company. It was housed in a huge building on the waterfront, not too far from where they had been the day before.

Fringing the curving banks of the river, the warehouse cargo consisted of various types of furs such as beaver, fox, otter, mink, and buffalo. Michaella covered her nose at the pungent smell of cured hides and muddy river. Rotting wood and marine life lent a brisk spice to the morning air.

She stood uncertainly for a moment, her gaze traveling up the line of warehouses and along the riverbanks. Michaella's gaze sharpened. A keelboat bobbed in the brackish water close to one of the warehouses. Riding the gentle waves beside the keelboat was the graceful curve of a canoe she had first seen the day before. She knew it belonged to Jean Patrick.

Her fingers tightened around the silk strings of her reticule as she suddenly recalled his intense blue eyes and hard, lean body. The memory brought a rush of warmth, an odd lurch of the heart, and a shortness of breath. Vaguely surprised at her reaction, Michaella sternly tried to compose herself. Such thoughts could only lead to trouble, and she had enough of that already.

Turning away from the waterfront, she strolled briskly to the warehouse and then went inside. It took a moment for her eyes to adjust to the change from bright light to a soft haze, and she blinked rapidly. Men were busily stacking furs along the walls, piling bundles of cured pelts high along the sides and back of the vast warehouse. As her gaze shifted, then focused, Michaella saw Jean Patrick, and her heartbeat quickened again. She wanted to go down to where he was working, but she did not want to be too forward. It would be awkward standing there, just staring at him and trying to think of what to say. Her first priority was to inquire about her father; she would stay away from Jean Patrick.

Michaella swept into the company offices and was surprised to see a gentleman she knew: Nolan Ketchman, Mrs. Wright's nephew. He was talking to a tall, dark-haired man just inside one of the offices.

She watched him silently for several moments.

Neither Michaella nor Mary Catherine had known or cared to know Nolan Ketchman very well. He had been snobbish toward them, and they had been happy he seldom visited his aunt. Michaella now noticed with a vague feeling of distaste that Ketchman still affected the use of a cane, and he leaned on it as he talked, his bony fingers absently caressing the gold-studded top.

It seemed odd to Michaella that he should be here in St. Louis. She knew that he was associated with the company in England in some minor way. And though the company regularly sent its senior officers back and forth from England to America, Nolan Ketchman was not one of those. Yet here he was.

There was no way Michaella could walk farther into the building and avoid him. He was, in fact, talking to someone who looked as if he was in a position of authority, someone she would want to converse with herself. She couldn't escape making a formal greeting.

She watched Ketchman a moment longer. He droned on, until the man to whom he was talking made an impatient gesture and turned away from Ketchman and saw Michaella. Then Ketchman followed his gaze, turning to stare at her with narrowed eyes. His small mouth pursed into a disapproving circle, and his features sharpened, as if he had been caught in some act of wrongdoing.

"Why, isn't this a pleasant surprise," Ketchman purred as he straightened and walked toward Michaella, swinging his cane with determination. Pausing in front of her, he tipped his hat with an awkward motion.

Yielding to convention, Michaella dipped in a slight, stiff curtsy of recognition. This man always gave her the shivers, tiny ripples of warning that tickled along the curve of her spine and made her hair stand on end. Ketchman still had the same trick of smiling a thin, catlike smile when he wished to make a good impression—a trick that had never fooled Michaella for a moment.

"Mr. Ketchman, I am equally surprised to see you here," Michaella commented. "You must be on holiday."

"Actually, I am here on business," he said. He turned back to the man he had left standing alone. "Allow me to introduce Mr. Stricker. He has been overseeing some new projects the company is considering."

Michaella's gaze flicked over the man without much interest. Stricker was tall, thin, and middle-aged. His face was lined with hundreds of tiny red-blue veins that looked like miniature lightning bursts against his sallow skin. Her nose wrinkled as she detected the scent of sour whiskey on the man's breath. Bowing over her wrist with a grand flourish, Stricker pressed his lips to the back of her hand. Her flesh shrank from the touch, and Michaella drew back her hand, wishing it was possible to wipe away the press of his lips without appearing too rude.

"Are you visiting this fair city?" Ketchman asked Michaella with his thin, flat smile.

"No. My sister and I are searching for our father," she said boldly, her eyes daring him to comment. When he did not, but merely exchanged a glance with Stricker, she continued, "We have reason to believe our father is living out in the mountains somewhere."

Stricker and Ketchman lifted their eyebrows, then looked at one another with an expression Michaella could only deem as surprise. So—they hadn't known. That was one conjecture answered, she decided, and waited for the question she knew was coming.

"Where do you think your father might be?" Ketchman asked, attempting to mask his anticipation with a smile.

"I have no idea," she answered blithely, now certain that he knew about the gold. She almost smiled at their obvious disappointment.

After a moment of silence, Stricker said to Michaella with a tinge of malice coloring his tone, "You *are* aware that your father is still an employee of this company, aren't you?" His tight smile widened. "The company has been providing a comfortable allowance to you and your sister. In return, you are expected to confide in us, to tell us everything you know about what he is doing. We haven't heard from Chattilion in some years, and we are sincerely concerned about his welfare . . . indeed, for his life."

"What makes you think he might be in danger?" Michaella asked carefully.

"The mere fact that he hasn't been seen for some time is reason enough to wonder. Those mountains are vast, but our men do travel through them a great deal, bringing news of other trappers back to St. Louis. We are taking care of you and your sister for him, and it seems odd that he would not return every few years to confer with us."

Michaella stiffened, her gaze narrowing on Stricker. "What might you want from him now?"

Clearing his throat, Stricker flicked a glance at Ketchman, who was leaning on his cane with his mouth pursed as he studied Michaella. Noting the glance, Michaella was certain these two men hoped to learn something from her, something that would confirm a course of action for them. She was just as determined they would not.

"Your father is indebted to this company," Stricker began smoothly, "and we want him to pay the debt in whatever way he can. Don't you think that is only appropriate in our circumstance?"

After a moment of silent study, Michaella answered, "So you are saying that my father owes this company, perhaps more than pelts. Am I correct?"

"Don't you agree?" Stricker inquired testily.

"Are you forgetting, Mr. Stricker, that my father helped *build* this fur empire you are now referring to as yours? I am certain *you* were not out in the mountains working and fighting against warring Indians and other fur companies to gather profits. In fact, I doubt you were even employed when this company first began! Correct me if I'm mistaken, Mr. Stricker."

When Stricker's face darkened, Ketchman stepped in to come to his aid. "You can be assured, Michaella, that Mr. Stricker has worked a good many years for this company and has contributed a great deal. He knows company policy. And policy states that as long as employees are paid by the company for their work they are required to contribute whatever they acquire on their own to the company. With no exceptions."

"But my father is not an employee. He is part *owner* of this concern."

"That is incorrect," Stricker put in with a smile. "Your father no longer owns any stock whatsoever in this company."

Feeling as if she had just been struck in the stomach with a hammer, Michaella managed to demand, "What do you mean?"

Stricker shrugged casually. "Your father has been absent from board meetings for a number of years. It was voted by those on the board that since his continued absence indicated his probable demise, his ownership should be distributed equally among the present owners. I can show you the documents, should you like to see them."

"That won't be necessary!" Michaella snapped, fury shadowing her eyes. "I'm certain it has all been tidied up legally with every 'whereas' and 'thereby' in place! But tell me: if that is the case, why did this company continue to provide for myself and my sister? Did you know that eventually we would come looking for our father, and that we should very likely find him, perhaps? I'm certain you wish to know where he is, for whatever reason. Why haven't you tried to locate him yourself?"

Neither Ketchman nor Stricker had a ready answer to soothe her. The company had sent many men out to find him; most had returned with the conviction that Chattilion must be dead, while others had never returned. Old Henry Chattilion was known to be an independent and clever man. No doubt he could avoid anyone he chose to. While no one knew for certain if he were alive, there was every indication that he was.

"You haven't answered my question," Michaella persisted doggedly. "Why haven't *you* located my father yet?"

"Because we do not know where he is," Stricker replied with a heavy sigh. "Believe me, we would have told you immediately if we had found him."

Michaella's chin lifted slightly. "I doubt that. I believe you want to get rid of him. He knows where something is that you want, and when you find it you will no longer need him. You have been waiting for just the right time to let my sister and myself know he might be alive. You knew that we were the only ones he would allow to find him—isn't that true?"

Avoiding her direct, hostile gaze, both men stood with their eyes averted. Michaella obviously knew more than they had guessed she would. Now things would be more complicated than they had anticipated. A wave of frustration swelled inside Ketchman as he realized how much easier matters would have gone if this chance meeting had not occurred. Now they could only send men to trail the two sisters, but it was such an obvious ploy that it would be expected.

Clearing his throat, Ketchman said smoothly, "You must believe that we wish only what is best for you," he began. "And as for 'getting rid' of your father, why, that is preposterous! We have only the best of intentions, and that fact can be proven by asking any of his old cronies. Why . . ."

"Including Sorrel? I understand that he knows a great deal about all this. . . ."

"How do you know Sorrel?" Stricker demanded.

"It is sufficient to say that my sister and I both know him, and have already conversed with him. So you see, I am not so dull witted as you may think!"

"It appears that you are very sharp, indeed," Ketchman said wryly. "You must remember, however, that Sorrel is a man much like your father. He does not listen to orders well, and he is not very loyal."

Bristling at the insinuation that her father was disloyal—though privately she thought him rather a rogue to have abandoned his daughters as he had—Michaella retorted, "I hardly think 'loyal' is the correct term! People are not required to be *loyal* to a company that conducts their business affairs underhandedly."

Ketchman's fingers tightened on the gold-studded head of his cane, and for a moment it appeared as though he would like to strike her. It was Stricker, however, who bit off a sharp answer to her blunt remark. "My good lady, I am of the opinion that you are too brazen for your own good! It hardly seems genteel for such a young woman to be so bold and viper-tongued!"

"You are entitled to your own opinions, sir, but they mean very little to me," Michaella answered coolly.

Stricker's eyes bulged, and while he slowly reddened to the color of a ripe plum, Ketchman watched with detached interest. It hardly seemed necessary to form a reply.

"I don't need any *assistance* from you gentlemen," Michaella said at last. "I have learned quite enough, and I am afraid I have divulged as much as I wish to now. You can rest assured that when we find our father, he will learn everything that has happened at this company. And I am equally certain that he will demand restitution."

Swirling about in a froth of lace petticoat and cotton skirts, Michaella stalked from the dingy little office without another word. Fury blinded her to her surroundings, so that when she rounded a corner of the wide doors leading from the warehouse and collided with a lean male form, she could not utter a sound—even when she recognized Jean Patrick. As she looked up at him, she was unable to form a greeting. Stammering was definitely not showing herself to advantage, she agonized silently.

A slow smile had begun on Jean Patrick's wide, sensual mouth, stretching to his eyes. "Excuse me," he drawled, stepping slightly back and away from her. He had automatically put out a hand to catch her, and now it fell away.

Recovering her voice and balance at approximately the same instant, Michaella flashed, "Don't pretend to be polite! Anyone who works for this company is not to be trusted, in my opinion!" Her curled fists came to rest on her hips as she glared at him and ended with, "In fact, I'm willing to bet even our *chance* meeting yesterday was contrived!"

Only the faintest glimmer of surprise showed in Jean Patrick's eyes as he studied Michaella's snapping eyes and flushed cheeks. "Willing to bet?" he echoed after a moment, his smile never wavering. "How much would you wager, I wonder?"

Ignoring his amused arrogance, Michaella insisted, "You did not come paddling along the shore in your canoe just by chance! I would bet that you were waiting in the trees until you saw my sister and myself. Then you followed in an effort to . . . to . . . to obtain as much information as possible from us."

"Did I? How clever of me," Jean Patrick said, his eyes narrowing at her obvious agitation. His mind worked swiftly to make sense of her accusations, and he realized that, as she was coming from the direction of the warehouse offices, she must have just encountered a rather nasty duo. Ketchman and Stricker, of course. He'd been wrangling with them himself over the past day, and was almost at the end of his admittedly limited patience. Stricker was putting off paying him for his load of furs, using meetings with Ketchman as an excuse. His threat to denounce Ketchman to the officers of the Intermountain Fur Company had not been an idle one. He had done so, and now awaited further action from them although he had no confidence the company would take action against Ketchman. His furs lay unsold, yet he had not been able to retrieve them from the warehouse, due largely to Ketchman's machinations, he was sure. Now the girl was rushing on in a heated tumble of words, pushing the hair back from her eyes and storming at him as if he were responsible for all her troubles. Jean Patrick decided to end this annoyance.

"Don't be so quick to judge me. I don't like it and won't listen to it. Now, if you wish to discuss things calmly and tell me what's troubling you, I'll be glad to listen. Otherwise, I will be forced to be rude and walk away from you."

Gaping at him, Michaella was momentarily taken aback by his bluntness and the raking assessment of his cold blue eyes. Her anger cooled and she realized she'd been unfair. She smiled contritely. "I apologize. *I* was the one being rude."

Jean Patrick's answering smile took away her breath as he offered her his arm. "Then shall we take a short stroll while you tell me what has happened? There's a small public park not far away."

So Michaella found herself strolling arm in arm with Jean Patrick up the narrow cobblestone street to the small green patch of grass overlooking the flowing Mississippi. She slid furtive glances at the powerfully built man at her side, wondering why he was bothering to be so polite and courteous. Somehow, she sensed it was not in keeping with his character to go out of his way like this.

When they reached the grove of large oaks on the river bluff and Jean Patrick had chosen a suitable spot for them to sit, he lowered his lean body to sit beside her. Michaella was demurely spreading out her skirts to drape in graceful folds over her legs, stalling for time in which to think. The day was clear and beautiful, with the sounds of river traffic below and birdsong trilling in the park all around them. Jean Patrick reached out a lazy arm and picked up a fallen acorn from the ground to toss at a curious squirrel that had paused to investigate the newcomers.

"I don't know why I came here with you," Michaella said quietly as she watched the squirrel dash away with its acorn. "I don't even know you."

Jean Patrick's gaze was as soft as a caress. "Are you sure?" he murmured.

Meeting his astringent blue eyes, Michaella felt a sudden rush of warmth through her veins, liquid fire that seared a path straight to her heart. She took a deep breath and asked with studied innocence, "What do you mean? How could I know you? I've never seen you before yesterday."

"Nor I you, but somehow I feel as if I've known you for a long time." His smile was potent, filling the short space between them with tiny charges of jolting current. "When I first saw you standing on the levee with your sister, I felt the same way. I can't explain it."

Speechless, Michaella's earlier anger began slowly to dissolve as she gazed into Jean Patrick's thick-lashed blue eyes. Perhaps she had misjudged him. He certainly did not seem to be the same kind of man as Ketchman and Stricker. Indeed, he did not seem to be like any other man of her acquaintance! This lean, bronzed frontiersman had a special quality that relaxed her, that made her feel as if all her troubles could rest in his very capable hands. And—as perilous as this might be—she felt that she could trust him.

Chapter Five

✦✦✦✦✦

WHILE MICHAELLA WAS sitting on a grassy knoll beneath the spreading branches of an oak, her sister was in a turmoil of anxiety. Mary Catherine fretted quietly, lacing and unlacing her gloved fingers, staring out the carriage window at the crowded streets. How were she and Michaella going to get upriver to Independence? St. Louis was so crowded and everyone seemed to have the same idea at the same time: booking passage on the *Lucy Janine,* a steamboat that was leaving early the next morning. Failing to secure passage on the steamer would mean traveling overland, a much longer and much more dangerous journey.

So Mary Catherine perched on the edge of the uncomfortable carriage seat and peered out the small windows as the vehicle rocked along the streets from the Mansion House to the docks. The driver had warned her that the steamboats were already full, and that the odds of their getting upriver to Independence in time to move out with the wagon trains were slim. This dismayed her more than a little, but Mary Catherine had not come this far to be turned back in defeat. Besides, Michaella would manage to take care of the necessary details. She always had.

When the carriage jolted to a halt and the driver informed her that they had arrived at her destination, Mary Catherine descended in a graceful swoop of flounced skirts. As she lifted her trailing hem from the filthy street, the driver pointed toward the levee. An impressively large steamboat was being loaded with supplies and provisions.

"That's th' *Lucy Janine*, ma'am," he said with a shake of his head. "Good luck to ya," he added, noting the alarm on her delicate features.

Mary Catherine didn't need to hear his muttered, "You'll need it," as he turned away to know that for herself. She tried to think of what Michaella would do in this situation and straightened her shoulders immediately. Striding forward with a determination she didn't feel, Mary Catherine picked her way carefully through the throng. Workers and sightseers blocked her way, while frontiersmen and emigrants of every description pushed their way forward, all desperate to book passage. She was shocked by the smell and nearness of the livestock, the many horses, mules, and oxen being readied for transport. The dizzying reality of the movement west struck her with full force.

The *Lucy Janine* was indeed an admirable craft. With two wide decks surrounded by strong railings all the way around, she was painted in wide stripes of bright blue and white. Her tall twin stacks rose majestically from the forward section. A huge paddle wheel jutted out from the stern, dripping muddy water while workers busily reinforced the individual blades.

Pausing uncertainly, Mary Catherine noticed a man garbed in tailored cotton among the busy throngs on the lower deck of the steamboat. He stood a head taller than those around him, shouting orders in French to the workers loading the cargo. Mary Catherine stepped closer, drawing up her dainty flowered skirts above trim ankles as she worked her way through the crowd toward him. He was obviously a man in charge.

"I must book passage for the next trip to Independence, sir," she said when she reached him. She had to shout to be heard over the noise, one hand holding her wide-brimmed straw bonnet on her head and the other holding her skirts. She smiled prettily when he turned to look at her, and added, "Are you the gentleman I should see about securing passage?"

The voyageur answered in broken English that he was only a foreman, much to his regret. "For I like veree much to 'elp such a lovely ladee," he added with a wide smile that revealed white teeth lined with gold. His smile glittered in the bright sunlight, and Mary Catherine took note of heavy golden earrings dangling from his earlobes and sparkling with dull brilliance. She had never before seen a man adorned thus, and it was a novelty she could not ignore, even for the sake of courtesy. After a moment in which the Frenchman openly admired Mary Catherine's fresh beauty, he directed her toward the captain's quarters located in the middle of the boat.

Thanking him, Mary Catherine pushed her way back into the confusion milling about her. Animals, foremen, and dockworkers created a deafening roar as the livestock objected to being loaded aboard the massive boat. Hooves slipped and slid on the slick decks and animals went down, panicked by the unnatural surroundings and the unsteady footing.

Just up the deck, Mary Catherine noticed an

older man dressed in worn trail clothes who was trying to get a half-dozen mules to settle in peacefully among the other livestock. The mule driver's patience with the beasts was obviously nearing its limit. He was trying to tie their halter ropes to the railing, but the mules were balking, tugging against him and disturbing the other animals and people around them.

A loud argument broke out between a farmer who was holding some spooked draft horses and the muleteer. The two men continued to argue with lifted voices and brandishing fists, while the mules became more and more excited. Mary Catherine paused to glance into the rows of windows lining the upper deck when she heard the clamor grow even more rowdy. A loud yell pierced the thick fog of shouts.

"Runaways! Clear the deck! Runaways!"

Whirling about, Mary Catherine was just in time to see the terrified mules charging wildly across the deck toward her. A crush of people rushed to get clear of their path, tumbling over one another and slipping on the wet deck. Two of the mules jumped blindly from the boat into the water, splashing the crowd. The other four beasts continued wild-eyed and lathered, charging through the throng of people unable to get out of the way.

Mary Catherine flattened herself against the steamer wall, but because of the incredible press of people, was thrown off balance. She slid sideways with a cry, and found herself in the direct path of a plunging mule. It crashed into the railing next to her, twisting and turning in its frantic search for escape. Braying loudly, the beast lashed out with a hind foot that glanced painfully off Mary Catherine's upper thigh. As she doubled up in agony, the mule leaped over her, scattering passengers and deckhands in its mad flight along the deck. She was vaguely aware that it had leaped the railing also, landing on the muddy levee and clambering up the banks to join the other runaways, with the owner in hot pursuit of his animals.

When she was able to sit up, she leaned back against the broken railing and sucked in sharp, painful breaths of air. Nothing was broken, she decided a moment later, exploring the tender portion of her leg. Yet the pain remained intense and her eyes welled with tears.

A shadow fell across her, blotting out the hazy light filtering through the press of bodies, and she looked up. It was the French foreman, and he was bending down beside her with a frown on his sharp features.

"Are you hurt?" he asked, putting his hands under her elbows to help lift her.

"I . . . I think I am all—oh!" she ended in a cry as her leg buckled beneath her weight. Walking proved to be an agony as the foreman assisted her in hobbling to one side and out of the crowd. "Truly," she said, swallowing her tears as best she could, "I can manage by myself."

"No, you must allow me to help you, my good lady," came another, commanding, voice. "I insist."

Mary Catherine felt a strong arm usher her away from the foreman and the other workers. Startled, she glanced up and into the handsome face of a man in captain's uniform. He ordered the Frenchman to get his men back to work cleaning up the mess left by the recalcitrant mules.

"And hurry, as we are behind schedule," he added before turning back to Mary Catherine. His voice softened. ""I am Captain Bringham Howe, and I cannot express how sorry I am about this unfortunate incident. Let me take you to my cabin so that you may rest. . . ."

Nearly overcome by pain, Mary Catherine allowed herself to be led away. "I haven't the time," she told him as they walked slowly down the narrow passageway. "I simply wish to book passage to Independence. My sister is waiting for me back at the Mansion House. She'll be worried." Choking back a sob, she clutched more tightly at the captain's arm.

"Nonsense," Bringham Howe responded immediately. "You are in no condition to go anywhere right now. I will send word to your sister about your mishap. Allow me to care for you. After all, you were injured on my boat, so let me make amends."

Studying him through the thick fringe of her long lashes, Mary Catherine considered briefly. With her leg injured, she could not fight her way back through the crowd to her carriage and then endure a long, jolting ride to their hotel. Perhaps . . . well, after all, the captain *did* appear to be a gentleman, and a very handsome one at that! Dark blond hair of the color her mother used to call "dishwater" curled from under the edges of his cap, and she could see kindness in the clear blue eyes fixed so earnestly on her face. How could she leave now, especially when her mishap seemed to have guaranteed passage to Independence on the *Lucy Janine*?

So Mary Catherine smiled demurely and allowed as how the captain was too kind, and yes, it would be best to send someone in a carriage to retrieve her sister, Michaella, and their belongings from the hotel. The gallant captain delighted her further by insisting that their passage and all expenses would be courtesy of the *Lucy Janine*. She was only to ask for whatever she might want, and it would be delivered.

"My quarters are on the upper deck," he said, sensing her capitulation. To Mary Catherine's mortification he swept her from her shaky feet and into his strong arms, holding her against his body and staring into her eyes. "I assure you that my intentions are only honorable," he said so sincerely that she had to believe him.

The captain's quarters, Mary Catherine noted as he pushed inside the heavy door, appeared to have been custom designed and built. She was certain it was much more luxurious than the usual room afforded most steamboat captains. A lavish expanse of dark hardwood partially covered with thick red carpeting covered the floor. One large window offered a clear view of the helmsmen and the slow-moving river stretching in front of the boat.

Captain Howe carefully pulled out a large oak chair by hooking his foot in the lower rungs, then seated his burden as gently as possible. She sagged into the chair, grimacing from the pain in her leg, and flashed him a grateful smile. Spread in front of her was a table set with fine crystal glassware, linen, silver, and pale bone china. Servants poured through the doorway, and she watched, amazed, as they set a sampling of hot teas and laid out a meal of crayfish in exotic sauce before the captain and his young guest.

Lifting one eyebrow, Mary Catherine asked, "Is this the normal fare on river steamboats?"

"I own this boat," Captain Howe replied with a laugh threading his deep voice. "Therefore, I make all the decisions."

Too tired to guard against his charm and hospitality, Mary Catherine felt herself beginning to relax at last. Time passed slowly as she picked daintily at her food, wishing she dared be rude and gobble like a common milkmaid. When she was full at last, she sat back in the cushioned chair and patted her mouth with the edge of a fine linen napkin.

She sipped hot, delicious tea from a bone-china cup, thinking that she had not had good tea since leaving England. Everything in the elegantly appointed cabin was nice, as nice as the captain himself, and as she sipped tea and cast covert glances at the handsome young captain, a thought occurred to her.

"You appear quite young to have your own steamboat," she observed, shyly watching Howe's reaction through her lowered lashes. "You must know the river and the boat business very well."

Chuckling slightly, he replied, "I grew up on the river. It seemed a natural decision to become a captain."

She considered the captain for a long moment. He had placed his silver knife and fork across his plate and was smiling at her. Mary Catherine suddenly wondered what Michaella would do in such a situation. Her older sister was always so suspicious, but her suspicions were ofttimes borne out as all too true. Perhaps she should be careful. And perhaps the captain was trying very hard—a little *too* hard—to charm her. So Mary Catherine listened politely, if a bit skeptically, to his lengthy explanation.

"My father had one of the first steamboats," he was saying importantly, "and I helped him work up and down the river, hauling everything you can imagine. After people became interested in going west, I decided the best money was in transporting emigrants from here to Independence, and taking those who fail to make new lives for themselves back. I'm doing very well at it."

"Very well indeed," Mary Catherine murmured. "I am grateful that you have shown me so much kindness. But you must not feel obliged to take my sister and me on as guests. It was not your fault that wretched mule chose to kick me in the leg."

Captain Howe studied Mary Catherine for a time. "Young women with your beauty are very rare on this river. I don't mean to appear forward, but I am certainly curious as to your destination. I would hate to see further misfortune befall you. By the way—how *is* your leg? Better, I hope."

"Much better, thank you." Her deep blue eyes shone with determination. While he seemed honest enough, she sensed she should not tell him about their quest. She decided to tell him they were on their way out to the frontier for the same reasons as many of the women they had already met.

"My name is Mrs. Mary Catherine Morgan," she said. "My sister's name is Mrs. Michaella White. We are going to join our husbands at their outpost."

The captain nodded. He watched her a moment. "Which outpost, if I might be so bold as to ask?"

"Santa Fe," Mary Catherine said quickly. She had heard the post mentioned often along the docks and at the hotel. It seemed to be one of the major destinations of many people both in and out of the military. Everyone was headed either there or to California to find gold or out to Oregon to settle.

Captain Bringham Howe raised his eyebrows. "I must say, that is a long way from here. And the country is certainly dangerous. Do you and your sister plan to travel out there unescorted?"

Mary Catherine shrugged. "I cannot see any alternative. Besides, there are many women who are in our predicament."

The captain did not nod in agreement this time. He looked at her a moment, then refilled their teacups. Why was she here? he wondered. Who was responsible for sending her west?

Mary Catherine could tell that the captain was not even remotely convinced of her story. He finally shrugged and slanted her a sideways smile as he commented, "It seems to me that a woman of your means, and I assume your sister's as well, would be traveling *en escorte* with other military people . . . possibly a contingent of women and their husbands also on their way to Santa Fe. Of course, there *are* women who have husbands in the military, but a great percentage of them will never locate their men. And it seems that there are any number of common wives who are struggling to find their spouses, who have no doubt run off from them. Although I hardly think a man with any sense or reasonable eyesight would run off from you."

Mary Catherine blushed. "Well, I am appreciative of your hospitality, but I will be going ahead with my sister. We intend to meet our husbands." Which was not entirely untrue, she thought guiltily, for after all, they *did* hope to meet suitable husbands one day!

Captain Howe cleared his throat. "I know your leg must be terribly painful, and I apologize for taxing your strength with my questions." Sensing her discomfort, he changed the subject. "I will have your leg treated by a wonderful woman who can help relieve some of the pain. She's treated me several times, once for snakebite. Let me show you to the room where you and your sister will be staying. You must want to rest."

With some misgivings, Mary Catherine took Captain Howe's arm and limped beside him until they reached a large room decorated in lavender velvet and satin upholstery and drapes. Again she was amazed by the luxury of this boat, which from the outside did not appear to be all that different from any other. Inside the room there were two spacious beds and two large oak dressers decorated with fresh flowers and small ornate crystal bottles of imported perfume. In most steamboats, she knew, several women shared one room.

Turning in the open doorway, Captain Howe smiled at her. "If there is anything else you need, please tell any one of the porters."

After he shut the door, the room was quiet, with only the muffled sounds of the men on the deck filtering through. Mary Catherine suddenly felt very alone and out of place. She wanted to leave. But then there was a knock on the door.

"Anyone to home?" came a pleasant voice from behind the hickory paneled door.

Mary Catherine limped to the door and opened it to see a large Negro lady with a broad smile and big warm eyes standing in the hall. The woman was short and wide, with hair and eyebrows of mixed white and gray. She was holding a large pan filled with a thick, dark mush immersed in steaming water. It had an exotic smell, almost sweet. Towels were draped across both arms, and she smiled as she waited to be let in.

Mary Catherine gestured her inside, wondering at the contents of the large pan.

"Don' be 'fraid o' me, chile," she said with a good-natured laugh. "I got somethin' here that's sure to help yo' leg. You jus' lie down on the bed yonder and let ol' Clara do the res'."

Mary Catherine hobbled over to the bed. Clara was humming while she set the pan down on one of the dressers and laid the towels beside them. She noticed Mary Catherine sitting on the bed watching her.

"Them men outside is sure noisy, ain't they?" she said. "You need to take off thet dress so's I can help your leg."

While Mary Catherine removed her dress and

pantaloons, Clara worked with the herbs, smearing a large mass of the mixture onto one of the towels.

Lying on the bed, Mary Catherine looked at the side of her leg. It was swollen badly, with a lump in the muscle tissue where the mule's hoof had struck her. Already a patch of dark blue was forming.

"I heard an ol' mule kicked you. They's not to be trusted, them mules." Her smile widened as she gazed at Mary Catherine. "Chile, you got the prettiest dark red hair."

Smiling back, Mary Catherine thanked her for the compliment. It was plain that Clara knew how to make people feel at ease.

Clara pressed the mixture onto Mary Catherine's thigh, singing quietly as she worked. The herbs were hot, almost blistering, but Mary Catherine did not flinch. Soon the heat became a steady warmth that worked at the pain in her leg. It was a soothing feeling, and Mary Catherine found herself very relaxed.

"Tha's not so bad, now is it?" Clara said, stopping her singing to smile at her patient again.

Mary Catherine peered dubiously at her leg. "What is it you put on me?"

Clara shrugged. "I don' know the name of the roots, but I do know they work good. I learned it as a chile from my gran'mother. She could always cure an ailment."

"Could she? My grandmother was the same, I understand." Then embarrassed she asked, "How do you know Captain Howe?"

Clara didn't pause in her ministrations, but kept

working, her blunt, strong fingers massaging the injured leg. "His pappy was good to my family. He's good to my family, too. He's a good man. You jus' res' easy, you hear?"

"I have no plans to leave for anywhere," Mary Catherine said with a laugh. "I can't walk very well with a lump tied to my leg."

Clara laughed. "That's a mighty big lump there, too."

"I want to thank you."

Clara smiled. "I'm happy to do it. You jus' rest easy now."

Clara went back to singing, and Mary Catherine took a deep breath. She felt herself relaxing even more as the poultice worked its magic on her leg.

"Tha's it, chile," Clara said between songs. "Now I'm goin' to tie this aroun' your leg and come back later. Bes' rest for a while. You'll be good as new."

Clara sang her way out the door, and Mary Catherine allowed herself to close her eyes. The throbbing in her leg had been reduced a great deal, and warmth had spread throughout her body. She could not get the image of Captain Howe out of her mind, and his face was the last thing she saw as she drifted off to a dreamless sleep.

Chapter Six

MICHAELLA LOOKED OUT from the hillside toward the deep waters of the river. As Jean Patrick sat watching her, she felt a pleasant warmth rush over her, and she struggled to control her feelings. She was drawn to this mountain man's charm, but she was terribly afraid. After a meaningful silence, he turned and spoke, curious to learn what had upset her so.

"What happened with Ketchman and Stricker? You looked like you were arguing with them."

Michaella didn't know if she should even trust Jean Patrick. She believed she could, but there was the risk that he was trying to succeed where Ketchman and Stricker had failed.

"Let's just say we had a disagreement," she said finally, wrapping her arms around her skirt to cover her knees.

"I understand," Jean Patrick said soothingly. He resisted the urge to smooth back a lock of her dark hair. "I can see how you would be sensitive to talking about your father." His strong fingers were twisting stalks of grass as he continued. "I couldn't imagine not knowing whether someone I loved was dead or alive."

"It's been hard for both of us," she said, nodding. "But my sister and I are both here now. We have to find him."

"I'm just thinking that I might be able to help," Jean Patrick said, still twisting the grass.

"I honestly don't know how much to tell you," Michaella confessed. "I know you work for the fur company, so I don't know if I can trust you. I don't mean to be harsh, but that is how I feel."

Dropping the grass, Jean Patrick met her worried gaze. "I am a free trapper, and I sell my furs wherever I can get the best price. Until now, that was the Intermountain Fur Company." His mouth twisted in a mocking smile. "As the old saying goes, 'A bird in the hand is worth two in the bush,' and I don't have anything in hand yet. Ketchman may find out that he has tangled with the wrong man as soon as the company officers take action. Anyway, that is why I'm still here. Our meeting was purely by chance."

"Then you know Mr. Stricker? And Mr. Ketchman?"

Jean Patrick was slow in answering. "I"ve known Stricker a long time. I can't say I liked him, but I've dealt with him any number of times. As for Ketchman, I just met him. He strikes me as no different from Stricker—two peas in a pod."

"Mr. Stricker told me my father was in debt to the company for considerations to my sister and myself."

"I doubt that," Jean Patrick said. "Unless he can show you a signed document that proves your father asked the company to care for you and your sister on his behalf, they have nothing to hold him for. I think they're just trying to gain control of you the way they try with everyone else."

Michaella knew those scoundrels would never gain control of her. She would always be true to herself. She turned back to stare out at the river. From their place on the hill they could see boats in the distance moving downriver on their way to

Cairo. The wind blew her hair around her face, and Michaella had never felt so free. She wanted to touch Jean Patrick's face, but instead she reveled in the glorious feeling of the afternoon.

"Do you think Ketchman and Stricker know where your father is?" Jean Patrick asked.

"I don't believe so," Michaella answered slowly. "They certainly wouldn't be interested in my sister and myself if they did. I am wondering about another man . . . a big man named Sorrel. Have you ever heard of him?"

Jean Patrick nodded. "He is well known in the mountains. How do you know of him?"

"Mary Catherine—that's my sister—and I met him when we were children. You can't forget a red-haired giant when you're six years old. But finding him gambling in a grog shop was quite an experience."

Jean Patrick listened to her story of how they had come across Sorrel.

"A grog shop is no place for a lady," Jean Patrick said with a laugh. "But he is the man to talk to—he knows a lot about the frontier."

"Maybe," Michaella said. "But when we tried to talk to him, he wouldn't tell us much."

Jean Patrick nodded. "He's stubborn. But don't let that stop you. If you really want to, you can find your father—whether or not you and your sister get any help from anybody."

Michaella now knew for sure that Jean Patrick was telling her he would help in any way he could. She thought about what he had said earlier.

"What would you do if you weren't a trapper?" Michaella wondered aloud.

"I've thought about that. There is a great demand for guides to take wagon trains through the mountains to California and the Oregon territories. I just might hire on and take a train through."

"Out of Independence?"

"There or St. Joe. There're a lot of people headed into the new land in the West. They don't really know what's out there, but they're calling it the Promised Land. I don't know who promised it to them, but I do know the Bible well enough to be sure that nothing is promised for free. I hope those folks realize they are going to have to work just as hard, or harder, than where they came from."

"Is it as dangerous as they say it is?" Michaella couldn't help a surge of excitement from running through her.

"Every bit," Jean Patrick said with a nod. "The country is a lot different from what you see here and in the East. For the most part, there's not nearly as much rainfall out there. It's dry and a long way between stops for water. Deserts lie between the mountain ranges, deserts so hot they can kill even a man who knows how to cross them. And the mountains . . . the winters freeze the land up tight and cover it with snow you can't walk through. It's not a good place to be unless you're ready for it."

"Mary Catherine and I are ready for it," Michaella said without hesitation. "It won't be easy, but we're ready."

"You know," Jean Patrick began slowly, "I know your sister's name and you know mine, but I still don't know yours. . . ."

Smiling shyly, she answered, "Michaella."

"Somehow I knew your name would be as lovely as you are," he said softly, smiling when she blushed.

Jean Patrick studied Michaella for a time. He could sense her determination. Underneath the fashionable exterior was a woman whose spirit could likely withstand a great many tests. Though she had obviously been raised to know and appreciate the best that money could buy, he had no doubt she could fend for herself whenever necessary.

Again Jean Patrick realized how much he already admired this woman whom he had just met. With a woman like this, there could be a future, maybe. There had been times in his life when he'd not thought beyond the moment.

Jean Patrick had always wondered how his life would have turned out had his parents lived. He could still see his aunt's face when she told him, tears streaming down her face. She had held him so tightly he could barely breathe. His aunt had wanted to raise him, but his uncle had stolen him out of bed before dawn early one morning and had stowed him away aboard a keelboat. The Missouri River had taken them away from civilization for a long, long time.

He had lived with his uncle among Crow, Shoshone, and Nez Percé Indians. His uncle had always believed in the Indian way—that a child came into the world to learn and to teach the parents something. When one or the other was finished with the learning, he left the world as we know it.

From the Indians Jean Patrick learned many lessons: much that goes on cannot be explained, and while it is not necessary to understand everything, one must have respect. Visions had come to him as a young man, some of which he was only now beginning to understand. And now, sitting next to this woman he had met by chance, a dark-haired lady more beautiful than any he could remember, he was struck by the feeling that he knew everything there was to know about her.

Michaella watched his eyes as he gazed over the water, lost in thought. Finally he turned to her and smiled. "I guess I went back to the mountains there for a while. I shouldn't have abandoned you like that."

Tilting her head to one side so that a drift of dark hair spilled over her shoulder, she said quietly, "I'll see the mountains for myself soon enough." She slanted a bold look at him from beneath her lowered lashes. Michaella was startled by her interest in this man, startled by the thoughts she was having. . . . She yearned for him to hold her while she looked out at the river and beyond.

Then he was leaning over and gently touching his warm lips to hers, catching her by complete surprise. When her eyes opened, he whispered huskily, "You are so very beautiful."

Shaken, Michaella pulled away and sat back, embarrassed and flushed with emotion. "Oh, I didn't mean . . . I only . . . But enough of this! Why am I kissing you?"

"Because you were meant to," Jean Patrick answered in the same husky whisper. "Don't make me a stranger when I'm not . . . or never could be."

Wildly searching for a distraction, anything that would remove her from this dangerous spot with this dangerous man and her even more dangerous emotions, she blurted the first thing that came to mind. "I have to find Mary Catherine!" Struggling to her feet, she tried to keep from looking into his eyes.

He rose in a lithe, easy motion, and she was certain a smile was lurking at the corners of his mouth as he said, "Allow me at least to accompany you and your sister to Independence. We'll decide what happens from there."

Helpless to deny the fact that she was as taken with him as he seemed to be with her, she stood for a moment and looked into his deep, soulful eyes. Her breath was short, and her heart was pumping madly to supply her oxygen-starved brain with enough air to enable it to function again. Everything was so mixed up, and if only he weren't standing there waiting for an answer, that silly, attractive smile crooking his mouth, she could form a decently scathing reply. But he was and she couldn't. "That would be nice. . . ." Michaella heard herself say, adding, "I must get back to Mansion House or my sister will be worried. Please! I must go soon."

Jean Patrick escorted Michaella to a carriage and reassured her that he would board the steamboat and travel with them to Independence while his crew watched over his furs. He knew the *Lucy Janine* was leaving the next morning. Emigrants going west would need a guide such as he, and there would be good money in it. But most of all, there would be Michaella.

Staring out the small, square window of the coach, Michaella saw him wave as the vehicle lurched forward, and she wished he was beside her still. It was a frightening thought. How could she want him near her like this? She could not allow her emotions to get in the way now, not when she had so much to do. And besides—how did Jean Patrick feel about her? It was a question that bothered her the entire journey back to her hotel.

The carriage bumped to a halt in front of the imposing Mansion House. Michaella stepped out, paid the driver, and turned toward the hotel doors. By this time, she had come to the decision that, should Jean Patrick indeed show up on the riverboat, she would speak to him only casually and not at any great length. They could always find another guide. That decided, she walked briskly into the hotel with her head up, determined to think only of the trip out into the mountains to find her father.

In the lobby she was approached by the manager of the Mansion House himself, a Mr. Richards. He smiled and gestured to their luggage, which was near the door.

"I am pleased to tell you that you and your sister are the guests of the steamboat *Lucy Janine*," he said. "Her captain is a friend of mine, Captain Bringham Howe. He has sent word that your sister is already aboard and awaits your arrival."

Michaella stared at him blankly, trying to absorb what he had said and displace the other thoughts whirling madly in her head. Finally she repeated, "My sister is now on the boat waiting for me? She didn't come back here first?"

"She is on the boat," he confirmed with a nod

and a toothy smile. "I don't wish to alarm you," he added in a confidential tone that irritated her, "but it seems your sister—I believe her name is Mary Catherine?—has met with a slight accident. She is well, I am told, but does not wish to come back to the hotel in her condition."

Alarm clutched her throat, and Michaella reached out to grasp his coat sleeve. "What condition?" she demanded.

Giving her a pained glance, Mr. Richards intoned, "All I have been told is that it is nothing serious and that she is resting at the moment. Please do not be alarmed . . . there is no need. She is waiting for you."

While she watched porters loading their belongings into a carriage, Michaella struggled in vain to keep calm. It was only when she was seated in the carriage and alone once more that hundreds of different possibilities swarmed into her mind, gnawing at her forced calm like ravening beasts. She had no idea what to expect when she saw Mary Catherine.

Awakened from a deep sleep by the sudden opening of the cabin door, Mary Catherine turned slowly over in the bunk to see her sister step inside. A smile curved the soft line of her mouth, and she rubbed sleepily at her eyes.

"What happened?" Michaella demanded, as she stared down at her sister with an anxious frown.

"Happened? Oh, oh, yes," Mary Catherine murmured, wincing as she sat up in the bunk. Upon receiving the full brunt of her older sister's gaze, she said hastily, "You needn't worry! I was kicked in the leg by a mule, but a Captain Howe—who is such a nice gentleman, despite his being a boat captain—had a dear lady apply some sort of poultice to it. You would be amazed at the improvement, Michaella, really you would!" Her voice faltered slightly at her sister's exasperated grimace, and she gave her leg an experimental shake. Glancing up in genuine surprise, Mary Catherine exclaimed, "Oh! It *is* almost well!"

"Thank God!" Michaella snapped, dropping her reticule on the end of the bunk. "I wasn't at all certain which mule I should shake first. Now I know."

"Oh, don't be angry with me," Mary Catherine begged. "It was not at all my fault, and I am sorry to have frightened you. Perhaps I should have sent a more detailed message."

"Yes. Perhaps you should have." Michaella plopped down on the bunk beside her sister. "I didn't know what to believe. First I got back to the hotel to hear that you were on board waiting for me, and then I learned you were injured. And then the captain of this boat—Howe, I believe his name is—why, he talked to me as if you were his wife."

Mary Catherine dimpled. "A lady could do worse, don't you think?"

"No doubt," Michaella said dryly. "But in such a short time?"

"Speaking of a short time," Mary Catherine said, "it seems you were occupied at the fur company for quite a while. You must have learned a lot about Father and Sorrel and the mountains."

"Ah, any change of topic will be welcome, is that it?" Michaella smiled fondly at her sister. She considered telling Mary Catherine about her long conversation with Jean Patrick, but decided against it. There was no need to bring him up when she was trying her best not to think of him. She decided instead to relate in detail the problems she encountered upon finding Nolan Ketchman in the offices.

Mary Catherine's round eyes grew even rounder when she heard that Ketchman was in America. And the details Michaella added reinforced her suspicions about Ketchman's intentions toward their father.

Their conversation was interrupted when a porter knocked at the door and told them that the captain was now in his quarters and wished them to join him for dinner. "It will be served as soon as you ladies arrive," he added.

Michaella's frown deepened when she saw Mary Catherine's wide, delighted smile. There must be something special about this captain to so attract her sister, and she intended to discover just what it might be. After all, her brief meeting with him had not impressed her as it obviously had Mary Catherine. This, Michaella thought grimly, could well be an interesting dinner!

Chapter Seven

WITH MICHAELLA'S HELP, Mary Catherine dressed and tidied her hair, and the two of them went to the captain's quarters, where Bringham Howe was giving orders to the servants. Standing tall and handsome near an oak table set with silver plates and crystal glassware, he turned to greet his guests.

"I trust you are feeling much better," he said to Mary Catherine, his gaze lingering on her heart-shaped face.

"Yes, thank you," Mary Catherine said softly, staring down at the rich carpet instead of daring to look up at the captain. "Clara is wonderful. Please give her my thanks."

"I shall," Bringham Howe said. "Please, both of you, enjoy your dinner."

They sat down to generous helpings of roast duck, hominy, and French rolls. Three bottles of fine French wine were at the captain's disposal, and he encouraged Michaella and Mary Catherine to try each one. Neither of them partook to the extent the captain did, though it was obvious he hoped to put the ladies at ease.

While the three of them ate, the conversation centered around the crowds of people coming into St. Louis and the beckoning frontier. Independence, the captain said, was seven to eight days of river travel away, depending on conditions and hazards encountered in the water. Just beyond there was Westport, the jumping-off place for emigrants headed into the wilderness. The captain cautioned his two guests that both settlements were jammed with people from all walks of life, and that they could expect just about anything to happen.

"And stay off the streets after dark," he added with another soft gaze at Mary Catherine. "It's not safe.

"However, most menacing of all is the wilderness. Although I've been content to stay on the river, I've heard a great number of stories from traders and mountain men. It's a challenging, often deadly place.

"I cannot understand why military men would not take wives such as you two with them when they left for their frontier posts. Were I married to either of you, I wouldn't let you out of my sight."

Michaella had to smile. The captain had been staring directly at Mary Catherine throughout most of this speech. He was obviously so infatuated with her that he could not contain himself. And she knew very well that the tale of being army wives was not fooling him in the least. But that was no reason to give in to his curiosity.

Placing her waterglass on the linen-topped table, Michaella said easily, "Please understand that life does not always go as smoothly as one wishes. Don't you think there are many army husbands who would have given the world to have their wives with them when they first were sent to the frontier? Surely you must realize that at times circumstances frustrate our hopes."

"I confess I have been wondering what those circumstances might be for you two ladies," the captain said.

Michaella looked down at the napkin folded in her lap. "I am certainly grateful for your hospitality, and Mary Catherine shares my feelings, I'm sure, but I don't wish to give you the impression that you are responsible for us."

The captain blinked in momentary confusion. "Please, I didn't mean to offend you. I was merely stating my concern for your welfare and offering to help, if I might."

"Of course," Michaella said. "No offense has been taken. But Mary Catherine and I have a destination that we cannot be dissuaded from. We do appreciate your thoughtfulness, however."

Nodding, the captain sighed. There was little doubt in his mind that these two women would persevere in whatever they determined to do. And he could only wish them the best of luck. And wish to himself that they would be back.

The captain had little else to say, other than describing landmarks to watch for during the trip upriver to Independence. He continued to feast his eyes on Mary Catherine and remarked offhandedly that though many women rode the river, none of them had ever caught his fancy. "Perhaps I shall never marry," he declared with a burning gaze at Mary Catherine.

Deciding enough was enough, Michaella stood up. "Thank you so much for your kindness. But I'm afraid that we are both very weary, and as my sister is still rather sore . . ."

"Oh, of course, of course," Howe said immediately. "Forgive me, please! I forgot my manners."

Once back in the spacious cabin, Michaella paced the floor and gazed thoughtfully at the furnishings. She admired the beautiful pieces and remarked—as Mary Catherine previously had—that this vessel was one of a kind in almost every way, including the personality of its captain. Pausing, she lit the stained-glass lantern resting on one of the dressers and then turned to Mary Catherine.

"I do believe Captain Howe is quite taken with you," she said. "He is very handsome. And I noticed the feeling seems to be mutual."

Mary Catherine was gazing dreamily out the window, watching as night shadows drifted over the Mississippi River. She didn't want to admit to her sister that she found the captain attractive, if a bit demanding. From his conversation, she had decided he was hard to please in many ways, and he seemed very choosy regarding women.

"I think he liked your smile very much," Michaella added, continuing her teasing.

"Oh, I can remember our first hour here in St. Louis," Mary Catherine retorted quickly. "It seems to me there was a frontiersman in a canoe who did his share of smiling at you. Don't you recall?"

Mary Catherine noted how quickly her sister fell silent. Nothing was said as Michaella undressed and put on a long white cotton nightdress with lace collar and sleeves. There were only the unfamiliar sounds of boards creaking and ropes straining, and in the distance muted footsteps that were evidence of nighttime activity aboard the steamer. Mary Catherine waited until Michaella had gotten into bed before she spoke.

"What are you thinking about so hard?" she asked in a soft voice.

Peering over the edge of the blanket spread atop

her bunk, Michaella narrowed her eyes at her sister. "Nothing really," she said finally.

"Nothing really?"

"Go to sleep!" Michaella exclaimed in exasperation.

A smile rode her full lips as Mary Catherine blew out the lantern. "Sweet dreams, Michaella," she said.

The *Lucy Janine* was loaded heavily, so heavily that she sat low enough in the water to allow an occasional wave to splash over the deck. Though it was spring and the water was high, the boat was so laden that there was doubt it would be able to clear the many snags and sandbars waiting in the river.

The dawn had broken clear, but clouds had moved in since and a sudden thunderstorm sent big drops of water slashing down to wet decks and passengers. Michaella and Mary Catherine, holding umbrellas, stood near the bow of the boat, marveling at the sights now before their eyes. People from everywhere were headed west. They were a curious mixture, to say the least: immigrant farmers and shopkeepers from all points east; Negroes, Spaniards, and Frenchmen; and all manner of drifters and adventurers, including the many types of frontiersmen and mountain men Michaella and Mary Catherine had grown accustomed to during their first day in St. Louis.

Though the sights were fascinating, Michaella had noticed Jean Patrick moving toward them, and was watching him too intently to devote her full attention to the comings and goings around her.

"You're getting all wet," she told him. "Move over here and I'll share my umbrella."

When he did, and his arm brushed against her, she felt a small shiver dance up the curve of her spine. It was like tempting fate, tempting lightning to strike by standing on a hill in a storm, and it felt wonderful. She felt wonderful standing beside him. He told her he had arrived on deck early in the morning with just a small buckskin bag. He didn't need much on the frontier, he had said. His eyes were their usual sparkling blue, visible through the thick, almost girlish fringe of his dark lashes. Michaella sucked in a deep breath of air, which tasted rain-scoured and fresh in spite of the muddy river water that swirled around the boat.

To Michaella the morning had been glorious, cloudy or not. To see Jean Patrick had been exhilarating. He stood out in a crowd, noticeable among the other men with no effort on his part. She hoped he would decide to lead their wagon train out from Independence. If he didn't, it was going to be very hard to forget him.

The rain stopped as quickly as it had begun. When they reached the juncture with the Missouri, the sun came out to reveal the numerous islands and ragged sandbars pushing up through the strong current. Along the shores rolled dense green forest that covered the land in all directions. It was beautiful and reminded the sisters of the English countryside.

"Tell me," Michaella asked as they leaned against the railing, "does the land look like this all the way upriver?"

"The country changes a lot when you get farther

west. You had better enjoy the trees while you can. There is a lot of country between here and the mountains where trees don't exist."

"What's out there if there are no trees?"

"Grass. Oceans of grass. Grass that grows higher than your head in some places. And it goes on farther than you can see."

Michaella and Mary Catherine exchanged dubious glances. They had seen tall grass, but not that much of it at one time.

"And there is a lot of game—deer and elk and antelope, and buffalo in herds so vast they cover the entire landscape as far as the eye can see," Jean Patrick added. "You have never seen anything like it in your lives, I'm sure."

"Surely there can't be so many of those buffalo that they cover the prairies," Mary Catherine said.

"You'll see," Jean Patrick promised.

Michaella and Mary Catherine were both silent, trying to imagine what it must be like to see so many buffalo at one time. This strange land certainly must hold fascinations far beyond their wildest dreams.

The boat surged through millions of tons of water, its prow pushing through brown and cream foam and displacing it on each side.

"Right here is the widest and deepest the river will get. Near the headwaters, you can usually wade across it."

"It's that shallow?" Michaella asked in amazement.

"It stays wide, for the most part, but it is very shallow in places."

Mary Catherine gave her frilly parasol a twirl that dispersed raindrops over her sister and Jean Patrick. "It is truly beautiful here."

"You'll be seeing it for a while, I'm afraid," Jean Patrick said. "From the looks of the debris in the river, we could be in for a slow trip up to Independence."

Michaella and Mary Catherine soon discovered he was right. Underneath the water, eddies swirled and snags awaited the boat. The spring runoff from the mountains was unusually heavy, and the river was muddy and swollen. Large uprooted trees were driven through the water past the steamboat, often slamming against its sides. Other obstacles hid themselves in the brown current and rocked the passengers when the boat ran aground. During that first day, Jean Patrick soothed both sisters' exasperation more than once while they waited as long as three hours for the steamboat to come off a sandbar.

"This river changes all the time," Jean Patrick told them. "Whole chunks of bank will fall away and get washed across to the other side. The channels move. The bottom changes. Trying to negotiate this river for very long takes an enormous amount of skill."

They spent much of the first three days watching the shoreline. Monotony was broken on occasion by Captain Howe's visits. He would explain to them what was happening when they would hear the odd scraping sounds of trees and snags and sandbars under the boat. Once they had to stop to repair a paddle. But all that quickly became routine, and the hours began to take on a sameness characterized by an endless parade of muddy water and passing shoreline.

Michaella and Mary Catherine ate in the captain's quarters each evening. Captain Howe no longer delved into anything that could be deemed private. He spoke in generalities about the river and his life on it and the frontier. He talked a lot about growing up on the river and seeing the growth of St. Louis.

With each new day spent strolling the decks and staring out over the railing, it became obvious to Michaella that Mary Catherine was drawn more and more to the captain. She would sparkle when he came on deck and paused to speak to her, and her mouth would curve in a coquettish smile as she laughed at his jests—some of which Michaella privately thought rather inane. But not Mary Catherine. She took interest when he spoke and made it obvious that she liked being with him. Several times during the course of the journey Michaella expected to hear Mary Catherine announce her intentions of remaining on the boat. And when she could stand it no more, Michaella asked her about it one evening.

Mary Catherine was startled. "Michaella, why would you think such a thing? Why, no! I would never make any such decisions until after we find Father. You must surely know that."

Michaella did not want to say, "No, I know no such thing when my sister is making a cake of herself over a man," so she remained silent on the subject. Perhaps Mary Catherine wasn't growing too emotionally attached to the captain, but merely enjoying her trip upriver. And anyway, justice demanded that she acknowledge her own growing attraction to Jean Patrick. It had been difficult to disguise her own disappointment that he appeared to be avoiding her now. Instead of strolling the decks and watching the sunsets with her, he spent more and more time around fellow frontiersmen who were journeying out into the mountains. While he was still as pleasant as ever, there was an indefinable difference in him that left her with the vague impression he wished to keep some distance between them. Had she offended him in some way? she couldn't help but wonder. Then she knew that she could not have done so. Unlike Mary Catherine and her boat captain, her conversation with Jean Patrick had remained light and topical, rarely touching on the serious.

On the fourth evening aboard the *Lucy Janine*, she saw Jean Patrick standing alone near the stern. The sun was lowering over the horizon, a huge ball of fire and blazing color, and Jean Patrick was watching the clouds slowly become infused with crimson.

Standing several yards away, Michaella studied him for a time before gathering up the courage to approach him. Then she began to step boldly toward him, rationalizing that he could not eat her but would only be remotely polite again—an even worse fate!

Before she could reach him, a man stepped in front of her and tipped his high top hat. He was a tall, thin man with uneven teeth, and his dark gray clothes reminded her a lot of Nolan Ketchman. His manner was every bit as presuming. His suit was stained in front by drink, and his breath smelled of whatever it was he had spilled. And he leered at her!

"Now, why should a fine lady like yourself be alone on such a lovely evening?" he asked in a raspy drawl. "I certainly would like your company."

As the leering man leaned toward her, Michaella stepped back. She was certain he was one of the many gamblers on board who spent their time filching whatever they could from the emigrants who crowded the boat. He looked like an elongated version of Mrs. Wright's obnoxious nephew.

"I would just as soon remain here by myself," Michaella snapped in her best haughty manner.

The gambler looked at her in polite disbelief. His lips stretched in a feral smile, exposing uneven teeth.

"I have had a winning evening at the card table," he continued. "Come with me and I will offer you a drink."

"Thank you, but no," Michaella said quickly. "I am just out here for a short while longer, then I will retire."

"But I insist," the gambler persisted, reaching out to curl his fingers around Michaella's arm.

Instinctively, she shrank away from him, alarm surging through her as she saw the glints of anger in the gambler's eyes at her repulsing movement. From the corner of her eye she could see that Jean Patrick had turned and was staring in their direction, but he made no move to assist her.

"No, I told you I don't care to join you," Michaella said as she wrenched her arm away. "I appreciate the offer, but thank you, no. Do not force me to be impolite!"

The gambler reached for her again, but Michaella lost her patience with the entire situation and put out both hands and gave him a hard push on his chest. Recovering his balance, he glared at her with his harsh little eyes.

"I was *inviting* you to have a drink with me," he said in a surly tone. "Now I expect you to oblige me."

"How unfortunate! I find myself extremely busy at the moment, and if you do not leave right now, I will have the captain of this boat throw you off. Do you understand? I know the captain personally, and he might not be especially nice with you."

Beady eyes narrowed in reflection as he weighed Michaella's words. It could be a bluff, but then again it could be the truth. At any rate, a run-in with the captain would not endear him to those he wished to impress.

"I'm not going to warn you again," Michaella added in a stronger voice that began to rise loudly enough to be heard by those nearby. "If you don't believe me, I'll just call for him right this instant."

Turning nervously, the gambler glanced around as if expecting to see the captain bearing down on them. Finally he moved away from her, pressing his hat back onto his head. He stormed past Jean Patrick, into the crowd of men along the forward rail.

Jean Patrick sauntered over to her. "You handled him very well," he told Michaella with admiration. "A persistent cuss, wasn't he?"

Gripping her reticule tightly in order to keep

from striking him with it, Michaella flashed him an angry glance. The rude gambler hadn't bothered her nearly as much as seeing Jean Patrick merely sit back and watch from a safe distance.

"Well, I was certain you weren't going to offer any help on my behalf," Michaella said, her voice shaking. "Why did you decide to come over here now—because it's all clear?"

Jean Patrick smiled. "Yes, it is safer," he admitted with a teasing light in his eyes. "But not from you."

Startled by the caress in his tone, Michaella jerked her head back up to look at him. In the gauzy light afforded by river mist and twilight, Jean Patrick was even more handsome than ever—a most dangerous fact, she decided, stiffening against him.

"Do you think so? I, however, find it odd that you should have been so concerned about our welfare when you first met us, and now you show very little interest—even when I am on the verge of being attacked by a disreputable gambler!"

Jean Patrick gazed down at her, lifting a dark brow inquiringly in an infuriating manner. "I rather thought you had all the odds in your corner, little one. Besides," he added, reaching out to stroke back a curl of her hair that had fallen into her eyes, "I was told you both are married. The good Captain Howe took it upon himself to inform me of that fact—only as a friendly warning, I'm certain."

Jean Patrick's slightly mocking tone and the sardonic twist of his mouth should have warned Michaella. But she was too unfamiliar with him to notice. She swallowed hard and managed a smile. Their lie had caught up with them, and how could she explain it without looking a fool now? So she gave him a shaky sigh and shabby concession.

"I guess I should have told you," she conceded with an inward groan. "It was my fault."

The dark brow lifted even higher, and his mouth quirked in a grin. "I had no idea," Jean Patrick said smoothly. "Of course I am still concerned about your getting out to the frontier, but at the same time I must keep my distance as a gentleman."

"I understand," Michaella grated. "I should not have expected you to be chivalrous and rescue me from a loud, rude, overbearing villain. After all, a married woman has no rights, correct?"

"Something like that. We would not want my intentions to be misconstrued by others, now would we?"

"No, of course not! It would be detestable for anyone to think you might be gentleman enough to protect a woman! Heaven forbid!"

"Do I detect sarcasm, Mrs. . . ?"

"Morgan . . . no, White!" Michaella snapped, too angry with him and herself to remember the correct name.

"Ah, Mrs. Morgan White. How lovely. I hope your husband is hale and hardy out in . . . was it Albuquerque?"

"Santa Fe!"

"Yes, that was it. Santa Fe. An army post, I think?"

Flashing him a scathing glance, she said in her most quelling tone, "Well, it certainly isn't the navy, sir!"

"How silly of me," Jean Patrick replied with another polite smile that didn't fool Michaella for a moment.

"Yes, it certainly is." There was a brief, awkward silence that seemed to stretch forever, then she added in an attempt to lend respectability to her story, "My father is said to be out there also." *Oh, why didn't I remember to ask the captain not to repeat our story? Jean Patrick knows that we are searching for Chattilion!*

"Santa Fe is a long way from here," Jean Patrick observed. "Do you expect to find your father there?"

"I can only hope he is in Santa Fe or nearby," she replied irritably. "Though I have no way of knowing."

Jean Patrick nodded solemnly. "Well, I hope you and your sister can find your father as well as your husbands. I am certainly glad I was able to meet you, and I wish you all the best."

Michaella politely thanked him for his concern, then watched him walk away with a loose, easy stride that reminded her of a tomcat. How could a man be so well made, and how could she be so interested in a total stranger who could offer her nothing but heartache? He was arrogant, infuriating, and she knew he had seen through her story of being married. Drat that Captain Howe for being a nosy, interfering busybody! Just because he was staking claim to Mary Catherine, it did not mean he should eliminate her from the—from the what? Marriage field? Race for a husband?

Filled with self-disgust, Michaella turned her gaze toward the river and looked out to where the last crimson streaks were fading from the sky. Closing her eyes, she ignored the frustrating sting of tears behind her lids as she reflected on the impossible situation.

Chapter Eight

✦✦✦✦✦

SHIFTING ATOP HIS piebald mare, Nolan Ketchman gave a disgusted glance at his attire. He was decidedly uncomfortable in the ill-fitting buckskins given him from the company stock. They had not allowed him to pick out his own garments; a clerk had simply given him a mismatched set from a towering pile and instructed him to wear them. What bothered him most was the mysteriously neat, round little hole in the chest of the fringed buckskin shirt. It was surrounded by an ugly stain, but the clerk who issued him the clothes insisted it was not blood. And, feeling rather queasy, Ketchman gladly accepted his assurance.

Ketchman was now five days out of St. Louis, riding the trails along the river. He hadn't bathed or shaved in all that time, and he was certain that should he happen across a mirror, the scruffy, bearded face in it would be one he wouldn't even recognize as his own.

The five company men with him were leading him toward Independence. And never far from their sight was the steamboat *Lucy Janine*. Ketchman knew that the Chattilion sisters were aboard. He had to keep them in his sight from now on until they led him to their father—and the gold. It was what urged him onward, what enabled him to endure this pestilence-ridden land with the swarms of mosquitoes and flying gnats, the snakes, and other wild creatures that lurked in the trees and thick foliage. He'd ridden horses in fox hunts, of course, but never for hours and days at a time without stopping, His aching muscles screamed for rest, but there was no stopping, not if he wished to successfully complete his mission. He had hated every moment he had spent in America, but it was the prelude to incredible wealth.

So Ketchman endured the motley bunch of company men as best he could, rationalizing that they were seasoned trappers and traders, hand-picked by Stricker for this particular job. All of them seemed to be alive with a variety of vermin that crawled in their hair, beards, eyebrows, and fell into their food when they ate. Repulsed, Ketchman had taken to eating apart from the others.

This attitude naturally encouraged the men to scoff at him behind his back, jeering at his aloof demeanor and his inexperience on the trail. Ketchman, in his turn, scorned the deficiencies of his companions in the elementary fundamentals of education, as only one of them could read or write his own name, and that almost illegibly. And this contempt for the men extended to his refusal to learn their names. They were not of his class, and he didn't care to know anything about them. It was only when he needed something from them, that he unbent in the slightest, becoming at least polite if not friendly.

So, a cane in one hand and a Hawken percussion rifle in the other—a rifle he disdained to use with the excuse that it was old—Nolan faced the frontier.

Today, as every day for Nolan, he considered the problem of the two young women—Michaella and Mary Catherine. It kept his mind active during the long hours of riding the narrow trail. To kill their father might not prove difficult, Nolan considered. After all, old Henry had at least six men after him.

Michaella and Mary Catherine presented a different problem. They would have to be handled in a precise and delicate manner.

Pursing his lips, Ketchman considered the possibility of selling the two young women to some Indian tribe for use as slaves or wives. It would have to be done discreetly so that if they were ever returned to civilization, he could be absolved of any blame in the affair. By the time of that unlikely occurrence, however, he would be as rich as Croesus and far distant from this primitive land where white women were a precious commodity to bands of roaming savages, and scalps even more in demand. Ketchman shuddered at the thought.

Slanting a glance at the five men riding ahead of him, he hoped they had not seen his reaction. Stricker had taken particular care in describing Ketchman as the leader of the men, the key to their promised bonanza from the company. He did not want to endanger his position by showing signs of weakness. Stricker had also been careful to instill in them the notion that once old Chattilion was located, great care must be taken with Ketchman's safety. All five men had been promised more money than they had ever dreamed of having should the mission be a success. Should it fail, the company would consider their efforts worth only a small compensation.

One of Ketchman's compensations on this wretched journey was his education in the manner of people who chose to travel the wilderness trails. As the band of men drew closer to Independence, he noticed a great number of emigrants camping along the river. Makeshift tents and wagons dotted the landscape, while frontier types mixed with farmers and their families. Women worked constantly, cooking and washing clothes while their energetic offspring romped through the trees and open fields.

Ketchman was having difficulty adapting to his surroundings. No one out in this uncivilized country knew or cared anything about how a business was managed or that political decisions being made along the East Coast could easily affect their lives in just a short time. None of these silly people cared about much of anything but heading west, he decided contemptuously. It was a new start for them, one that they believed would divorce them from the wretched lives they had once lived. All that was important was making it across the plains and mountains. Life would start fresh from there.

Late the evening of the sixth day out, Ketchman and the other five men rode into an encampment of emigrants and were welcomed. The other travelers were a contingent of farmers, most of them related to one another. They had journeyed out from Ohio, and at the time Ketchman stumbled across them, they were busily painting signs reading "CALIFORNIA OR BUST" on the sides of their wagons. Succumbing to hearty invitations, Ketchman and the others sat down to heaping bowls of beef stew, the best meal they'd eaten since leaving St. Louis.

While they ate hungrily, small children gathered to gawk at the strangers. Giggling and whispering behind cupped hands, they stared at them until their mothers called them away. Ketchman did his best to ignore them, having a great disdain for children that was shared by his companions. Unlike their leader, however, the five men did seem to enjoy staring at the women of the emigrant party, a fact that escaped Ketchman's comprehension.

While the five liked what they saw in the raw, sunburned women with freckles and straggly hair, work-worn hands and care-wrinkled faces, Ketchman did not. There wasn't a beauty among them. They were all peasant stock as far as he was concerned.

But later that evening he wished he had paid more attention to the situation. As he was talking with the camp's teacher, one of the five men with whom Ketchman traveled rushed up to him and spun him around with a hand on his shoulder.

"Mr. Ketchman! Mr. Ketchman, I . . ."

Brushing away his hand with an impatient gesture, Ketchman glared at the man. "What do you mean, accosting me in such a manner, Crenshaw?"

Taken aback by Ketchman's brusqueness, Crenshaw shifted his gaze to the teacher, then back to Ketchman. "Sorry," he muttered sullenly. "But you'd better come quick if'n you want to avoid trouble."

"Trouble? What kind of trouble? Well, speak up, man!"

"LaRange. It's that LaRange, and he's pesterin' some woman. Her ole man is gettin' his rifle an' he ain't none too happy, neither."

Appalled by this turn of events, Ketchman hurried after Crenshaw without a word of farewell for the teacher. The mere mention of rifles frightened him, for he knew that he could not match any of them as a marksman. What was he supposed to do about this? And why on earth had Stricker chosen such a ragtag band of thugs and thieves to guide him out west, anyway!

Sucking in a deep breath of air to bolster his courage, Ketchman rounded the edge of a wagon to see LaRange standing with a woman clutched in front of him, a beefy arm wrapped around her waist and a knife at her throat. Dismay filled Ketchman. The poor terrified girl seemed to be only in her teens, and soft blond hair fell over her forehead and into her eyes as she sobbed quietly. LaRange was speaking in broken, barely comprehensible English to an angry young man with a long rifle.

"Ze *femme,* she goes weeth me. Eef you follow, I weel cut 'er throat, *comprenez-vous*?"

"What is he saying?" the distraught young man asked as Ketchman approached. "Doesn't he know he can't do this? Is he crazy?"

"Probably," Ketchman shot back in annoyance.

Damn that LaRange! This could delay them indefinitely, and all for a scrawny girl with pale hair and skin like that of a plucked chicken! "Let her go, LaRange," he called out loudly, not even certain the big Frenchman would listen to him. "We do not want trouble here."

As suspected, LaRange ignored Ketchman. He continued walking backward, holding the terrified woman in front of him. When Ketchman repeated the order and LaRange again paid him no more attention than he would have a sand flea, Ketchman felt a rising surge of fury.

That this primitive backwoods baboon with the intelligence of a muskrat should defy him threw the Englishman into a rage. Disregarding completely the girl's welfare—not through intention but because of temper—Nolan Ketchman stepped quickly up to the surprised Frenchman and brought the head of his gold-studded cane down on the man's skull. LaRange immediately sagged to the ground with a stunned "oof!"

"I told you to let her go, dammit!" Ketchman snarled, and lifted his cane again. The knife had dropped to the ground, and he kicked it aside as he aimed another blow at the Frenchman's head. The girl, released at last, managed to crawl away from LaRange's heavy weight and the slashing of the cane. Ketchman paid her no heed whatsoever.

All the past week's frustrations were concentrated in the head of that cane as he brought it down again and again on LaRange's head. Only when he felt his fury ebb did he pause. No one lifted a finger to stop him, not even the wide-eyed trappers who were LaRange's friends.

Ketchman glanced at the girl being embraced by her husband, but did not offer a word of apology or comfort. Instead, he pulled a clean linen handkerchief from the pouch at his side and began to clean the head of his cane.

This action served to galvanize one of LaRange's friends to action, and he came forward to help the burly Frenchman to his feet. Dazed and stumbling, LaRange sagged into his companion's arms.

"Bisler? Izzat you?"

"It's me," Bisler confirmed. "Here. Let me help you. No, I don't think you want to do that," he said hastily when LaRange bent as if to retrieve his knife. "Stricker said we were to take care of him—not kill him."

"But ze leetle peeg damned near killed me!" LaRange protested feebly.

"That don't matter none," Bisler assured him as he tried to lead him away from the watchful Ketchman. Lowering his voice, he said, "He's Stricker's man, remember? And you don't want to get in bad with him, do you?"

Sucking in a deep breath and wincing at the pounding pain in his skull, LaRange's complaint subsided to an indistinct mutter at his circumstances. He left Ketchman with a baleful glare in his direction, hobbling in his companion's wake.

Though he appeared outwardly calm, inside Ketchman was shaking with apprehension. He knew that if it were not for the deal with Stricker, LaRange would have slit his throat for certain. It was not an easy fact to absorb. And a glance at the emigrants was not exactly reassuring, either. They were gathered in little clumps, armed with rifles, pistols, pitchforks, and pickaxes, waiting for LaRange to pass from view.

Intercepting covert glances from the trappers, Ketchman realized he had altered the way they thought of him by his actions. They were gazing at him with dislike, yes, but they had done that since the beginning of the trip; now there was fear, and maybe respect in the glances they flicked in his direction. Ketchman wasn't certain if this was good or not. These five men were troublemakers, rabble-rousers, and street fighters. They were all veterans of many dockside fights and tavern brawls, and he had no intention of confronting them again if it could be avoided.

When Ketchman sensed someone behind him, he whirled, the cane at ready and his stringy muscles taut. "Wait!" the teacher said, holding up his hands. "I merely wished to speak with you."

"Yes. Of course," Ketchman said, lowering the cane.

"Why are you traveling with these men?" the teacher asked, his eyes straying from Ketchman to the crew of five.

Annoyed at the man's temerity in asking such a personal question, Ketchman shrugged it away. Remaining silent, he let the teacher walk away without an answer.

Afternoon light had faded into deep purple shadows, and as night fell, Ketchman retired to his bedroll close to a fire. Perching on the spread blankets, he looked up to find LaRange gazing at him with narrowed eyes. The beefy Frenchman's malignant stare was unnerving, and when LaRange rose from his own bedroll and crossed the space separating them, Ketchman snatched up his cane. LaRange paused a few feet away and pointed a blunt finger at Ketchman.

"Maybee you no get to ze mountains, eh?" LaRange said softly. "*Oui,* I think maybee you no even live to see ze mountains, leetle man!"

Independence bustled with people preparing for the long journey into the mountains. Wagons were being repaired and strengthened for the long, wearying trip west, and droves of people crowded small dry-goods stores that sold fabrics and other provisions for making and mending clothing. Everywhere were the sounds of blacksmiths' hammers and the incessant bawling of livestock. Children scampered in the streets or watched from the backs of huge wagons that looked like ivory-backed land turtles occupying every available space.

Two major wagon trains had been organized. One was bound for the Santa Fe region and then on to California, and the other was bound for Oregon, taking a trail that eventually branched toward northern California.

Steamboats docked frequently, and the *Lucy Janine* nudged into the seemingly endless stream of boats crowding the docks. Michaella and Mary Catherine were waiting on the deck to leave. They had earlier said their farewells to Captain Howe. Mary Catherine left him with a mixture of regret and relief. She had liked him very much, but, as the trip progressed she realized that although he was a charming man, his charm wore thin after spending several days in his company.

In Independence, the sisters decided to first search for a small shop they had been told was owned by Sorrel. Michaella thought that perhaps if he were confronted again, he might be more forthcoming about what he knew of their father.

For the better part of the afternoon they scoured the streets, until finally they saw the big man standing inside a crude shop, studying a wolf skin stretched upon a table.

As they walked inside, an eager apprentice came over from where he was sorting goods and asked, "Can I help you ladies?"

"Yes, thank you," Michaella haughtily informed him, "we must speak to Sorrel at once."

Awed by her manner and her decisive English accent, the apprentice backed away immediately.

The two women followed the young man over to where Sorrel stood studying a skin. "Do you remember us?" Michaella asked abruptly, disturbing him so that he looked up with a frown.

"What is it you want?"

Undeterred by his narrowed gaze, Michaella answered, "We need more information about our father. I'm certain you haven't told us everything you know."

After a moment's deliberation, Sorrel turned back to the trapper with whom he was conducting business. "Take the two rifles I offered, and two axes. No more."

Shrugging in defeat, the trapper nodded, picked up two rifles that were resting against the counter, and then selected two axes. He strode leisurely past Michaella and Mary Catherine and out the door.

Turning back to face the sisters, Sorrel crossed his arms over his broad chest and regarded them from beneath his bushy eyebrows.

"We've come for your help. My sister and I don't have enough to go on in our search for our father." Michaella paused for a heartbeat, then added softly, "Please."

Sorrel's eyebrows lifted a fraction, then straightened across the bridge of his nose. Pushing away from the counter on which he leaned, he pulled a stoneware jug from a shelf and tipped it back, pouring a large amount of liquor down his throat. Finally he lowered the jug and wiped his mouth on his shirtsleeve.

"Well . . . it's been chewin' at my craw for a lot of years," he began grudgingly. "That whole business with your father. I guess I ought to tell you."

Michaella folded her hands and waited silently for him to begin. Sorrel was her only link now, the only way she could begin to put the pieces together like a giant puzzle that had been scattered in a hundred different directions. It was so important for him to help them, and she had no idea of how to go about it, no idea of the right way to coax him into searching for their father. And there were moments when she wasn't even certain he knew anything at all about Henry Chattilion.

"Well, years back Chattilion found a vein of gold way out in Sioux country. The Sioux called those mountains the Sacred Hills—it's a special place to the Indians, a holy ground. And they didn't take kindly to trappers and traders traipsin' over their ground. In fact," Sorrel said, looking at them closely, "it's said that to step foot in that area was to court death.

"It's dangerous," he warned with a shake of his head. "I've known a man to go in there and die in the most . . . ah, die anyway."

Shuddering, Michaella listened impassively to the rest. "It's hard for you ladies to believe, I know, but when gold was first discovered no one was too excited about it. At that time, trapping was expected to be the biggest source of wealth for years to come. And the Indians had no use for gold—never have. To them it's a soft metal that can't be worked into much of anything useful like cookware or weapons.

"We didn't care at the time that gold was bound to drive men crazy sooner or later," Sorrel added with a heavy sigh. "We shoulda thought 'bout what would happen when word got out, but we didn't. All we cared about then was livin' wild and free out there. I guess we should've figured what was up when the Intermountain Fur Company sent out some men with a map."

"To search for the gold?" Mary Catherine asked a little breathlessly.

"No. To have your father find the gold for 'em. Oh, it was a big deal. See, awhile before that, old Henry Chattilion drew out a right good map and sent it back with some fur company employees, detailing the location of the gold. Natcherly, they sent some more men back pronto to find old Henry and have him take them to the gold." Sorrel shook his shaggy head. "I was with old Henry when those men got there that day. They wanted to get to that gold right away, right then, forget the furs and pelts we was skinnin' for them! It was pretty plain that once Henry showed them to that gold, his life wasn't worth a moth-eaten old rat hide."

"Then . . . then our father was killed by those men?" Mary Catherine asked with a little catch in her voice.

"Now, I didn't say that, missy. I ain't sayin' that at all!" Sorrel stared at her peevishly. "I told you before, I ain't sure if'n he's dead or not. You see, we was attacked by Sioux—Oglalas and Tetons—and then it blew up a terrible thunderstorm. Lightning and thunder to beat the band boomed and cracked all around us—scairt those Sioux so bad they dropped everything but their drawers tryin' to get away. Took off on their ponies, and for all I know are runnin' yet!" Guffawing, Sorrel slapped his meaty thigh and shook his head. Sobering, he added, "I got away in one direction and never saw what happened to the others—your father or the company men. I just plain don't know if they got him or not. I wouldn't care to wager either way."

"Did you say this place is known as the Sacred Hills?" Michaella asked.

Sorrel shrugged. "The Indians call it the Sacred Hills. Trappers and the like call 'em the Black Hills, on account of they look so dark from afar off. No snow on the tops like higher mountains, just trees black as sin."

While Michaella mulled over this information, Mary Catherine asked brightly, "How do you get there? Do *you* know?"

Sorrel stared at her earnest expression for a moment, then threw back his head and laughed. "I surely do, missy, I surely do know. But there ain't likely no wagon trains headed that far north. Like as not, you'll have to break off from the main party and head on up into the hills by yourselves. It's a far piece, and I wouldn't bet a Chinaman's shoe on yer chances of survival."

"Perhaps our odds would improve if you were to lead us," Michaella pointed out. "After all, you were supposed to be our father's friend, weren't you? And you escaped the company's hired killers while he did not. Shouldn't you feel some sort of obligation to pay your debt to him?"

"Mebbe I should," Sorrel answered roughly, "but I don't! Now don't you go and start puttin' any guilt on me, little lady, 'cause that was years ago and I can't change it none now! Losin' my topknot ain't gonna bring old Henry back."

"So it really doesn't matter to you if our father is dead or alive?"

"I didn't say that. It matters, but I told you I can't do nothin' about it now."

"Mr. Sorrel?" Mary Catherine said timidly, "if Papa is alive, he knows where there is a fortune in gold. We have reason to believe the Intermountain Fur Company would like to know where that gold is located, and they have already sent out men to follow us in case we find it."

Narrowing his eyes, Sorrel asked, "You sure of that?"

"As sure as I'm standing here," Mary Catherine answered solemnly.

"Well, I'll be damned," Sorrel breathed.

"Probably," Michaella observed tartly, "but we

do know there is a man who has followed us from England to America for that very purpose. He is acting on behalf of the company. And there is little doubt the company will send other men with him."

Sorrel stared at Michaella for a moment, rather liking this tart-tongued young female with the steady eyes and cold voice. She was the strong one, while the bit of fluff that was her sister would blow away in the first good wind that came down the pike. It was women like this steely-eyed girl who survived in this land, not the fragile flowers. And he'd bet a nickel to a horseshoe that she didn't give a fig for her father's whereabouts, but was interested in the gold. It was the young one with the idealistic eyes and her head in the sky who was mooning after a father who had never even bothered to contact his daughters. Sorrel smacked a fist into his open palm.

"Why don't they let well enough be?" he demanded. "That means you two ladies got to dodge hired killers as well as Injuns."

Michaella gave a curt nod of her head. "Correct. Perhaps now you understand why it is so important that we have help, the right kind of help—your help."

"And if I do?"

"We would share whatever gold we find," was Michaella's prompt reply.

Sorrel nodded. He'd expected just that answer from this determined young woman. "What makes you so sure there is any gold, missy?"

"I'm not. I'm just going under the same assumption as the Intermountain Fur Company, who would hardly waste time and expense if there was not good reason to do so. And of course there is a map which plainly indicates gold."

Sorrel nodded. "Wait here a minute."

Michaella and Mary Catherine exchanged baffled glances as they watched Sorrel walk over to the apprentice and say something to him. Their curiosity grew when the young apprentice's mouth dropped open in surprise and then delight.

"What did you say to make him so happy?" Mary Catherine asked when Sorrel returned to them.

"Him? Oh," he said with a careless shrug, "I just told him he owns the store until I get back." When both young women stared at him blankly, he added, "Let's go find your father and some gold. . . ."

Chapter Nine

✦✦✦✦✦

THE NEXT MORNING found Michaella and Mary Catherine in a canoe with Sorrel, traveling the river's edge up to Westport, where the wagon trains were to depart. At Sorrel's urging, they had left their nicer dresses in storage and were wearing the brightly patterned everyday cottons that they had just purchased. Sorrel had convinced them they would be better off purchasing clothes in Westport that were more suited to the harsh frontier.

Leaning over the side of the canoe, Michaella let her hand drift in the water, creating small currents. She was thinking of Jean Patrick again. Since the evening she had been accosted by the obnoxious gambler on the *Lucy Janine,* she had not spoken to Jean Patrick. Oh, there had been occasional glimpses of him, but from a distance or across a crowded room. She had not been able to bring herself to speak to him, and he must have felt the same way. Once they had reached Independence, she had not seen him again. And, oddly, there was a void in her days that had not been there before. It was frustrating, and she wondered why. She didn't know him that well, yet somehow there had been *something*.

When Mary Catherine excitedly pointed out deer and birds and other animals glimpsed through trees on the bank, Michaella managed an absent smile. She wondered if Jean Patrick had decided to go ahead with his plans to guide a wagon train into the mountains. It would not be outside the realm of possibility for him to be . . . no, she admonished herself sternly, she must not borrow trouble!

When they reached Westport, both women gaped in awe. It must be the largest gathering of people all going in the same direction since the exodus from Egypt, Michaella muttered under her breath. Westport must be even more prosperous than Independence.

These people and their families were planning to make their way into the West via every mode of transportation available for overland travel. Most common were wagons with heavy canvas covers, including the large and impressive Conestogas with flared bows and sideboards that hung over both the front and back of the wagon. Everywhere were smaller wagons with more upright bows, carriages, coaches, flatbed wagons, and buckboards, in which people expected to safely traverse the rough terrain that lay ahead.

The wagons were drawn by either oxen or mules in teams of six to eight. Vehicles of all description were filled to overflowing with everything civilization had to offer. There were cattle and sheep and hogs, as well as chickens, ducks, geese, and various fowl roaming the site. Farmers had brought along their scythes and sickles and plows, as well as bushels of corn, oats, wheat, rye, flax, and even sacks of seeds for apples, pears, plums, and cherries for orchards in the promised land. Crowded in alongside were beds and chairs and butter churns, carefully wrapped china dishes and windows, household goods and food supplies. Someone had even brought along a church bell and, as it was Sunday, was striking it to get people to pay attention and stop their work. Unfortunately, the insistent clanging scattered nervous livestock in every direction.

Shaking his head, Sorrel mumbled, "Never seen anything like it! I ain't rightly sure now why I ever agreed to come along."

Michaella was inclined to agree. The mass of confusion was unlike anything she'd ever witnessed. Turning to Sorrel, she asked, "Is there another way to get out into the mountains? Must we travel with a wagon train?"

"Only if we want to stay alive. Injuns ain't too fond of attacking big bunches of settlers. Increases the odds, see? They ain't particularly fond of gettin' themselves shot up if they can help it, neither. But small groups by themselves—why, that's just like ringin' a dinner bell! Them Injuns will have hair on a coup stick quicker than you can spit."

Hastily, before he added any details that she'd rather not know, Michaella said, "We shall stay with a crowd, then! It might be slower and more frustrating, but at least we will be alive to complain."

Scratching his grizzled chin, Sorrel asked, "Can both you gals ride?"

"Yes," Michaella answered for both. "In England we had our own horses, and would ride daily."

"Then figure on riding all the way," Sorrel said with a note of satisfaction. "Don't figure on no carriage or the like—it'll split into kindling at the first river crossing and be more aggravation than the comfort's worth. What comfort there is in a bouncing crate set on wheels, that is. We kin load all your supplies on a couple of mules or good packhorses. But don't be surprised to find out this ain't gonna be no Sunday picnic," he warned.

Michaella had no such illusions, while Mary Catherine was only vaguely interested in the conversation. She was gazing off into the distance, her blue eyes fixed on a far-off spot.

"I'm goin' shoppin'," Sorrel announced, abruptly leaving them standing in the middle of the confusion.

A few hours later, the girls found a seamstress who showed them how to alter their long skirts for riding. She was a middle-aged woman with a deep, husky voice, and her blue eyes sparkled brightly, giving the lie to her age. Her brisk manner suggested that she had plenty of experience on the frontier, and had decided to make her tailoring shop one that would cater to the needs of women instead of fashionable styles.

Her name was Fran, and from the first introduction, Michaella liked her immensely.

"I don't give a hoot what other women think of what I'm doing," she said, punching a pin through a fold of material. She talked around the pins in her mouth without losing a single one or pricking her tongue. "There's a practical way to look at wearing clothes when not in the city." She held up an altered dress and regarded it critically for a moment. "I'm going to teach you two something," she said, apparently deciding the dress would suit. "Some of the women might frown at you, but by God, you'll be comfortable on a horse! And the men love it!"

The skirt Fran showed them was sewn into two sections for the legs, providing an open skirt that was usable on a horse. It seemed totally appropriate and practical to Michaella who knew from experience that riding sidesaddle was very tiring—and would be unbearable for weeks and months on end.

"Would you show us how to divide our own skirts ourselves?" Michaella asked, pushing forward a length of material.

Fran nodded and laughed. "I don't plan on going out with you!"

Michaella had selected a light blue cotton dress, and watched while Fran deftly scissored up through the middle of the material in both front and back, then pinned the cut edges and sewed them together.

"Huge pantaloons!" Mary Catherine said with a laugh.

The sisters selected more of the cotton dresses, looking through many with high-button fronts before finding some with a looser, Y-cut front. They could alter some of the high-button dresses to suit themselves, but it would be time-consuming and neither of them were extremely confident of their dressmaking abilities.

"You'll learn fast enough," Fran assured them with a laugh. "You'll learn a lot of things out there on the prairie."

Once outside the shop, they rejoined Sorrel at the hotel he'd indicated, wearing their new skirts and feeling quite daring.

It was now only a couple of days until the wagon train departed for Oregon. Michaella busied herself by learning from Sorrel how to pack the horses and mules with the provisions. Mary Catherine was reluctant to go near the mules at first. But after repeated insistence from Michaella, she at last became able to approach them and tie packs across their backs. Both women became proficient at arranging the great variety of supplies that Sorrel had taken with him from his store, including various types of rifles and "fowling pieces," as he called them, and scatterguns used for shooting wild turkeys, ducks, geese, and other wild birds that lived on the upland prairies and along the river.

It was important to know how to secure the provisions in the correct manner. Sorrel showed them again and again how to tie knots that would not slip or allow the packs to swing under the mules' bellies. Should that happen, Sorrel explained, Mary Catherine was apt to see a kicking demonstration that would make the incident on the deck of the *Lucy Janine* look like a square dance.

The day before departure, Sorrel went into Westport again to procure some more supplies while the sisters remained behind. The time had come for the vast number of people to divide into two different factions—those who were going along the northern trail toward Oregon, and those going the southern route to Santa Fe. Michaella watched the group leaving for Santa Fe depart.

By late morning most of those going south had moved out, and there was a long line of wagons trailing out into the distance. They were hoping to get at least past the Lower Delaware Crossing before sundown. Soon they were a large wall of dust in the distance, and those readying for departure to Oregon and California the next day at sunrise continued to prepare for their own journey.

Michaella and Mary Catherine had finished washing clothes earlier in the morning; now that it was late afternoon, they were dry enough for packing. The sisters had a campfire burning already and were boiling some soup in a huge pot over the flames. The rich smell of coffee filled the crisp air and mingled with the other aromas of the camp.

Travelers moved leisurely from wagon to wagon to chat and become acquainted with fellow emigrants from all over America and elsewhere.

Mary Catherine gathered the sun-dried dresses spread over bushes, hugging them to her and inhaling the sharp scent of their fresh fragrance. She went into the tent she shared with her sister, leaving Michaella to gather the rest of the garments spread over the juniper bushes.

Accustomed by this time to her sister's lackadaisical method of packing, Michaella heaved a soft sigh and began to collect cotton undergarments and blouses still draped over the branches. As she was reaching for a chemise, she was startled by the sound of hoofbeats approaching. She turned with the chemise clutched in one hand, and flushed when she saw Jean Patrick's bronzed, handsome face only a few feet away. Her heart raced, and realizing she was standing there with her undergarments in her hand, she quickly put her hands behind her back.

"You missed your wagon train," Jean Patrick said with a smile, his eyes crinkling at the corners as he gazed down at Michaella. Her flushed face and disheveled hair only made her more lovely in his eyes, a fact that was vaguely surprising to him. "I saw them roll out, yet you're still here. Any particular reason?" he asked, lifting a dark brow when she remained silent.

Caught with her unmentionables in one hand and her heart in her eyes, Michaella found it difficult to say anything at all to the man she had been dreaming of for the past week. Instead, she stood awkwardly, like a schoolgirl called upon to recite an unfamiliar passage, drinking in the sight of Jean Patrick's lean, hard body and his laughing face.

He had a new rifle, she noticed when he dismounted in a leisurely fashion, tied up his horse to a wagon tongue, and strode toward her. The rifle stock gleamed in the light of the setting sun, and dull glints reflected from the blue-gray barrel as he leaned it against the wagon. Michaella fastened her attention on the rifle in order to keep from having to look at Jean Patrick, and her first words to him were not what she would have wished to say if she had had more time to consider.

"That's a nice rifle," she commented, then flinched at her own inanity.

Grinning now, Jean Patrick replied, "Yes, it is. But you are going to have a hard time reaching Santa Fe with the route this train is traveling," he observed, gesturing toward the long-departed train.

Michaella finally looked up into his bright blue gaze. "I am not going to Santa Fe, as you well know," she said bluntly.

"Ah, the truth is out! Does this mean your dear husband must languish without his lovely wife while stranded in a lonely Santa Fe outpost? Poor man, I . . ."

"Oh, be quiet!" Michaella snapped. "You know very well that I am not now nor have I ever been married."

Jean Patrick leaned against the side of a wagon. "Right enough, but why bother lying in the first place?"

"If you will only recall, it was Captain Howe who told you those ridiculous tales, not me, and he was told that story by my sister. We came up with the idea upon first reaching St. Louis. You can imagine why."

"Yes, I suppose I can. Two women—and lovely women at that—alone in a city with no male protectors and a pocket full of questions. Yes, I can well understand why you would invent husbands." Jean Patrick's expression hardened. "I can't understand why you felt it necessary to continue the deception with me, however. Call me foolish, but somehow I had the impression we understood one another better than that."

Meeting his deep blue gaze, Michaella finally understood why he had avoided her on the steamboat. He had been hurt by her unwillingness to confide in him, not put off by the story of her marriage. "I guess I was wrong," she said quietly.

"I guess you were," he returned in a soft, husky voice.

His tone sent shivers dancing down Michaella's spine. When he reached out for her—as she had somehow sensed he would—she lifted her arms to embrace him. The cotton chemise dangled from her fingers, and before she could fling it away Jean Patrick lifted a dark, mocking eyebrow. His amusement stilled her sudden impulse, and the moment was lost as Michaella took a step back.

"Laundry," she explained unnecessarily.

"Ah," he acknowledged wisely. His arms dropped to his sides.

Wadding up the clean, dry garments, Michaella shifted from one foot to the other, once more feeling shy and uncertain of herself. How did he make her feel this way when other men did not? It was a mystery, and an irritating one at that! She tried to avert her eyes from his spare frame, from the wide shoulders and deep-muscled chest, from the curls of hair visible at the open collar, and the taut sleeves of his shirt where thick biceps strained against the buckskin. And, inexplicably, she was finding it very hard to keep from reaching out and touching him, running the pads of her fingers over the hard planes and hollows of his lean body. Clearing her throat, she decided her only salvation was to talk to him.

"Have you decided if you intend to lead a wagon train?" she inquired, sternly berating herself for the slight quiver in her voice.

Jean Patrick's smile was slow and easy. "Sure have. I'm leading this one."

Stunned and more than a little confused by the reaction of her madly pumping heart and accelerated breathing, Michaella managed a smile. "That's wonderful," she said in between the pops of her heartbeat, and was pleased that her voice did not betray just how wonderful she thought it was.

But somehow Jean Patrick must have known, for he was reaching out for her, sweeping her into his arms and pressing her body close to his. As his mouth descended over her half-parted lips, she dropped the wadded-up clothing, closed her eyes, and put her arms around his neck. For a generous instant she found herself suspended in another time. His hard male body against her curves seduced her senses, lured emotions she hadn't known she possessed from deep within, satisfying that empty aching of her heart.

Mary Catherine chose that moment to emerge

from the tent, ducking through the low opening and straightening up with a dress clutched in one hand and her mouth open to speak. Words died unuttered as she skidded to a sudden halt and stared at Michaella and Jean Patrick. Her amazement faded slowly and was replaced by a warm smile.

"Goodness me," she said impishly, "I certainly didn't mean to interrupt anything!"

Drawing away from Jean Patrick's embrace, Michaella smoothed her rumpled dress and replied coolly, "You didn't. We were just . . . just saying hello."

"Hello?" Mary Catherine echoed. A sly grin squared her mouth as she said, "*That* is hello? I'd hate to see good-bye!"

Jean Patrick chuckled. "Maybe you won't for a while."

"I hope not!" the irrepressible Mary Catherine exclaimed. "My sister was unbearable to be around after we left the *Lucy Janine,* and I have a feeling it was because she . . . ouch!"

Michaella's toes found her sister's shin with unerring accuracy, and she didn't flinch from Mary Catherine's reproachful glance. "I'm sure Jean Patrick is not interested in such trivial details, Mary Catherine. Why don't we sit by the fire and have a cup of tea? Or coffee, if you prefer, Jean Patrick?"

Jean Patrick did, and they sat by the cheerily burning fire as the sun set and night fell around them in soft shrouds of purple and black. Sipping from tin mugs, they discussed the trail to the mountains. Michaella repeated what Sorrel had told them about the Black Hills and the various Sioux tribes that considered the region their private hunting grounds. And, with her shoulders hunched against the slight evening chill, Michaella quietly related the tale of the gold and the company's search for it. She even retrieved her map from the tent and showed it to Jean Patrick, pointing out the trails leading from where they were now camped.

"See? They end at this torn edge, somewhere between Kansas and the mountains," she said in frustration.

Drawing his brows into a knot, Jean Patrick studied the map carefully. "Whoever drew this map really knows the mountains," he said slowly. "I assume it was drawn by your father?"

Nodding, Michaella said, "Yes, we are certain of that. But we don't know where the other half is, or who has it."

Refolding the map, Jean Patrick gave it back to her. "Of course, the missing half shows the location of the gold," he observed.

"Of course." Michaella sighed as she tucked the map into the sash of her dress. "And that is the piece we lack, I'm afraid."

Night birds called loudly, while the pioneers settled in for the night. Darkness seemed to muffle the harsher sounds, muting them into a pleasant hum of distant activity as the three sat around the fire and discussed the coming journey.

Glancing around uneasily, Mary Catherine ventured, "I wonder what is taking Sorrel so long? He should have been back by now."

Jean Patrick turned toward her. "Sorrel? The old codger is probably knee-deep in trouble somewhere. Don't worry about him."

"That's just what *is* worrying me," Michaella put in dryly. "He has a knack for attracting trouble, and we can't afford to lose him now."

"Do you want me to look for him?" Jean Patrick asked, leaning back against a log and crossing his long legs at the ankle. His lazy gaze rested on Michaella's fire-lit face, the rosy hue of her cheeks and the sparkle in her dark eyes, and he smiled. "Do you?" he repeated when she hesitated.

She nodded. "Yes. Would you mind?"

"Would it matter?" he shot back with a grin. "No, I don't mind."

Rising in a lithe motion, he reached for the rifle he'd placed nearby, and turned back to see Michaella pulling a shawl around her shoulders. When he gave her a quizzical glance, she said calmly, "We intend to go with you."

"Oh, no! It's not safe in Westport after sundown. All kinds of drifters and worse roam the streets, drinking rye whiskey until they can't see straight, if at all. No, with all the Indians and ruffians, you ladies need to stay here."

But in the end, Michaella and Mary Catherine prevailed. Michaella didn't pause to examine her motives for going along with him, realizing that somewhere deep inside she feared his disappearing again. It was too silly a reason for her to examine too closely, and she chose to ignore it as she mounted her pony and rode close beside Jean Patrick.

True to his warning, the streets were crowded

with men who staggered about and argued vociferously with one another. Among the drifters and voyageurs and frontiersmen were a number of Delaware and Kansas Indians, as well as Shawnee and Sac and Fox, all moving freely from one place to another. The numerous log structures built for the purpose of drinking and gambling were now well lit by lanterns and doing a flourishing business.

Michaella and Mary Catherine exchanged glances and nudged their ponies closer to Jean Patrick's big bay. It was more than likely that Sorrel was in one of the drinking establishments, playing the hand game and winning money.

They rode through the streets for a short distance before coming upon a large group of men gathered in a circle in the middle of the street. All were shouting, waving, and gesturing. In the center of the circle two men were seated cross-legged and facing one another. As expected, one of the men was Sorrel.

"He's at it again," Michaella said in resignation. "One of these fine days, he's going to get himself killed!"

"Wait here," Jean Patrick ordered, then he moved in closer. Torch- and lanternlight danced in wavering patterns across the scene as the sisters waited in their saddles, able to see over the heads of those crowded around the men on the ground.

In the flickering light they could see Sorrel was winning handily over another Frenchman, in much the same fashion as he had back in St. Louis. It appeared as if the game would end in the same way. Then suddenly the other man rose and Sorrel leaped up with him.

This time someone grabbed Sorrel from behind before he could get to the man he had beaten. The man who grabbed him was almost as big as Sorrel, and Sorrel was struggling to break his hold. Meanwhile, the Frenchman who had lost his money started swinging his fists at Sorrel.

Jean Patrick leaped gracefully from his bay and pushed his way through the crowd until he reached Sorrel. The burly Frenchman who had lost his money turned and swung a meaty fist at this new opponent. In a blur of movement Jean Patrick ducked the blow and countered with a swift right into the Frenchman's face, sending him reeling backward into the hooting crowd.

Sorrel by now had worked his way free of the big man and was punching him unmercifully. Two other men waded in to assist the big man, and Sorrel turned on them, throwing one against the other. They tumbled to the ground in a tangle of arms and legs.

The Frenchman Jean Patrick had put down was back on his feet, considering whether to come at his opponent with a knife. But Jean Patrick had drawn a knife of his own, a huge bone-handled blade that dwarfed the Frenchman's puny weapon. The Frenchman's eyes widened. He backed slowly away from Jean Patrick and was swiftly lost in the milling crowd.

Seeing his defection, the big man and his two cronies abandoned the fight as well. Laughing hugely, Sorrel clapped Jean Patrick on the back. "So you like to fight, eh?"

"No," Jean Patrick answered with a shake of his head, and gestured to the sisters perched atop their ponies. "But those young ladies seemed to think you might need help."

"So I did, so I did! Come along, and we shall let them do the introductions, eh?"

"Where did you find this stout young hoss?" Sorrel asked Michaella once they had left the middle of the street.

She smiled. "On the river. Actually, his name is Jean Patrick, and he says he knows you."

Glancing at Jean Patrick in surprise, Sorrel squinted in the dim, hazy light. "Umm, why I think he does! I ain't seen you since you was a whelp of a kid, trackin' a bear with your old daddy out on the Bighorn!" He laughed loudly. "You've grown a mite since that time!"

"A mite," Jean Patrick agreed affably. "That was a few years back. I heard you run a good shop in Independence. What made you agree to go back into the mountains now?"

Motioning toward the listening sisters, Sorrel said, "I knew their pappy as well. I'm fixin' to help them find him, if I can keep the Sioux from liftin' my hair."

"That might take some doing. That Frenchman you just beat wanted to lift your hair, too. I'm thinking maybe it's not too smart to be cleaning up on everyone the way you do."

Sorrel snapped back testily, "I'll be the judge of that! I ain't too old to handle my own when it comes to a good fight!"

"I didn't mean to imply that you were too old," Jean Patrick assured him. "But there's men nowadays who don't care much about honor, Sorrel. They'll jump on you from the back while their *compadres* stick knives into you. You'd be better off if you had someone you could trust with you."

Sorrel's face split into a huge grin, and Jean Patrick had to step nimbly to avoid another heavy clap on his back. "Yeah," Sorrel boomed, "maybe you're right! And maybe I'll take you along next time, and that way they won't want to jump me—you think?"

"I think maybe we should avoid it completely," Jean Patrick said dryly.

As the sisters waited for Sorrel to get his horse and join them, Michaella noticed a familiar shape standing in the far shadows of a building. She nudged her sister. "Look! That man—doesn't he look something like Nolan Ketchman?"

Surprised, Mary Catherine turned to look, squinting into the shadows. She shook her head. "It can't be. That man is dressed in buckskins."

"But look at his hat! And if you look closely, isn't that a cane he's carrying?"

Gasping, Mary Catherine whispered, "It does look like one, doesn't it! My God in heaven. . . ."

Chapter Ten

✦✦✦✦✦

DAWN BROUGHT A brisk breeze and slowly lightening sky as the order was given to "stre-e-etch out!" Wagons lurched forward and mules brayed and oxen bawled. Dogs barked, men swore at stubborn cattle, and the long line of eighty wagons snaked across the broad, flat land beyond the Kansas River. Westport being at the fork of two rivers—the Kansas and the Missouri—it was easy enough to avoid an extra river crossing by traveling a mile north. There wouldn't be another river crossing until the wagons hit the Big Blue on the northern border of Kansas.

Dust boiled up from beneath rolling wheels, whisking past Michaella's face and making her cough. She pulled up a lace handkerchief to cover her nose and mouth, and motioned for Mary Catherine to do the same. Even the morning dew could not dampen the clouds of dust swirling in the air and up noses and into clogged throats.

For Michaella, the only consolation to her discomfort was the pleasant sight of Jean Patrick riding ahead. He sat tall and straight in the saddle, a commanding figure that was instantly obeyed by the men and ogled by the women. The last fact intrigued and irritated Michaella. He was handsome, of course, but his hard, hawklike features and lithe body did little to inspire confidence in a woman. Indeed, just the opposite held true. Jean Patrick was the kind of man who would bewitch and betray a woman in the same breath.

Perhaps it was the sight of him with an eagle feather tied onto the trigger guard of his Hawken rifle, and a little bag, which he called a medicine bag, on a cord around his neck that attracted the feminine stares. Today Jean Patrick looked more like an Indian than ever.

Expertly flicking her wrist and guiding her mare down a shallow ravine, Michaella thought of how concerned she had been earlier in the day. Jean Patrick had risen long before daylight, and when the sun had first begun its slow ascent into the sky, he had stood with outstretched arms and his head thrown back, speaking in a strange tongue.

When she'd asked him about it, Jean Patrick's blank stare and casual shrug had been his answer, then he had teasingly told her to hurry and get ready before she was left behind. Michaella was left with even more unanswered questions.

Wagon bosses had been elected the day before, but as Jean Patrick was the hired guide, Michaella worried that the emigrants would become concerned about what were probably Indian practices. Surely he could see that? But apparently not, for he did nothing to change them. His terse answer to her repeated question was the admonishment that he had no intention of discussing his actions with anyone. And that had been that.

Edging her mare closer to her sister, Michaella lifted a brow at Mary Catherine's sullen expression. "What's the matter? Are you ill?"

"No," Mary Catherine answered shortly, and pointed with the end of her riding crop. "It's those wretched beasts! I can't bear having them so close to me!"

Turning to look in the direction she pointed, Michaella could not hide her smile. "Do you mean Jack, Jenny, and Clarence Mule?" she asked innocently.

Mary Catherine favored her with a glare. "Don't dare speak of them as if they were human—or even animal! I can't see why Sorrel insisted upon tying the creatures to *our* horses! Why doesn't he lead them, or let someone else do it?"

"Don't be peevish," Michaella said. "They're tractable beasts if you get to know them."

"Get to know them? I should say not! Do you see how that gray mule . . ."

"Do you mean Clarence?"

"Whatever! That gray mule hates me. The other two aren't so bad, but that gray mule has it in for me, I tell you!"

"You're just angry because he won't let you feed him grass, while Jack and Jenny don't mind at all."

"Hmmph! Do you recall yesterday when we came out of our tent after that brief rain? I brought a parasol with me, and the wretched animal behaved as if I'd poked him with a stick! He snatched it—my best parasol, too—right out of my hands and stomped it to pieces with his hooves!"

"Mary Catherine, don't you recall Sorrel telling us that Clarence hates parasols? That his former owner used to poke him with one all the time? I would have thought . . ."

"Well, really! I can't be expected to remember *everything*, can I?"

Swallowing the laughter pressing against her throat, Michaella did not answer her younger sister for a moment. Poor Mary Catherine. Everything was such a trial for her. There were no in-betweens, no gray areas, only black and white, ecstasy or agony.

"No, I suppose you can't," she said finally.

They rode in silence for a time, gazing out across a rolling sea of grass almost as high as a horse. It waved in the breeze, glowing a pale green in the sunlight. Along the riverbanks there were thick groves of maple, wild plum, and Indian thorn apple, their white blossoms coating the dense growth for miles and miles. Scattered in the clumps of foliage was an occasional log dwelling belonging to a family of Delawares who seemed to be making a half-hearted attempt at farming. For the most part, they saw only wild shrubs and trees garbed in spring finery, opening the way into the unsettled wilderness.

Days began to roll slowly past, and with each new light Michaella and Mary Catherine grew more accustomed to sleeping in the open under the stars. Lying wrapped in their blankets, they would point out various constellations to one another. At times, staring up at the dark sky spreading above, Michaella would feel a rush of awe at the vastness. She lay listening to the distant howl of coyotes that hung in the air in shivering wails, and drew comfort that Jean Patrick in his blankets was only a few yards away.

The days passed in an endless blur of dust and sunlight, and they came to understand Sorrel better. They learned to their frequent exasperation that he was a natural tease. Spiders were discovered folded in the clothes laid out in neat stacks for the next day's wear; burrs were hidden under the packs of the mule Mary Catherine was to lead; salt was substituted for sugar in their evening cup of tea; and their water pouch was laced with a strong dose of rye whiskey. Sorrel continually delighted in seeing bewildered faces and hearing cries of dismay. Then he would arrive and know exactly what to do to save the day, taking the credit without a qualm.

"Old mountain men are like that," Jean Patrick explained when Michaella complained. "They love to pull tricks on one another. I'll bet your father is that way, too. You just have to learn what they're thinking before they know it. That way you can stay one step ahead, but you better be pretty damned quick."

The wagons followed the trail westward, making a slight detour to avoid a group of Mormons camped near a grove of cottonwoods. Jean Patrick had no intention of allowing the various missionaries, zealots, and hard-minded emigrants he was leading to clash with the Mormon group. There were enough problems ahead without walking into certain trouble.

Each evening the wagons were drawn up and the teams unhitched and taken to water and pasture. Prayers were said individually and in groups for the journey to be safe and successful. Campfires were built and exhausted children fell asleep while their plates tipped from their laps into the dirt. Men and women, equally as weary, worked before retiring to keep clothing washed and wagons repaired.

At the end of the first week, Jean Patrick had the party stop early at a large spring, where there was plenty of grass and water and the trees grew thick. After traveling in the hot, searing sunlight, it was an oasis for the sunburned pioneers. Everyone feasted that evening, as game and fowl were plentiful. Sorrel took it upon himself to bring in a wild turkey with his fowling piece. He carried it proudly into camp, set it down near the fire, and began to singe the feathers from it. A jug sat near his elbow, and occasionally he would lift it over his shoulder and turn his head to take a long pull from it. Then, wiping his wet mouth on his shirtsleeve, he would go back to pulling feathers from the turkey.

While Sorrel was plucking feathers, Mary Catherine followed her sister to the still loaded mules. "I don't see why you ever agreed to do this," she grumbled, casting sour glances at the waiting mules. "I'd rather clean a turkey than unload these worrisome beasts!"

"But could you have shot the bird?" Michaella asked. "Somehow—recalling your limited experience with guns—I rather doubt it."

"Minor details! It's still better than this. Just look! That ornery mule is waiting for me!"

Pausing, Michaella turned to look at her sister. "Look, are you going to allow some dumb animal to frighten you? To force you to behave like a timid mouse? I cannot believe that you would do so."

Mary Catherine gave the gray mule a grim smile and flexed her arms. "I suppose you're right," she said with a sigh. "I'll take care of Clarence." With that, she strode directly to the waiting beast, fixing him with a firm eye as she grasped his halter.

Clarence immediately dug in his forefeet and hunched his laden back.

"Come along, Clarence," she coaxed sweetly. Plucking a handful of clover, she waved it under his nose. Clarence turned his head in disdain. Mary Catherine flicked a glance at her watching sister and shook her head. This did not bode well for her struggle for supremacy. "Here, Clarence. Thirsty? There's water in the stream, and if you come along like a good boy—mule—I will take you . . . hey!" she ended when Clarence took umbrage and yanked his head.

Holding tightly to the leather halter, Mary Catherine just barely managed to keep the mule from bolting. Exasperated beyond good judgment, she glared at the balky animal and shook her small fist, lifting it high and bringing it down right between his eyes. Though not a hefty blow, it was sufficient to startle the mule. He blinked, brayed softly, and was still. Mary Catherine approached his side warily, still not trusting the animal. To her surprise and her sister's, Clarence was as docile as a lamb.

"See?" Michaella said when they had completed unloading the mules and seen to their food and water. "I knew you could do it!"

"That remains to be seen. Tomorrow is another day," Mary Catherine said darkly.

Laughing, Michaella remarked, "If you can handle a stubborn mule like Clarence, a husband should be no problem whatsoever."

If Michaella and Mary Catherine had successfully completed their part of the bargain with Sorrel, he was having trouble with his. Squatting by the cooking pot, he was still struggling with the turkey. Sorrel sighed heavily and took another swig from his jug.

"Damned turkey," he mumbled, gazing at it dolefully. He had been instructed to baste it with a mixture of herbs and sauce, but for the life of him, he could not seem to get it to taste right. After sliding a furtive glance around to insure that no one was watching, Sorrel poured a generous helping of rye whiskey into the bowl, tasted it, and decided it was greatly improved.

"You there!" a gruff voice shouted, and Sorrel started guiltily. "You, Frenchman! For pity's sake, bring that poor bird over here!"

Rolling his eyes, Sorrel turned to see a large middle-aged woman standing with arms akimbo, staring straight at him. She shook her head and gestured to her fire and cooking pots.

"Yes, you! You heard me, Frenchman. Bring that turkey here before you ruin it!"

Accustomed to women being soft spoken, Sorrel glanced at her askance. She was stout with gray streaks in her flaming red hair, and her cheerful face was liberally sprinkled with freckles and what some would kindly call "character" instead of wrinkles, and her generous mouth was pursed into a frown.

"What for should I bring you this good turkey?" Sorrel asked belligerently.

"Because if you don't, you'll ruin it for those poor girls with you. If nothing else," she added in a thick Irish drawl, "be for caring of their needs!"

Relaxing slightly, Sorrel considered his options. He could allow her to cook it and take the credit, after all. Or he could ruin it and be forced to accept the blame. No competition.

Rising, he carried her the pan of turkey. "You're not much of a one for cookin', are you?" the woman asked when she took the bird and inspected it. "Almost scraped this poor thing's skin from the bones, you great buffoon!"

Speechless at this unwarranted assault, Sorrel merely watched as she set the pan down on a rickety table and set about removing unnoticed pinfeathers. Beyond an occasional "Hand me the pepper" or "Dish out a tablespoon of lard," little was said as the woman repaired the turkey.

"There," she said at last as she shoved it toward him. "Now put it on the spit and keep a'turnin' it! Even like, now mind, or it'll burn on one side and be raw on the other."

"But . . . but there was a special sauce I was supposed to baste it with," Sorrel argued.

"I'm sure there was. Did it include corn liquor, by any chance?"

Glancing sheepishly at his half-empty jug, Sorrel gave a helpless shrug of his shoulders. "Mother's milk," he corrected.

She snorted. "Indeed! And who do you think you be talkin' to, laddie? This is Meg Magoffin, and I wasn't put into this world yesterday! Mother's milk, indeed!" Putting her hands on her hips, Meg Magoffin gazed at Sorrel critically, then said, "Put some potatoes on to cook so the little ladies will have else to go with that bird. I've a feeling they'll be needin' it."

"No need to go talking bad to me, now," Sorrel said in self-defense. "I did the best I knew."

"Which is a spot above wretched!" Meg said with a sniff of disdain. Then, more kindly, she added, "Why don't you just sit down and let me tend this bird? What sort of special sauce was it you were to make?"

"I don't know the first thing to put in it," Sorrel admitted. "Do what comes right to you."

Meg was doing just that when Michaella and Mary Catherine returned from tending to the mules and horses. As Sorrel noticed their approach, he stood and, pointing to the Irish woman, said, "She stole our bird! What do you make of that?"

Meg Magoffin only laughed heartily, never pausing in the basting of the turkey, her blue eyes sparkling slits in her full cheeks. Michaella and Mary Catherine immediately joined her with ringing peals of merriment. Baffled by this unexpected reaction, Sorrel began to get angry.

"You make fun of Sorrel, yes?" he demanded, and was further incensed when Michaella gave a gasp of laughter and nodded.

"Yes, we are, Sorrel! We thought it rather a good joke to watch while you tried to explain your methods of cooking to Meg."

"*Meg*? You know her, then!"

"Of course," Michaella replied. "Did you think we could travel so closely with her and not become acquainted? But it was good fun to watch you pluck feathers and try to make a sauce."

"Damn!" Sorrel bellowed in outrage. "Was this ,ned?"

No, how could it be? But never let it be said I n't know when to take advantage of an opporнity," Michaella shot back.

"What opportunity is that?" Jean Patrick asked

as he sauntered up to join them. He pushed his wide-brimmed, flat-crowned hat to the back of his head and gazed at the group in mild curiosity. When told, he grinned widely. "I gotta say, it's about time you got a little of your own medicine, Sorrel!"

"So you think so?" the big Frenchman muttered, but he had to grin. "Well, maybe this time! But I'll know better than to say I'll cook any more turkeys in any way but the way I know best!"

"No more sauces?"

"No more sauces!"

While they ate the roast turkey at Meg Magoffin's linen-draped table—it was dressed up for company, she said—Meg told them a little about how she had come to be in the train of wagons going westward. She'd emigrated from Ireland to New York only two years before, but had not been able to locate her relatives. Since she couldn't find them, she had decided to travel westward, and had ended up in Kansas, where she had met and married Sergeant Thomas Magoffin. Sergeant Magoffin was now stationed at Fort Laramie, and she was on her way to join him.

"So here I sit!" she ended cheerfully, wiping her greasy fingers on a linen napkin edged with Irish lace.

"But aren't you a little frightened at the prospect?" Michaella asked.

"Yes," she admitted after a moment. "I suppose I am, a wee bit. I've never lived on an army post, you know. But I says to myself, 'Meg, old girl, you've done whatever you pleased in life without a thought. Now should be no different!' And so I keep that in mind when I get to thinkin' about what might—or might not—happen."

"An excellent philosophy," Michaella said, and began to understand that beneath her gruff exterior, Meg Magoffin was as frightened as the rest of them.

In the following days, Meg did whatever she could to help Michaella and Mary Catherine. Her outgoing, jovial nature made harsh tasks easier, and she came to look upon the two sisters as the daughters she had never been able to have. She insisted upon helping them and mothering them, yet remained distant enough to keep from becoming too possessive. It was a welcome change for them in a way, for the help was sorely needed and the companionship of an older woman was welcomed.

"Wisdom and knowledge are nothing to send away," Michaella told Mary Catherine, "not when we're headed into a broad and unknown wilderness."

And sometimes, when she was alone with her thoughts, Michaella would wonder about the future. Not just hers, but her sister's—and Jean Patrick's. What did the future hold for her? Love, perhaps? Marriage and a family? At such times, she would push those thoughts to the back of her mind with great determination. No, she must concentrate on the gold, on finding her father and seeing that Mary Catherine was cared for. First things first, she would scold silently.

But it was hard not to think of Jean Patrick, to recall their last brief kiss and embrace, his strong arms around her and the feel of him beneath her fingertips. And when she closed her eyes at night, she could see him, see his lean face and mocking smile, the bright blue eyes that were so striking in such a dark face. Then she would long for him, wish he could be with her even though she knew he was busy with the wagons. He had a great responsibility, and Michaella had always respected a person who took care of life's duties, perhaps because she had been forced to do so at a young age. So while she missed him, she respected the time he was devoting to the emigrants. Perhaps soon they could linger together, walk along a stream or beneath the hanging branches of a tree. It was a mental picture she held to tightly. . . .

Chapter Eleven

THE WAGON TRAIN moved westward. The Kansas River was now a week behind them, and both the Little and Big Vermillion rivers became but moments lost in time. With each crossing came more sweat and work and broken wagon wheels and tongues that required repair, or harnesses for the mules and oxen. But the river crossings brought relief at the same time, in the form of baths and clean clothes. Water was always welcomed, for despite the strong pull of the current it brought the sensation of starting afresh—crossing another boundary that lay between them and the eventual new land that existed somewhere far to the west.

Now Meg Magoffin regularly took her meals with Michaella and Mary Catherine, while they all pitched in to prepare the game brought in by Jean Patrick and Sorrel. There was the normal fare of prairie grouse and fowl from along the streams and bottoms, and occasionally Jean Patrick or Sorrel would shoot one of the graceful animals known as pronghorn antelope. With his usual flair for the pithy, Sorrel referred to them as prairie goats, and showed the women how to cut the meat into strips for drying.

"This I do know!" he declared with a grin. "Dry it, and we shall not go hungry for some time."

In the past week and a half Michaella and Mary Catherine had learned what was important and what wasn't when it came to hunting and preparing game. They listened well, and learned quickly. And Michaella asked questions when Jean Patrick or Sorrel spoke of the land and what lay ahead. Both men considered themselves at home in the wilderness and could subsist normally on fare that would invite starvation to another man. Michaella recognized the importance of learning to live on very little and maintain strength at the same time.

Besides knowing the land and how to live off it, Jean Patrick and Sorrel had both developed their personalities in the wild country. They were as untamed as the antelope that bounded across the trail ahead of the wagons, and the frequent hawks that circled the grasslands and rode the prairie wind currents.

Being in the prime of life, Jean Patrick seemed never to tire. Often he rode out great distances ahead of the wagons to scout for grass and water and suitable camping spots. He maintained his constant watch for hostiles as the buffalo grassland stretched just ahead of them.

When he had extra time one day, Jean Patrick suggested to Michaella that she learn to shoot a rifle accurately. Sorrel had given each sister a rifle, and they were getting used to the feel of the rifles and learning how to load and fire them. But neither had yet learned to load and shoot rapidly and accurately.

It was a wonder to Michaella that Jean Patrick found time for anything after his hard days out scouting ahead of the wagons. She marveled at his fortitude. No matter how long a day he would put in, he was still willing and able to help someone fix a broken wagon tongue or reset a wheel, or just talk to someone who needed encouragement. And if he wasn't giving her a lesson in marksmanship or seeing to someone else's needs, he would be repairing a frayed harness or finding some other little task to occupy him.

Sorrel, on the other hand, found it more relaxing to lounge around camp and give Meg pointers on the art of cooking. It took no time at all for Michaella to figure out that Sorrel was a selfish old goat in many ways—rivaling, Mary Catherine claimed, the mules. Sorrel spent more time thinking of ways to avoid manual labor than he would have if he'd just completed the task without argument or attempting to avoid it.

In spite of Sorrel's constant teasing and bantering with both sisters and even Meg, they came to realize that in his way, he respected them. And indeed, Sorrel expected that Michaella and her sister would be able to survive in this land if they had to do so.

The two sisters made a good combination with Meg, a strong woman of virtue who genuinely cared about people. She seemed always to be on hand to help someone with a sick child or an injury. Meg was especially attuned to the other women. Many had left behind comfortable homes and the security of a daily routine to follow their husbands' dreams, which might or might not benefit them in the end.

In many cases, their children complained of the long journey and wanted to go home. The smaller children were especially uncomfortable most of the time and rarely got a good night's sleep. Expectant mothers found the strain of travel made their time that much harder. Some were confined to lying in the back of a hot, musty wagon, sick and miserable most of the day. And each day brought more of the same: boring, tiresome travel. Even for those in the best of health, long days and nights on a high wagon seat or walking along the packed ground were taking their toll.

Meg had a way of getting the women to understand that when they finally reached Oregon or California, they could look back and say they had accomplished something that would forever stand out in their lives. The new land would give them renewed vigor, and the despair they now felt would turn into jubilation. None of it would be easy, but the reward would be worth the effort.

The days passed in a blur of sunshine and the ever-present wind that blew up dust and untied bonnet strings. It was a constant, unceasing roar in the travelers' ears. The wagons rolled on, finally reaching the Big Blue River that snaked along the Kansas-Nebraska border. It was swollen with run-off, and they were forced to linger a day in the hopes it would lower.

When they were finally able to cross, they had to navigate the strong current on rafts or tack buffalo hides over the bottom of their wagons to keep precious provisions and belongings from becoming drenched. They crossed slowly, only two or three wagons at a time, with Jean Patrick shouting orders from the banks or riding his horse into the middle of the river to give directions.

When the crossing was finished, the elected council members of the wagon train decided they should rest for a few days before pushing on, arguing that they were ahead of schedule and the delay would not matter. Though dubious because of the importance of crossing the Rockies before the early snowstorms, Jean Patrick had to agree. He had spotted a smaller wagon train ahead of them, and he wanted to let that train move farther ahead.

Everyone welcomed the brief respite. Some of the men had brought along their fiddles, and for the first time they got them out and tuned them up. While the music echoed on the evening air, the children delighted in scampering along the riverbank. Everyone felt a sense of relief, and it was as if tomorrow were far away. Clean clothes soon hung over wooden barrels and wagon tongues, and even bushes and the low branches of trees. Fresh water soon filled water casks to overflowing.

Jean Patrick spent his evening with Michaella for a change, describing to her the features of the country ahead. They were both delighted to have time to be together.

Later, before they retired, Michaella was sitting with Meg and Mary Catherine, drinking coffee and mending clothes. Night had fallen and Sorrel was already asleep in his tent, having spent the entire day hunting. He had been bringing in as much antelope meat to dry as possible, for there was no telling when game would become scarce. The women were listening to his snores and laughing quietly when Jean Patrick arrived in their camp, his handsome face set in grave lines.

"Meg, they want you at the other end of the wagons," he said. "A woman there is having a baby, and from what I understand, she isn't having an easy time."

"Certainly!" Meg said briskly, immediately putting down her mending and rising from where she sat beside Michaella. "Please fetch my little leather kit, Mary Catherine," she asked, "and some lye soap!"

"What are you going to do?" Michaella asked.

"Going to do? Why, child, I'm going to deliver a baby!" Meg replied with a laugh. "My kit has all the things I will need, and the lye soap is for washing my hands and anything else that needs to be cleaned! Care to come along?"

Hesitating, Michaella might have refused if not for the odd light in Jean Patrick's eyes. It was the way he was looking at her—sideways, as if he thought her too soft for such a sight. That decided her.

"Of course," she answered. "I'll do all I can to help."

But once they arrived at the mean little tent where the seventeen-year-old girl lay on a dingy cot, Michaella wasn't certain she had the stomach for this. *Don't be silly!* she scolded herself. After all, it was very much like birthing a foal, and hadn't she helped with her prize mare once? But that had been in a clean stable on piles of clean, sweet-smelling hay, not in a dusty tent that was musty and stifling.

Meg seized control at once, ordering out the women who had gathered to hold the girl's hand and offer unwanted, unnecessary advice.

"Put a pair of scissors under the cot to cut the pain in half," one woman said as Meg firmly shoved her out the tent flap.

Meg snorted indignantly. "Fool," she muttered. "I will never understand how babies come to be born sometimes, what with all the foolishness that goes hand in hand with this sort of thing." Busily rolling up her sleeves, Meg sliced Michaella an inquiring glance. "Well? Aren't you going to ask me what you can do?"

Feeling rather faint, Michaella managed a weak nod. "Yes, of course. What . . . what do I do?"

"Well, for one thing, you stop wearing such a long face! This is a birthing, not a wake. And put water on to boil so I can clean my knife good."

Mary Catherine, who preferred waiting outside, helped Michaella with the heavy pot of boiling water. "I always did wonder what boiling water was for," she said as she helped her older sister lift the pot. "I sort of thought it might just be to get everyone out of the way."

"No, I think it's used to clean the knife and . . . and other things."

"Oh."

There seemed to be little to say after that, and both young women listened to the expectant mother's moans with trepidation. But if they were taking it hard, the father was in even worse shape. At least a dozen men walked with him to calm him down, without much success. The husband appeared to be nearly ten years older than his wife, yet he was as frightened as a schoolboy.

An older man leaned against a wagon, smoking a pipe. "His first baby," he commented to Michaella and Mary Catherine. "He's not slept in two days, waiting on this."

The men finally got the husband to sit down with them outside a nearby wagon. Someone suggested a game of cards but was talked down by a number of them, who insisted angrily that card playing was the devil's work, and sinful.

Michaella lifted a brow, but suggested calmly that the argument cease, no matter the reason. "It is important that the young mother have peace while she labors."

Though several of the men exchanged glances, they did cease the argument.

Michaella and Mary Catherine brewed a pot of tea. Then Michaella took the tea and hot water into the tent. Meg dropped her knife into the still bubbling water, along with two slender lengths of cord. She drank the tea, saying that the patient should not have any until after the birth. Then she began to lay out her utensils.

Perching on an upturned bucket, so she was level with the patient, Michaella did her best to comfort the terrified young woman, who gazed up at her with deep brown eyes. She spoke to her soothingly, asking her questions to distract her during the worst of the pain. It seemed to help for the young woman to focus her attention on something else at those times.

Finally Meg moved to the cot and stroked the girl's damp hair back from her forehead. She wiped her face with a clean cloth and arranged the blankets, sliding a clean white towel beneath the girl's hips. "It won't be long now," she assured her with an encouraging smile. "You're doing fine, child, just fine. This will be an easy birth."

"It doesn't . . . doesn't *feel* easy!" the girl said between heaving pants.

"You go ahead now, do like you've seen a mama dog do," Meg instructed. "That's right, pant. Take short breaths at the worst of times, then rest with long, easy breaths to relax you. It'll help if you just concentrate."

An hour passed, then Jean Patrick appeared at the tent flap. "Here," he said, holding out a tiny piece of root. "Give this to the mother. Tell her to put it under her tongue and not to spit it out. It's bitter, but it'll help her."

Nodding, Meg didn't question his gift, but took it straight to the girl. Though reluctant, the young mother did as she was instructed, and a few minutes later began to breathe more easily. Her belly grew taut as the muscles contracted, and in a very short time, Meg was delivering the child.

Grinning proudly, Meg held up the baby for the mother and Michaella to view. It was a little red-faced, wrinkled, wizened apple of a girl, with dark wet hair that would be a pale blond when dry. Michaella—who had thought she might be repulsed—instead found the process somewhat of a miracle. She wasn't even disturbed when Meg cut the umbilical cord and disposed of the after-birth. It was all so natural, so miraculous, and she felt as drained as the mother must feel!

Staggering from the tent, Michaella sucked in several huge gulps of fresh air. She leaned wearily against a nearby wagon as the father was fetched and practically dragged into the tent to see his new daughter.

"Tired?" Jean Patrick asked softly, and Michaella turned with a jerk to see him at her side.

Relaxing slightly, she said, "Yes, but I don't know why I should be. The mother did all the work. By the way—what was that miracle you brought for her to eat?"

"That? It's just an old Indian remedy. It is a medicine food and a healing food. The Indians call it 'bitterroot' because it is. It doesn't grow around here, but I happened to have some in my bags, so . . ."

"So you brought it to that girl. That was very nice, Jean Patrick," she said softly.

"Was it?"

A smile curved her mouth. "Yes, it was. Don't

try to hide a sense of decency. It will show every time."

"Maybe I should hide it under a bushel?" he suggested with a quirk of his mouth, turning back to face her, his eyes searching her face in the light from the half-moon that was shedding its silvery light on the land. Jean Patrick reached out a hand and pushed back a stray tendril of dark hair from Michaella's face. Wisps of hair fluttered around her face most becomingly. "Care to go for a walk?" he murmured.

There was something in his voice that had not been evident in the past weeks, a low, husky tone almost like a caress. Hearing it made Michaella's stomach lurch, and her heart began to beat faster. "Yes," she replied after a moment of what she hoped looked like calm deliberation instead of panic. "I would like that very much."

Taking her hand, Jean Patrick tucked it into the crook of his arm and walked her through the camp toward the river, just as they had done in the past. It was a friendly gesture, but somehow, tonight it held overtones of sensuality that made Michaella's nerves vibrate and her tongue cleave to the roof of her mouth. How could she speak intelligently if her vocal cords refused to work? How could she speak intelligently when she was near Jean Patrick? her logic demanded.

The night was soft and windless, pierced only by the occasional howl of a wolf or the lonely yap of a coyote. The half-moon was suspended at the end of a band of stars flung across the sky in a wide, milky strip, outshining the cluster with a brilliant, silvery light and brightening the trails. Nighthawks flapped past on muffled wing beats, and the river snaked through Kansas in a surging rush. It was, she was to later reflect, a night woven of magic and moon dust.

When they paused on a bluff overlooking the river and the flat land beyond, Jean Patrick stood gazing across the frothy current, his expression remote and . . . was it sadness she saw in his eyes? Michaella asked softly, "What do you see out there?"

"Mountains."

She followed his gaze, and beyond the flat land she could see nothing that resembled mountains, nothing but deep shadows. "You can't wait to get back to them, can you?"

A gentle smile touched the corners of his mouth. "There's something in the land that draws me. I can't stay away from it for very long at a time. It's like a voice in the wind, calling to me, whispering sweet songs. Ah, I guess I sound pretty silly."

"No. No, you don't," Michaella replied. "You sound like a man who knows what he wants."

Moving away from the bluff, Jean Patrick took her hand, holding it in a warm clasp. She entwined her fingers through his, and walked beside him in silence as they strolled through a thicket of cottonwood trees. Long branches swung delicately in the breeze from the river, a lacy net that tickled her face and caught in her hair. They paused while Jean Patrick gently disentangled a slender branch from her thick coils of hair. The clearing where they stood seemed like a good place to rest, and when she was free of the clinging branch, Michaella sat down on a thick clump of bear grass.

"How do you think the mountains will affect me?" she asked after a moment of silence. He turned quietly to face her, lifting one hand to cup her chin in the gentle cradle of his palm, and gazed into her eyes.

Moonlight silvered Jean Patrick's hair and hawk-like features with a pale, iridescent glow, and his blue eyes were shadowed by some emotion she didn't recognize. Michaella's breath slowed, and she could feel the bruising force of her heart thumping against the prison of her rib cage as he drew her slowly to him.

"I'm sure you will feel the same way I do," he murmured in a low, husky voice that penetrated all the way to her spine. "You are a child of the earth. I've watched you the past weeks. The land and the rivers have released something inside you, I think. Something you can't resist."

Her senses were swirling, rioting with tiny bursts of fiery sparks that should have ignited an inferno, and Michaella had the swift thought that the something she couldn't resist was Jean Patrick, not the mountains. He was an embodiment of the wild, free, untamed land. Jean Patrick was a free spirit, a man who could not be forced into a mold.

Michaella shivered as his hand moved from her chin to caress the arch of her throat, slowly shifting to cup her shoulder and draw her into his embrace. She yielded gladly, fiercely happy to be held in the circle of his strong arms. His dark head lowered, and his mouth brushed across hers, lightly at first, then more insistently, drawing the breath and will from her body with his gentle touch. When his lips moved from her mouth to her neck, trailing warmth in a searing path, she closed her eyes and let her head fall back.

It was sweet madness, and she was lost in it. She felt his fingers at the buttons of her dress, felt it fall away and the cool night air whisper across her heated flesh. Then the dress was gone, along with her chemise, petticoats and unmentionables, and she was before him clad in only silvery moonlight and the glow of his admiration.

"You're beautiful," he murmured, "but I knew you would be."

Jean Patrick's warm lips went once again to her mouth and to her neck, pausing to kiss the tiny flutter in the hollow of her throat, then moving down to the gentle swell of her breasts. He held their weight in his palms, cradling them tenderly, kissing them lingeringly. Michaella moaned softly, a throaty love sound that made Jean Patrick pull her closer to his lean body.

Burying his face in the cleft between her breasts, he moved his hands under her, caressing her back with his splayed hands, roaming from the high, sweet curve of her shoulders down the gentle ridge of her spine to her slender hips. His hands cupped her buttocks and lifted her to him so tightly that Michaella could feel the surge of his desire against her stomach. Her senses reeled, and she could think of nothing as she existed in a shadowy, cottony world where everything was colored by passion.

Then Jean Patrick was moving away from her, withdrawing and leaving her suspended in anticipation as he shrugged out of his buckskins. Michaella drew in a quick breath at the sight of him. His lean body was perfectly formed, with wide shoulders and ridges of muscle that flowed smoothly over his frame. Bronzed skin gleamed in the pale light, and a wide pelt of dark hair furred his chest, dipping in a V down to his flat belly and below. Michaella's gaze jerked quickly upward, and her cheeks flamed.

"Don't be shy, love," he whispered, putting his fingertips beneath her chin and tilting back her head. "God intended us to be like this with one another."

Nodding wordlessly, Michaella let him lay her back on a cushion of thick grass, let her mind drift into that hazy half-world of desire as he caressed and explored her body with his mouth and hands. His burning mouth and inquisitive hands sent racking shudders through her, and she was hot and cold at the same time. The moment had a dream quality about it, a hazy, unreal atmosphere made of moonlight and night birds and soft river breezes.

Then, cautiously, shyly, Michaella allowed him to take her hand and move it down to caress him. He shuddered at her touch, and growing bolder, she moved her hand in the gentle motion that he taught her. Jean Patrick groaned huskily, and his warm breath fanned across her face.

When he could stand no more, he shifted, levering his body across hers, his knees nudging gently between her soft thighs. Michaella opened herself to him, as eager for him as he was her, on fire with need for an end to the burning ache inside. She gasped when he entered her, her slender body arching upward and her heels digging into the grass.

"Be still, love," he murmured in her ear. "It's all right, you'll see. . . ."

And it was all right after that first, sharp pain. A slow wave of sensation built into a towering rush that seemed about to consume her as he moved against her body, his lean hips driving in a slow rhythm. Michaella heard a soft cry, realized dimly that it was her own, and felt a starburst of release that shattered the world into a thousand pieces. She floated gently back to reality, opening her eyes and gazing at Jean Patrick with an overwhelming feeling of love.

He turned his dark head, his mouth quirking into a heart-stopping smile that never failed to make her melt inside. Putting out a finger, Jean Patrick rose to prop himself on his elbows, looking down at her. He pushed aside a sweat-damp strand of hair from her eyes, then kissed the tip of her nose.

"I had no idea a woman like you existed," he said.

Reaching up, Michaella let her fingers drift through the springy mat of curls on his chest as she said, "No one has ever made me feel the way you have. I never thought I would be so completely . . . captured by a man."

His smile deepened. "Captured? I like the sound of that. It makes me feel like I have fought for and won you from a band of hostiles, or have battled in a joust for the hand of my fair lady." When she laughed softly, he grinned, then added soberly, "I want you with me always, Michaella."

Her eyes widened. She thought about what lay ahead for both of them. Jean Patrick was committed to taking the wagon train on to its final destination, but she wished in her heart of hearts that he could come with her to find her father. She knew that she and Mary Catherine would have to break off from the party sooner or later to look for Henry Chattilion. From the details of the map, they could tell he wasn't in California or Oregon.

After a brief, pregnant silence, Michaella asked slowly, "Will you be able to come back from wherever you take this wagon train? To help us find our father, I mean."

"I don't know. I was hoping you and your sister would come with me."

Michaella's heart sank. She'd known all along that he might want that. She wondered if he thought that she and Mary Catherine were wasting their time looking for their father, that he was probably dead and they would only be disappointed if they continued. But Michaella also knew, no matter how strong her love for Jean Patrick was, that she could not give up the quest. She had never quit in her life and would not start now.

"You know we have to find our father," she answered in a small voice.

"And if you never find him? What then? What if he is dead, Michaella?"

"But he is alive!" she insisted. "I know he is. He has to be or . . . or everything is ruined! Everything!"

"Whoa, whoa, sweetheart," he said against her hair as he pulled her to him. "I didn't mean to upset you."

"Then don't say that he might be dead," she whispered into his shoulder. "Jean Patrick—do you know something you aren't telling me?"

"No, no, sweetheart. It's only that you may never find him, you know. This is a vast country, and it's easy for a man to get lost out there. I don't know if you've considered failure, but it's a possibility."

Sniffing, she muttered, "Well, I don't want you to think for a single moment that Mary Catherine and I are ever going to give up our search for our father. We won't."

"I know, sweetheart, I know," he said gently, tucking her into the angle of his shoulder and arm. "I'll help you all I can."

He began to kiss her again, his mouth moving softly and tenderly over her closed eyelids, cheeks, and the straight line of her nose until he reached her trembling lips. Then he kissed her deeply, hungrily, and the kisses stirred a passion that had only been slumbering instead of satisfied. Michaella responded with a surprising surge of desire, and the feeling was so powerful and fulfilling that she felt as if she belonged in another world. She could not bear the thought of a world without Jean Patrick.

Chapter Twelve

✦✦✦✦✦

EARLY THE NEXT morning as she lay in her blankets and watched the rising sun, Michaella touched her bruised lips with the tip of her tongue. Love bruises, she reflected, and a smile flickered for a moment on her mouth. She rolled onto her back and stared up at the gray and pink sky, misty with morning light and shrouds of low-lying fog.

Somehow, she now felt she could see Jean Patrick for what he truly was—a strikingly handsome, bold man who was not embarrassed to display the tender side of his nature. She had seen evidence of his courage, and now his more vulnerable emotions. As far as she was concerned, he was far ahead of most men his age—or any age, for that matter.

At times Jean Patrick seemed as wise as Sorrel in the ways of the land. He could recognize animal tracks in the dirt that Michaella couldn't even see, and tell her what kind of animal and how long before it had passed that way. He could smell rain on the wind and knew where there was water even when there was only a dry, barren stretch of land ahead of them. The call of a bird—which sounded like any other to Michaella—was a cry of alarm to Jean Patrick, and he would know there was a natural predator lurking in the tall grasses or thicket. He also knew when death lay ahead, for he followed the flights of the scavenger crows and magpies that circled and swooped over carrion. To

Michaella, it often seemed as if he could sense things before they even happened.

Three days from the Big Blue, Jean Patrick returned from a scouting foray in a rush, reining in his bay in a billowing cloud of dust. Michaella immediately straightened from bending over the cooking fire, shading her eyes with a cupped hand against the dying light from the sun.

"What is it?" she asked tersely as he dismounted and strode toward her. "What has happened?"

"Where's Sorrel?" he asked instead of answering.

"Hunting." Michaella handed him a tin mug of coffee and watched quietly as he took a deep gulp. Lowering the mug, he pushed his hat to the back of his head and looked down at her, his gaze somber. "It's the wagon train ahead of us. Most are dead, from what I can tell. Cholera or something like it." While that penetrated he took another sip of scalding coffee, watching Michaella over the rim. She didn't panic, but her thick-lashed dark eyes widened slightly, absorbing light like a mirror. "It looks like a lot of graves up there, shallow ones scratched into the dirt in a hurry. Wagons filled with goods have been abandoned," he added after a moment.

Stunned, Michaella couldn't speak. Cholera. It could mean the deaths of all the people on this wagon train. Jean Patrick was watching her closely, waiting for a reaction, and she steeled herself for what he might say. She was half expecting his next words.

"If there were any way to go on without passing close to it, I would. But there's not." He took a deep breath and continued, "The trail cuts right through a ravine only a few yards from there, and to go around would add needless miles and time."

"But are we in danger of contracting cholera if we go that close?" Michaella asked.

He shook his head. "I don't think so. If we all just pass the wagons, wearing scarves over our noses and mouths and don't stop to touch anything, then I think we'll be all right."

There was a tinny clatter behind them, and Michaella turned to see Mary Catherine's pale, taut face. "Does this mean . . . are we . . . Oh, my God!" she exclaimed in a whisper.

"Don't!" Michaella said, stepping forward and gripping her tightly by the wrist. "Above all else, we must not allow anyone to panic." She gave her arm a slight shake. "Do you understand that, Mary Catherine? Do not say anything to anyone!"

Sorrel chose that moment to ride back into camp, his bearded face creased in a huge grin of expectation as he led a packhorse burdened with the carcasses of three fat deer. His grin faded when there were no shouts of welcome or hurrahs for his hunting skill, and he pulled his mount to a halt and swung down.

"What is it, hoss?" he asked Jean Patrick, tossing his reins over a wagon tongue. "Somebody die or something?"

"There are times, Sorrel," Jean Patrick said grimly, "when you are right and don't even know it!"

Sorrel's bushy brows swooped lower over his eves. "Where?"

"Up ahead. There are some fresh graves. My

guess is cholera. I imagine we'll lose some from our party because of it—they won't want to go on once they're confronted with mortality. Some folks fool themselves about this trip out west, thinking it's a Sunday outing until something like this happens."

Sorrel nodded. "There's nothing like graves to scare people into turnin' back."

Which is exactly what some of the emigrants decided to do when Jean Patrick called them together to inform them of what lay ahead. It took some fast talking to settle them down enough to call a meeting of the governing council, but it was finally decided that the wagon train would stay intact. Only nine wagons had wanted to abandon the train, and that small a number alone on the prairie would be suicide. Everyone would stay—for now.

It was the next morning before they reached the place where the first graves had been dug and bodies buried just off the trail. A number of the graves were marked with crude wooden crosses. One tiny grave, however, had been marked with a small headboard that seemed to have been taken from a bed frame. An inscription had been engraved on it, leaving a pitiful epitaph:

Here rests Martha Jean Pratt
Age 3
Gone to her Maker on June 3, 1849
God rest her Soul

Michaella turned away from the small marker while Mary Catherine gazed at it with brimming eyes. There were other small graves marked only by crosses, and the size of the mounds indicated that many children had passed away as well as a sizable number of adults. It must have been a devastating time for the survivors. Michaella wondered where they had gone. There must have been survivors or no one would have been left to bury the dead, yet there were no wagon tracks or signs of flight.

Jean Patrick gave the signal and the wagons rolled forward again, soon leaving behind the empty wagons, the graves, and the dust blowing across the desolate spot. For a time people were quiet as they walked or rode along. They didn't seem to have much to say beyond a word or two. But as time and miles passed, they began to talk about getting farther on and eventually seeing the mountains. It would be cooler in the mountains, with more to see than empty plains and waving grasses and hot blue sky. Their worry about disease and other calamities faded, and the optimistic side of human nature prevailed.

As the days blended into one another in a haze of hot sun and constant wind, Michaella and Jean Patrick drew closer to one another, spending each evening walking away from the camp and discussing what lay ahead of them. The future was a mystery, frightening and hopeful at the same time. They spoke of the mountains and how beautiful they were in spring and summer, yet how treacherous they would be when the winter snows fell. Survival was a feat of ingenuity and endurance, and Michaella wondered if she would pass the supreme test.

Although she discussed a hundred different topics with Jean Patrick, Michaella avoided mentioning Chattilion again. She didn't want to think about the inevitable time when she would be separated from Jean Patrick, when he would go on with the wagons to Oregon and leave her behind. It wasn't that she hid from the truth, but more that she put off thinking about it.

Jean Patrick, however, had not forgotten Chattilion. Nor had he forgotten the shadow in Westport. He'd recognized the shape, with its top hat and cane, and wondered why Ketchman was following him. Or was it the sisters he was following? The latter made more sense. If Nolan Ketchman was on the prowl, it was best to be wary, best to watch every distant dust cloud and every solitary shadow. . . .

As they traveled, the landscape gradually changed. The tall, lush grass that had surrounded them at the beginning gave way to a drier, more arid part of the prairie. Here the grass grew tall only along the river bottoms and where water regularly overflowed the banks of streams and rivers. No longer did the growth reach well above the stirrups of horses, but grew to just above the knees.

With the change in the land, Michaella and Mary Catherine could see that they were entering the high plains, a huge, empty expanse that lay between the wagons and the mountains. It stretched toward the horizon, a mixed sea of flatland and rolling, grass-covered humps. They were reaching the edge of the region Jean Patrick had spoken of often before—the territory of the ferocious Plains Indians.

Early one morning when the sky was still gray, Jean Patrick and Sorrel awakened Michaella and her sister. They told them to bring their rifles and be quiet. Alarmed at first, Michaella took a few minutes to fully waken and notice Sorrel's smile. He didn't smile when there was danger.

Dressed, the sisters met Jean Patrick and Sorrel outside their tent. It was still quiet, as most of the emigrants had not yet risen. It was unusual for the wagon train to delay departure this late. Normally the wagons were hitched to oxen and mules, and everyone was ready and rolling by the time the sun rose. It was cooler in the early morning, and more miles could be made while the animals were still fresh.

Jean Patrick already had their horses saddled and waiting, as well as Clarence the mule, and Michaella mounted with a skeptical glance at the guide. He was certainly behaving mysteriously this morning! When he handed her the rifle and told her to make certain it was loaded, she asked him bluntly if there was trouble ahead.

"Not for us," he said with a grin, and refused to say more.

They rode away from the wagon train, finally stopping about two miles out and reigning in their mounts at the crest of a low rise. Michaella—irritated with the mystery—turned to demand an explanation from Jean Patrick. But a blur of movement caught her eye and she jerked her head back around to gaze out across the plain, squinting in the dim light. A great dark wave seemed to be undulating, and even as she gasped she knew what it was.

"Buffalo!" Mary Catherine cried out, and Jean Patrick nodded.

"Right. Thought you might be interested in seein' them while they're grazing peacefully."

Sorrel put in, "Yeah, they've already watered this mornin', or we might have quite a wait with the wagons."

"Quite a wait?" Michaella echoed.

He nodded. "When buffalo go to water, you just sit back and wait until they're finished. If yer smart, you don't try and drive a wagon train through a herd of buffalo!"

"Oh," Michaella said, remembering all Jean Patrick had told her about the buffalo and its importance to the Plains Indians. The animal was used for food, clothing, lodging, needles and thread, eating utensils, and a hundred other things. The shaggy beast, with its poor eyesight, surly nature, and tendency to stand and let itself be slaughtered, was sacred to the Indians. It meant the difference between their survival and starvation.

"Look," Jean Patrick said, rising in his stirrups to point out a pack of coyotes that was prowling at the edge of the herd. "They feed on the weak and dying, or the leavings from a hunt."

"Well, they shall eat well this morning!" Sorrel said with a boom of laughter. "We're goin' to make some meat! Does either of you ladies want th' privilege of the first shot?"

Mary Catherine shuddered delicately and Michaella gave him a quelling glance. "No," she answered for both of them. "I don't think so. You shoot one for us."

"That I kin do! But watch close where I shoot

him, in case you ever have to drop one yourself one day."

As Sorrel rode downwind toward the herd and finally dismounted, stealing stealthily toward what Jean Patrick identified as a young bull, Michaella watched with her heart in her throat. What if the animal lowered its massive head and charged at the aging Sorrel? He would be killed, if not gored, for the mass of the beast would be enough to crush a man in seconds.

"Look," Jean Patrick said softly, pointing with the barrel of his Hawken, "he's going to shoot it low, just behind the shoulder, so that the bullet will pierce the heart and lungs. It'll die instantly if it's a good shot. No decent hunter likes a bad shot, or making an animal suffer," he added upon noticing Mary Catherine's pallor and set face.

A single shot rang out, startling Mary Catherine but not affecting the rest of the herd. Beyond a few snorts and lifted heads, they did not see the intruder in their midst, and the noise was soon forgotten. If they had caught his scent, it might have started a stampede.

Jean Patrick rode down to join Sorrel, leaving Michaella and her sister on the safety of the hill. He helped dress out the fallen animal. Soon a small pack of prairie wolves gathered, slinking close to peer hungrily at the scraps of meat and offal being disposed of by the men. When the two frontiersmen had finished, they would move in to take care of the rest of the carcass.

Michaella watched in curiosity as Jean Patrick turned toward the sun, lifted something in his hands for a moment, then buried it in the ground.

The brief ritual completed, he joined Sorrel and rode back toward the waiting women.

No sooner had the horses moved away than the wolves were snarling and fighting over the slain buffalo, while vultures and crows hopped aimlessly, hoping for a quick meal.

The meat was packed on Clarence, and the four rode back to camp. Slanting a glance at Jean Patrick, Michaella finally asked, "What sort of ceremony was that you performed after cutting up the meat?"

"Ceremony? Oh, that. That was just an old Indian way of saying thank you to the Great Spirits for giving us the buffalo. By burying the heart, more buffalo will be given to the Indian."

"I see. Sort of like saying grace before a meal, is that it?"

"Exactly. And the Indian never forgets."

Smiling, Michaella nodded. "I'm beginning to think you're more Indian than anything else," she teased.

"To tell the truth, I feel that way sometimes. The Indians live close to the land, respect it for the most part, and take care of it. They don't own the land, nor do they want to own it. They just consider themselves as caretakers, I guess. It's on loan, and if mistreated, it will be taken away."

Michaella gazed at him skeptically. "*All* of them? I seem to recall . . ."

"No, not all tribes do, of course. There are Indians who care for nothing more than whiskey or fighting, just like there are white men who feel the same. But those tribes aren't respected by the others, just treated with contempt."

As they rode back to the wagons, Michaella thought about what Jean Patrick had said. She wondered why, if he felt such a kinship with the Indians, he didn't stay with them more. He had so many traits and customs that belonged to a native American, yet he traveled in another world when it was obvious he preferred that of the Indian.

There was no opportunity to ask him, for when they arrived back in camp everyone was packed, ready to go, and wondering where their guide had gone. The wagons soon pulled out, and throughout the day the emigrants marveled at the buffalo from a distance. Thousands upon thousands of them carpeted the plains in a dark brown mass, stretching as far as the eye could see.

Later that day when the wagons had halted and pulled into several circles, as was normal for the train, Michaella and Mary Catherine had their first taste of buffalo meat. After picking at her portion, Mary Catherine decided she would prefer beans and salt pork instead of the strange slab on her plate.

"I just can't eat anything I saw die," she complained softly, earning hearty guffaws from the men and even a smile from her sister and Meg.

"See if you feel that way a month from now, missy!" Sorrel boomed, chuckling to himself as he pierced a juicy chunk with the point of his knife and wedged it into his mouth.

Michaella ate hers more delicately, and was surprised—after her initial reluctance—to find it quite tasty. It was tender, with a fine texture and not at all as stringy as it looked. Perhaps survival wouldn't be too difficult after all!

It was two days before the wagon train left the herd of buffalo behind. They were only a few days away from the Platte River, considered by many to be the real beginning of the journey. More and more often they passed remnants of cargo that had been abandoned by previous wagon trains. There were pieces of furniture bleached white by the sun, much of it broken into fragments. Some things, like plows and heavy farm implements, were still intact. The animals pulling the wagons must have been under considerable strain, and their loads had to be lightened.

Until they arrived at the Platte, grass and water had been plentiful, but now there was mostly sand along the riverbanks instead of forage. It had been a dry year, and the wagon trains ahead of them had worn down a lot of the grass. Jean Patrick advised everyone to take the same precautions as the wagon trains before: any cargo not absolutely necessary should be abandoned. The draft animals in particular were going to be under tremendous strain from the shortage of grass, and if the teams gave out, the people who owned them would either lose their entire wagonloads of goods or be forced to pull them with human labor.

Some families took Jean Patrick's advice, with tearful debates over what should be abandoned and what saved. Keepsakes handed down from generation to generation ended up in piles beside the trail, to vanish in the distance as the wagons moved onward.

But there were some who refused to discard anything. They sat resolutely in their wagons and ignored their neighbors' advice, which quickly became warnings not to come begging for help when their oxen gave out. Jean Patrick knew that he could advise, but would not overstep himself and interfere in their individual decisions. Besides, other concerns troubled him more.

For one thing, they were now traveling into Pawnee country. The Pawnees were known to make life miserable for invaders on their hunting grounds. According to Sorrel and Jean Patrick, the Pawnees fought nearly every other tribe in the region. During a previous midsummer's ceremony, they had sacrificed a woman captured from another tribe.

Trouble, it is said, often comes in threes. Along with the worry about the Pawnees came a swarm of black insects that clung to everything—wagons, clothes, food, and livestock. Jean Patrick and Sorrel called them "dorbugs" and insisted they were only harmless nuisances. But the worrisome insects created a constant humming as they moved, clinging everywhere and bringing screams from sleeping people who felt them invading their bedrolls and crawling over their faces.

When the dorbugs finally left, a spell of terrifying weather set in. Rain swept across the plains in a series of violent thunderstorms, with sheets of lightning that bolted across the sky and made hair stand on end and the skin prickle. The storms were frequently accompanied by black funnels of deadly wind that snaked down from the clouds and tore up whatever lay in their path. The emigrants could only watch and keep moving in spite of the storms pummeling them and their belongings with deluges.

Michaella noticed that the storms seemed most frequent during the afternoon hours, when the clouds built up against the hot, moist air rising from the ground. It was odd to watch distant sweeping currents that rose high into the sky and boiled back down again in black masses of twisting power. Neither sister had ever witnessed such storms before, and they found them fascinating and terrifying at the same time.

There was no predicting what the twisters would do. Some of them were small and others were very large. Often they would descend only partway down, while at other times they would loop quickly from the clouds and churn across the plains until they either blew themselves out or rose back up into the sky.

When the twisters became more frequent, everyone's concern grew. The travelers debated what to do in the event of a serious storm, and those who had been in such storms offered advice. But nothing prepared either Michaella or Mary Catherine for what happened just two days after they reached the Platte River.

The wagons had halted for the day, and the livestock had been let out to graze. Michaella and Jean Patrick had walked out from camp to watch the sunset. All at once the sun vanished behind a mass of dark clouds shot through with veins of lightning. The air began to hum with a strong, menacing sound. Jean Patrick quickly grabbed Michaella's hand and they ran for the wagons to take cover.

As they skidded into camp, they were greeted by Sorrel, who was swearing and trying to calm the mules. "These mules smell a heap of bad weather," he said. "I've a mind to set them loose and follow them wherever they go."

"Not a bad idea," Jean Patrick muttered, raking a hand through his hair. A steady stream of livestock was already moving out from camp toward the west. When the mules were released, they ran the same way. After a brief exchange of glances, Sorrel shrugged, grabbed Mary Catherine's hand, and took off behind them. Jean Patrick shouted that he would warn the others, and Michaella moved protectively closer to him.

She glanced around nervously as he tried to hurry the people along, urging them to follow the animals' instinct. Suddenly the wind swept through the camp and rain fell heavily. The others wouldn't leave their wagons; they remained huddled inside and underneath. Plead as he might, Jean Patrick could only get a few of the travelers out of their wagons and headed out onto the prairie with the livestock.

Michaella stared in anguish at Jean Patrick, silently pleading with him to flee with her. Through the odd, muted calm that suddenly shrouded the camp came Mary Catherine's distant scream. Michaella whirled to look and saw Sorrel motioning for them to hurry, pointing frantically to the sky. She looked up to see a large funnel cloud drop down out of the sky.

Jean Patrick snatched Michaella and yanked her beneath a wagon just as the twister touched the ground and bounced. Michaella held her ears against the thunderous whining roar as the funnel tore a swath outside the camp, sucking up everything in its path. Everyone panicked, their screams drowned out by the heavy drone of the funnel as it continued to bear down on the wagons.

Covering Michaella with his body, Jean Patrick put his arms over his head as the howl of the twister became overpowering. She felt a sweeping sensation, then a smothering blast of dirt and grass and debris sucking the breath from her lungs. The wagon they had been under was completely gone, torn from the ground. Everything was in confusion.

At once it was over as fast as it had begun. The heavy whining sound vanished and rain fell again. Jean Patrick lifted his body off Michaella and carried her to a nearby wagon. Michaella looked at him, dazed and coated with mud and grass as he knelt over her. Others came running. She could see and hear everyone—Sorrel, Mary Catherine, and Meg Magoffin—but their voices were jumbled and made no sense to her. She lay back, dizzy and numb.

The entire party was in an uproar. People ran in every direction to see what damage had been done. Three wagons had been drawn up into the funnel and dropped at various distances from the camp. Two of the wagons were splintered; the third had been set down on its wheels with only minimal damage. Five people were dead, including three children, and three had been badly injured.

By morning the rain had stopped. Michaella awoke and walked slowly to the river, her muscles aching. She felt bruised and battered, but glad to be alive. Kneeling on the bank, she was washing traces of mud from her arms when Jean Patrick approached.

"I was afraid I had lost you yesterday," he said gravely, and she stood up to face him.

"So was I," she said simply. She put up a hand and caressed his cheek, a faint smile curving her mouth. Jean Patrick swept her into his embrace and lay his head against her hair, closing his eyes and sucking in a deep breath.

"I don't ever want to lose you," he whispered fiercely.

Strengthened by the force of his words, Michaella relaxed in his embrace. She felt the warmth flow over her once again.

Chapter Thirteen

KETCHMAN AND HIS crew had been following the wagon train at a distance ever since it left Westport, staying close enough to always keep it in sight, yet remaining far enough so as not to be detected. Ketchman was glad that Jean Patrick was concentrating mainly on scouting up ahead and not behind, and that those who hunted usually rode ahead of the train as well. That made it easier for him to keep Michaella and Mary Catherine within sight and not be noticed.

Ketchman had watched in suspense as the twister churned through the camp. At first he was certain Michaella had been killed and that his hopes of locating the gold were damaged. But Michaella proved to be of hardy stock, and when he saw her walking about the next morning, Ketchman had shouted and clapped with glee. He was so obsessed with the gold that he couldn't contain himself.

Seeing Ketchman's outburst, both Bisler and LaRange had hissed at him to quiet down. The tension between Ketchman and the company men was growing worse as time passed. Instead of acting together on a mission that would benefit them all, they were suspicious and resentful of one another.

Sorley, the youngest of the five, stayed off by himself and seemed to be in another world much of the time. Like Ketchman, he was something of an outcast. Ketchman considered him a good deal smarter than the rest and often wondered why the younger man had even come along. Before secrecy was so necessary, Sorley had often spent the evenings reading in front of a low fire, a fact that had impressed Ketchman until he had discovered they were not real books. The thin paper novellas were considered trash of the worst sort by Ketchman.

And the man known only as "Itch" because of his disgusting habit of constantly scratching at the vermin-infested garments he wore, grew even more disgusting to Ketchman as the days went by.

Crenshaw continued his boasting to whoever would listen. By night, he slept as close to the others as he could, fearing the strange sounds of nature. But by day he bragged of past conquests and the dangers he would soon lead them safely through. But once Ketchman and the others realized his stories were only that—stories—they ignored him completely.

Bisler, the big man, seemed always to be talking to LaRange. Ketchman became more concerned about this over the days of travel. The night way back along the Missouri when LaRange had held the young woman at knifepoint was still vivid in his mind. It frightened him more each time he thought about it. Ketchman could not remember reacting so violently to anyone in his entire life. But what else could he have done? If he had just stood by and let LaRange abduct the woman, the entire band of emigrants would have come down hard on all of them.

Nevertheless, Ketchman was having trouble sleeping nights. It was bad enough that the ground was hard and the food distasteful; having to keep his senses alert all the time was bringing him to mental and physical exhaustion. He could still see LaRange with the knife, and he could see the trapper's enraged eyes glaring at him through the light of the fire while his hand wiped blood from his head where the cane had split the scalp. Ketchman was worried that when LaRange had said he might not live to reach the mountains, it had not been an idle threat.

As the countryside changed, Ketchman and his party no longer bothered to hide themselves. The plains along the Platte were flat, sandy, and treeless, and Jean Patrick would soon see his pursuers. But Ketchman wasn't concerned. He reasoned that Jean Patrick would not be able to tell their identities. After all, he had no idea Ketchman had ever left St. Louis!

The Platte was the oddest river Michaella had yet seen. Trees were almost nonexistent. Scrubby brush grew in a few places, but it was obvious the buffalo kept it browsed down to gangly stubs. The river was a murky color and flowed very slowly, almost at a trickle in some places. It was wide but often shallow enough to allow a woman to walk across without getting her knees wet. As a result, the water frequently stood in foul pools filled with grit and sand.

"This must be the worst water we've had in our entire lives," Michaella commented in disgust one evening. They had made camp, and she was gazing into a tin pail of water she had fetched from the river. She couldn't even see the bottom.

Mary Catherine shrugged in resignation. "With all those huge buffalo trampling through the river, I suppose there's no reason to expect anything but murky water."

"But we need to *drink* this water," Michaella pointed out reasonably. "I refuse even to try this!"

"Let it settle some," came a familiar voice, and Meg Magoffin stepped into their camp. She grinned, knowing what must be running through their minds. "Or use a sieve! You've heard the saying about the Platte bein' too thick to drink and too thin to plow?"

"I hadn't, but I must say I agree with it!" Michaella returned shortly.

"Here, let me show you a trick or two. . . ." Meg

showed the sisters a fast way to boil water and keep it for drinking later. After that, whenever they paused for any length of time they would boil pots of water and store it in barrels strapped to the wagon sides. Before long, others in camp were doing the same.

With the absence of trees, a new fuel had to be used. Dried buffalo droppings were collected for the cookfires. The sun-hardened chips burned like peat, and the aroma was surprisingly pleasant. "Not at all like peat from the bogs in Cornwall!" Michaella reported with a laugh. "I was expecting a foul-smelling cloud to rise from the flames, like something on Judgment Day!"

In a week's time they arrived at the newly established Fort Kearney, an outpost constructed to keep travelers safe from warring Indians. Michaella noted that the fort's structures were crudely constructed from mud bricks, but the mere presence of military dragoons made the members of the party more confident that they were being protected—which proved to be an illusion.

While Mary Catherine began cooking the evening meal in the open fireplace of the tiny cabin they had been assigned, Michaella went with Meg Magoffin to inquire after her husband at Fort Laramie.

"Will they have a record of him here?" Michaella asked.

"They should. It's not like it's that far away by military standards," Meg replied.

They met the commanding officer, Colonel Wilson, who had just finished putting his dragoons through their maneuvers on the parade ground.

"I would like to know if my husband is still stationed at Fort Laramie, please," Meg said to the commander. "Would you have any way of knowing? And if you do, could you help me find him?"

Colonel Wilson was small and whipcord lean. He glanced only fleetingly at Meg, but his gaze lingered on Michaella. She stiffened, lifting her chin and staring back at him in a bold manner that indicated her disdain. The colonel averted his gaze.

"My name is Mrs. Thomas Magoffin," Meg explained. "My husband is a sergeant at Fort Laramie. . . ."

"Ma'am, would you also like to know if your husband is well?" the colonel asked Michaella abruptly, ignoring Meg, whose face was slowly growing red and angry.

"That won't be necessary," was Michaella's cool reply.

Wilson preened, smoothing a thin mustache that looked to Michaella like a smudge of soot beneath his thin nose. Clearing his throat, he straightened his coat and invited Meg and Michaella to accompany him to his office. When he was behind his desk, he shuffled through several ledgers, finally skimming down a page with his forefinger.

"Yes, I see that he's still stationed there," Wilson said.

"Thank you," she managed to say calmly, and turned to leave, her back stiff and straight.

The office door swung open before either woman reached it, however, and Jean Patrick strode into the room. He swept his hat from his head, his gaze instantly moving to Michaella. A warm smile curved the sensual line of his mouth, and his gaze lingered for a moment before shifting to the colonel.

Noting this silent exchange, the commander stiffened and snapped, "What can I do for you, sir?"

Jean Patrick's attention returned to the colonel. "I am Jean Patrick Malloy, scout for the wagon train. I would like to request an escort from your command as far as Ash Hollow. I understand the Pawnee are becoming ever more dangerous to travelers."

Wilson's brows rose. "That's rather an understatement, Malloy," he said dryly. "However, I must regretfully refuse your request. Yours is the fifth wagon train to come through here in less than a month. If I sent escorts with every one, I would find myself with a severe shortage of men in an emergency."

Shrugging, Jean Patrick crooked a smile in Michaella's direction and moved to open the door. "Good day, Colonel," he said, slapping his hat back on his head as they left the small office.

"You're not angry?" Michaella asked when they stood outside in the sun.

"Angry? No, I didn't expect him to agree. I only asked because the committee insisted. They're afraid to go on without military escort."

"You mean the governing council of our wagon train has so little faith in our guide?" Michaella teased.

"Can you blame them? After all, there's only one of me, and I can't be everywhere at once. Besides, most of the soldiers and officers stationed in the posts and forts have less experience than I do at fighting Indians. The dragoons might just incite the Pawnee to attack us instead of letting us go."

"Do you really think we'll be attacked?" Michaella asked, taking his proffered arm and stepping down the wooden steps into the dust of the open yard.

Meg gave a snort of derision. "I'll take my frying pan to the first red face I see poking his nose into my wagon!"

"You may have to," Jean Patrick commented with a grin. "You can head up the frying-pan brigade!"

His jest was recalled in the following days when the wagon train moved out of the safety of Fort Kearney's shadow and into the open. With the passing of the days, the trail became more difficult to traverse, and fewer miles were put behind them at the end of each day.

Michaella could see that Jean Patrick had been right about the need to lighten the loads in the wagons. She watched in dismay as oxen gave out, lying down in traces and harness to die. Wagons were abandoned, and it was not at all unusual to see mules hitched with horses and oxen in the harnesses. Often the beasts were simply played out and would be turned loose to fend for themselves, exhausted and near death, easy prey for wolves and scavengers.

Michaella was grateful that she and her sister had brought little more than a tent and a few changes of clothes. She watched the emigrants grow weaker, seeming at times to be as close to giving out as the oxen. But they rallied and resolved to make the best of things, shouldering what possessions they could carry on their backs.

Late one afternoon Jean Patrick came back early from a scouting foray to announce there were a number of Pawnees just ahead. Everyone was to stay close to the wagons and obey orders. Michaella noticed with trepidation that Jean Patrick was more worried than he appeared. She watched him, her heart aching for the burdens he carried on his broad shoulders. There were times she wanted to help him, to aid him in carrying such heavy responsibilities, but of course, she could not. Only her love for him could comfort him now, and she made certain he was confident in that.

Shaking his dark head, Jean Patrick admitted that there was no way to know what might happen. "There are some French-Canadian trappers with the Pawnees—and that could mean trouble."

Nodding silently, Michaella did not know what to say. There was little she could do, so she put her head against his broad chest and circled him with her arms, hugging him to her. She could feel the slow, steady beat of his heart beneath her cheek, and felt the subtle relaxing of his tense muscles beneath her caressing fingertips.

"Have I ever told you," Jean Patrick murmured into her hair, "how much you comfort me?"

She shook her head no, and he laughed huskily. "Good. I wouldn't want you to get overconfident."

Turning her face into his buckskin shirt, Michaella smothered a laugh in the soft hide. His chest hairs tickled her nose, and she tilted back her head to look up at him. "Liar," she said softly, and he nodded.

"Only about some things, love, only about some things," he said.

Close to evening of the next day they reached the Pawnees, who looked as if they had been traveling hard. Their horses were gaunt and weary from constant use. The warriors were dressed only in breechcloths and moccasins and were painted in bright colors, with bows, arrows, and lances in their hands. Most of the men wore a roached hairstyle, front to back, the roaches interlaced with feathers and the skins of small animals.

Michaella noticed the French-Canadians among the Pawnees' group. They were rough-looking men dressed in skins and painted in as many colors as the Pawnees. Except for their heads and facial bone structure, they looked like another Plains tribe.

Jean Patrick and Sorrel rode out from the wagons to talk to them, making hand signs and speaking in a guttural tongue that was quite alien to those at the wagons who were straining to hear. Squinting, Michaella watched closely as she tried to make out what they were saying. She had learned a few hand signs from Jean Patrick, but not enough to make her proficient.

She went with Mary Catherine to help Meg calm some of the women in the party who had grown hysterical at the sight of the decorated, armed Pawnees. Michaella tried to explain what she had seen—these Indians wanted some of their goods and that was all. They weren't dressed or painted for battle; they wanted to barter.

But Michaella soon realized that neither Jean Patrick nor Sorrel had assured her that the French-

Canadians were harmless. The trappers resented the flow of emigrants into the wilderness and preferred that the country remain wild and open, without settlements. It was even rumored that the trappers were inciting attacks by the Indians.

After a long, agonizing wait, Jean Patrick and Sorrel rode back into camp. Swinging down from his bay, Jean Patrick told the council that presents would have to be offered or there would be certain trouble. When packages of sugar, flour, and coffee had been given out to the Pawnees, the wagons were allowed to move ahead.

"They said they are satisfied with the gifts and won't bother us," Jean Patrick told Michaella, "but I don't trust those French-Canadians. They could be up to something."

Michaella had been practicing with her rifle for some time now. She had become proficient enough to hit buffalo chips propped against dirt clods. Glancing at her now, Jean Patrick told her to be sure she kept her rifle close by at all times.

"And stay by the wagons!" he admonished. "No one is to leave camp for walks tonight."

"Where will you be?" she asked anxiously.

"I'll be outside of camp on guard duty," he replied with a smile that was intended to ease her fears. "Don't worry about me. Just keep your rifle close at hand."

While the night closed in, all the men took turns at keeping watch. Michaella thought they should be safe on a night like this one; a full moon and clear skies soared overhead. Surely the Pawnees—who were said to be the worst thieves—or the Sioux would not come to steal horses and mules on a bright night but would wait until the moon was shadowed or the night was dark.

Reassuring herself that nothing would happen, Michaella ducked into her tent and rolled up in her blankets with her rifle close by. She fell asleep easily in the quiet of the camp, drifting into a sleep filled with dreams of Jean Patrick. He was always in her dreams, inhabiting every moment of her life, awake or asleep. There were times she wondered with a sense of despair how she would ever be able to let him go, to allow him to ride away from her when they came to the inevitable parting. But Michaella had learned to be strong during her early years, had learned to accept what life gave her and to make the best of it. She would do so now.

It was late, with the moon waning and the bright light fading when the camp was awakened by the loud braying of a mule. Jerking up in her blankets, Michaella flung them back and grabbed up her rifle. Her heart was pounding, and she went to the closed flap of the tent and pushed it back to peer out.

"What's all the fuss?" Mary Catherine murmured sleepily. She stared at her sister through a tumble of chestnut hair in her eyes.

"It sounds like Clarence," Michaella answered shortly, struggling to pull the gaping edges of her gown together. With all the tension in camp, she had gone to bed fully dressed.

"Clarence? Oh, that *mule.*"

The incessant braying had been embellished by the nervous whinnies of the horses, and oxen had begun lowing and cattle to bawl. Dogs barked and in the midst of all the chaos could be heard the shouts of the men on guard.

"Sounds like a regular party out there," Michaella said as she tugged on her shoes. "I'll be back."

"Michaella!" came the scandalized exclamation. "You can't go out there! Why, there might be danger."

"Which is why I need to go. Jean Patrick may need me."

Exploding with cries of "Jean Patrick! Jean Patrick!" Mary Catherine sat up in her blankets and glared at her sister. "What about me?"

Michaella flicked her a glance as she pushed open the flap and stepped out. "Stay here. You'll be safe enough."

As the tent flap fell back into place, she could hear Mary Catherine's scathing comment that Jean Patrick seemed well able to take care of himself, while she wasn't so sure about Michaella. A smile curved Michaella's mouth as she strode determinedly toward the cause of all the confusion.

Mary Catherine was right, of course. He had done an excellent job of caring for himself in the past, but that didn't mean he didn't need her help now. And, as she expected, she heard her sister's footsteps behind her a moment later.

"I often wonder if there's anything left in that bone-box of yours," Mary Catherine huffed as she caught up with Michaella. "Of all the insane, ridiculous notions, this beats the band!"

"I knew you'd come with me," was all Michaella said, and Mary Catherine sniffed.

"I couldn't let you be insane alone, you know."

What had seemed like a good idea in the safety of the tent seemed rather foolish as they neared the spot where the mules and horses had been picketed. Frantic livestock were veering to and fro, and several men were running among them. Thinking that it must be some men from the camp, Mary Catherine ran forward, hoping for protection.

"Wait!" Michaella yelled, grabbing for her and missing. "Mary Catherine, they might not be . . ."

Realizing that she had misjudged in the dim light, Mary Catherine tried to turn and run back, but a tall man spotted her and gave chase. Frozen in place, Michaella did not dare attempt to shoot for fear of hitting her sister, and she watched helplessly as the man with roached hair and a lance in one hand swept her sister from her feet and into his arms. Mary Catherine dropped her rifle and began kicking her feet and screaming at the top of her well-developed lungs.

Her struggle was so energetic that the man was soon wheezing and puffing with the effort of trying to hold her, and he growled a warning at her to be still or he'd cut her throat. The warning was delivered in a thick French accent.

While Michaella hesitated in indecision, a Pawnee warrior raced forward to capture her. Now, at last, she had something to do, and Michaella coolly raised her rifle, aimed, and fired. The recoil staggered her, but the warrior dropped to the ground with a loud cry.

Seeing his comrade fall, the angry trapper holding Mary Catherine lost his grip on the squirming girl. She twisted in his cruel embrace, lashing out with both feet to catch him on his shins, then shoved as hard as she could with the flat of her hands against his chest. The trapper stumbled, and before he could catch his balance Mary Catherine took advantage and gave him another hard push. Sprawling backward, the trapper fell beneath the flashing hooves of a rowdy gray mule. He rolled frantically, trying to avoid the deadly hooves, but the mule seemed determined to wreak vengeance upon this intruder. The lance the trapper held was splintered beneath the attack, and Mary Catherine turned away with a shudder and ran to Michaella.

Michaella was busily reloading her rifle, and urged Mary Catherine to help. Her fingers were shaking, and she looked up long enough to ask tersely, "Are you all right?"

Mary Catherine nodded, her face pale in the dim light. "Yes. Just bruised and a little shaken, but unharmed."

"Good. I was afraid to shoot for fear of hitting you."

"I know."

The sisters took refuge behind a huge wagon, watching as the commotion began to die down. Orange bursts of rifle fire split the night, and there was the sharp, acrid smell of gunpowder in the air. The thunder of hooves and running feet seemed louder than any storm, and they huddled beneath the heavy wagon bed and waited. Michaella kept an arm around her sister's trembling shoulders, murmuring sounds to keep her calm, wishing she felt calm herself. Her hands were quivering, and her heart was a stone weight in the middle of her chest, her stomach tight and her throat almost closed. What was there about danger that did such dreadful things to one's internal organs? It was as if they all rebelled at once, refusing to function normally.

It wasn't until Jean Patrick and Sorrel found them beneath the wagon that Michaella's body began to return to normal. She managed a shaky smile and reached up silently to lay a hand along Jean Patrick's cheek when he pulled her to him.

"What happened?" he asked gently.

"Michaella saved my life!" Mary Catherine blurted, adding in a tone of awe, "And so did that wretched gray mule!"

"Clarence? What'd he do?" Sorrel asked in surprise.

Sagging weakly against Jean Patrick, Michaella began to laugh. Between gasps, she said, "Clarence . . . stomped a man. I think he thought he had an . . . an umbrella in his hands! But it was . . . a war lance, and Mary Catherine . . ."

"Got away," Mary Catherine finished with a reproachful glance at her sister. "And I think Clarence saved my life on purpose. I believe he knows how wretched he's been and is trying to atone for his stubbornness."

"There is that possibility," Jean Patrick said with a straight face.

Rubbing his bearded jaw, Sorrel observed, "Well, if it hadn't been for that gray mule, we'd likely have lost a lot of stock. Those Pawnees were serious."

"It wasn't just Pawnees," Michaella said quickly. "I heard French accents."

Jean Patrick nodded. "French-Canadian trappers. The ones we met yesterday. They needed our horses. Theirs look worn out."

Stomping her foot, Mary Catherine put in testily, "Well, they shouldn't have been so hard on them. Imagine! Trying to steal our horses because they've been too rough on their own. And look what it cost them! Why, Michaella shot one man who was . . ."

Turning Michaella to face him, Jean Patrick stared down into her face. "Did you?"

She nodded. Reaction had begun to set in, and her entire body was quivering. "Yes. I had to. He was . . . coming at me, and Mary Catherine was in trouble, and . . ."

"You don't need to explain, love. You did the right thing." He folded her into his embrace again. "I just hope you remember that in the days ahead."

She stiffened. "Why?"

Answering slowly, Jean Patrick confirmed her fears. "I didn't want to bring this up until I was certain, but those men needed fresh mounts in order to ride fast. They're doing their best to get back to their village before they're overtaken by the Sioux war party."

"Sioux war party?" Michaella echoed weakly, feeling all the blood drain from her head and congeal in the pit of her stomach.

Jean Patrick's arms tightened briefly around her slender body. "We're on the edge of Sioux country, sweetheart, and they aren't noted for their hospitality."

Chapter Fourteen

✦✦✦✦✦

KETCHMAN WISHED THE journey would end. He reckoned that the gold lay somewhere to the north, and perhaps if they just headed out from where they were, they would soon be near the Black Hills. His guides had also informed him that they were now in Sioux country, and traveling in small groups in hostile territory meant certain death.

As the days passed, the land grew more barren and the hardships of travel intensified. Ketchman suffered terribly, longing for the cool green hills of England. He wondered how the emigrants in their slow-moving wagons were able to manage without suffocating from the stifling heat. It was bad enough with just the six of them bedding down at night, eating very little and finding whatever grass they could for their horses, but the emigrants' needs must be even more pressing.

But with almost eighty wagons in the emigrant party, Ketchman thought it unlikely they could keep traveling against the odds now facing them. Each day they lost more oxen, and lately some mules as well. Ketchman couldn't understand why the emigrants continued to press on.

The days dragged slowly. Ketchman watched the wagons churn through the quicksand of the Platte. Oxen were double yoked and mules teamed in sixes and eights to haul the wagons through. It took nearly three days to accomplish, because the riverbed was soft and wagons became mired easily. More cargo was dumped, and Ketchman laughed with the company men as they watched people mourning the loss of their cherished dressers, dishes, beds, and farm tools.

"Stupid fools," Crenshaw muttered to no one in particular as he shifted atop his horse and watched the emigrants. "I wouldn't have carried along all that junk they got in them wagons."

A few days past the North Platte crossing, conditions eased for both the wagon train and for Ketchman's crew. They reached Ash Hollow, a pleasant area filled with ash trees, waving stands of lush grass, and a gurgling stream. To reach Ash Hollow, however, the wagons had to navigate the most rigorous slope yet. Coming down into it was Windlass Hill, a descent so steep that no one in the train could speak for some time. The wagon wheels had to be locked by chains, with all the ablebodied men hauling back on ropes to keep them from crashing down the almost perpendicular slope. The glimpse of paradise, of the promised rest and haven lying within view, was the only thing that kept them going.

Ketchman watched the emigrants' resurgence with apathy. He needed rest as badly as they did, but he also felt a pressing need to push on. It was galling that the emigrants would have a day of rest when he must be ever on his guard.

Even as exhausted as he was, Ketchman was impatient with the delay because he knew gold was waiting at the end of his journey. The longer they dallied, the harder it was going to be to find Henry Chattilion and the riches of a lifetime.

And when the emigrants finally, reluctantly, left Ash Hollow behind—having loaded up with extra axles cut from tree limbs in case of wagon breakage farther on—Nolan Ketchman pronounced himself satisfied at last. He kept the wagon train barely in sight, lagging back and riding past their abandoned furniture and heirlooms without a glance, anxious to put an end to his wearisome journey.

This satisfaction quickly faded the second morning out. The emigrants had risen before first light again, and by dawn had begun to move on with a creaking of wagon wheels and the muffled clatter of hooves against the hard-baked earth. Ketchman and the company men could barely hear them as they loaded their horses. The sun was just peeking over a distant ridge when Bisler happened to glance up and spy a lone rider topping the ridge and riding toward them at full speed. Ketchman and the others quickly grabbed their rifles and swung them to the ready.

"Injun!" Crenshaw yelled, swinging up his rifle and firing in almost the same motion.

The ball hit the approaching Indian and he jerked, but managed to stay mounted, swerving out of range with an effort. Bisler and LaRange yelled simultaneously at Crenshaw to put down his rifle and stop shooting. Bisler ran forward and yanked away the rifle, while Crenshaw stared at him in amazement.

"What the hell did you shoot for?" Bisler was yelling. "Now if there's more of 'em, they'll be after our hair, you fool!"

Crenshaw shrugged. Turning away in disgust, Bisler shouted an order for everyone to mount. If there were more Indians nearby, they might end up having to take refuge with the wagon train.

•

"Oh, no, we're not!" Ketchman paused to snap. "I've no intention of risking all I've worked for by . . ."

"You won't have a choice," Bisler shot back. "An' if you don't want to, you can always stay here. Hey!" he ended in a shout, dropping his reins and starting off at a sprint.

When Ketchman turned to see the cause of his action, he saw LaRange atop Crenshaw, pounding into his face with a fist and screaming imprecations. "There'll be more o' them Injuns, you damn crazy fool! We'll all be killed because you're itchin' to pull your trigger, damn you!"

Bisler managed to pull LaRange off the fallen man, giving him a shove toward his horse and telling him to mount and ride. It might have ended that way had Ketchman not looked up then to see a thin line of mounted riders silhouetted against the horizon. Stiffening, he called out a warning to the others and vaulted into his saddle with surprising speed and agility. Bisler, Sorley, and Itch did the same, while LaRange was a bit slower in following. The battered, dazed Crenshaw was left to his own devices as the others raced away. The line of Indians gave a concerted whoop and started down the slope in a rush.

Jean Patrick looked up from getting the wagons into a tight circle—a circle within a circle for extra protection against attack—and saw the men riding hell-for-leather toward the wagons. Far ahead of them was a lone rider, listing to one side as if wounded, bent over his horse's neck as he rode straight toward them.

"Arikara," Sorrel announced, squinting at the

Indian. "Must've been shot by them stragglers 'as been followin' us for a while. I heard the shot. Damn fools. So did the Sioux."

Rushing out from behind a barrier of overturned furniture and barrels, Michaella paused at Jean Patrick's elbow. "Shouldn't we help him?" she asked.

"What fer?" Sorrel wanted to know. "He's Arikara! A Ree! They're murderin' bastards, and if'n he don't die soon I may help him on his way to the happy hunting grounds!"

"No," Jean Patrick said, putting out a hand. "Leave him be, Sorrel." The Indian had ridden close now, and was sliding from his horse and hobbling toward the wagon, waving his good arm to indicate friendly intentions.

"Are you crazy?" Sorrel spat. "He'll kill us all in our sleep! I kin remember my first trip into th' mountains under General Ashley. We were goin' up the Missouri on a keelboat, and those murderin' Arikaras kilt twenty-three of us a'fore it was over with!"

"That was a long time ago," Jean Patrick said. He shook his dark head and went out to help the Arikara into the camp. Blood dripped from the wounded Indian's arm, and he was weak and stumbling. Jean Patrick handed him over to Meg and Michaella and turned back to watch impassively as five other riders approached at a dead run.

He recognized Ketchman in the lead, and a grim smile pressed at the corners of his mouth. He'd been expecting him sooner or later, but it was pure luck that brought Ketchman in under these circumstances. Things had a way of circling back on a man, as he was certain Ketchman was discovering for himself now.

"Hold your fire!" Jean Patrick shouted, raising one arm in the air. Ketchman and his men rode in and reined to a halt just outside the circled wagons.

"Give us leave to come in!" Ketchman shouted. "Sioux!"

Looking beyond Ketchman, Jean Patrick had seen the Sioux form a line and ride down. The warriors were painted in bright red, yellow, and black, and they carried guns or bows, as well as lances and shields. Most were clad only in breechcloths. They were grouping again, and Jean Patrick didn't need a map to know where they were headed next.

"Kind of brassy of you to be riding in here, isn't it?" Jean Patrick drawled, looking at Ketchman from beneath the brim of his hat. "I mean, you've been following us for a while without wanting to talk. Why get friendly now?"

"Hurry, man! Pull down those barriers and let us in!" was the frantic reply. "Would you have us killed?"

"That's a pleasant possibility. You should've thought about that before you went sneaking along behind us. Now that there's trouble, you come skulking in here like you belong. Well, you don't."

"Please!" Ketchman babbled. "We need protection! We were just riding behind, not meaning any harm . . . for God's sake, man! Let us in!"

Coming up behind Jean Patrick, Michaella stared at Nolan Ketchman with distaste and contempt. His face was pale and he was sweating. His beard had grown long and was unkempt and tangled. He'd lost even more weight, so that instead of looking like a scarecrow, he now looked cadaverous. His top hat was absent and so was the cane, and Michaella felt a surge of animosity toward the man.

"Don't trust him," she spoke up, and Ketchman's bulging gaze shifted to her.

"So, it's Mrs. Wright's little niece!" he said with a brief return of his old spite. "And you certainly don't look so uppity now!"

"Neither do you," Michaella remarked, and turned away. Her barb had struck home, for Ketchman swallowed any hasty retort he might have made, flushing a bright shade of scarlet.

"I don't like your being here a bit," Jean Patrick said into the sudden silence. "If your intentions had been honorable, you would have joined our party from the outset. I find it hard to believe you didn't mean us any harm."

"Then you'll leave us out here to be murdered within ten feet of you?" Ketchman asked with a quiver in his voice.

"I haven't decided yet." Jean Patrick's steady gaze was fixed on the thin man who looked much older than he had a month before. A glance beyond the men showed him that the Sioux had already butchered the man left behind, and were now regrouping to do the same to the rest.

Several options flicked through his mind. He could, as the leader, challenge a single warrior in hand-to-hand combat and possibly win and thereby save the entire wagon train. But that was risky. More than likely, the Sioux just wanted to display their prowess in battle and return to their village in glory. That was the Sioux way. Catching coup—or getting within reach to touch a live enemy—was considered much more courageous than merely killing a man. The Sioux respected bravery.

Straightening, Jean Patrick signaled to Sorrel to open the barrier and allow Ketchman and his men inside. Then he asked for his horse.

"Are you loco?" Sorrel demanded. "You ain't gonna do what I think you're gonna do!"

"Just get my horse, Sorrel."

"But if you think they're gonna be impressed by one single idiot ridin' out to . . ."

"Get my horse, Sorrel!"

"But . . ."

"My horse! Unless you're anxious to ride out there and parley with them?"

"I'll get your horse," Sorrel capitulated, adding in a low mutter, "but I still think you're the craziest man who ever got hisself kilt!"

"Jean Patrick!" Michaella said, starting forward and putting a hand on his arm. "You . . . you aren't . . ."

"Don't worry, love. It's not my day to die."

He smiled down at her, and her heart felt as if it were breaking. She blinked back the hot sting of tears pressing against her eyelids, and managed a smile for him. If worse came to worse, she wanted his last glimpse of her not to be blurred with her tears.

"I love you, Jean Patrick."

He cupped her chin in his palm and bent to give her a fleeting kiss. "And I love you, sweetheart," he finally said, then was gone.

Michaella swayed, and Mary Catherine caught her. "Just say a prayer," her sister murmured.

Jean Patrick rode out with his spine stiff and straight, walking his horse slowly toward the grouped Sioux. When he was more than halfway there, he reined his bay to a halt and waited. The Sioux watched as they discussed their next action, then finally sent out a cortege of six warriors to meet him.

Michaella moaned, and Mary Catherine's hand tightened around her arm. "Pray!" she said firmly, and Michaella gave her a slight smile as she formed a silent, heartfelt plea in her mind.

Straining, Michaella watched as the Sioux and Jean Patrick conversed in a mixture of sign language, English, and the guttural patois that passed for Jean Patrick's command of the Sioux tongue. Then, incredibly, the Sioux were laughing, pointing toward the wagon train and making signs so swift Michaella could not read them. It was only when Jean Patrick wheeled his bay and rode back to the train at a leisurely lope while the Sioux rode in the other direction that she could relax.

Her muscles collapsed, and Michaella's rebellious knees deposited her in a heap on the ground. She was quivering with relief, and could not imagine why Jean Patrick looked so calm as he dismounted and came to her.

"What did they say?" she demanded, piqued at his easy grin and offhand attitude. "By all rights you should have been killed doing something that foolish!"

"Is that what you wanted?" he teased, then gathered her in his arms as the waiting tears rolled slowly down her cheeks. "Aw, love, I didn't mean to scare you. We just shared a few jokes, and I explained to them that we meant no harm. Seems that the warrior leading them is an old friend of an Oglala Sioux I used to hunt with sometimes. We shared a few memories, and . . ."

"And I sat back here terrified that there would be nothing left of you but your scalp!" Michaella blurted with a tearful sniff.

"No, no. You've got it confused, love. That's the only thing they *take*, not leave."

"Whatever. You would have been separated from your hair, and that wouldn't be good."

"No," he agreed with a grin, "it wouldn't." Ruffling her already mussed tresses, he stood up with her and turned to Ketchman.

Nolan Ketchman lifted a brow, bracing himself to be invited to leave the safety of the wagon train. He was genuinely astonished to hear Jean Patrick say tersely that they could stay with the train as far as Fort Laramie. "But no farther—understood?" he ended, and Ketchman nodded with great satisfaction. Matters were going much better than he had hoped.

Chapter Fifteen

✦✦✦✦✦

Leaning against the wheel of Meg's wagon, Meg oversaw Michaella doctor the Arikara warrior's arm. The wound was not severe, but he had lost a lot of blood. The warrior was grateful, and she felt his eyes on her as she worked. Though she thought she should be more wary, she was intrigued instead.

This Arikara was garbed only in a thin breechcloth wrapped around his middle. Moccasins covered his feet and ankles, and all the rest of him was bare. He had a lean, hard body rippling with muscle. When he stood, he rose to a height almost as tall as Jean Patrick, who stood a little over six feet. The warrior seemed to be younger than Jean Patrick, maybe in his late teens. His hair was long, thick, and straight and the color of jet, trailing down past his shoulders in heavy strands.

Fastened atop his coarse hair with lengths of painted rawhide was a cap of sorts, a gray-and-black-spotted fur with the ears still intact. Michaella thought immediately of the wolves that had haunted the fringe of the buffalo herd. Jammed into the skin of the cap were two large feathers trimmed with horsehair. He was a strange-looking sight indeed, she thought as she finished tying off the strip of clean linen that bound his arm.

"There," she said, rising and looking down at the young warrior. "I'm finished. Perhaps Mary Catherine won't mind bringing you a bowl of rabbit stew now."

"Oh, no," Mary Catherine assured him with a dazzling smile. She had been gazing raptly at the Arikara warrior the entire time Michaella had been bandaging his arm. "I won't mind at all."

Michaella slanted her a quizzical glance, but said nothing as she moved a few feet away and began cleaning up the pan and rags she had used. Meg had given her a poultice made of some kind of plant to smear on the wound, and it was sticky and gummy, still clinging to her fingers. She knelt beside a wooden wash barrel, idly listening to the conversation between her younger sister and the Indian.

Staring at him in fascination, Mary Catherine handed him a brimming bowl of stew and smiled shyly. He took it carefully, balancing it with his one good arm and smiling back at her.

"What is your name?" Mary Catherine asked after a moment, and he swallowed his food before answering.

"I am called Spotted Wolf," he replied in reasonably good English. "And you are Mary Catherine."

"Yes," she acknowledged, pleased that he had noticed and remembered her name. "Where did you learn to speak such good English?"

"I learned the words as a child," he replied with a smile. "Many different fur traders, and a Black Robe. . . ."

"A priest?" she guessed, and he nodded.

"*Ai*. Yes. They spend much time in our village. I learn other tongues, too. *Français. Italiano, Deutsch*. . . ."

"My heavens!" Mary Catherine exclaimed. "I don't know any of those! Oh, perhaps a tiny bit of

French, but I never learned much. So where is your home, Spotted Wolf?"

He gestured toward the mountains with his bandaged arm. "On the river you know as the Missouri."

Her eyes widened. "Aren't you a long way from home?"

"*Ai.* But I had to seek my vision. I sought it in the Black Hills and was on my way back to my people when the Sioux war party saw me. I ran, and now . . . I am here."

"I'm glad," Mary Catherine said softly and, blushing at her forward remark, stared down at the ground.

Michaella looked up, her brows knitting in a frown, and met Meg's steady gaze. Nothing was said, but each understood the other's unspoken message: Mary Catherine was not to be left alone with this handsome young Indian brave!

"Tell me," Mary Catherine said after a moment, "what do those feathers and paint you're wearing mean?"

The top half of Spotted Wolf's face and his entire forehead were painted red. Three lines of black streaked down from his chin and over his throat, coming together in a point on his chest. Surrounded by all the paint was a pair of dark eyes that had been very hard when he'd first ridden into camp, but now they were soft and filled with light.

"To a warrior," he answered, "the feathers and the paint have many meanings. With the feathers we can be like the great eagles who soar above the clouds—we can fly over our enemies. The paint must be the proper color and be put on carefully. If it is done incorrectly, it will endanger the warrior's prowess in battle. Do you understand?"

"And are you ready for battle?"

Spotted Wolf shook his head. "No. I was painted to seek my vision."

"And did you find your vision?"

A slow smile curved the young man's mouth. "I think I have now," he said softly.

Startled, Mary Catherine could only gaze at him in speechless astonishment, while Michaella and Meg exchanged glances of alarm. It was no surprise to hear the young man ask if she was promised to another.

"I would pay many ponies for you," he added, and Mary Catherine shrugged helplessly.

Deciding to intervene before the scene went any farther, Meg and Michaella both arrived at the same time. As if on cue, Jean Patrick also approached, and he had some questions for Spotted Wolf.

Hunkering down on his heels beside the young warrior, Jean Patrick paid no attention to the tight-lipped gaze of Mary Catherine's sister as he asked, "How many Sioux are there? Are there more Brule in the direction we are headed? More Oglala? Where are your people?"

While Spotted Wolf attempted to answer, Michaella drew Mary Catherine aside. "Come and help us wash the dishes," she said.

"Dishes? But they're already done, and I wanted to talk to Spotted Wolf some more," Mary Catherine protested.

Biting her tongue to keep from saying something sharp, Michaella managed to say pleasantly, "But

Spotted Wolf is occupied right now, Mary Catherine, and we really need your help." There was no point in making a scene, especially as her sister had a mind of her own and might decide to devote even more attention to the Indian if there was firm opposition to her choice. It was quite possible, and Michaella had no intention of forcing her sister into such a decision if it could be helped.

"Well . . . all right. But when we're through, I want to talk to him some more. He's very interesting, Michaella!"

"Yes, I should think he would be. I've been told that the Indian way of life is very different from ours. . . ."

Jean Patrick was asking Spotted Wolf about the Sioux and Cheyenne tribes in the west, and the young man was shaking his head.

"The Sioux and the Cheyenne fight each other, but now are angry with the white man for coming into their hunting grounds. The white man—they say," he added craftily, "uses all the wood, grass, and game without giving any back to the Earth Mother. One cannot take too much and still have plenty, and they say the white man does this."

"I agree," Jean Patrick said simply, and Spotted Wolf stared at him for a moment.

"It is so," he said finally. "Now the Sioux and the Cheyenne think to band together against the destruction."

"Nothing can stop the flow of wagons westward."

"The Sioux believe differently. Soon there will be much trouble along this trail! There will be war against the wagons. It will happen much sooner than anyone thinks."

Narrowing his eyes, Jean Patrick mulled over the warrior's warning. He'd known for some time that there would be trouble one day. Anyone with any sense could see that, as the white man moved westward and decimated the Indian's hunting territory, there would be reprisals.

With the many oxen, mules, and horses coming through each summer, the Indian horses' grazing land was being lost. The buffalo were becoming more wary as well, so that it was harder to hunt them. Besides, most whites didn't know the custom of giving presents when crossing unfamiliar territories. It seemed that instead of placating the Indian with gifts, they felt they owned the land themselves.

Then Spotted Wolf spoke briefly of returning to his people along the Missouri River. Jean Patrick told him that it would be dangerous for him to try to go back through Sioux country alone, especially with an unhealed wound.

"I know that it will be dangerous. If it was not for you, I would not be alive to make the journey."

"Then stay with us awhile until you mend," Jean Patrick advised. "There's no reason for your quick return, is there?"

"No. When a warrior from my village goes out to seek his vision, it sometimes takes many moons."

"Then you'll stay?"

Reflecting for a moment, Spotted Wolf finally nodded. "*Ai.* My people expect me to come back with honor. My arm must heal before I can do that."

"Good." Jean Patrick rose, and Spotted Wolf rose also. They stood eye to eye, measuring each other, and then Jean Patrick smiled. "You can help us, my friend."

"That I will do. I will help you guard the men who shot me," he answered. "They are not good—they are evil and will make trouble."

"I could use some help watching them," Jean Patrick agreed. "Just keep an eye on them and tell me if they try something. Don't attempt to handle them yourself."

"I will not do anything on my own," Spotted Wolf promised.

When Jean Patrick stepped away, he found Michaella waiting for him, her expression anxious. "Is everything all right?" she asked.

He pulled her into his arms. "Yes, love. Everything will be fine."

"I think Mary Catherine is quite taken with our new friend," she ventured rather uneasily.

"That bothers you?"

"Some," she admitted. "Do you trust him?"

"I never make the mistake of trusting *any*body," he responded, then paused to look down at her. "Almost anybody," he amended.

Smiling, she teased, "Thanks for your faith in me!"

"Well, you are kind of special," he said softly.

"Jean Patrick, what will you tell everyone in camp about him? They may feel rather uneasy at having a painted warrior in our camp."

"I'll tell them the truth," he said with a shrug. "It usually works."

But the truth didn't work as well this time. When Jean Patrick informed the governing council that Spotted Wolf was going to stay with the wagon train, there was immediate protest.

"The hell he is!" one man said loudly, and was joined in his sentiment by two others.

"It's invitin' trouble to have an Indian a'sneakin' around in our camp," another said.

"He stays," Jean Patrick said flatly, his deliberate stance daring them to argue further. "I personally vouch for him."

"And that's supposed to make a difference?" one man sneered. "You look half Injun yerself! How do we know you ain't in cahoots with this'n, and intend to rob and murder us in our sleep at night?"

"You don't," was the laconic reply, and there was nothing else said for a moment.

"Then you ain't denyin' it?" the man demanded.

"Don't be stupid. I've had plenty of chances to get rid of all of you before now. Why would I wait for one single Indian when I just got rid of a whole war party?"

Silence again, then a grudging agreement. "But we don't like it," the man added sourly, "not one damned bit!"

Ketchman felt naked without his cane. He found himself reaching for it constantly and finding nothing there to grab. He noted with annoyance that

LaRange and Bisler thought his distress very amusing. Those two delighted in doing whatever they could to cross him.

But now Ketchman knew he had to concentrate on the matters at hand. Here they were, surrounded by a bunch of emigrants who did not want them along and made no secret of it. Jean Patrick had come back to tell Ketchman that he was letting them stay with the wagon train against his better judgment.

Ketchman had told his men about the remark, not wanting LaRange to accost another emigrant woman. If that happened, they would quickly find themselves booted out among the Sioux.

As the days went by, Ketchman grew ever more certain that LaRange was spoiling for a fight with just about anybody. LaRange continued to watch the big man, Sorrel, waiting for an opportunity for vengeance. LaRange obviously had not forgotten that night in Westport when Sorrel had taken his money in the hand game. Ketchman remained on edge, afraid LaRange would once more get them all in trouble.

Late one evening Ketchman saw LaRange approach Sorrel. It was obvious that LaRange wanted to test him in the hand game, but Sorrel kept shaking his head no. LaRange eventually backed away with his fists clenched and fire in his eyes. Ketchman was certain that Jean Patrick had told Sorrel not to gamble with LaRange during the trek.

Ketchman himself was growing angry with his so-called companions. It seemed as if all they wanted to do was rob and kill. It wasn't within their mental capacity to understand that they could have all the wealth they desired if they would just keep themselves out of trouble until Michaella and her sister led them to the gold.

His problem needed to be solved quickly. To help him decide what to do, Ketchman chose Sorley. Since Sorley seemed to have a better set of brains than the others—a perception of him based solely on the man's affinity for reading penny novellas—Ketchman thought he must be wondering about LaRange's motives, too.

It was late one evening when Ketchman finally caught Sorley alone. He was by himself, huddled close to the light of a lantern and reading one of the tattered pages of his thin novella. Immersed in his reading, Sorley did not notice Ketchman's arrival at first.

Ketchman cleared his throat. "I hope I'm not disturbing you."

Glancing up from his reading, Sorley frowned. "As a matter of fact, you are. But you look troubled. Sit down."

Taking a seat on an overturned wooden crate close to the fire, Ketchman folded his hands in front of him. "I shall come right to the point. I believe that you are the only one besides myself in our party who has a lick of sense. I also believe that if we are to succeed in our mission, you and I must unite so that we can keep the others from causing trouble."

Sorley put down his novella and stared at Ketchman. His expression was wary, much too wary for a man of his young years. Etched deep within his features was an innate distrust of his fellow man.

"I take it you're worried LaRange is gonna try

and kill someone before too long, is that it?" he asked finally.

"That's part of it."

Grunting, Sorley shifted on his seat of stacked crates. "You're worried that he's going to kill you—right?"

"Admittedly he wants to, but I believe even inside that thick skull lurks the knowledge that it would be too bad for him if he did. I'm necessary."

Another grunt, then Sorley said, "LaRange doesn't know anything. How long have you wondered about the others on this mission?"

"Ever since we left Westport," was the prompt reply.

"Then why'd you wait so long to talk to me?"

"Well, I suppose I wasn't certain you would understand or be sympathetic."

"What changed?"

"Nothing." Pausing, Ketchman reflected, then added, "I just have this feeling about you, that's all. Call it instinct if you like, or a sixth sense, but often I know a man's true character by just a few signs. I sense that you don't really want to be here. Is that why you joined us at the last minute?"

There was a long pause during which Sorley studied the man next to him intently. "I wasn't supposed to come," he said in a low voice, so low Ketchman had to lean closer to hear. "But I told them I wanted to come along. See, a few years ago LaRange killed my oldest brother in a fight. I decided that sooner or later I'd find him and kill him. This seemed like a good opportunity."

"And you aren't worried about telling me this?"

Sorley shook his head and grinned. "Naw. LaRange wants to kill you. Why should you interfere?"

A slow grin squared his thin lips as Ketchman nodded and said, "You're right. But aren't you afraid that LaRange will find out your identity?"

"Why should I be? He didn't even know my brother when he killed him," was the bitter answer.

"You've been planning this for a long time," Ketchman observed shrewdly, and Sorley shrugged.

"Ever since my brother was murdered. But you came out here to get rich."

"Yes. I intend to live the rest of my life in comfort. No—luxury!"

Laughing, Sorley shook his head again. "What makes you so certain there is any gold?"

Ketchman leaned forward, his fingers forming a bony steeple. He rested his chin on the point of his fingers and gazed into the fire. *"I just know!"* he whispered so fiercely that Sorley was impressed.

"It may interest you to know that I have a map that shows the location of the gold."

Stunned, Ketchman slowly straightened, his wide-eyed gaze leveling on Sorley's face. "You what?"

"I have a map. It was my brother's—the one who was killed. He had it for years."

"A map? Uh, where . . . how . . . who?"

Grinning, Sorley said, "Yeah, it's just what you're thinking, Mr. Ketchman! And I have it right here." He tapped his shirt pocket with one finger.

"Do you mind?" Reaching out, Ketchman's hands were shaking so badly he could hardly take the map from Sorley.

"My brother, he got it from an old trapper. Chattilion, I think they called him. That name familiar to you?"

Ketchman glanced up. "You must know that it is."

"Yes, I do. All this is so odd, what with LaRange here and me knowing where you're headed and why, and me having the missing piece. Reckon that's worth a share of the gold—or maybe all of it."

Resisting stuffing the map into his own pocket and fleeing with it, Ketchman forced his voice to remain calm as he said, "Why be greedy? After all, you would not be able to get there by yourself. Not in this territory, with the Sioux on the warpath and swarming all around us. And there is the small detail of the missing half of the map, of course."

"Of course. And I wouldn't suppose you have that half?"

"Actually, no. But I know where it is." Leaning forward and giving Sorley back his map, Ketchman began to feel a bit better. Sorley still needed him. One hand could wash the other in this case, he told himself.

"So where do we go from here?" Sorley wanted to know.

"We wait. And we watch. We take the protection now being offered, and at the right time we split from the others." Ketchman hesitated, then added, "And we don't draw attention to ourselves.

Stay away from LaRange, and I will try to keep him away from me."

"Sounds easy."

"It will be, for a while."

"Sure you got your part of the map?" Sorley asked in sudden suspicion.

"Don't worry. I can lay my hands on it whenever I wish," Ketchman replied confidently. And he could. Those two foolish sisters would never stand against him for long. Except for the older one. Ah, she was a canny one at times, always staring down her nose at him. But she'd fallen in love now. He'd seen her looking at the guide with those sheep's eyes, and women in love had a habit of being careless about anything else, especially *young* women in love. Yes, it would all work out nicely.

Chapter Sixteen

MICHAELLA WATCHED with increasing anxiety as Mary Catherine spent more and more time with Spotted Wolf while his arm healed. The two obviously enjoyed being together and grew closer as the days passed. At first he told her little about his past, but finally he began to confide in Mary Catherine.

Spotted Wolf was destined to become a great chief among his people. It had been prophesied by the elders and medicine men. In order to become a leader, he was now on the path to obtaining power and wisdom. He had been traveling to a sacred place in the Black Hills called Bear Butte, where the medicine was powerful and life could change for those blessed by the sacred presence on the summit.

Mary Catherine knew nothing at all about Indian customs and the way a warrior found his individual power. But she realized quickly that Spotted Wolf did something to her—touched some inner core in a way that she could not deny. While all the other women seemed deathly afraid of him, Mary Catherine found him even easier to be with than old Sorrel.

But Spotted Wolf seemed as calm as if he were among his own family. As his arm continued to heal, he accompanied her whenever he wasn't helping Jean Patrick or Sorrel. Mary Catherine confided in Michaella that she cherished that time more each day. And Michaella grew even more concerned to learn that her sister was learning to speak Arikara and to use sign language. Mary Catherine, however, was elated.

"There's so much I want to learn!" she enthused to her less than enthusiastic sister. "Spotted Wolf has taught me about his people and how they revere the land and all the elements. And he seems so happy to know that I am truly interested and want to learn."

"Just remember who you are and why we're here," Michaella warned gently.

Mary Catherine stiffened. "What do you mean by that?"

"Nothing. Only that you're both so different, and come from such different worlds, that . . ."

"And you and Jean Patrick don't?"

There was nothing Michaella could answer to that, and so she grew silent. It disturbed her to see her sister with the Arikara, not because of any ingrained prejudice, but because she foresaw heartache and problems ahead. It was hard enough to fall in love with a man of one's own class, but to choose a mate from such a different background could be disastrous if not dealt with properly.

To Mary Catherine herself, it often seemed that events were moving too quickly. She was falling in love with this warrior and didn't know how to stop it.

"I don't know if we should be spending so much time together," she told him late one afternoon as they sat on the sandy shores of the river and watched a bird swoop gracefully over the water.

"You like spending time with me," Spotted Wolf said. "And I know I like to be with you."

"Yes, but my sister said something— Oh, it's not that she dislikes you, for that isn't it. Michaella is not that way. But she is worried that our ways of life are so different. Maybe I should not allow myself to fall in love with you."

"And maybe you should," he said softly, turning her to face him.

It was this scene that Michaella stumbled upon, and she made the best of it, calling out gaily and approaching them as they quickly pulled apart.

"Just out for a stroll," she said, pausing to smile at Mary Catherine. "Spotted Wolf, I understand that you are a very adept musician."

"I do not know what you mean," he said with a puzzled frown.

"That you play a wind instrument. A flute?" She made a sign with her hands and he brightened, finally understanding her.

"Ah, that. *Ai,* I do. I shall show you later this evening. I do not have one now, but I will show you," he promised.

And as he had promised, Spotted Wolf came to their campfire that evening at dusk and proudly thrust forward a flute he had carved from a slender reed. The liquid notes trilled into the soft air, lingering like the sweet melody of a night bird, haunting and beautiful. Michaella grew quiet and relaxed as she listened, and she could tell Mary Catherine was quite impressed.

The entire camp heard the lilting music in the days that followed, for Spotted Wolf serenaded Mary Catherine night and day. Music played in a nighttime lullaby, and ushered in the morning with the first song of the day. It was played in the middle of the day, when they would pause to rest the animals, and played at odd times, whenever he felt moved to serenade his love.

Mary Catherine was enchanted with his devotion. She eagerly awaited the moments when she would hear the first soaring notes, and then seek him out along the river or wherever he waited for her.

And Michaella found it increasingly difficult to hold her tongue when Spotted Wolf presented Mary Catherine with two small figurines he had carved from a cottonwood tree. They were images of a man and a woman and were obviously love charms. When Mary Catherine stared at them uncertainly, the young Arikara gently took her hand and placed the figurines in her palm, closing her fingers around them.

With her heart in her throat, Michaella watched her younger sister stroll away with Spotted Wolf. There was nothing she could do, nothing she could say. One could not live another person's life for them, even when that person was beloved. And when night fell and Mary Catherine and Spotted Wolf returned from their walk, Michaella knew from the dreamy expression on her sister's face what had happened.

As the wagons moved ever westward, traveling conditions remained harsh. The wagon train passed through a huge prairie dog town, and Michaella was intrigued as the large rodents sat up on their hind legs, making little barking sounds that reminded her of small terriers. She marveled at how agile their small, round bodies were, and how they scampered from burrow to burrow.

"May I try to catch one?" Mary Catherine asked, and Jean Patrick laughed. "I wouldn't if I were you. They may not be too hostile, but there are some rattlesnakes that aren't known for being too friendly."

"Rattlesnakes?"

"And bull snakes. They hide in holes, too, and if you happen to stumble across one under a patch of sage or rock, well, you'd be dead before too long."

Mary Catherine shuddered. "How awful!"

"Do they live in the same holes as the prairie dogs?" Michaella asked curiously.

"No, not the snakes. Owls do, though."

"*Owls?*" Michaella stared at him incredulously.

"Small burrowing owls. Less than a foot long. They only hunt at night, so unless you're watching after dark it's unlikely that you'll see one."

"How can they exist with the prairie dogs? I mean, do they get along with one another?"

"Not too bad, I guess, though I've never bothered to watch that closely. Owls are lousy nest builders, see, and have to take what they can get." He grinned, and Michaella felt her heart lurch. "All in all, owls don't do so bad—kind of like humans who happen to fall into something good once in a while."

"And are you referring to yourself, by any chance?" she asked lightly, feeling the burn of his eyes scorching her face. Why was it that all he had to do was look at her and she'd melt? It didn't matter where they were or what they were doing. If Jean Patrick happened to pass by and give her one of his lopsided smiles—or even glance her way—she could feel her defenses crumbling. Desperately, Michaella sought for a way to avoid this soul-searing reaction to him. The time would come when he would be gone, she daily reminded herself. Then what would she do? It was highly unlikely that he would seek her out again, in spite of his declaration of love. He had told her of his feelings only once, and she couldn't bring herself to ask him about them again.

So when he looked at her curiously and spoke to

her in his warm, husky voice, she felt shivers course through her. But when he asked if she had minded taking him in as if he were an owl, she replied coolly, "No, of course not. Why should I? After all, women are known for their nesting abilities, right?"

Faintly puzzled by her suddenly distant tone and the cool withdrawal he sensed, Jean Patrick just looked at her. What had happened? Hadn't they just been bantering with one another? He shook his head, and the ebony wings of hair framing his face gleamed in the bright sunlight. Women. They were more complex and confusing than any animal or man he had ever run into in his life, he decided. Maybe that was why he'd never gotten close to one before. But there was something about Michaella, an indefinable quality that both lured him and frustrated him beyond belief. It wasn't just her slender beauty, or the feel of her warm, satin skin beneath him when they could steal away from the others. Though he often felt as if he could drown in her—lose himself in her body and warm embrace and never even try to come up for air—Jean Patrick also recognized that his feeling for her went much deeper. She'd touched some long-buried chord within him, had coaxed a response from him when he had only meant to dally a short time, and he didn't know yet if he should be grateful or angry. After all, he'd spent half a lifetime mistrusting other people, women in particular, and it was difficult to accept this new emotion.

Shrugging at her inexplicable change of mood, Jean Patrick turned to point out to Mary Catherine the reeds along the Platte. "Stay away from them unless you've got a rifle or pistol with you. Snakes. Lots of 'em. Be careful."

Shuddering again, Mary Catherine said, "Oh, I will!" Her keen senses had picked up on the tension between her sister and Jean Patrick, and since meeting Spotted Wolf, she now understood completely. She smiled sympathetically.

The wagons rocked on over the ever-changing land of sun and wind. Huge, wind-sculpted mounds of sand slowly altered to coarser, rocky ground that tore at the animals' hooves and made those walking moan softly. Rocks were pried from between the metal horseshoes and the tender frogs of the animals' hooves; pebbles were emptied from shoes covering bruised feet. The rolling, monotonous landscape melded into higher hills and wind-scoured ridges. Grass still grew in scarce, tufted clumps, and the oxen and mules strained at their traces as they labored to climb the steepening grade.

Jean Patrick rode beside Michaella, and he pointed out the blur of foothills in the distance. "Beyond those are the Rocky Mountains," he said. "And there is where the real test begins."

Filled with dismay, Michaella only nodded. There was nothing to say. The prospect loomed ahead like a grim specter, and she shuddered to think of the cost in human life and effort.

"What are those?" she asked a few minutes later, pointing out a clump of sharp-needled plants. "They look deadly."

"On the contrary, those plants are called Spanish bayonets, or soapweed. The roots are used for cleaning clothes and washing hair. If we gather some while we're here, they'll be useful in the coming months."

Months? Michaella wondered sadly, her thoughts returning, as always, to the future and what might lie ahead. Did she have *months* with Jean Patrick, or only a few weeks? Or perhaps . . . only a few days. Her heart ached, and she longed to tell him how she felt. If only she was certain of him, knew that he would return for her, then she could open her heart. But long experience had taught her that life was not always fair, and often a person's intentions—though well-meant—were not always lasting.

The wagons passed through a field strewn with brightly colored flowers; leggy stalks bearing blossoms of a delicate lavender, which Jean Patrick identified as blazing star, were interspersed with black-eyed Susans and occasional daisies. Curious pronghorns grazed in the chest-high field, lifting their heads to watch the wagons roll past, their huge, liquid eyes soft and wary. Prairie chickens scurried into hiding, and the noise of wheels and hooves even coaxed a burrowing owl into peering out from its den of rocks and sticks.

In spite of the beauty, the dry air was almost intolerable. Lips cracked, nostrils dried up, and the hooves of the animals split so badly they had to be treated with hot tar. And the wind was a constant presence, never ceasing, always blowing across the flat, treeless land in a moaning whistle that at times made Michaella want to scream. High bluffs rose on each side of the trail, sometimes deflecting the wind, but never halting it.

The wagons strained forward, climbing a hill Jean Patrick called the "ox killer." The slope seemed gentle enough at first, rising with a deceptive gradualness, but the wheezing of the oxen as the yokes bit into their necks and sand clutched at their hooves indicated how steep it actually was. It wasn't until they reached the crest and Michaella looked eastward that she realized their height. A herd of buffalo spread below like a thick brown carpet, and from where she sat on her mount, they looked like toys. She had not realized before how vast the herds could be, but now they stretched in an endless sea. Jean Patrick commented that it would be difficult to ride around them without causing a stampede.

"Stampede?"

"Yeah. Believe me, you don't want to see one of those. Imagine several thousand buffalo coming at you full speed. There wouldn't be enough left of you to bury. . . ."

"I understand your meaning," Michaella said hastily before he embellished his word picture.

He grinned. "All right. Pass the word along that no one is to fire a gun. Just go slowly and keep the dogs quiet or there'll be trouble!"

Pushing on without further problem, the emigrants encountered strange rock formations in towering red sandstone, one of which was shaped roughly like an old castle. Close by squatted a more square version of a castle, and a few miles farther on rose a tall, slender spire that brought an old chimney to mind as they gazed at it in awe. The red sandstone surrounding it rose gradually, and the chimney-shaped formation jutted proudly into the air as if aspiring to touch the sky. Green meadows spread in a thick carpet around it, and though they did not pause, it remained in everyone's memory for quite a while.

Scott's Bluff would remain etched in the emigrants' memories for quite a while, too. It rose so sharply on the south banks of the North Platte River that some were reminded of an old medieval fortress, with turreted domes and rock windows. Michaella's gaze strayed to it again and again, and when they camped in its shadow that evening she asked Jean Patrick if they could explore some of the lower regions.

"Climb that?" He stared at her as if she'd gone mad. "Sweetheart, that rock shoots eight hundred feet into the air! We'd need to be spiders to climb that high!"

"I didn't mean *climb* it like that," Michaella explained patiently. "I only meant perhaps walk around the fringes of it, and . . . look up," she finished lamely.

"Ahh! Look up." Cocking his head to one side, he gave her his lopsided grin again, tempting her to turn her back on him. "No, wait," he said when it looked as if she might actually walk away. "I was only teasing. I'll walk around with you. Besides—I have something to say to you."

Immediately apprehensive, Michaella opened her mouth to ask what it was, but he shook his head.

"No, no, sweetheart—on our walk. I'll meet you by Meg Magoffin's wagon in, say, a half hour?"

"And what clock do I use to tell the time?" she asked with a lifted brow.

"Use the sun. When it's right over"—he paused to squint up at the lowering sun—"that third peak from the left, it'll be a half hour."

Michaella watched him walk away. He never ceased to amaze her. And if she still had her watch, she would probably time him and find out he was correct to the minute!

That's what she told Meg while she waited, and the older woman listened with an amused smile on her broad face. "You two should get married," Meg said with a laugh. "Ah, and I've never seen two more suited to one another!"

"Because we disagree?" Michaella asked in some surprise.

"No, lovey. Because of the *way* you disagree." Meg gave her a wink as she expertly flipped a frying corn cake in the heavy black skillet over the fire. "There's a way to agree and a way to disagree. You'll know what I mean when you see it in someone else."

"Well . . . I suppose," Michaella said, though she didn't quite understand.

"No, you don't. But you will. Ah, and here's your handsome man now!"

Turning, Michaella saw Jean Patrick striding across the camp toward her, and as usual her heart did its peculiar flip-flop. He was so handsome, with his jet hair and azure eyes, his strong features and easy grin, and she could hardly keep from running to him. Instead, she forced herself to remain where she was, forced herself to make him come to her when she really wanted to run to him. There were no certainties in life, she reminded herself, and that included Jean Patrick Malloy.

"Ready, love?" he said when he reached her, gazing down at her with soft eyes.

She nodded. "Yes. I even have on my walking shoes."

He glanced down and laughed. Michaella wore a pair of moccasins on her feet, compliments of Spotted Wolf. The Arikara had made a pair for each of the sisters, and if she had not been so concerned about Mary Catherine's future, Michaella would have gladly admitted that the young warrior was really in love.

Taking Jean Patrick's arm, Michaella strolled through the camp with him. Close up, the bluff was even more impressive, and she craned her neck to gaze up at the rocky crags and spires.

"Rather overwhelming, isn't it?" Jean Patrick asked quietly, and she nodded.

"Yes. And it's so quiet here. I thought the wind would be even louder against this rock, but it's not."

"Michaella."

There was a note in his voice that she'd not heard before, and she turned to look at him with a steady gaze. His blue eyes were serious, his mouth in a straight line instead of curving into a smile.

"Yes?" she said softly, and waited.

"I've got something I want to say, and I think a place as majestic as this is the best setting," he said after a brief pause. "Have a chair?" A ghost of his normal smile flickered on his lips as he gestured to a stone seat etched by wind into the rock. She sat and folded her hands in her lap, looking up at him expectantly.

The air seemed to vibrate with tension, and there

was a dull weight in her chest. Perhaps this was the time he would tell her that he could not stay, that when they separated it would be forever. A chill danced up her spine. Maybe that was what he would try to say. But when he sat down beside her and took both her hands between his, she betrayed none of her fear.

"Michaella, normally I don't interfere in other people's lives, but since I've gotten close to you, and feel responsible in a way, I just want to . . . well, what I want to say is that . . . dammit!" He shook his head impatiently. "Look, let me just be blunt: I think your sister is in love with Spotted Wolf and that's bad. I'm sorry. I probably shouldn't have asked him to stay, but of all the possibilities that occurred to me, that wasn't one of them. I know you might be angry with me, and I know it won't do much good to say I'm sorry, but . . . hey! Are you crying?"

Michaella had buried her face in the cup of her palms, and her shoulders were shaking. Jean Patrick stared at her in numb misery. He hadn't meant to upset her so, but he'd only thought she should know. Tentatively reaching out a hand to comfort her, he was more than a little startled when she lifted her head.

"You're . . . *laughing!*"

She nodded. "Yes . . . yes, I am! Sorry. That was such a pretty apology, and I hate that you wasted it, but it is hard for me to believe that men can be so slow!"

"Slow?"

"Slow," she confirmed, laughing again. "I've been concerned about Mary Catherine since the first day, Jean Patrick! Did you just now notice their infatuation?"

"Well, it's not as if I haven't had other things on my mind," he defended himself. "And you certainly don't sound concerned!" he added crossly.

Wiping her eyes with the cuff of her sleeve, Michaella said, "Well, I am. And as for laughing, I thought you had some horrible secret to tell me! I'm just relieved!"

Jean Patrick bent down and scooped up a pebble, tossing it and listening to it patter and roll down the slope. "What kind of horrible secret?"

She waved a hand. "Oh—anything." She wasn't about to admit to her true thoughts.

Putting his hands on her shoulders, Jean Patrick pulled her to him, and his mouth descended on hers in a smothering swoop. His hands splayed across her back, moving down the column of her spine to her hips. He pulled her up with him, pressing her against him, chest to chest, hip to hip.

This was not the Jean Patrick she was accustomed to, the gentle, considerate lover. This Jean Patrick was on fire with a fierce, driving urgency. There was no time for protests or warnings about possible intruders stumbling across them or about the possibility that they could be seen from below. There was no time for anything but surrender.

Michaella felt herself carried along by his passion, lifted on the waves of desire and swept into the regions where only Jean Patrick could take her. Closing her eyes, she leaned back and yielded to it, let the raging fire in her veins heat her flesh and light up the dusk. There was nothing or no one but Jean Patrick.

Roughly, impatiently, they pushed their clothes aside to form a thin cushion against the rough stone pallet beneath them, and Jean Patrick took her against the sandstone. Her blouse was gone, her divided skirt pulled away, and she was left with only the dying rays of the sun to clothe her curves and hollows. The brisk evening air did nothing to chill her bare flesh. Michaella had the vague thought that steam should be rising from her heated skin. Was it possible to melt from the delicious flames of passion? she wondered hazily. If not, it should be. She felt as if she were melting, slowly dissolving into a shapeless mass in Jean Patrick's warm embrace. She could feel the heated length of him against her, pressing closer and closer, and she was opening to receive him with sweet release. The stones were sun-warm beneath them, and the air seemed to sizzle with passion as Jean Patrick's mouth seared a fiery trail from her lips to her throat to her breasts.

Moaning and arching upward, her back pressed against the rough slope of the rock, Michaella was hardly aware of the abrasive scratch against her tender skin. Jean Patrick filled her world, and he was the sky, the very air that she breathed.

And when release came, shuddering through them, she wept against his shoulder. Huge tears rolled down her cheeks and wet his skin.

"Did I hurt you?" he murmured against the sweat-damp curls of her hair. She shook her head, and his arms circled her slender body in a tighter embrace.

"I'm just happy," came her muffled reply against his skin. She could feel the thread of laughter when he said, "I'd hate to see you when you're sad then, love."

Pushing away, he kissed the tip of her nose, lovingly kissed away her tears, then reached down for her blouse. She took it from him and put it on, her fingers fumbling with the buttons until he helped her. In the end, Jean Patrick had to help her with all of her clothing. She was weak, drained from the storm of passion that had swept across them.

After they had walked back down the rocky slope and reached the fringe of the camp, Michaella paused. "I rather enjoyed our little talk," she said primly. "Perhaps we can chat again sometime." Jean Patrick gave a shout of laughter.

"You minx! Have you no shame?"

She stared up at him with glowing eyes. "Not where you're concerned."

Whatever Jean Patrick might have answered was disturbed by the sudden, noisy appearance of Sorrel at their side.

"There you are!" he boomed jovially. "I've been looking everywhere for you!"

"Why?" Jean Patrick asked. "Is there trouble?"

"No! Better than that! There is fun!" He put out a huge hand and grasped Michaella by her wrist. "Come along, missy, and dance with me. There are fiddles playing, and a flute, and even a violin or two. Come along and dance with an old man!"

Pulled along, Michaella laughed helplessly, hoping no one noticed her disheveled hair and rumpled clothes. There was no point in being too forward about her love for Jean Patrick. Not that it was a secret, but . . .

"Oh, there you are!" Mary Catherine cried out as Sorrel dragged his captured prize into the circle of dancers. "I have been looking everywhere for you!"

"I feel quite popular this evening," Michaella said with a shrug of laughter. Sorrel swung her energetically, and her skirt swung above her ankles as she tried to keep up with him. Everyone seemed to be dancing, men with their wives, daughters, or even other men, and women doing the same. It didn't matter about the choice of partner; the main idea was to enjoy oneself, and that everyone was doing as enthusiastically as possible.

The rigors of the day were forgotten as the music soared and the sky darkened. Campfires blazed brightly. Sleepy-eyed children rubbed their eyes with their fists and were finally tucked into waiting blankets. Dogs barked and fiddles scraped.

Spotted Wolf stood at the edge of the circle of onlookers with Mary Catherine. They had danced until she'd pleaded exhaustion, and now he leaned against the side of a wagon and watched with his arms folded across his bare chest.

He noticed that Ketchman and his men were scattered through the crowd and dancers. Up to this point they had done very little to disturb anyone, staying apart from the others and causing no trouble. But Spotted Wolf could sense that tonight would be different.

Something felt wrong to him as he gazed around the crowd for Ketchman and his men. He saw the man called Itch laughing in a ridiculous, boisterous manner off by himself, as no one would let him near them. Ketchman and Sorley were together, closely watching the proceedings.

The big man, Bisler, was also standing off by himself. Usually he was with LaRange. Spotted Wolf looked everywhere but couldn't find the Frenchman. Where was LaRange?

Spotted Wolf noticed movement in the shadows just behind the wagons. Leaning forward, he whispered in Mary Catherine's ear, "Stay right here and do not move. I must leave for a moment."

She turned in surprise to see him drift away from the dancing, slipping into the shadows and melding with them so that he could not be seen. He moved silently, on cat's feet, lightly and quickly. Mary Catherine frowned, wondering what he was doing.

As Spotted Wolf got just outside the circle, he saw LaRange position himself with a rifle across the top of a wagon. He knew LaRange was about to do someone harm. Recalling his promise to Jean Patrick, the Arikara hesitated. Jean Patrick was too far away, and if he did not stop LaRange now it would be too late.

Spotted Wolf made a swift decision. The rifle barrel had been lifted and was gleaming dully in the lanternlight. Leaping agilely, the young Indian reached LaRange just as the rifle fired. No one was hit, but the lead ball smacked into a sandstone rock with a shattering whine, ricocheting and echoing in the still night air.

Ordinarily, this would have been the end of it. But the ball crumbled the ridge of rock, which fell in a storm of sandstone onto the neighboring rock, which in turn fell onto the next ridge in a chain reaction that started the line of rocks tumbling like a house of cards.

Jean Patrick raced toward the wrestling men on the ground. LaRange had pulled a knife and was attempting to stab Spotted Wolf, while the young Arikara was doing his best to avoid the razor-sharp blade. His injury was still stiff and sore and was hampering his efforts so that Jean Patrick had to leap in and help him. As LaRange lifted his arm with the knife poised over Spotted Wolf's chest, Jean Patrick reached them and wrested it away. There was a brief struggle; then the two men managed to overpower the panting, swearing Frenchman.

"Let him go!" Jean Patrick shouted at Spotted Wolf as LaRange sagged to the ground in a daze. "It doesn't matter now! We'll take care of them later. Listen!"

Turning, the Arikara gave Jean Patrick a puzzled glance, then his eyes widened. With a dull roar like the sound of thunder, the earth began to vibrate. In that instant, Spotted Wolf understood.

Stampede. Both men had seen stampedes, seen the death and destruction one could cause. And this stampede was even more destructive than most, for the buffalo herd that was roaming the plains was now thundering across rock and grass with a force much more terrifying than that of domestic cattle.

As the men pulled away from him, LaRange took advantage to leap to his feet and stumble into the night, headed in the direction of the tethered horses.

"It doesn't matter," Jean Patrick repeated, and Spotted Wolf agreed. There were more important things to contend with now. "Get the people into the wagons while I tend to the stock," Jean Patrick shouted. "Sorrel is already rounding up what he can."

Nolan Ketchman, having watched the entire scene, was frozen with fear. He stood like a statue while people jostled past him, yet until Bisler gave him a hard shake he didn't move. Blinking as if just awakening from a dream, Ketchman looked around him. People were scattered in panic, and even in the dark he could see the dust rising into the air from the thousands of hooves. He turned back to look at Bisler, the words finally penetrating.

"Stampede, you fool!" Bisler yelled in disgust, then added that he wasn't waiting around to see what Jean Patrick or the buffalo would do. "I'm riding out of here!"

"But you can't go without me," Ketchman said automatically. "Stricker said . . ."

"Stricker, hell! If you want to ride with us, get on your horse or be left behind!"

These last words were thrown over Bisler's shoulder as he began to run, and a glance told Ketchman that the other company men were following suit. As they disappeared into the night, he began to run.

By now the buffalo and cattle had reached the outer fringe of wagons, and dust rose in thick, misty clouds. Michaella could smell it and turned blindly to grope for Mary Catherine in the sudden darkness. Lanterns had been doused in case of fire, and only the campfires still burned to throw grotesque patterns across the ground. A wagon went down in a splintering crash and screams filled the air as the herd plummeted into camp.

"Mary Catherine!" Michaella screamed, poised for flight and panic-stricken at the thought of not finding her sister. "Mary Catherine, where are you?"

There was a thin wail that rose above the chaos, and Michaella turned hopefully in that direction, starting to run forward, then pausing, calling for her again.

"Here," came a weak cry, and Michaella, narrowing her eyes in the dim, dusty light, dashed forward. She found her sister pinned beneath the wreckage of a stack of wooden crates, and bent to pull her loose. "No," Mary Catherine said. "My leg . . . it's caught on something."

The thunder of hooves lent speed to her efforts as Michaella worked frantically to free her sister. Where was Jean Patrick when she needed him? Or Spotted Wolf? But even as she was wondering that, she knew that Jean Patrick had a responsibility to more than just her sister and herself. He had an entire wagon train of people to keep safe, and he depended on her common sense to keep her from harm.

Finally freeing Mary Catherine from beneath the wreckage of the crates, Michaella put her shoulder beneath her sister's arm and helped her as quickly as possible to the safety of a wagon. The world seemed to be made of dry, choking dust, the roar of beating hooves, and the smell of musky hides while fear permeated everything. As the sisters huddled in a wagon, shaking with fear and relief, the tide of buffalo and cattle swept past only a few yards from where they were. Mary Catherine cringed and put her hands over her ears while she squeezed her eyes shut and crouched on the floor of the wagon. Michaella could offer no words of comfort when she herself wasn't at all certain they were safe.

It was only when Jean Patrick and Spotted Wolf found them that she dared to hope the worst was over. "Are . . . they gone?" she ventured, gazing up at Jean Patrick with wide, frightened eyes.

"Probably in Oregon by now," he assured her, reaching up to help her from the wagon. "Along with Ketchman and his men," he added as she got down and stood on shaky legs.

"They ran in the middle of a stampede?"

Jean Patrick nodded. "Fools. I should have shot them while I had the chance, and if the buffalo didn't get 'em, I just might do that after all."

Michaella turned to survey the ruined camp. A few fires still burned, and one wagon—which the owner had foolishly left with a lit lantern—was burning nicely. The family was doing their best to put it out with buckets of water from the river, but it looked hopeless. Dirt had been churned so badly that the campsite looked like a plowed field, and she shivered at the destructive power of the stampede.

"Did we lose all our cattle?" she asked Jean Patrick.

"Some. Most of those that ran will end up circling back. They can't survive on what those buffalo live on."

"I wonder why there was a stampede because of a rifle shot, when they don't even care when you shoot one of them and dress it only a few feet away!" Mary Catherine burst out petulantly. "The silly beasts! They deserve to be shot if they're that foolish."

"It wasn't the rifle shot, but the avalanche of rocks that spooked them," Spotted Wolf explained to her. He smiled as he pushed back the burnished hair from her eyes.

"Oh. What avalanche?"

"Didn't you hear? No, I suppose you didn't," he said when she stared at him blankly. "It doesn't matter. You are safe now, and that's what matters most."

"What about Ketchman and his men?" Michaella asked Jean Patrick in a low voice as Spotted Wolf soothed her sister. "And where is Sorrel?"

"Right here, missy!" came a voice from the shadows, and the big, grinning Frenchman stepped into the circle of light thrown by the still-burning campfire. "I've got something to say to that young *ami* courting your sister."

Stiffening, Spotted Wolf's head lifted as he gazed at Sorrel warily. But the Frenchman held out his hand and smiled. "You saved my life, Spotted Wolf. I won't forget it."

Nodding, the grave-faced Arikara took Sorrel's hand in a warm clasp. "You are a man worth saving, Sorrel."

"Oho!" the Frenchman burst out with an embarrassed grin on his broad face. "I'm glad we both know that now!"

Glancing from one to another, Michaella cocked

her brow questioningly. "I take it that our young friend has acquitted himself in your eyes, Sorrel?"

"More than that, missy! He risked his own neck to get me out from underneath the wagon that got overturned. I shoulda known better than to get caught out, but I reckon I got careless."

"I reckon you did," Jean Patrick put in. "Do you suppose we could all stop congratulating ourselves now and see what has to be done so we can move on in the morning? I've kind of lost my partiality to this particular spot. . . ."

Chapter Seventeen

LATE IN THE night the last of the herd disappeared from the area. The next morning broke clear, and although the dust had settled, the sky was still hazy. The two wagons that had been destroyed were beyond repair, and what goods could be salvaged were taken and placed into another wagon.

Jean Patrick had gone out to scout around for the missing cattle and came back into camp with the news that he had found two bodies lying not far from camp.

"Bodies?" Michaella asked with a gasp. "Who?"

"Two of Ketchman's men—Itch and the one called Sorley, I think. Both of them are pretty gruesome. It's amazing what a thousand tons of moving meat and sharp hooves can do to a human body."

Michaella blanched, and Mary Catherine grew pale and fled from their tent with her hands over her ears. "How did you . . . uh . . . *identify* them?" Michaella asked after a moment.

"By the remnants of their clothing. And by a broken bit of a pistol one of them carried, and by this. . . ." He held up a thin leather satchel no larger than a man's hand. It was badly battered, but barely visible on the outside was the engraved name *Jim Sorley*. Jean Patrick rubbed his thumb across the letters cut into the leather. He looked up at Michaella with a faint frown and added softly, "There's more."

"More? What . . . what do you mean?" She recoiled from touching the satchel he held out. "I don't want to . . ."

"Look inside," he insisted. "I think you will find a very interesting piece of paper."

It was the map. Michaella held the worn fragment and gazed at it wordlessly for several long minutes. There was no mistaking it—it was not a forgery.

"If you fit that piece with the piece you already have, won't it lead to the gold?" Jean Patrick asked when it looked as if she couldn't talk.

She nodded. "Yes . . . I'm sure of it."

"Then your troubles are over, right?"

"I suppose," was the slow answer, though she was thinking that in some ways they might have just begun. Now that she had both pieces, Ketchman would certainly redouble his efforts to find her, and while she should soon leave the train, what about Jean Patrick? He was committed to going on to Oregon, and yet the thought of finding the gold and her father was not as important as it had once been if Jean Patrick was not there to share the experience with her.

And later in her tent, when she and Mary Catherine fitted together the ragged edges of the map, she saw at last that her father—if he was still alive—was north of Fort Laramie. There was no question that what lay just ahead was the most important part of the journey. If Henry Chattilion had remained near the gold, he would be in the Black Hills. However, there seemed to be another smaller mark in the Bighorn Mountains. He would remain near the gold, of that she was certain. But had he made the larger mark to throw others off the track?

"But which?" Mary Catherine asked in bewilderment. "He could be in either area for all we know, and the gold is . . ."

"Is well hidden," Michaella said, taking up the map and folding it. "From these maps, it's obvious that the ranges are two hundred miles apart. But I think that even at that distance, it shouldn't be that difficult to find our father."

Sitting back, Mary Catherine studied her sister for a long moment. "You don't really care if we find Papa, do you?"

"Why do you say that?"

"Because you always seem more concerned with the gold than anything else."

Michaella took her time in forming a reply. "No," she began slowly. "I *do* want to find Papa, if for no other reason than to ask him why he never came back or sent word to us. I want to see his face when he answers, and then I will decide if I want to find him again or not."

"And the gold?"

"Is small recompense for many years of neglect. Our mother died of shame and . . ."

"She did not! She loved Papa!"

Her delicate features hardened as Michaella stared at her sister, but she could not bring herself to tarnish Mary Catherine's ideal of their father any more than had been done already. "Yes, you are right," she said gently. "I had forgotten how much she loved him."

After a moment of sniffing and tear wiping, Mary Catherine said, "Spotted Wolf said he would guide us to find him if we wished."

Turning, Michaella stared at her. "He did?"

She nodded. "Yes. But I didn't know if you would like that or not."

"Of course I do! That would be wonderful!"

Brightening, Mary Catherine said, "I am so glad you feel that way! I . . . I've been afraid to say anything to you about him because I knew you didn't like me to be with him as much as I have."

"Only because I worry that you will be hurt," was the soft reply, and Mary Catherine's head bobbed.

"Oh, I know that. But it's still been awkward. Oh, wouldn't it be wonderful if the four of us could be together, Michaella! Why, then, we could . . ."

"That's impossible," came the unintentionally curt answer, and Michaella turned away before her sister could see the pain in her eyes. It hurt too much even to think about the lonely days ahead of her.

Swinging down from his weary horse, Ketchman let the animal drink deeply from the little stream winding between the rocks. There was no sign of LaRange or Bisler, and as far as he was concerned, it was better that way. He still hadn't recovered from Sorley's untimely death; he'd nearly been trampled himself, but fortunately his horse was stronger and had maneuvered its way out of the buffalo.

Now the map was lost along with Sorley. Ketchman hadn't gotten to see it more than once, and that hadn't been enough. He could not recall many of the details, and he'd intended to talk to Sorley later, when LaRange and Bisler couldn't hear. But now that time would never come. There was nothing for him to do but hope Michaella and Mary Catherine headed north from Fort Laramie.

Ketchman realized he shouldn't stay too near the wagon train. Bisler and LaRange no doubt planned to follow it as well. Ketchman knew his only hope now was to stay out of sight, keeping just far enough off the main trail to watch the wagons, yet able to outdistance anyone who detected him.

Survival was no longer his biggest worry. He knew he could shoot game if he had to, and make do on the ground at night. His biggest worry was the Sioux—they were close. He'd heard drums during the previous night. A war party was probably ready to ride any time.

If he could only evade the Sioux and also keep away from LaRange and Bisler, Ketchman knew he would be able to fulfill his dream of getting the gold. Or so he told himself for three days straight. He had to make it; he had come this far, hadn't he? But he well knew that the odds were against him now.

Though he traveled only at night and then not very far, the time seemed to pass slowly. As the fourth day dawned, Ketchman began to worry that he might have guessed wrong. He knew the wagons would have to come this way when they left the fort, and he had insured his seeing them by working his way into dense, rocky foothills.

Just below him was the Oregon Trail, snaking across the hills and bottoms west of the North Platte River. His position overlooked a massive natural bridge—a stopover point where wagon trains watered and allowed their animals to graze. The trail led around the north end of the mountains and continued westward. Ketchman could see for miles from where he was, and anyone riding below him would be clearly visible.

After another day hidden in the rocks, Ketchman felt safer. For the first time since he'd been alone, he decided to risk building a fire. He waited until it was completely dark, then struck flint to a small pile of bark and dry leaves he had collected during the day. It took time, and Ketchman fumbled and cursed until finally a small blaze grew out of the tiny slivers of bark.

As the flames rose, so did Ketchman's spirits. He took some jerky and mixed it with pieces of a rabbit he'd just shot, then threw in some roots dug from familiar-looking plants. He'd seen LaRange and Bisler use the same method, and though their cooking had lacked a great deal in taste, it had assuaged the pangs of hunger well enough. The thick mixture cooked rapidly and gave off an aroma that made his mouth water in expectation. He could hardly wait for it to be done, and when it was he ate until the pan was empty, then cooked more.

While he washed up with creek water, Ketchman thought again how easy things would be for him now if only he had been able to keep the map, or even get a better look at it. As it was, he was going to have to find it or rely on his tricky memory. And the thing was, if he took the map, he'd have to take the sisters, and he didn't intend to have anyone with him when he got his hands on that gold.

The more he thought about it, the more aggravating it became, until finally he was feeling sorry for himself. He lay back on his bedroll and stared up at the night sky. The air was now incredibly still, a marked contrast from the wind that had scoured the trail and tugged at his clothes during the earlier part of the evening. There was a sense of peace in this spot he could not ignore. Reflecting on his past, Ketchman thought of his aunt and how she had managed to hold on to their wealth and position through the years. She was financially secure—but he knew she would try to disinherit him.

Beyond what he was entitled to simply by family ties, he had never been able to make any money on his own. As a result, he went without respect in a family known for its ability to accrue wealth. Members of his own family mocked him!

This was the reason he had seized upon the opportunity to blackmail his aunt in the matter of Henry Chattilion's daughters. Here was a fortune he would not have to share with the family, not if he handled matters right.

Ketchman smiled and stretched lazily, gazing up at a dark sky peppered with thousands upon thousands of bright stars. When he found the gold and it was his, he would have the last laugh. His family would no longer ridicule him or make jests at his expense. He would have the respect and position he craved. . . .

Sunlight washed the sky in blinding light as the wagons rumbled into Fort Laramie from the southeast. Against the drying hills of July, Michaella saw the buildings of the fort gleaming white in the distance. Riding up front with Jean Patrick, she noticed a contingent of army dragoons riding out to meet them as they drew closer to the fort.

Jean Patrick gave the signal and the wagons creaked to a halt. Sorrel, on Michaella's other side, gave a signal and Spotted Wolf drew abreast of them. Mary Catherine hung back a bit, but kept her gaze trained anxiously on the Arikara.

More and more emigrants came forward to get an eager look at their first sight of frontier soldiers. As the dragoons rode up and halted in formation, Meg Magoffin pushed through the line of emigrants and stopped. She stared hard at the sergeant leading them. A heartbeat passed, then she was lifting up her skirts and racing forward.

"Thomas!" she cried. "Thomas, it's me! It's your Meg!"

The column remained in position as the sergeant in charge dismounted in a smooth running movement and ran toward Meg. Michaella watched with a smile as the short, brawny sergeant managed to get both arms around his hefty wife and give her a huge, enthusiastic hug. He was so enthusiastic, Meg's feet actually lifted from the ground for an instant. All those in the wagon train who knew Meg and her journey to her soldier husband broke into a loud "Hurrah!"

Grinning sheepishly, the sergeant finally broke off his embrace and walked forward hand in hand with Meg while his men remained in place. Sergeant Magoffin saluted smartly to Jean Patrick, and the guide returned it with a snap. Then the two men shook hands and introduced themselves. A short, stocky man with a light complexion and gray-blue eyes as friendly as a puppy's, Sergeant Magoffin had an easygoing manner and winning charm.

"I must certainly commend you on bringing these people this far," Magoffin told Jean Patrick. "You are one of the youngest guides I've seen lead a group this large. I'd venture to say your wilderness experience makes up for your age."

Squeezing her husband's arm, Meg said fondly, "He's one of the best, Thomas."

For the first time since she'd met him, Michaella

was astonished to see Jean Patrick flush with embarrassment. His dusky complexion glowed with rosy highlights, and she had to hide a smile.

"Thank you, Sergeant," Jean Patrick replied with a self-conscious cough. "Uh, Meg . . . your wife has been a great asset to our party and an inspiration as well. We shall miss her sorely when we push on."

"Pshaw!" Meg broke in, and sudden tears filled her eyes. "You won't be leaving for a few days yet, so don't get me started in a'weepin' now! Let's laugh while we can, and have the wake later."

The emigrants made camp outside the walls of the fort, settling in a short distance from the trees on the river's edge where a number of Indian lodges stood. Jean Patrick explained that the Indians were a permanent encampment of Miniconjou Sioux. Alarmed by this news, the emigrants had to be reassured by Jean Patrick that this particular band of Sioux was peaceful.

The Miniconjou were for the most part docile, sadly reduced in some instances to the level of beggars. They lingered near the fort dressed in torn clothing, begging whatever they could. Already they were approaching the emigrant families for handouts. A number of them asked for something to drink; trade whiskey had taken its toll. Michaella was reminded of the demoralized Indians they had seen in Independence and Westport. Gradually the white influence was making its way into the wilderness, and she wasn't certain that was entirely good.

Even Fort Laramie was changing. Jean Patrick and Sorrel both recalled the post when it had been owned by the American Fur Company to serve as an outpost for the expanding trade in buffalo hides. Now it belonged to the Army, and the cottonwood storerooms and sleeping cabins were being replaced by adobe buildings made from local mud bricks and whitewashed to conform to army standards.

Fort Laramie was the first garrisoned outpost along this part of the Oregon Trail. Increasing pressure from the Sioux to stop the steady flow of wagon trains had caused alarm in Washington, and Companies A and E, Mounted Riflemen, and Company G, Sixth Infantry, were all assigned to the fort.

The fort commander in chief, one W. F. Sanderson, made it plain to Jean Patrick and Sorrel that he did not welcome a long stay by them.

"The grass around the fort has already been grazed down by previous wagon trains, gentlemen," he said, "as well as continuous use by army horses. I trust you do understand my dilemma?"

"Of course, sir," was the expected—and quickly given—answer. "We would like to resupply ourselves with flour, salt pork, beans, sugar, coffee, tea, and other necessities if possible."

Permission was granted, and the emigrants bought whatever goods and food they could afford from the sutler's. Prices on the frontier were as much as ten times higher than in Independence or Westport, but that was to be expected because of the cost of transporting goods. Besides, it would do little good to complain.

Michaella stayed with Jean Patrick as much as she possibly could while he worked to keep order.

She was searching for a way to avoid their final farewell, but time was shortening and the day was drawing near when it would come. There were other farewells, too, such as the one to Meg. It was surprising how close they had grown to the older woman in the two short months they'd been traveling.

On the evening of the second day's rest in the shadow of the fort, word came in from a young Miniconjou that a large party of Crow Indians had come through the Laramie Range and was sounding the drums of war. The Miniconjou had heard them, and he had also seen a war party of his own nation, along with some Oglala and Brule Sioux, traveling in the direction of the drums.

Jean Patrick explained to the worried settlers that the Crow who lived to the north were bitter enemies of the Sioux nation. The two tribes warred with one another continually. Since the early fur trade had caused a shift in the migration pattern of the buffalo herds, it was now common to see roving bands of Crow this far south from their traditional hunting grounds. Their endless fighting with the Sioux nation had frequently made life at the fort uneasy.

"Does that mean we can't leave the fort now?" Michaella asked Jean Patrick, uncertain whether she wanted the answer to be yes or no. "Yes" would mean a quicker end to her quest, but "no" would mean more time with Jean Patrick. She watched his face—the same beloved features that inhabited her dreams, her waking hours, her very soul—as if her life depended upon his answer. Did he realize how much a part of her he was? Did he feel the same way? Michaella agonized silently.

As she looked up at him, he reaching out, letting his fingers trace the smooth line of her throat, his fingers working beneath the loose cotton collar of her blouse to stroke the golden hollow that beat with every pulse throb. Michaella leaned into him, her eyes heavy-lidded and gleaming with a light he recognized, her lips parted and moist. The heavy weight of her breasts was pressed against his chest, and he could feel their scorching heat through his buckskin shirt. Hot, fluid heat coursed through his veins as Jean Patrick forgot her question, forgot his answer, forgot the world waiting outside her tent. Nothing mattered but the moment and the warm, lovely woman in his arms.

Chapter Eighteen

THEIR DEPARTURE WAS delayed while the Indian situation remained unclear. Two days passed with no sign that a battle had been fought. Miniconjou scouts sent out from the fort returned with the news that both the Crow and Sioux war parties had moved north. The battle would likely be fought there.

Finally Jean Patrick gave the order that they would have to move out. The commander at the fort gave permission to Sergeant Magoffin to take a detachment of fifty dragoons and escort the wagons as far as the natural bridge some four days distance from the fort, but no farther. Jean Patrick argued, with good reason, that the battle would probably be fought just up from there, in the spot where the mountains parted. This was where the buffalo regularly migrated and also where traveling war parties ran into one another.

But Jean Patrick was not successful in coaxing the commander to allow the escort to accompany them any farther than the natural rock bridge. If the Crow decided to attack the Miniconjou settled at the fort, the army would have to step in. In that event, a messenger would be sent out to recall Sergeant Magoffin and his men back to the post. It would not matter where the wagon train was or what danger the emigrants were facing.

Jean Patrick began to wonder if it was worthwhile to have the escort along for such a short distance. But Sergeant Magoffin had become a friend of the emigrants, and both Michaella and Mary Catherine wanted the extra days with the Irishwoman. Chances were, this might be the last time the sisters would see Meg Magoffin again.

Finally the wagons rolled out. Though Sergeant Magoffin had a great deal of fighting experience, most of the dragoons in his command were hardly more than teenage boys. They were almost as afraid as the emigrants, riding at the edge of the wagons and starting at every leap of an antelope or rustle of the wind.

Jean Patrick and Sorrel made a concerted effort to bolster the young soldiers' confidence. Having spent long periods of time with his uncle among the Crow people, Jean Patrick knew the Indians would not want to attack the wagons. They were adept at horse stealing and cattle rustling, but they did not usually choose to attack white people.

"The Crows were early allies with whites during the first days of the fur trade," Jean Patrick explained to Michaella. "The mountain men fought with the Crow against a lot of their enemies, so they've remained friends, for the most part."

"If we don't have to worry about the Crow, then what about the Sioux?" Michaella asked anxiously. Her brows drew into a tight knot over the bridge of her nose as she considered all the possibilities ahead.

"We have a lot to worry about where the Sioux are concerned," was the blunt reply. "But we have a big company of soldiers with us, and the Sioux won't want to risk losing their best warriors—not when there's a Crow war party close by."

During the second night out, war drums began

to throb. They came from opposite sides of the valley, indicating that both the Crow and the Sioux were making ready for war. A few hours before dawn, the drums stopped.

"Get down," Sorrel told Michaella and Mary Catherine in a low voice. "You're about to see something that may not be pretty, but it's damned impressive!"

Shivering in the early morning air, with the dew still on the ground and the wind brisk and chill, Michaella watched as the sky slowly lightened from gray to pink, the first faint rays of sunlight brightening the land. At least four hundred Sioux and Crow warriors faced one another in two mounted lines. The warriors on both sides were either nearly or totally naked. All were covered in paint from head to toe, and their ponies were likewise marked with round circle signs, jagged streaks of red or blue or black, or other marks of distinction.

The warriors wore combinations of feathers, quills, and animal or bird headdresses. War cries rang out from both sides in shrill male voices, but the battle did not begin right away. Individual warriors displayed their strong medicine by riding their ponies in a dead run and doing agile tricks from atop the bare backs while their enemies looked on. Then came a time of insults shouted back and forth. Warriors on both lines shouted obscenities in their native dialects and gestured with sign language so the meanings would be clear.

The hair on the back of Michaella's neck rose as she watched two warriors—one from each side—ride toward one another and clash in the middle of the field. They were followed by other individuals who each picked an enemy to charge in the opposing line, and the battle began in earnest.

Soon the dust was thick, masking much of what was going on. In the haze Michaella could see forms that fell from their horses with arrows or lances protruding, and she turned away from the sight. She had to hold her hands over her ears to block out the screams of wounded men and horses.

The battle continued, with heavy losses on both sides. Above the ceaseless screaming and yelling came the shrill noise made by the Sioux warriors blowing on eagle-bone whistles. When a hapless warrior went down, many enemies would ride by and ram their lances into him or shoot arrows until the body bristled with them.

Just after noon the battle ended and both sides began to seek out the dead and wounded. The field was littered with warriors both living and dead. As the dust slowly settled, the rank smell of blood grew so heavy the emigrants' livestock became difficult to control.

That night in camp one of the dragoon guards ran shouting to Sergeant Magoffin and Jean Patrick that Indians were approaching the wagons. Three Crow warriors, riding ponies still worn out from the battle, announced in faulty English that they wished to come into the camp. One of them was leaning over in his saddle. As the sergeant hesitated, Jean Patrick stepped forward to gaze closely at the wounded Crow.

"Do you remember me?" the wounded warrior wheezed in a mixture of Crow and broken English.

Jean Patrick nodded. "I have seen you, but it seems we were children then," he replied in Crow.

"Yes, we were children. I am Little Coyote. I have come here to die."

"And what do you want me to do?" Jean Patrick asked, sensing there was a reason for Little Coyote's visit.

"We were separated from our friends and left behind because of my wound. I want you to see that my young brothers, Yellow Horse and He Who Knows Buffalo, get safely back to the Bighorn. I fear for them. . . ."

He broke off in a painful spasm of coughing, and Jean Patrick called for someone to help him assist the warrior from his pony.

Later, while Little Coyote lay on a blanket by the fire with his eyes closed, Michaella edged close to Jean Patrick. "Will he really die?"

He nodded. "Yes. The wound is bad."

"And you knew him when you were a child?"

Again he nodded. "I haven't seen him since I last hunted in the Bighorns. Michaella . . ." When she turned to look at him, he said, "Little Coyote claims he has seen Henry Chattilion at the Medicine Wheel in the Bighorns."

She stared at him blankly for a minute. It did not make sense that a dying Indian would come into their camp and say he had seen her father. "Why would he say that?"

"Because he knew I had once hunted with old Henry. I suppose it was an effort to give me good news, but that doesn't matter. You know what this means."

"That the map is right."

"Yes. And that you aren't too far away now."

Somehow the thought frightened her. It was all

coming too fast now after taking so long to develop, and she was confused, wanting yet not wanting the gold, and wanting Jean Patrick without reservation.

These thoughts tormented her during the long night alone in her blankets. When she rose the next morning, it was to discover Little Coyote had died and been taken away by his brothers. Sorrel had gone with them.

"Gone?" Michaella asked incredulously. "I cannot think why he felt it necessary to leave us now! Why did you let him go?"

Jean Patrick looked at her strangely. "I gave my word," he said in a quiet tone that made her flush. "I gave my word to these people, and I gave my word to Little Coyote. I don't give my word lightly."

Ashamed, Michaella just nodded. "Will he be back soon?"

"I think so."

Sorrel returned by the time the emigrants reached the natural bridge. He reported that the brothers and their sad burden had made it safely around the Sioux, and were headed back into their home country.

"Thanks," Jean Patrick said, and the big Frenchman just grinned.

"It wasn't so bad, hoss! Bein' around you, I'm beginnin' to get used to Injuns!"

Jean Patrick matched his grin. "Good. You can never tell when you might decide to grow your hair long and braid it with rawhide, Sorrel! I expect to see you wearing a breechcloth and painting your face one day."

"Now, that you'll never see, hoss!"

While the emigrants bathed and washed clothes in preparation for the next leg of the journey, around the end of the small Laramie range and onward to the Sweetwater River and South Pass, Meg faced the reality that she would soon see the last of Michaella and Mary Catherine. It was time for her and her husband to go to Fort Laramie. The extra few days had been nice, but they were now over. The three women chatted amicably, and when they finally parted, all three were weeping profusely.

Michaella and Mary Catherine waved their farewells until the rolling hills hid Meg and her sergeant husband from sight. For a long time, neither girl felt like talking or doing anything. They rode with heavy hearts.

Chapter Nineteen

As the sunset flamed in colors of crimson and orange, Michaella and Jean Patrick walked along the river. It was their last night together, for the next day the wagons would roll on and she would ride in the opposite direction. Her throat tightened, and she fought the tears stinging her eyes.

"Sad, love?" Jean Patrick asked softly, and because he knew her answer, he pulled her into his arms beneath the drooping branches of a cottonwood tree and held her tight. "It won't be forever," he murmured, kissing her brow, her closed lids, her quivering mouth. "I'll be back before you can even turn to look for me."

Michaella could not speak around the huge lump in her throat; she merely nodded and rubbed her face into the rough material of his buckskins. Her fingers curled into the fringe stretched over his chest, and she drew in a deep breath.

Then there was no need for words, for Jean Patrick was making a place for them beneath the green bower of the tree branches, pulling her gently to the ground and stretching out beside her. Michaella put her palms on each side of his face and kissed him deeply, hungrily, her mouth exploring every harsh angle and plane of his face. She drank in the essence that was Jean Patrick, absorbing him through touch and taste and smell, her senses storing up every particle for the coming drought ahead. There would be no more Jean Patrick—maybe forever. Too many dangers faced both of them so that there was a special urgency in their lovemaking this evening.

The wind blew softly across the river and stirred the lacy branches, whisking over bare, heated flesh and mingling with the steamy passion beneath the cottonwood tree. Jean Patrick's lean, hard body gleamed in the dying light of the sun. It was bronze and primitively beautiful, and Michaella thought that there would never be another moment like this one. Her hand explored the flexed muscles that flowed across his chest, her fingertips skipping downward over the flat-muscled ridges of his belly and moving lower, making him suck in a sharp breath and hold it as she curled her fingers around him.

When he could stand it no more, Jean Patrick shifted quickly, moving onto her, wedging between her willing thighs, murmuring love words in English, French, and a language she didn't recognize but knew to be Indian. She didn't need to understand the words to understand his heart, and Michaella arched upward in a singing sweetness to accept him. His heart pounded against her chest, and the world seemed to move in a honeyed languor as he moved against her.

Half sobbing, she clung to Jean Patrick with feverish urgency, and when the sweeping rush of release came, she had the vague thought that it had never been so sweet. Spent and drained of all but the will to lie in his arms, Michaella refused to allow her thoughts to wander toward the inevitable parting. Nothing mattered but now and the moment and Jean Patrick.

Her eyelids drifted upward when she felt him shift, and she stared up into his lazy blue eyes and smiling face.

"First you exhaust me, and now you want more?" she murmured in contentment.

"Are you complaining?"

Her eyes kindled with fire. "Ah, never that, love, never that," she said softly.

"Good. I detest complaining females!" Jean Patrick's smile faded, and he reached for her hand. His fingers were warm, and Michaella could feel the weight of something being placed in her cupped palm.

"What is this?" she asked, lifting her hand to gaze curiously at the leather pouch.

"My medicine bundle. It has a special magic, love."

"A special magic?" she echoed in confusion. "What . . . what do you mean?"

"Yes, a magic of sorts. You see, if you keep this with you and don't lose it, I will always be with you. You will think of me and remember our times together whenever you feel this between your breasts. . . ." He paused to kiss the ripe peak of one breast, his tongue flicking across the rosy crest in a movement tantalizing and breath stealing. "I want you to remember me, love," he said huskily, "as I will be remembering you. And someday we will come together again . . ."

Hot tears coursed down her cheeks, and she bit back a sob. Jean Patrick never finished his sentence. He began to kiss away her tears, and Michaella's response was so urgent and fevered that the medicine bundle was momentarily forgotten. It rolled from her palm to the grass and nestled among their discarded clothing.

From his place among the gritty rocks and sand-scoured wind sculptures, Ketchman looked down onto the rolling bottomland. Everything was quiet and peaceful, and he was actually enjoying himself. Maybe he was a better frontiersman than he'd ever given himself credit for, for he was still alive and in reasonably good health. The wagon train was nearly out of sight to the west, and the small party that had broken away was now headed toward the Bighorn Mountains.

Shifting in his saddle, Ketchman narrowly regarded the four horses and their riders. Michaella, Mary Catherine, Sorrel, and the Indian Spotted Wolf were riding at a fast pace along the timeworn trail. It was still early in the day, and he had plenty of time to catch up to them.

He didn't know exactly what had made them decide on going into the Bighorns, but he didn't care as long as they led him to the gold—before Bisler and LaRange showed up. He was thinking of the two men when he heard something, or someone, moving in the rocks above him. A trickle of stones rolled down the hill, and Ketchman leaned forward to snatch up his rifle just as a shot was fired. The ball zipped past him and smacked into the rock just behind, showering him with splinters.

Ketchman fumbled with the rifle in its saddle scabbard and dismounted in a frenzied rush. At the same time he heard LaRange cursing, saying that he had missed an easy shot.

Ketchman ran low and took cover behind a gnarled, wind-twisted tree. He tried to pinpoint their location. He knew they were above him in the rocks, but he couldn't tell how far up. He waited for them to shoot again and give their position away, but nothing happened. Then Ketchman realized they were trying to circle behind him.

Frantically racking his brain, Ketchman decided to try a trick that the braggart Crenshaw had always included in his stories about his exploits in the mountains. Crenshaw had always won in his stories in spite of overwhelming odds, of course, but Ketchman hoped that in this one instance the trick would work.

He tossed a pebble to draw their fire, determined their approximate location, then snaked over the rocks on his belly until he managed to get several yards away. This time when he threw a pebble and received rifle fire in return, he gave a loud cry. Then he threw a large chunk of rock a distance from him and waited.

In a matter of moments, he heard Bisler's and LaRange's satisfied voices as they descended from the rocks above. He could see them moving slowly and cautiously. Their eyes were riveted on the spot where the thud of the rock had sounded so much like a falling body. It was obvious they were expecting to see Ketchman's bloodied body sprawled among the rocks.

Ketchman measured his chances. He had a rifle and a small pistol. He could shoot one with the rifle, then use the pistol on the other. Praying that neither weapon would misfire, as they so often did, Ketchman took careful aim and waited for a good shot. As soon as they were close, he rose swiftly from behind the rock.

"Drop your rifles! Put your hands in the air—now!"

Both men were taken completely off guard. LaRange started to swerve, and Ketchman aimed his rifle at the man's midsection. His voice was low and thick with menace.

"Go ahead, LaRange," Ketchman said. "Just try and make a run for it! Nothing would please me more than to put a ball into your worthless hide!"

Halting, LaRange cut his eyes toward Ketchman, not daring to move anything else. His mouth worked in silent hatred, and if his fiery gaze had been bullets, Ketchman would have been cut to pieces.

"How do you think you'll manage to get us both?" Bisler demanded. A sneer twisted his face as he glared at Ketchman and complied with his demands. Both hands lifted slowly into the air.

"I don't think I'll get both of you, but I will get one of you. Care to take a chance?"

"Then the other of us will get you," Bisler said.

"Perhaps so, but in either event, *one* of you will be dead. That will leave only one man alone out here in hostile territory with no notion of how to find the gold or Chattilion, and if that Frenchman or that Indian ever find you, it should make for an interesting last few hours. . . ."

Snarling with frustration, Bisler retorted, "And how do you figure on getting away by yourself, Ketchman? You couldn't find your way out of a burlap bag!"

"Not without a map I couldn't."

The implication struck Bisler forcibly. His features altered from fury to grim amusement. He began to laugh. "What do you think you're trying to pull?"

"Why do you think Sorley kept to himself?" Ketchman waggled the gun barrel when Bisler took a step forward. "Oh, no! Stay where you are and listen! Sorley had a map, or I should say, part of a map. He got it from his brother, a man your friend LaRange killed a few years before. It seems that

Sorley hadn't forgotten or forgiven that trespass on the good LaRange's part. Ah-ah! I said stay where you are, gentlemen!"

Bisler and LaRange once more paused to glare at the thin man with the long rifle. The sun had burned Ketchman's pale face to a deep brown, and his protuberant eyes gleamed with a fanatical light as he grinned at them. To Bisler's superstitious mind, he looked like a death's-head.

"Sorley said his brother and some others, including that old trapper Sorrel, were out here in the mountains and attacked by the Sioux. They were separated, but Sorley's brother had this piece of a map. He gave it to Sorley before he was killed. I, in turn, got it from Sorley before he was killed. Rather providential, wouldn't you say?"

"I'd say a mite *too* providential! I don't believe you, Ketchman. Show us the map."

"My dear fellow, you seem to be confused. *I* am the man with the rifle. I need show you nothing. Besides, I have committed the map to memory and destroyed the physical evidence. Now the map is here. . . ." He tapped a forefinger against his head.

"How convenient."

"Yes, isn't it?"

After a brief hesitation, Bisler asked, "Mind if I lower my hands?"

"Not at all, but first kick your rifle over here. Both of them, please," Ketchman ordered.

"We could parley, bargain about this," Bisler suggested when he had done as Ketchman demanded. "You can't go after the gold by yourself when there's a bunch of screamin' Sioux on the warpath."

"Perhaps not. And perhaps one man alone would not attract as much attention."

"What about those girls? And Sorrel?"

"I have the map, remember?" Ketchman lied.

"And not the chance of a snowball in hell if you go it alone," Bisler shot back. "You need us. And what do you intend to do when you get to the gold? Can you mine it by yourself? No, you'll need help. That's where me and LaRange can come in."

"I hardly think so," was the cold reply. "Your big dumb friend has the nasty habit of making repeated attempts on my life, remember? I do not intend to find myself with a knife in my back one fine evening!"

Bisler slanted a glance toward LaRange. "And if I promise to keep him in line?"

"*Promise?* Are you suggesting your word might be good, Bisler?"

"Keep our weapons, then," was the bold suggestion, "if it makes you feel better. Should there be danger, you can always give them back."

Stroking his straggly growth of beard with a thoughtful, narrowed gaze, Ketchman finally gave a brief nod of his head. "Very well. But if either of you even look as if you may be plotting against me, I will shoot without compunction. Understood?"

"I understand you'll shoot if you have to," Bisler replied.

"Excellent! Then perhaps we can deal together."

There was a grim satisfaction as the three men stood in wary silence for a moment. One common goal united them—gold.

Chapter Twenty

MICHAELLA AND MARY CATHERINE felt a new excitement working within them now. The Bighorn Mountains were rising in the distance, and though the snow still lingered high atop a landmark known as Cloud Peak, the summits of layered rock seemed to be bathed in warmth.

For two days they had traveled from the crossing on the North Platte River and were heading up through foothills along the base of the mountains. The slopes were timbered in many places and the creeks lined with quaking aspen. Their delicate leaves fluttered in the soft breeze of the morning, and below them next to the water, thick bunches of wild roses spread their colors of delicate red.

Many small birds that Michaella had never seen before sang as they darted through the branches. Though she could still see antelope farther out from the trees and frequently in the open, the area they rode through contained large herds of big deer with floppy ears that Sorrel called mule deer. They would bound out from the creeks and meadows and stand in uniform fashion for a time before dashing off for cover.

These deer seemed bigger and darker than the varieties encountered along the rivers and bottomlands on the way out. Michaella thought them spectacular, especially the bucks. Their antlers were large and still covered with a velvety fur that Sorrel said would wear off in the fall when they began fighting for territorial rights during the mating season.

It was all new and different for both women. They kept their eyes open and learned what they could from observation, as well as by questioning Sorrel and Spotted Wolf. They were now in an immense expanse of wilderness, and it was continually offering them something different to learn—as if each section had its own personality.

Though she was learning new things and increasing her wilderness skills even more each day, Michaella still felt as if she were only half alive. Being without Jean Patrick was proving harder than she had anticipated. Even with his medicine bundle tied around her neck, she found herself wishing she could hold him when darkness came, and see him riding nearby during the sunlight hours. She found herself stopping to look back at the crest of every hill, hoping to see a distant wisp of dust coming ever nearer, the dust from a horse that would be carrying Jean Patrick.

When they camped each night, Michaella thought every noise she heard was Jean Patrick riding in to join them—to be with her and make her whole again.

Mary Catherine realized how much her sister missed Jean Patrick and did what she could to help her. At the same time she was struggling with her own uneasiness. She feared something was coming between herself and Spotted Wolf. It wasn't anything she could readily identify—they hadn't quarreled—but it troubled her greatly.

Late one evening after they had made camp,

Mary Catherine sought out Spotted Wolf. She decided it was time to ask him what he intended.

"I have been thinking a lot," he began. "I have told you some about myself, but I haven't told you very much."

"I want you to feel you can tell me anything you want," Mary Catherine said. "I know you've never lied to me."

"No, I have never lied to you, and I never will lie to you," Spotted Wolf said. "But there are things I haven't said to you that I think I should."

"Is something wrong?" she asked. "Do you have a wife back at your village or something like that?"

"No," Spotted Wolf said with a laugh. "I have no wives. I have not taken any because I have not yet wanted to. I am glad that I didn't." He smiled at her tenderly.

"Then what is it you want to tell me that worries you?" Mary Catherine asked, her blue eyes wide and serious.

"I am not completely of Arikara blood," he said quickly. "My mother was part Hidatsa and part Arikara, and my father was a fur trader who worked for the American Fur Company. I hope you do not think less of me."

"Why, of course not," Mary Catherine said in surprise. "Why should I?"

Spotted Wolf shrugged. "It seems to me that white people think everything should be pure, when nothing is really pure. Among most white people, it is in their heads that they are all pure and everyone else is not."

"I don't feel any different about you," Mary

Catherine said, coming close to him and curling her fingers around one of his strong arms. "I love you more all the time. Nothing can change that. I know you would never do anything to deliberately hurt me."

The taut muscles in his face relaxed as Spotted Wolf seemed to feel more at ease. Mary Catherine wondered what harmful experiences he had had in his village. Something must have happened to him as a child—or possibly as an adult—that would make him concerned this way. Mary Catherine wondered if it had anything to do with his fluency in English.

"How did you learn to speak English so well?" she asked him. "I know you said fur traders influenced you. But was there anyone else?"

"Yes. I told you my father worked for the American Fur Company," Spotted Wolf began. "My people, the Arikara, did not like that. They have never really liked white people. They have been friendly at times, but they have made war a lot. My father left my mother and myself when I was young, because he was afraid he would soon be killed."

"I'm sorry," Mary Catherine said. "That must have been hard for you. I . . . I know how it feels to lose a father like that."

Spotted Wolf nodded. "Yes, I loved him very much. But I realized he might lose his life if he stayed. Then, only a year after he left, my mother caught a fever and died. I knew I must go to live with my father, and I left the village and traveled to St. Louis with some Flathead Indians. I wanted to find my father."

Mary Catherine was listening with interest. This

was a side of Spotted Wolf's story that he had kept hidden from her. Now he felt he should tell her, and she was glad he trusted her.

"My father was an owner of the company," Spotted Wolf continued, "much like your father and his company. When I arrived in St. Louis, he put me in a private school. I didn't want to go, but he insisted. I spent six years there. That is how I know English so well, and the ways of the white people."

"Why did you leave St. Louis?" Mary Catherine asked.

"My father seemed to have little time for me. And no one else cared about me, either. So when I was older, I found my way back to the Arikara. They did not know how to take me at first—they could not understand some of the things I had learned. But I have a brother and a sister there, and they welcomed me back."

"That must have been interesting, coming back to your people after being educated in St. Louis," Mary Catherine said.

Spotted Wolf looked at her. "Sometimes it was interesting," he said. "Sometimes it was dangerous."

Mary Catherine learned that Spotted Wolf's people were worried that he would bring more whites out to live with them. That was something they didn't want at the time. Whenever he spoke to the Arikara about the school in St. Louis, they frowned. And having come back from the white culture made it that much harder for him to prove himself as a young man training to become a warrior.

But he had been strong, capable of beating all the

younger men in the village at wrestling and the other games that tested strength and skill, and that was very important in the eyes of the older men. Strong warriors brought strong sons into the world to help defend the tribe. He had proven to be the very strongest.

"Now they want you to be a chief among your people?" Mary Catherine asked. "Even when they weren't sure if they wanted you back?"

"I am to be a chief among the Arikara people," Spotted Wolf repeated. "That is what is important to me now."

Mary Catherine thought about what he had said. It seemed that he was denouncing the white culture and looking forward again to life among his people. Where did this leave her?

"Do you intend to come back to St. Louis with my sister and myself after we find our father?" Mary Catherine asked. "I thought you said our future was together."

Spotted Wolf thought for a time. "I want our future to be together," he said. "If you are going to St. Louis, then I will go to St. Louis with you. Is that what you would like?"

"I believe that is where we plan to make our home," Mary Catherine said. "Neither Michaella nor I want to go back to England."

"I have heard of England," Spotted Wolf said. "If you do not like it there, I know I wouldn't like it."

Mary Catherine laughed. "No, you wouldn't like it. I don't think the people would know what to make of you."

Spotted Wolf laughed. Then he became suddenly serious. "And what of your sister and Jean Patrick?" he asked. "He has to take the wagons on toward the west."

Mary Catherine shrugged. "I don't know what they'll do or how they'll figure it out."

"It would be hard for both of them if they had to live apart," Spotted Wolf observed. "And it would be hard for us as well."

"It would be very hard," Mary Catherine agreed.

"I am glad that I have found you," Spotted Wolf finally told her. "My life is much better because of you."

"You have done a great deal for me, too," Mary Catherine said. "I don't ever want to be without you."

"Nor I without you," Spotted Wolf said. "Let us hope you and I never face that."

Jean Patrick missed Michaella so much that it was hard for him to concentrate. He continually wondered where she was and whether she was safe. He knew the Sioux war party was still somewhere out in the hills, and he feared that Michaella and the others would run into them.

Ever since their parting, Jean Patrick had not really been himself. His zest for life was now merely a drive to get the wagons to move as fast as possible. A number of the emigrants got into arguments over how fast they could go. The country was not easy to travel.

Late in the evening of his third day without Michaella, Jean Patrick stopped the wagons for the night at the Sweetwater Crossing. Many of the people were complaining about how long the day had been. As he watched the wagons pull into a circle, Jean Patrick wished with all his heart that his trip to Oregon with them was over. He longed for Michaella's arms, and with so many miles left to go, it would be a long time before he held her again.

As the wagons pulled into formation, Jean Patrick looked out toward the mountains and saw a group of riders heading for camp. He immediately called for the men to get ready with their rifles. But it turned out to be a party of trappers and mountain men, and Jean Patrick knew their leader.

"Caleb?" Jean Patrick yelled out as the riders neared the wagons. "Caleb Marshall, is that you?"

Jean Patrick heard a husky laugh as a grizzled old mountain man jumped down off a brown pinto pony and shook his hand. Caleb Marshall had been a good friend of Jean Patrick's father when they lived among the Crow. Caleb had taken a Crow wife at the time, and he and Jean Patrick's father had hunted together regularly. Jean Patrick could remember how Caleb used to coach him on stalking elk.

"Why, Jean Patrick, you weren't no more than a whelp when I last saw you," the mountain man said. "Look at me . . . I'm so old I can't remember when my hair wasn't white. And I'm stove up like some snake-bit cow." He favored one leg, but his blue eyes sparkled in the light of the fire, and he rubbed a beard as silky white as his long hair.

"What brought you riding pell-mell into camp like that?" Jean Patrick wanted to know.

"Injuns," Caleb answered as he stroked his beard. "Sioux. A war party fit to be tied out there. We got a good head start, though, and beat them down outa the mountains."

"Which way did you come from?" Jean Patrick asked.

"The Bighorns," Caleb said. "I figure those Sioux want revenge for something."

"They were just in a big battle with the Crow," Jean Patrick told him. "They got beat pretty bad in that fight."

"That explains it," Caleb said, rubbing his white beard. "No wonder they want somebody's hair."

"What were you doing in the Bighorns?" Jean Patrick asked. "Aren't they all about trapped out?"

"Everyplace is all trapped out," Caleb said with a shrug. "We went up to the Medicine Wheel. The Crows were havin' a ceremony and wanted us to come. After it was over, we had all planned on goin' down to Fort Laramie. We was just comin' down out of the mountains when we met those Sioux."

Jean Patrick invited Caleb and the trappers with him over to his fire for coffee and a hot meal. There was some fresh antelope roasting over a fire, and it went well with the wild greens Jean Patrick had cut from along the river.

While they ate, Caleb introduced him to the other men and they all talked about the old days when trapping beaver was easy. They talked also about Jean Patrick's father and their days with the Crow people. But now that was passed and times had changed.

"Not many old cusses like me left out here,"

Caleb commented, taking a cut of antelope. "Just me and old Henry Chattilion over in the Black Hills."

"Who did you say?" Jean Patrick asked quickly.

"Henry Chattilion. You know him?"

Jean Patrick couldn't believe his ears. Here was an old mountain man whom he hadn't seen for years, and he was telling him right where Michaella's father was.

"Yeah, that crazy old man was hidin' out in a small cabin back in a canyon on the north side of the mountains. I figger if you're a friend of his, it's okay for you to know.

"Anyways, old Chattilion had a score the year before when the hillside had been burned by lightnin'."

"I was traveling with a woman and her sister, old Henry's two daughters," Jean Patrick said. "They came clear over from England to find him. They should be somewhere in the Bighorns now, traveling with an Arikara warrior and a trapper named Sorrel."

"Sorrel?" Caleb laughed loudly. "That crazy Frenchman! I remember when he ate all my sourdough pancakes up on the Three Forks. Ate every one before any of the rest of them even woke up." He was still laughing. "I thought he'd given up a long time ago and went to Independence to set up a trade shop."

"He decided to come out and help the Chattilion girls find their father," Jean Patrick said. His mind was working swiftly, and he had the spark of an idea. "I intend to join them myself as soon as I get these wagons safely to Oregon. Ever been to Oregon Territory, Caleb?"

"Ah, Oregon! Beautiful country out there!" Caleb said.

A satisfied smile slanted his mouth as Jean Patrick gazed at the grizzled old mountain man. "I hear it's ripe for a man to settle if he's got a little money and the time," he said carefully. "Ever thought about settling out there, Caleb?"

Cackling, Caleb said, "I got the time, young feller, but I ain't got the money! Oncet I sell my furs, I spend it all on whiskey and women. Now I ain't got nothin' to show for my time 'ceptin' achin' bones."

Shrugging, the old man speared a slice of antelope with the point of his knife and wedged it into his mouth. "Don't know I'd want to," he said around the juicy mouthful.

"If you had a lot of money, perhaps?"

Another shrug, then: "But I don't, so that don't come inta mind, ya see."

"I could see that you did have some money," Jean Patrick said slyly, and the old man's head jerked up.

"How?"

"I'm getting paid very well to guide these folks on to Oregon. You know the trail better than I do, Caleb! Hell, you probably blazed it yourself."

A gap-toothed grin spread across Caleb's face. "I prob'ly did! But just 'cause you're getting paid, don't mean I would!"

Jean Patrick leaned forward. "Caleb, there's a young lady I want to see, and if I could shift my responsibility to these people to a qualified man, I would be able to join her. Do you understand?"

"How much?" the old mountain man asked after a moment's deliberation.

"All they've already given me, and the rest of what I would earn—a thousand dollars, Caleb."

Rheumy eyes widened as the old man's mouth drooped in astonishment. "A thousand *gold* dollars?"

"A thousand *spendable* dollars, Caleb. What do you say? I couldn't leave these folks with just anybody, but I know you're a dependable man and a damned good guide."

Scratching his bearded jaw, Caleb reflected for a long moment, then nodded. "Done! I'm Oregon-bound!"

Leaping up from his seat by the fire, Jean Patrick grabbed the old man's hand, gave it a pump, then hurried to call together the council members of the wagon train. He told them that their guide from here on out would be Caleb Marshall, and that they were to pay him all the monies owed from the trip. Some of the emigrants expressed disappointment, but most had always been wary of the guide who looked so much like an Indian himself. Switching guides was not unheard of, and so they all agreed.

Without hesitation, Jean Patrick gathered his things and saddled his horse. Caleb and the other mountain men warned him against leaving so soon while the Sioux were still close, but Jean Patrick would not wait.

"You're goin' to lose your hair, young feller,

Caleb said with a shake of his head. He had walked out from the campfire to stand beside Jean Patrick as he tied his belongings onto his horse.

Jean Patrick slanted him an irrepressible grin. "The Sioux won't catch me! I'm too slick for them. I still remember some of the old tricks you and Father taught me so long ago, Caleb!"

Laughing, Caleb clapped Jean Patrick on the back. "I'll bet you do, at that," he said. "If them Sioux do find you, head right for the Medicine Wheel. You know enough to do that. Sacred ground. They won't fight you there."

Jean Patrick nodded as he tightened the last strap on his saddle. "I know that trick, and a few others. I'll make it. You just take care of yourself and these settlers on the way to Oregon . . . and don't spend all that money on women and whiskey!" he added with a laugh.

Stepping into his saddle, he touched the brim of his hat with one finger and bid the old man farewell. He reined his bay around and rode into the darkness, putting the wagon train behind him. The future lay ahead, a future with the woman he had dreamed of at night.

Chapter Twenty-One

As they rode along the foot of the Bighorn Mountains, Michaella lost herself in the landscape once again. She marveled at the high peaks that rose into the clouds, the highest still capped with snow. Eagles soared in lazy circles overhead, their piercing cries echoing across the valley. It would all be so wonderful if only Jean Patrick weren't gone.

Meanwhile Sorrel was looking off in the other direction, across the wide, sweeping valley to the east. He had done so almost from the beginning of their ride north. Finally he stopped everybody and turned to Michaella and Mary Catherine.

"I figure we're headed into the Bighorns for no good reason," he said. "We ought to turn for the Black Hills. I've got a hunch that's where we'll find your father."

"What makes you think so?" Michaella asked, startled by his sudden actions.

"I've just got that feelin'," Sorrel said noncommitally. "I say we go down the creek from here and then turn to Powder River. That will take us south for a while, and then we can travel on to the mountains."

"What about the Sioux?" Mary Catherine asked. "They must be somewhere near."

"We've just got to take our chances. We'll travel at night and we won't have no fires. In a couple of days we'll be across, and I'd wager we'll find your father."

"You seem pretty sure of yourself all of a sudden."

"What makes you think we should go into the Black Hills before we've looked in the Bighorns?" Michaella asked.

"Instinct," Sorrel replied. "That's all. I just figure I know where he's at."

Even while she was speaking, Michaella found herself thinking about Jean Patrick again. He had flashed into her thoughts in a way that alarmed her, but she fought his memory. She reasoned that it was silly to be pining over Jean Patrick now, especially when she had told him that she couldn't be with him because of her mission. It was time to concentrate, and she could worry about Jean Patrick later. There was a lot of unknown country ahead, and working with her sister and Sorrel and Spotted Wolf to find her father was going to be an incredible task.

They decided to go along with Sorrel. They headed their horses down the creek to go across the Powder River. Sorrel knew the country well, having trapped throughout the entire region for a number of years. If anyone could get them across the shortest and safest way, it was Sorrel.

As they continued down through the rugged foothills, Michaella suddenly thought once again about Jean Patrick. For some reason she believed he was in danger. She thought possibly the wagon train had been attacked by the Sioux, or something equally bad had happened.

She continued to worry. It was as if the medicine bundle she wore around her neck was somehow telling her something. The premonition was something she just couldn't explain, but it was very real and something she could not ignore. She turned her horse around and contemplated going back in the direction of the wagons.

"What is it? What's wrong?" Mary Catherine asked.

"I don't know, I'm worried about Jean Patrick. I don't understand it."

Spotted Wolf rode his pony next to her and looked first at the medicine bundle and then at her.

"What are you feeling?" he asked.

Michaella shrugged. "I guess I'm feeling fear, but I don't know what I'm afraid of. . . . No, it isn't me that's afraid, it's Jean Patrick, and I'm afraid for him."

Mary Catherine asked Michaella if she was being affected by the heat. But Spotted Wolf realized what was happening. Michaella was wearing Jean Patrick's medicine bundle and by so doing, was also wearing his thoughts and emotions. What was happening to Jean Patrick at that moment was coming to Michaella through the medicine bundle.

Suddenly Michaella kicked her horse and rode onto a hill above the creek bottom. She peered into the vast distance toward the south, shielding her eyes from the sun. Far out in the distance she could see dust rising.

"What is that way out there?" she asked, pointing toward the lower end of the mountains.

The others were now up on the hillside with her. They, too, were looking out.

"Is that dust out there? Are those riders?" Michaella asked.

Spotted Wolf nodded. "Riders. The Sioux. And one man in front of them, riding alone." He had pushed himself up on his horse and was leaning over, staring far out.

"How can you tell all that?" Michaella asked. "I can only see the dust."

"The dust is parted so that it shows the rider in the lead," Spotted Wolf explained. "He is quite a distance in the lead, but they are all coming straight toward us. It is hard to tell unless you know the signs."

Sorrel was cursing. "My eyes can't make out what they used to. I'm too damn old."

"What are you complaining about?" Mary Catherine asked, trying to encourage him. "As it is, you can see better than most."

"I ain't worried about seein' the horses. I just can't make out the rider in the lead. Some years back, that would have been easy for me."

Michaella and Mary Catherine both looked at him with astonishment. The riders were miles away. But as the sisters looked to Spotted Wolf, they could see that he knew who the rider in the lead was.

"It's Jean Patrick, without his buckskin shirt." Spotted Wolf's voice held concern.

Michaella knew the fear that had suddenly welled up inside of her was justified. There was no question that Jean Patrick was riding toward them and the Sioux were right behind him.

Sorrel and Spotted Wolf were not particularly concerned that the Sioux would catch up with Jean Patrick; he had a sufficient lead on them and was riding a good horse. But they did worry about all of them outrunning the Sioux once Jean Patrick reached them. Jean Patrick's horse would be played out, while the Sioux had an extra horse or two apiece and would be able to jump from one to the other, often in midstride.

As Jean Patrick and the Sioux came even closer, it became evident to Michaella that Jean Patrick was not going to come to where they were waiting for him. He was turning off his course.

"Where's he going?" Michaella asked, her voice filled with worry.

Spotted Wolf spoke up. "He is turning to ride up the trails through the lower end of the mountains to reach the high country that much quicker."

Michaella became ever more distraught and said that she wished Jean Patrick would come to where they were.

"Hell, he don't know we're here!" Sorrel said in disgust. "He don't know where we are. He's just headed up into the high country, and I'll wager ten good horses I know right where he's going."

"Where?" Michaella demanded. "I have to know."

"What are you going to do, little lady, chase those Sioux away from him?" Sorrel asked.

"If I have to," Michaella said, her jaw tight. "I just want to know how we're going to find him."

Sorrel rubbed his chin. "Remember when Little Coyote said he had seen your father at the Medicine Wheel? That's sacred ground there. I'm sure that Jean Patrick is headed to the Medicine Wheel. If he can make it that far, the Sioux won't touch him. None of the tribes fight where there's a medicine wheel," Sorrel assured her.

Michaella felt her heart jump. As long as she new where he was going, she could find him. She vondered again why he had left the wagon train nd was now riding across the open by himself, vith the Sioux after him. But she could ask him hat question when she saw him again.

Sorrel pointed up to a switchback that led high nto the mountains.

"I figure if we go up that trail, we can likely get o the Medicine Wheel the same time as Jean Patick. If we don't get there at least by then, the Sioux vill find us, and we'll be the ones runnin' for over."

They began to ride up from the foothills toward he mountains once again. Spotted Wolf stayed in ront with Sorrel, stopping at times to look out rom a high place into the distance. Mary Catherne had wondered, ever since leaving the wagon rain, if Spotted Wolf didn't wish he had stayed with Jean Patrick to help him. But she realized his ove for her had kept him with her, no matter what his loyalty to Jean Patrick.

They reached the trails that led up into the high country. It seemed to Michaella as if endless hours had gone by while the horses took them ever higher. They rode as fast as they could without tiring the horses badly, easing them along over the higher, steeper trails.

They stopped to water the horses often and even let them graze on occasion to keep up their strength. All the while both Sorrel and Spotted Wolf were assuring Michaella that Jean Patrick was doing the same thing so that his own horse could last the distance and the climb.

"Does he know the way to the Medicine Wheel?" Michaella asked Sorrel.

"He knows all these mountains. He's young, but he's been all over this country."

But her worries would not leave her. "Can Jean Patrick fight that many warriors if they catch him?" Michaella asked.

"He's not crazy enough to stop and fight," Sorrel assured her. "Don't think for a minute that Jean Patrick ain't got it all figured out. That man of yours has a lot of tricks up his sleeve. He didn't grow up out here and keep his hair like he has without plenty of savvy."

The encouragement did little to calm Michaella's nerves. She wanted to reach Jean Patrick as quickly as possible. She would go out and fight the Sioux by herself, if that's what it took. Jean Patrick was coming back to her, and she wasn't about to let anything come in the way of that.

Bisler was in heaven, as was LaRange. They had found a full jug of whiskey sitting in an abandoned wagon along the trail. Someone had overlooked it or had decided it wasn't worth taking.

They drank in front of the fire and asked Ketchman repeatedly about the gold. Ketchman only said that the Bighorn Mountains were just ahead and that there was gold in them. He didn't want to say anything else. He knew he had to keep stringing them along some way.

Ketchman also noticed that in his drunken state Bisler kept taking a piece of paper out of his pocket and looking at it, then grinning at Ketchman. After a time it made Ketchman very uneasy, until Bisler slumped over with the paper resting on the ground just beyond his fingers.

LaRange had passed out awhile before and was snoring loudly. Ketchman became more and more curious about the piece of paper, and when he finally decided Bisler wasn't going to awaken, he began to sneak over.

Ketchman worked his way carefully. The fire popped once and it scared him, but then he continued ahead. Finally he got to Bisler and reached down for the piece of paper. Holding his breath, Ketchman stepped back from Bisler and into the shadows, where he read the note.

It was a letter written by one of the Intermountain Fur Company executives. It was addressed to Bisler and stated that he was to find the gold on behalf of the company and was to "proceed with every means available to insure that Henry Chattilion no longer controls any stock in the Intermountain Fur Company." Ketchman read on to where the letter stated in part that Bisler was also to "do whatever necessary to insure the safety of the gold then remove all those associated with it."

Ketchman was shocked and angered. It was obvious the company had been using him and had every intention of getting rid of him. He didn't sleep well that night, despite the fact that both Bisler and LaRange had passed out from the whiskey. He would keep the piece of paper in his boot under one of the soles, and Bisler would never know. With the wind that was coming up, Ketchman knew he would have no trouble convincing Bisler that whatever he had been looking at had blown away.

When dawn came, Ketchman fixed himself breakfast while Bisler and LaRange continued to sleep. He didn't want to think anymore about the note. Instead he would concentrate solely on reaching the gold. The Sioux were still a problem, but now he realized LaRange and Bisler were even more of a threat than he had originally thought.

Bisler and LaRange finally came awake, complaining of aching heads. Bisler seemed to have forgotten completely the letter he had fallen asleep reading, and went about fixing himself something to eat without any thought of it.

Ketchman worried that the Chattilion women would get too far ahead of them, and he tried to hurry Bisler and LaRange.

"Don't you think we should be getting on the trail?" Ketchman asked Bisler. "That gold is just waiting for us."

"What's your hurry all of a sudden? First you want to lay back for a couple of days and let them Sioux settle down, and now you want to ride right into the middle of them. I can't figure you out."

"I'm just anxious is all. Aren't you?"

"Wait till we finish breakfast, at least," Bisler snarled. "It won't be that long."

Ketchman grew even more anxious when a group of trappers appeared, their horses at a slow gallop. Both Bisler and LaRange stood up to see if they knew any of the riders. Ketchman tried to remain calm, but realized this could mean a further delay of anywhere from a couple of hours to all day. When trappers got together, they generally talked for a long time.

"Mornin'," Bisler said to the trappers as they rode into camp. "Where you be comin' from?"

"Back on the Sweetwater." The man who answered was young and blond and big, with a thick wolfskin cap down nearly over his eyes. "Care if we use your fire to cook? We ain't eaten all day."

Ketchman welcomed them and they made themselves at home. There were five trappers, and they all got down from their horses immediately. Some of them brought packs over to sit on, and another brought some buffalo meat that he started to unwrap to place in a pan over the fire.

The men began trading stories, and Ketchman fought to control his impatience. He didn't particularly care to hear any stories; he merely wanted to get on the trail of the Chattilion sisters. One of the trappers got to talking about a wagon train they had met at the Sweetwater Crossing, and how the young scout had invited them in for a meal.

"His name was Jean Patrick. Caleb Marshall was with us back there, and he recognized the young scout. Said he knew Jean Patrick's pappy way back when he lived with the Crows." The trapper shook his head and laughed. "Damnedest thing. Old Caleb led that passel of greenhorns in their wagons across the mountains. Craziest thing I ever saw a man do."

Ketchman was listening intently now. "Did you say the scout's name was Jean Patrick?"

The trapper nodded. "That was his name, for sure. When Caleb said he would guide the group, Jean Patrick headed out for the Black Hills. He was tickled to death to hear about old Henry Chattillion."

LaRange stepped forward and grabbed the trapper by the front of his buckskin shirt. "What did you just say about Chattilion?" he demanded.

The other trappers stopped eating. The big blond one grabbed his Hawken rifle and cocked the hammer back.

"LaRange! Let him go!" Bisler was yelling right in LaRange's face, and LaRange released the trapper and stepped back. Bisler stared hard at LaRange for a while longer.

"He's got something against Henry Chattilion it seems," Ketchman told the trappers quickly. "Don't mind him. He didn't mean anything by it. Now, what were you saying about Jean Patrick and Henry Chattilion?"

None of the trappers answered Ketchman. Instead, they gathered their things and began to walk to their horses. Without another word they rode off in the direction of Fort Laramie.

"You could have got us all killed!" Bisler yelled at LaRange when the trappers were gone. "I swear sometimes you ain't got the brains to piss downwind."

LaRange frowned.

"Enough of that," Ketchman said. "We've got to get to the Black Hills before those Sioux decide to come across. We haven't got a lot of time."

"Yeah, I heard that trapper say Chattilion was in the Black Hills," Bisler said, looking suspiciously at Ketchman. "I thought you said last night that Chattilion was in the Bighorns, and that you knew the gold was in the Bighorns."

"I didn't say that exactly," Ketchman stuttered. "I said that the map showed gold in the Bighorns, but Chattilion and the main strike are in the Black Hills. That's what I said."

"That ain't what you said," Bisler argued.

"You can't remember, you were so drunk," Ketchman said. "Besides, we've got to get going and quit arguing or that gold won't do any of us any good. The Sioux will find us."

Bisler suddenly remembered the letter. He felt in his pockets and when he didn't find it, he looked up at Ketchman.

"Was I readin' a letter from home last night?" Bisler asked. He wanted to refer to the letter, and hoped that Ketchman didn't know what the letter contained. "It was a letter from my family," he lied. "Did you see me readin' it?"

"I saw you reading a letter," Ketchman said. "But you fell asleep and so did I. Maybe the wind blew it away."

Bisler cursed loudly. He looked around camp for a time, still cursing, until he finally gave up and got his horse ready to leave. He looked at Ketchman a number of times while he saddled up and got his things packed.

Ketchman found himself tightening up inside. He was sure that Bisler knew he had seen the letter. He wondered what he would say if Bisler finally asked him if he'd taken the letter. Of course, he would tell Bisler the same thing—that the wind had blown it away. He could only hope Bisler would believe him, and not press the matter.

In addition to the letter from the company, there were other problems Ketchman had to deal with. It seemed to him that LaRange was itching to kill him, and could try it at any time. And now Bisler was suspicious about both the letter and the supposed map he had in his head telling where the gold was.

Fortunately the Black Hills weren't that far off. A few days' hard riding and they would be at the north end of the range—where the map had indicated GOLD. Ketchman knew that when they got there and found the gold and old Henry Chattilion, he would then have to make the decision as to whether it would be Bisler or LaRange who would be the first to die.

Chapter Twenty-Two

IT WAS WELL into the afternoon when they got to the Medicine Wheel. It didn't appear to be much more than a wide circle of rocks in a big, open meadow, but Spotted Wolf assured them that just from the feeling he was getting this was a place of real power.

Michaella could feel the power herself. There was something in the air, something that united the ground here with the high, wide sky, making it a very special place. With the power came a sudden feeling of peace and tranquillity.

Michaella, no longer as worried about Jean Patrick, felt sure that he was not far away and that the Sioux hadn't even bothered to follow him past the first section of low hills on the south end. They knew he was going to the Medicine Wheel, and they weren't about to kill someone at the Medicine Wheel, not without suffering dire consequences.

Michaella and the others had been at the Medicine Wheel but a short time when Jean Patrick appeared. Michaella raced to her horse with glee. She waved and yelled as she vaulted onto its back and kicked the animal into a gallop.

When Jean Patrick spotted her, he kicked his own mount into a run. Michaella met him in an open meadow, and the two of them jumped down from their horses and ran into each other's arms.

"Thank God!" she said with a catch in her voice. He felt warm and strong, and she rubbed her tear-streaked face against his bare chest. "We saw you running from the Sioux. Up until a short time ago, I was afraid they would catch you."

"I had too big a lead on them," Jean Patrick said, giving her a tight hug. "I didn't expect to find all of you up here."

"We certainly didn't expect to see you riding across the open with the Sioux right behind you, either," Michaella said. "What happened to your shirt?"

Jean Patrick pulled it from a parfleche bag he had tied to his saddle. "I was getting some sun and didn't have time to put it back on after those Sioux found me," he teased.

Michaella smiled. "Just out for a Sunday ride, were you? I can't believe you're here."

Mary Catherine rode up with Spotted Wolf and Sorrel, who both greeted Jean Patrick with handshakes and back clapping.

"You're lucky we saw your dust or we wouldn't have gotten up here to meet you," Sorrel said.

"I guess missing Michaella was what caused me to be so reckless in riding across the open like that," Jean Patrick said with a frown. He had taken a grave chance. "I should have traveled slower and at night, but I didn't want to take the extra time."

Michaella handed him his medicine bundle. "It worked. There is something in it that told me you were in trouble," she said. "You can have it back, now that you're staying with me . . . aren't you?"

Jean Patrick laughed. "I'm staying with you. Forever, if that's all right with you."

"Who's takin' the wagons on to Oregon?" Sorrel wanted to know.

"You'll never believe it," Jean Patrick said with a laugh. He told them the story about Caleb Marshall and the other mountain men riding into camp at the Sweetwater Crossing. "Caleb is taking the wagons onward. That was a good stroke of luck."

"Caleb Marshall?" Sorrel said with a wide grin.

Jean Patrick grinned too. "I told him who I had been riding with and he warned me to watch out for you, especially around mealtime. He told me that you and he and some others were once trapping up on the Three Forks and you ate all his sourdough pancakes before any of the other men in your party even woke up!"

Everyone laughed, and Sorrel shrugged it off, saying he had liked sourdough pancakes at the time. But he had eaten so many that day that he had gotten sick and hadn't touched one since. "Old Caleb kind of soured me on sourdough."

Everyone went back to the Medicine Wheel. Since it was getting late in the afternoon, Michaella suggested they fix a hot meal before moving on. They all worked together to cut some firewood and put together a filling stew made from wild roots and some buffalo jerky they had with them.

After the meal, Spotted Wolf lamented the fact that there wasn't a medicine man around so that they could have a ceremony within the Medicine Wheel. He said he knew the prayers they could use, but a pipe ceremony would almost insure that they would find Michaella and Mary Catherine's father.

"We have a good chance of doing just that," Jean Patrick spoke up. "I was going to keep it to myself until I was sure, but old Caleb said he knows where Henry Chattilion is."

Both Michaella and Mary Catherine asked Jean Patrick at the same time what he had learned.

"Caleb told me that a while back he ran into your father over in the Black Hills. He must certainly be over there still."

Sorrel looked at them and winked. "What did I tell you?"

The two sisters got up and hugged one another, then began to jump around. This was the best and most concrete news they had heard. Jean Patrick went on to say that according to old Caleb, he had come upon their father living in a small cabin nestled way back in a canyon on the north side of the mountains—just past a hillside that had been burned off by a small lightning fire just the year before. It wouldn't be hard to find once they got into the area.

Michaella and Mary Catherine packed right away. There were still the Sioux to worry about, but they were behind and would have to ride hard to catch up. The last phase of their long journey seemed to be filled with hope, and nothing must stop them now from getting over to the Black Hills.

Ketchman found himself in a battle of nerves with Bisler and LaRange. They had been pressuring him with every possible argument to lead them to the gold right away, to prove to them that he indeed had knowledge of where it was. Ketchman kept his counsel the entire time, pointing out sagely that it would be foolish to make a move anywhere until they were safe from the Sioux.

All three had been watching the Sioux for the better part of a day. The Sioux sent out scouts on both sides of the mountains to see where Jean Patrick would lead the group down and where they would go from there. The main war party had no reason to go up on top, for they knew that it would just cost them time to try and follow them back down again.

Two days of following the Sioux at a distance was tiring, and Ketchman became nervous. They had to be cautious at all times; certainly they could risk no fires, and they got very little sleep, as they moved by day and also by night to keep up with the Sioux. Ketchman had learned how to sleep on horseback. It wasn't nearly as restful as being

retched out on the ground, but it was better than
oing without any sleep at all.
Finally on the morning of the third day, Ketch-
ıan and the other two watched the war party
ather in a council. They spent a long time discuss-
ıg something. When they were finished, they all
ıounted their ponies and turned immediately
own a small stream that led out onto the flats.
hey were in a hurry and seemed to know right
here they were going.
"They're headed for Powder River," Bisler com-
ıented dryly. "That will take them to a place
here it's easy to cut off to the north end of the
lack Hills." Bisler then turned to Ketchman. "Is
hat where the gold is?"
"I'm not telling you where the gold is," Ketch-
ıan said.
"I'm tired of this!" Bisler flared.
"Don't you think Michaella and Mary Catherine
re headed into the Black Hills for the same reason
ve are?" Ketchman asked. "Hasn't it occurred to
ou that they are looking for their father, who
appens to be where the gold is?"
"Then we don't need you anymore, do we?"
isler said, rising to his feet.
"You can't shoot me," Ketchman said. "I have
our guns." He was trying to appear nonchalant.
'Besides, the Black Hills have an awful lot of can-
ons. You could never find the gold without my
ıelp."
"We can just follow the Sioux to Jean Patrick and
he rest of them now," Bisler growled. "Like I said,
ve don't need you."

Ketchman was still calm, which bothered Bisle
Indeed, Ketchman seemed even more sure of hir
self now.

"And what if the Sioux kill Jean Patrick and th
others before they reach Henry Chattilion and th
gold?" he asked. "Then where would you two be?

LaRange, who seldom spoke, sat gazing out t
where the Sioux were riding into the distance.

After a moment's thought, Bisler decided h
would rather find the gold with Ketchman leadin
them than kill Ketchman and take the chance c
not finding it.

"You can go with us and show us the gold
then," Bisler said. "But don't you try and get away
Sioux or no Sioux, we'll cut you up and hang yo
out to dry."

Jean Patrick and Sorrel led the way down th
west slope of the Bighorn Mountains and into th
valley below. It was a broad basin filled with hc
mineral springs and frequented by buffalo. Mi
chaella heard Jean Patrick say the northern en
was generally home to some Crow Indian band
while the southern end of the valley, near the Win
River Mountains, was Shoshone country. Becaus
of both tribes, the Sioux rarely came into this place

From discussions with Jean Patrick and Sorre
Michaella knew that the fastest way to get into th
Black Hills and avoid the Sioux was to go aroun
the north end of the Bighorns and cross the head
waters of the Tongue River; then cross the ope
and dangerous Powder River country and get int
the Black Hills from the north.

It was a tiring trip, as they kept moving day and ight. To give the horses rest, they often traveled foot. The north end of the Bighorns was filled vith rugged canyons, and Michaella began to tire f the rocks and steep trails. She knew they were ll suffering, but it would be worth it once they eached the Black Hills.

They left the Bighorn and traveled across the oothills to reach the red-canyon country of the 'ongue River. From there they crossed a wide ex-anse of rolling sagebrush hills where buffalo ran n large groups. This was Sioux country again, and nore than once Jean Patrick stopped them and had hem take cover wherever they could.

"There are scouts all over these hills," he told Aichaella in sign language. "We can't be too care-ul."

"I just want this to end," she signed back to him, ıer strength at a low ebb. "I want to find my ather."

"Soon," Jean Patrick said to reassure her.

Two full days of traveling slowly and carefully rought them across the Powder River country. They rode into the north end of the low mountain ange the Sioux called the Sacred Hills. The Black Hills, as the emigrants and frontiersmen knew hem, were impressive in their own unique beauty, hough they lacked the towering peaks of the Big-ıorns and the other ranges to the west.

Michaella was overjoyed. Traveling with caution ıad paid off—no fires and talking only in sign anguage had kept them from dying at the hands of he Sioux.

The day was hot and the flies bothered the horses

so badly they had to let them stand in creeks an
streams for a time to give them relief. As the
wound their way through the many canyons at th
north end of the mountains, they stopped often t
rest and take small naps. Michaella strove to kee
her frustration in check; they were so near, ye
they still hadn't found her father.

Late in the afternoon a mammoth thunderstorr
welled up from the west, and soon the thunde
and lightning were filling the canyons. The thun
der was deafening, and as the rain started to slas
down, they were forced to find cover as best the
could under a grove of cottonwoods near a stream

They dismounted and Michaella huddled wit
Jean Patrick under a tree. He was not bothered b
the sudden storm, but something he saw suddenl
made him jump nervously.

"Quick, everyone!" he said. "Get on your horse
and follow me."

Jean Patrick pointed and Michaella turned wit
the others to see what had caused his sudde
alarm. Just down the creek, partially obscured b
the storm, was a war party of Sioux. The Indian
had already seen them and were kicking thei
horses into a dead run.

"Ride hard!" Jean Patrick yelled. "And for God'
sake, don't stop!"

As the rain continued to pour down in sheets
Michaella and Mary Catherine stayed close to
gether, riding their horses blindly through the
storm. They could hear the three men behind them
firing their rifles and yelling at them to keep riding
not to stop for anything. Michaella turned aroun
to look, but the storm was so bad that it was im

possible to see where Jean Patrick was or what was happening behind them.

The downpour continued, and Michaella and Mary Catherine found themselves riding up a steep canyon. The horses were strong and were doing a good job of picking their way along the trail. Michaella worried about Jean Patrick and the other men, for there was still a lot of shooting going on down below.

The rain finally began to let up, and a short way farther they stopped briefly to let the horses rest. The rain let up even more, and Michaella heard Mary Catherine yelling with glee as Spotted Wolf rode up the trail toward them. He took them into a grove of aspens, where they hid the horses and began to look down into the bottom for signs of Sorrel and Jean Patrick.

"I don't know what happened to them," Spotted Wolf said. "I know Jean Patrick was with me not long ago, but he turned off up a canyon in the rain. We split up so that the Sioux would have more trouble catching us."

Once again thunder sounded from above, and the sky released heavy torrents of rain. Michaella couldn't stand just to wait and wonder about Jean Patrick—she had to find him.

"Please stay here with Mary Catherine," she said to Spotted Wolf. "I'm going to look for Jean Patrick."

Michaella did not want to listen as both Mary Catherine and Spotted Wolf pleaded with her to remain there, at least for a while longer. Michaella pointed out that she had suffered without Jean Patrick long enough and wasn't going to spend

another moment wondering as to his well-being
She rode back down the trail in the rain, searching as best she could for any sign of Jean Patrick. She rode back to the bottom and then along the trail they had taken into the mountains. The thunderstorm continued, and there was still no sign of Jean Patrick—or Sorrel either, for that matter—and she became gravely concerned.

Then, from the storm four riders appeared. They were Sioux warriors. Michaella knew they had split up to look for Jean Patrick, and now she was in trouble. She raised her rifle but realized she could do no good against four. Besides, they had seen her already and were kicking their ponies into a run.

Michaella turned her horse and started back up the hill, but her horse slipped and she felt herself falling sideways. The rise of the hill was right next to her, and she pulled her leg free of the stirrup and jumped off into the mud before her horse could slide down onto its side and pin her. Then the horse regained its footing and ran off into the rain before she could remount.

Now Michaella began to run. She held on to her rifle, knowing she would have to use it very soon. She kept falling in the mud, and the rain made visibility poor. She heard the Sioux coming up behind her and she turned to see them take shape in the rain. The warrior in the lead got off his pony and walked over to her.

Michaella raised her rifle, but the powder was wet from the storm and the gun would not fire. The warrior seemed to know this, for he did not hesitate when she aimed at him and pulled the rigger. He merely walked up and took the gun from her.

"What do you want with me?" she asked him in sign language.

He was smiling. He signed back to her and she understood every terrible word.

"You are mine," he said. "Now you are mine."

Chapter Twenty-Three

MICHAELLA WAS PULLED roughly to her feet. The face of the warrior leering through the rain terrified her. He held her arm tightly and turned back around to say something to the other three.

Shivering, Michaella wished she could speak the Sioux language. The warrior's fingers were like steel bands cutting into the tender flesh of her arm, and she knew there was no point in a struggle. It would be futile and dangerous. She closed her eyes against the pain of his grip and concentrated, wishing she had given Jean Patrick a medicine bundle of her own to wear around his neck. Perhaps it would have endowed him with the special magic he needed to find her.

Dear God, where is Jean Patrick? I need you, my love.

It seemed that even without the medicine bundle, Jean Patrick had used his own brand of magic to find Michaella. A shot rang out, burning past her in an angry buzz. Even as she flinched away, Michaella became aware of the warrior's loosened grip. Wrenching away, she watched as the Sioux pitched forward with an expression of stunned disbelief on his face.

In the space of only a few seconds—though it seemed to Michaella that events were moving at a turtle's pace—another shot rang out and a second warrior fell, plummeting from his horse to the ground with a wordless cry. After only the briefest of hesitations, the other two warriors abandoned their captured prize and whirled their ponies around. They fled up the rocky slope, the blinding storm swallowing them in an instant.

Rain poured down on her head, and she clawed at the wet ropes of dark hair in her eyes, turning to see her rescuer. It was Jean Patrick, of course, and she recognized his rough voice as he half slid, half climbed down the steep slope above her.

"Hurry!" came the swift order through the sheets of rain. "Let's get out of here before they change their minds and come back!"

He arrived at the foot of the slope in a shower of red mud and rock grit, his black hair plastered to his head and his features blurred with rain. But in the dim light Michaella could see his teeth gleam in a grin, and was reassured. Did nothing daunt this man's spirits?

"Here," he was saying, shoving something wet and limp into her hands. "Tie this on your rifle and sling it around your neck like I've got mine."

Only then did Michaella notice that Jean Patrick

had tied a thin leather strip to his rifle stock and trigger guard and was using it to carry his rifle and free his hands. Bending, she scooped up her rifle from the ground and followed Jean Patrick, who had already turned and was sliding along the rain-slick rocks of the trail.

His huge bay was hidden behind an outcropping of rocks, and he vaulted into the saddle and put out a hand for Michaella. "Come on!" he urged. "And hang on tight. The main war party isn't far behind."

With that comforting news ringing in her ears, Michaella was hauled onto the bay, barely having time to wrap her arms around Jean Patrick before the horse bounded forward. Rain pelted them unmercifully, and she thought longingly of drier weather as the horse slipped and slid along the trail. Jean Patrick's unwieldy rifle banged against her tender skin as they rode, and she could feel the harsh bite of the leather strap holding her rifle cutting across her neck and shoulder.

As uncomfortable as it was, she was grateful for the unusual method of carrying the rifle a few moments later.

"Grab the next limb and hang on!" Jean Patrick yelled as they rode beneath a huge cottonwood.

Startled, Michaella instinctively did as he commanded. She found herself dangling from a stout tree limb with her feet several feet above the ground. Following Jean Patrick's instructions, she edged her way hand over hand along the branch as he was doing.

When they reached the rain-slick trunk and

rested at the apex of limb and trunk, she looked at him. "Now what do we do?"

"Go from this tree into the next one," was his grinning reply.

Michaella wasn't certain if he was serious. She looked from him to the next tree several feet away and shook her head. "I can't do that! Do you think I'm a monkey?"

"Personal opinions aside, I think you can do it," he said, laughing at her indignation. "And besides—we don't have time to argue or think of anything else." He cocked his head in the direction from which they'd come. "The Sioux—remember?"

"Lead on," she grumbled, thinking that since arriving in this vast country, she had done things she'd never thought she could do. Though America was her birthplace, England seemed infinitely more civilized—and certainly less interesting!

Several minutes and several trees farther on, Michaella paused to blow on her bruised palms and fingers. The rough, wet bark had torn skin and left splinters, and she knew her hands would never work properly again, but they were quite a way from where they had begun. Once she had almost fallen while leaping from one tree branch to the next, but Jean Patrick had plucked her from the air and swung her next to him. She had banged against the trunk and jarred every bone in her body, but she had not fallen. Now they waited.

"They'll be following our tracks, and hopefully my old horse will lead them on a long, circling trail," he whispered into her ear, his breath warm against her chilled flesh.

Michaella nodded numbly. The rifle had grown heavier and heavier, and she sagged against the comfort of Jean Patrick's tight body. How was it that she was the only one who was so tired? Did the man's energy never flag?

Then his hand tightened on her arm as he motioned for her to remain still and quiet. Tensing, Michaella heard the faint clatter of hooves on rocks and saw the ghostly shapes of Sioux passing through the rain. They had gone much farther from the original trail than she'd thought, for the Indians were very far away.

When they passed on, he gave the signal and they slid down from the tree. Michaella stood shakily for a moment, then followed Jean Patrick through the thick undergrowth. She hoped Mary Catherine and Spotted Wolf were still hiding in the aspens, and that Sorrel had found them.

Reaching the aspen grove at last, Michaella fell into her sister's arms. She was too weary to weep, but Mary Catherine's face was streaming with tears as well as rain.

"I thought you were gone forever," she sobbed into her older sister's drenched blouse.

"No, Jean Patrick rescued me." Michaella sat abruptly on a rock and managed a reassuring smile. "I should have known he would. He always manages to arrive in time, it seems."

Slanting a glance at the lean-bodied man standing a few feet away and talking quietly with Spotted Wolf, Mary Catherine said softly, "I hope so. I think he is the right man for you, Michaella."

"You do?" Michaella looked at her in surprise. "Why do you say that?"

"A lot of reasons. One is that you are not the same girl you once were. Oh, you're better!" she added hastily. "I mean, it used to bother me that you never had any real emotions." A shy smile curved her mouth as she gazed at Michaella's stunned face. "Nothing ever bothered you on the outside. I knew you would be hurt, or that you wanted to cry, but you never would. It was only after you met Jean Patrick that you allowed your true emotions to show, and that has to be good. Do you see what I mean?"

Considering for a moment, Michaella finally nodded. "Yes, I think I do. I suppose I did keep everything inside. It seemed safer that way, not to let anyone know if I did or didn't care what they did and how it affected me. You know, after Papa left I was angry for a long time. I did not understand why he never came back, never wrote, and I used to dream of finding him and telling him how much I hated him. That's the real reason I came out here, to live out the fantasy I'd carried for years. Then, after meeting Jean Patrick and listening to him talk about the mountains and how they made a man feel, I began to understand a little of what our father must have felt. Not that what he did was right, but at least now I have some understanding. Jean Patrick taught me to love, Mary Catherine."

Her sister nodded. "Yes. I know," she said softly.

They gazed at each other in new understanding as the rain dripped from aspen leaves and the wind blew in chilly gusts.

Glancing toward Mary Catherine and Michaella,

Spotted Wolf asked, "Where is Sorrel? I thought he was with you?"

"He was. We got separated when Michaella was captured. Then I lost him in the storm. I don't know what happened."

"The Sioux?"

Jean Patrick shook his head. "I don't think so. Sorrel is too foxy to be caught by them."

"Why don't you sound more certain?"

Shrugging, Jean Patrick had no answer. He wasn't certain. He only hoped the old mountain man had not been captured by the band of Sioux.

"We'll wait for a while," Spotted Wolf said, and Jean Patrick nodded.

"Yes. We'll wait for a while."

They waited for over an hour, until the sky began to clear, the clouds scudding overhead in a breeze-whipped rush. Mary Catherine rode behind Spotted Wolf, and Jean Patrick and Michaella rode her horse. Clattering up the trail as the sun came out and brightened the hills, they realized they had come up the canyon to its end. It was a box canyon. Rising all around them were high, steep walls of rock, ascending to a small cliff at the crest. To leave, they would have to retrace their steps or climb the walls hand over hand, and that would be risky.

At the very top of the steep hill, resting at the edge of the cliff, was a series of large boulders. Jean Patrick whistled and commented that if any one of them ever came down the hill, the whole canyon would be blocked with rocks. He explained that it looked as if part of the hill had broken off at some time in the distant past, for the bottom of the canyon contained a large number of boulders and rocks. It was impossible to tell how long ago the boulders had fallen down, but it was apparent it had changed the canyon when it had happened.

Then Michaella noticed a small cabin nestled back near the base of the high hill and cliff. Her heart gave a start and she turned and pointed it out to Mary Catherine. It was hidden in the trees and hard to see at first. Jean Patrick and Spotted Wolf both showed interest but made the girls stay back until they had investigated.

"Who do you suppose lives there?" Michaella asked Jean Patrick.

"There's only one way to find out," Jean Patrick said. "But let's be careful."

Jean Patrick led the way, his rifle across his saddle, ready to use if need be. It didn't appear as if anyone had come up the canyon ahead of them, but the rain had wiped out all signs of old tracks and they couldn't be sure. They rode slowly, listening all the while and watching the entire canyon for any signs of movement.

From the outside, the cabin looked as if it had been abandoned for some time. It was weathered and there was a lot of brush growing in front of the door. Inside was an old stove covered with rust where water had run down through the leaky roof. The dirt floor was dank and musty from dampness and lack of sunlight. Remnants of crude, homemade wooden furniture showed where rodents had been gnawing on the arms and legs over the years.

Michaella and Mary Catherine looked at one another in disappointment. Michaella said out loud what both of them were thinking: "Do you suppose Father ever lived here?"

No one answered. It was obvious someone had, but not in the recent past. Jean Patrick pointed out that the cabin had been vacant for much longer than a year.

"You have to remember, old Caleb told me that he saw your father more recently than that," Jean Patrick told Michaella. "There's still hope. He's likely living in another canyon."

Michaella walked nervously around the inside of the cabin. She wanted to think that Jean Patrick was right—that her father was living up a nearby canyon. It wrenched her heart to think he had once lived here and something had happened to him.

She went to a back window and looked out at the hillside behind. Her eyes widened and her breath caught in her throat. Mary Catherine asked her what was wrong, and she told them all to come and see for themselves.

"Look at that," she said. "That's unbelievable."

They looked out the window through the trees to see a faint glimmer barely visible where the sun struck the rocks. Speechless with apprehension, Michaella cleared her throat and finally managed to ask, "What is it?"

"Pyrite," Jean Patrick answered decisively. "It's not what it looks like. But"—he paused for effect—"often pyrite is close to the real thing."

Disappointment laced her voice as Mary Catherine said, "I thought it was gold."

"Maybe it's not, but have you ever heard the saying, Where there's smoke there's fire?"

"What's that got to do with this?" Mary Catherine asked crossly.

"Let's get some picks and go see."

Michaella followed Jean Patrick outside and down a narrow path that was hidden by clumps of trees and thick underbrush on both sides. It had been a trick of the light, she decided as they drew near, for the glitter faded and disappeared the closer they got.

"It's probably only visible from a certain spot at a certain time," Jean Patrick answered. Shouldering a pick he had found in the cabin, he pursed his lips in a tuneless whistle that Michaella found particularly annoying.

What was even more annoying was his nonchalant reaction when he had labored with his pick for the better part of an hour and hacked away nothing but the metal known as "fool's gold."

"Is this what we came so far to find?" Michaella wondered aloud, unable to keep the bitterness from her voice.

Jean Patrick looked at her. "I thought you came to find your father."

"You know my reasons," was her terse answer, but she could not face him. It was all so mixed up in her mind now, the long years of hating an absent father melding with the realization that he might very well be dead. Henry Chattilion had been a myth. And the gold that might have made it all worthwhile seemed to have been a myth, too.

Letting the pick swing to the ground, Jean Patrick leaned on the handle and gazed at her closely. "So, have you decided if you're sorry you made this journey?"

Startled by his perception, Michaella's dark head swung up and her large, thick-lashed eyes widened even more, giving her, he thought, the look of a startled doe.

"Sorry?" She thought for a moment, then said slowly, "No, how can I be sorry when I have you?"

"Then I'm more important than finding your father? More important than finding gold?"

"Jean Patrick," she said feelingly, "you are more important than *anything!*"

He grinned. "That's what I've waited to hear, love!" Jerking up the pick again, he moved a few feet farther down the rock and swung it with all his strength. A large portion of rock came away, and the rock around it crumbled. Mary Catherine and Spotted Wolf leaped back in alarm as rocks showered down on them, but Michaella was riveted to the spot. A bright yellow vein snaked through the rock in a glittering, gleaming shine that was definitely not pyrite.

Ketchman sat his horse at the entrance to the canyon, listening to Bisler and LaRange argue about what had happened to the Sioux and to Jean Patrick and the others. They had followed the Sioux into the mountains, barely keeping ahead of a fierce storm. Now that the weather had cleared, they didn't know where to find them.

Hunkered on his heels, Bisler was studying the ground. "The rain ruined all the tracks. Maybe the Sioux got them."

As Bisler was talking, Ketchman caught sight of a stray horse wandering the edge of the timber along the ridge. He was certain that the horse belonged to the Arikara warrior Spotted Wolf. There was no mistaking the distinctive markings on the animal.

"I don't think the Sioux got them," Ketchman said, pointing to the horse on the ridge. "That horse up there belongs to that Arikara warrior. I'd bet good money on it."

Bisler looked to where Ketchman was pointing, and nodded. "Damned if you ain't got a keen eye for a city-bred type. I never would have thought it of you."

"You don't give me enough credit," Ketchman said.

"I'll give you credit when you make us rich," Bisler said. "Now that we know where they are, what do you say you take us to the gold?"

Ketchman thought a moment. "Maybe we had better find Henry Chattilion now and get him out of the way first."

"Take us to the gold first," Bisler said. "We can worry about Chattilion later. That gold is what's most important."

"It is important," Ketchman said. He was getting more uneasy all the time. "But if we don't get rid of everybody first, they might be harder to get rid of after I show you the gold."

"You know what?" Bisler said, leaning over with an ugly sneer on his face. "I don't think you even know where the gold is. I think you've been lyin' to us all this time. Ain't that right?"

"Listen, I'll take you to the gold first if you insist," Ketchman said. "If that's what you want.

But don't blame me if we have trouble because of it."

"No, you don't know where the gold is," Bisler repeated. "You've just been leadin' us on all this time." He reached for a hidden pistol tucked into his belt.

"Let me do it!" LaRange said with a sneer. "He didn't think about my knife."

"No," Bisler said, "we ain't got time for all that."

While the two men hesitated, Ketchman took the opportunity to kick his horse into a run. He ducked low over the saddle just as Bisler fired. The ball whizzed over his back. He kicked his horse as hard as he could and rode up the winding trail into the canyon. Bisler shot again and missed. Cursing, the pair kicked their horses into a run up the canyon behind Ketchman.

Ketchman had no idea where he was going. He was hoping the trail would take him up to the top, someplace past where he knew Jean Patrick and the Chattilion girls must be camped. He knew he had to get to the top and over if he stood a chance against Bisler and LaRange. Once on top, he knew his horse was fast enough to outdistance either of their horses.

Ketchman felt an icy fear come over him as he rode past a thick clump of trees and up to the end of the trail, where it stopped at a little abandoned cabin. Behind the cabin was only more trees, and he could see there was no trail beyond this point.

He cursed and jumped down from his horse. Taking his rifle with him, he ran behind the cabin and along a trail that led through a grove of trees.

He would have to make a stand and attempt to fight off Bisler and LaRange. He had no other choice.

Then Ketchman stopped in midstride to look at the hillside ahead of him. He couldn't believe his eyes. There was a solid patch of gold gleaming brightly. He could hear Bisler and LaRange running through the trees after him. Ketchman ducked behind cover.

"You wanted me to show you the gold," he yelled at them. "Well, is that enough gold for you?"

Bisler and LaRange broke through the trees to where they could see the hillside. There was a long silence and then Bisler began yelling.

"Yahoo! We're rich, we're rich!" he shouted.

Bisler and LaRange were both ecstatic. They ran past Ketchman, caring nothing at all that he might shoot them both. It didn't even cross their minds, so absorbed were they in getting up the slope.

Ketchman squinted at them and raised his rifle. He could do it anytime now, he thought as the two of them scrambled up the hillside, clawing and scratching at the ore with their fingers, completely oblivious of anything else.

He was just about to fire when he heard his horse nickering and turned around. His horse was turned, head up and ears pricked forward, looking down the trail at other horses that were coming up. Ketchman could see a number of horsemen making their way quickly along the trail. He couldn't see them clearly at first, but he didn't have to think long before he realized the Sioux had heard Bisler's gunfire and were coming after them.

Ketchman put his rifle down and turned from

he hill. He decided he'd better not shoot the two, s he might need all his ammunition later. Now he ad to get up the slope and over the cliff to get way from the Sioux.

Bisler and LaRange were still preoccupied with he gold. They weren't paying attention to the ickering horses, and they didn't even see Ketchnan run up the hill past them and begin the climb ip the cliff toward the top. Ketchman knew all he ad to do was get to the top. The Sioux would take are of Bisler and LaRange.

Chapter Twenty-Four

✦✦✦✦✦

MICHAELLA WAS STARTLED awake as the gunfire began n the canyon below. Jean Patrick had fallen asleep igainst the boulder and he and Spotted Wolf jerked iwake as well. Michaella shook Mary Catherine ind then grabbed her rifle and peered over the edge to see what was happening.

She could see the Sioux swarming through the rees behind the cabin. Behind her, Jean Patrick was cursing himself. The horses had disappeared, naving worked themselves loose from their hobbles, and Jean Patrick was saying, tired or not, he should have taken more care. Now they would have to stay under cover and forget about the horses—at least until this was over.

Michaella rested on her stomach at the edge of th
cliff. Mary Catherine worked her way alongside her
and Jean Patrick and Spotted Wolf joined them
Now, as they all peered carefully over the cliff, the
saw Ketchman and the other two headed up th
slope toward them, with Ketchman in the lead.

But the rain had made the footing treacherous
and all three men kept sliding back, all the whil
glancing down at the Sioux, who were yelling con
tinuously from the trees.

Michaella looked overhead and saw that anothe
thunderstorm that had been gathering on the hori
zon when she'd gone to sleep had moved in. Th
black clouds boiling ominously in the sky were rum
bling once again. She and Mary Catherine loade
their rifles with the last of their ammunition.

"Look!" Spotted Wolf said softly, nudging Jea
Patrick. "There are the horses!"

Leaning forward, Jean Patrick saw the flick of
tail and grinned. "Now if we can just get to them."

"I'll take Mary Catherine and go to the bottom,"
Spotted Wolf suggested. "We can take a position a
the opening of the canyon. We can hold off a lot o
men from there. They won't be able to come u
after us."

Agreeing, Jean Patrick squinted into the dis
tance. He muttered an observation that he an
Michaella were going to have a difficult time stand
ing everyone off from where they were, but tha
they had the advantage of shooting down fron
above.

Taking a deep breath, Michaella grabbed Mar
Catherine and gave her a hug. She didn't voice he
fears, but gave her sister a tremulous smile.

"Shoot straight," she said softly, and Mary Catherine nodded.

"I will."

Turning away, Mary Catherine gave Spotted Wolf her hand and they slid down the slope toward the grazing horses.

"She'll be fine," Jean Patrick said in Michaella's ear. "Don't worry."

Dry eyed and tight-lipped, Michaella managed a fleeting smile as she said, "I know."

They worked their way to the edge of the ridge and peered over. "There's Bisler and LaRange, but I don't see Ketchman anywhere," Jean Patrick murmured. "I can't understand where he went."

"What about the Sioux? They're not far behind and if . . . How will we manage to make a stand against all of them?"

Slowly shaking his head, Jean Patrick methodically loaded his rifle. "This is the last of my powder. We've got to make every shot count."

Staring glumly down the rock-studded slope, Michaella tried to think of all the military strategies she'd read about in the vast library at her aunt's house. The tactics of everyone from Alexander the Great to Napoleon had been bound in those dry and dusty leather volumes.

War whoops rose from below, and her throat tightened with panic. The Sioux. They must have sighted—who? Spotted Wolf and Mary Catherine, or Ketchman and his men? She closed her eyes, and in that moment of desperation an idea came to her.

"Jean Patrick!" she said, giving him a push. "The rocks can be pushed down on their heads!"

"What? On whose heads? Spotted Wolf and Mary Cath—"

"No, on the Sioux!" she snapped quickly "Hurry. If we can just get a large rock to start down the hillside—you remember what happened with the buffalo stampede?"

"What about your sister and Spotted Wolf?"

"They're on the other side," she said quickly "We'll shout down a warning."

Jean Patrick had stopped listening and begun looking for a suitable rock. A huge boulder was perched near the edge of the crest, but it was too large for them to send over the side.

"I'll make a lever," he said, and while Michaella peered anxiously over the edge and shouted down a warning to her sister, Jean Patrick found a dead tree. It went down easily, and he dragged it to the boulder.

Michaella worked alongside Jean Patrick, pushing and heaving, wedging the log at the bottom of the boulder and placing another rock beneath the log. Though not sturdy enough to send it over, it did loosen the boulder enough so that they were able to shift it. Sweat streamed down their faces in spite of the freshening wind and chill bite in the air. Rain began to splatter down again, and finally Jean Patrick felt the boulder grate loose.

"It's going!" he shouted, pushing with all his strength. He braced his palms against the rough surface and heaved again.

A pistol shot cracked and rock splinters flew, striking Jean Patrick on the cheek and leaving a long red scratch.

"Don't touch that boulder!" came the command.

Whirling around, Michaella and Jean Patrick saw Nolan Ketchman standing only a few yards away, aiming a pistol.

"If I don't, we'll have half the Sioux Nation in our pockets!" Jean Patrick snarled, rubbing at the blood trickling over his cheek.

"If you do, you're likely to bury that gold under tons of rock," Ketchman countered coolly. "I say leave it be."

"And do you know how else to keep the Sioux from decorating their lodges with our scalps?"

Lightning cracked, briefly illuminating the darker outlines of the approaching Sioux, and Ketchman hesitated. His eyes bulged and his mouth worked soundlessly as he saw the painted warriors, but the pistol didn't waver. "No, I—I have to have that gold!"

Realizing that he had no time to argue with Ketchman, Jean Patrick strained against the rock. His chest muscles flexed, and he gave a mighty push just as Ketchman fired his pistol at Jean Patrick.

"No!" Michaella screamed in horror, and acting quickly, stooped and flung a handful of pebbles into Ketchman's face. When he dropped the pistol, she reached down and threw a large rock, striking him heavily in the collarbone. She heard the faint crack of breaking bone and a choking, retching sound from Ketchman, but she had already turned to Jean Patrick.

"Are you hurt?" Blood soaked his right sleeve, and she grabbed anxiously for his arm.

"No, I'm not hurt. At least, not much. It's a flesh wound. Help me," he said in short gasps for air.

But the rock didn't need any more help to go careening over the side. Michaella leaned her hand against it to help him up, and it slid away from beneath her palm, arcing gracefully in the air for a moment before gravity forced it back down with a crashing thud and it bounced crazily down the slope.

Loud screams announced that someone was below, and she peered over the edge to see Bisler and LaRange clinging to the sides of the slope with frantic fingerholds. Below them were the Sioux, notching arrows to their bows. Realizing they were already dead no matter which reached them first, Bisler and LaRange let out more agonized howls that ended in high, keening screams as the boulder reached them first. Michaella turned away, shuddering as the huge rock crushed them into the side of the slope.

When she turned back, she saw that the Sioux had scattered out of the boulder's path. More rocks had begun to slide, and there was a loud rumble as they went rattling down the rain-soaked slope. The sound of rocks breaking loose almost drowned out the noise of the thunderstorm.

Not waiting to see if any Sioux escaped, Michaella turned back to Ketchman. He was groping for the pistol, and Jean Patrick surged to his feet and grabbed for it. Ketchman struggled. Both men were weak, and Michaella watched anxiously as they grappled for the pistol. They rolled on the ground, and when there was a sudden shot, she flinched. Neither man moved for a moment, and Michaella started forward with a horrified expression.

Then Jean Patrick rolled away from Ketchman and rose to his knees with the smoking pistol in his left hand. Blood was smeared from his face to his waist, and he was breathing harshly.

Ketchman lay sprawled on the rocks, his face pale and his mouth working. His fingers splayed over the wound in his chest. His thin legs shook, and he said hoarsely, "You killed me!"

"No, you've killed yourself," Jean Patrick disagreed, gazing dispassionately at the man. "You've no one to blame but yourself."

Michaella dropped to her knees, and Spotted Wolf and Mary Catherine arrived at that moment, surprised to see Ketchman lying on the ground. "We cut off the Sioux below," Spotted Wolf told Jean Patrick as he knelt beside him. "I don't think they'll be back for a while. Those that are still alive were running as fast as they could."

Jean Patrick grinned weakly. "Good."

"What's he doing here?" Mary Catherine asked, pointing a finger at Ketchman.

"I'm dying, that's what I'm doing here!" Ketchman said. He coughed again. "Here. Come here, girl!"

Glancing uncertainly at Spotted Wolf, Mary Catherine moved forward.

"There's a letter inside my left pocket," Ketchman said between coughing spasms. "I'll have my revenge if you'll do with it what I tell you . . . No, *left* pocket, girl! That's right, and don't tremble so. I'm dying and can't hurt you."

Mary Catherine handed the letter to Jean Patrick and shrank back against Spotted Wolf for comfort. Jean Patrick opened the folded paper and began to read aloud the instructions from the Intermountain Fur Company to secure the gold and then "remove all those connected with it."

"States it pretty plain, I'd say," he commented with a frown, refolding the letter and handing it to Michaella.

Ketchman nodded. "With that evidence, Henry Chattilion can have the company signed over to him."

"But first we have to find Henry Chattilion," Jean Patrick pointed out. "And that doesn't seem too easy."

Closing his eyes to conserve his strength, Ketchman said blindly, "There's a cabin in the canyon across from the gold. I saw it. It's being used, but I didn't see who lived there. Probably old Henry."

"Why do you want us to find him?" Michaella couldn't help asking. "You've done nothing but try to harm us."

A smile flickered briefly on Ketchman's bloodless lips. "Vengeance," he said simply. "The company has always tried to best me, always. . . ." Breaking off into another spasm, he shuddered once, then was still.

"He's dead," Jean Patrick said softly, more to himself than the others. He reached out and passed a hand over Ketchman's face.

"Do you think he was right about another cabin?" Mary Catherine asked.

"Hard to say," Jean Patrick responded. "Let's get him buried and get out of here."

They covered Ketchman with a cairn of stones. The rain had finally stopped, and they worked their way down the trail. Finding extra horses abandoned by the Sioux at the bottom, they each took a mount. A short way into the canyon, they rounded a sharp curve in the trail.

Sitting in the midde, astride his horse with two mules on a pack string behind him, sat Sorrel.

"By all hell!" he yelled. "I thought I'd never see the likes of you again! I thought maybe the Sioux had got you or you'd been buried in that rockslide across the way. Me, I think there are too many rockslides out here."

Laughing, Jean Patrick explained what had happened, then added, "What happened to you? We thought we'd find your scalp dangling from some Sioux lodgepole!"

"When we got separated during that storm, I found myself a cave to hide in," Sorrel replied with a grin. "The mules ran off. I still don't know why the Sioux didn't find them, but it would have served them right if there was feathers in the varmints' ears now. Anyway, I waited it out and then started searching for you, *mon ami.*"

Chapter Twenty-Five

✦✦✦✦✦

As they approached the second cabin, Sorrel called out, "Anybody to home up there, eh?"

They rode closer to the cabin and could see a figure framed in the open doorway. It paused, a shape against the darker background, then stepped into the open. Jean Patrick saw the glimmer of white hair shining in the fading light.

"Got some visitors!" Sorrel called again, cupping his hands over his mouth.

Michaella glanced nervously up at the cabin when there was no answer. Behind the cabin, framing it in a shimmering arch, glowed a large rainbow, stretching out across the canyon in a burst of color. The air was fresh and clean, and birds trilled in the dripping tree branches. The old man made his way down from the cabin and stood waiting, a hand over his eyes as he squinted toward them.

Mary Catherine gave a small gasp, and Michaella felt the hair on the back of her neck prickle. "Papa! Papa, is that you?" Mary Catherine cried out, sliding from her horse and running up the grassy slope toward the figure.

"Be careful!". Michaella called sharply after her sister as she bolted up the slope.

"Well?" Jean Patrick asked when Michaella made no move to go with her. "Don't you want to see if it is your father up there?"

Her dark, tortured gaze shifted from the man on the slope to Jean Patrick, and she whispered, "I'm afraid to. . . ."

"I understand. But you don't have to be."

She turned back to look as Mary Catherine raced—half stumbling, then lifting her tattered skirts with one hand—and suddenly envied her sister her simple emotions. It looked so easy, forgiving a human being who had hurt her, but it was so hard when the moment came. Why couldn't she be like her sister?

"You're not Mary Catherine, you know," Jean Patrick said, his uncanny ability to read her thoughts startling Michaella into jerking her head to face him.

"No, and I don't know if I want to be the daughter of a man who would leave without a glance behind him," she returned softly. "Jean Patrick—what do I do?"

"Talk to him. Then decide."

Nodding, she nudged her horse forward, her heart pounding in her rib cage like Sioux drums. Mary Catherine had reached the man and was throwing her arms around him and calling him Papa, and Michaella cringed. How could she call him Papa when he hadn't been there for her? When he hadn't cared enough to send word that he was alive?

Resolutely moving forward, Michaella finally reached them. She reined her mount to a halt and sat staring down with impassive features, watching as Henry Chattilion put his arms around his youngest daughter and gave her a welcome hug.

"So many years, so many years," he was saying over and over, and Michaella could not stop the words that tumbled from her mouth.

"Yes," she said sharply, "it *has* been so many

years! Why? Why did you abandon us? Why didn't you ever return? Did you know that our mother died of the flu after living a life of shame?"

Gently moving Mary Catherine away from him, Chattilion turned slowly to gaze up at his older daughter. "Michaella," he breathed softly, "you are the image of . . . How lovely you've grown."

"Am I supposed to thank you? Where have you been? Papa, *why* didn't you let us know you were alive?" she burst out in a surge of pent-up emotion.

"I couldn't," he said simply. "You were all watched. It would have meant my death."

"Your death? By whom?"

"Dismount, daughter, so that I may speak to you without craning my neck. I'm an old man, and I can't stand as long as I used to."

After a brief hesitation, Michaella dismounted and followed her father and sister into his cabin. It was scrupulously clean, with swept dirt floors and crude wood furniture bare of dust. She glanced around, then back at her father, waiting.

"I wanted to come back to St. Louis," he began, lowering his body into a sagging willow chair and gesturing for them to do the same, "but I would have been killed." He pointed to Sorrel looming in the open doorway. "He's been coming out for a long time to keep me up on what's been happening. He told me way back then that the company wanted to give my shares of stock to someone else. They knew I wouldn't stand for it, so they decided to have me killed. Old Sorrel here warned me."

Half turning, Michaella and Mary Catherine

ooked hard at Sorrel. "Why didn't you tell us!" Michaella demanded.

He shrugged sheepishly. "I wasn't sure if your papa was still alive. It's been a while since I was last out here, and I didn't want to tell you something that wasn't true. I wanted to wait and see what I found first. You see, he used to live in that little cabin by the gold, and the last thing I heard, he was gone from there. I'd already decided to come and check on my old friend myself when you two showed up in that grog shop."

"Grog shop!" Chattilion exclaimed with a skeptical glance at his daughters.

"We were looking for Sorrel," Mary Catherine explained when Michaella didn't answer.

Silence fell, then Michaella said slowly, "Well, Sorrel, perhaps that was the right thing to do after all. If you had told us our father was alive and we had come all this way to find him dead, it would have been very hard on Mary Catherine."

"And not you?" Chattilion asked softly, his keen eyes fixed on his daughter. "You would not care if your papa was dead?"

"Did you care if we were?" she countered.

"Hey!" Sorrel protested. "I never thought you would talk to your papa like that, Michaella!"

She turned on him. "Let him answer!" she spat, her hands curling into fists at her sides. Tension vibrated in her slender body, and Sorrel finally recognized her torment. He nodded.

Awkwardly, with outspread hands, Henry Chattilion said haltingly, "There was never a day that I did not think of you both. I missed your mother, and I missed my lovely little girls." When he saw her scornful disbelief, he gave a helpless shake of his head. "There is no way I can make up for those lost years, but I do have something to give you. I . . . I saved them over the years, in case this day ever came."

Rising painfully from the chair, he shuffled to a corner of the cabin and lifted the lid on a wooden chest. He bent over, and it took him a moment to collect several objects from the deep interior. When Henry Chattilion returned, he placed the things gently on his well-scrubbed table and stepped back.

"There they are. The things I made for you all these lonely years I spent away from my family. I had little to do, and I would think of you and wonder what you would like. I dreamed of you playing with this or that. . . ."

Tenderly, he lifted from the table a rag doll with a carved wooden face, the hair etched in great detail and the features painted with now fading paint. There were wooden picture frames and clumsily sewn scarves, cleverly detailed figures and blocks carved into the shapes of animals. As Michaella gazed at the pile of Christmas and birthday gifts Henry Chattilion had made for his daughters over the years, her throat clogged and her eyes filled with tears. She could barely see the face of the doll her father held out to her.

"Her name is Michaella," he whispered, and tears began running down the faces of parent and child.

Sobbing, Michaella put her arms around her faher at last. She cried for her mother, for the years lost to all of them, and for the bitterness she had stored so long. Then she cried for herself, for now she was free.

"I understand," Chattilion was murmuring over and over into her hair, his hand clumsily patting her back, her shoulder, the heavy mane of dark hair that was the exact shade his own had once been. "I understand. . . ."

Finally stepping back, Michaella stood with wet eyes and nose, and Henry handed her a scrap of cloth. "You never could remember a hanky when you were ten, either," he said practically, and Michaella had to laugh.

"But why is it the Sioux didn't kill you?" Jean Patrick asked Chattilion when they had gathered around the fire.

Smiling, Henry limped to a neat pile of pelts. He pulled a white one from the stack and held it up. "I used to have a lame white buffalo who would visit. The Sioux thought he was a spirit and I was calling him. I was sacred then. It scared them. They wouldn't come near me, and they still don't."

Mary Catherine and Spotted Wolf looked at each other and smiled. "Spotted Wolf and I saw a white buffalo way back along the trail coming out," she said. "It has brought us good luck as well."

Mary Catherine could see that her father was not wholly pleased by her relationship with Spotted Wolf. He, too, had been on the boat with Sorrel and the other men of the Ashley-Henry Expedition when the Arikara had killed so many of them.

"I've never felt good around a Ree," he said sternly.

"Times have changed," Jean Patrick said in behalf of Spotted Wolf and Mary Catherine. "Spotted Wolf has done a great deal for all of us. Mary Catherine couldn't have found a better man."

"Maybe not," Henry Chattilion said. "Maybe not."

Jean Patrick changed the subject to the Intermountain Fur Company and the piece of paper Nolan Ketchman had given him before he died. He explained to Henry all that had happened and what Ketchman and the five company men had set out to do initially.

"Well, I guess we don't have to worry about no gold no more," Henry laughed. "I never figured to ever mine it anyways. Nobody cares none about gold, really."

"There's a whole passel of folks who'd argue that," Sorrel said. "We brought a bunch out that's headed Californy way. They're crazy over a place called Sutter's Mill."

"I don't care about none of that now," Henry said with a wave of his hand. "I got my two girls back and I'm just as fine as fine can be."

"And you will have your share of the Intermountain Fur Company back as well," Jean Patrick said. "I believe your share is more than half. You will be able to get rid of everybody and start fresh."

"I ain't as young as I used to be," Henry said. "I'll need some young blood to get things off in the right direction. I've been hearing about you for years. I figure you'll do."

Jean Patrick smiled. "I'll do what I can."

Mary Catherine waited for her father to say something about Spotted Wolf and where he might fit in, but Henry didn't say anything more. He just mentioned that he had some things to pack before he could leave with them.

Spotted Wolf got up from where he was sitting and walked outside. Mary Catherine followed him out and found him sitting at the top of a small hill.

"Your father is happy that his two daughters have found him," Spotted Wolf said. "But he isn't happy about who is with his youngest daughter."

"He will change his mind," Mary Catherine assured him. "He's been cooped up here so long that he doesn't like anybody just yet."

"He likes Jean Patrick," Spotted Wolf pointed out.

"Please . . . things will work out," Mary Catherine said. "I know they will."

"Maybe," Spotted Wolf said. "Maybe they will. We will see after we reach my people. We must go there before we go anywhere else."

"I know," Mary Catherine said. "They will be expecting you back."

The others came out of the cabin, and after a time they had Henry's things packed on the mules. Henry wasn't too enthused about going up to Spotted Wolf's people; he said he hadn't spent ten years dodging the Sioux just to have his hair lifted by the Arikara. But Mary Catherine convinced him they owed it to Spotted Wolf to let him see his people. After all, he had done so much for all of them.

They kept their eyes open for Sioux as they began their journey back, but there was little chance that the remnants of the war party would be any threat. They had likely gone back to their band and would spend a long time mourning the many companions they had lost.

Henry Chattilion looked back one last time at the mountains he had called home for so long. The canyon that had caused all the furor was now choked with rock. It was strange to see it so changed and to think that just a few hours before it had been open and led to a fortune in gold.

That was all gone now, and no one seemed to care all that much. Henry was happy to be with his daughters, and Michaella and Mary Catherine were equally thankful they had found their father. Sorrel and Jean Patrick seemed cheerful enough, discussing the events of the day among themselves and the others. But Spotted Wolf was silent. He rode quietly and contemplated his future. He didn't know now how much Mary Catherine really loved him. As he thought about it, he resolved to himself that he would find out.

They traveled north and west from the Black Hills, across open prairie grasslands filled with buffalo. Mary Catherine offered her father many suggestions concerning Spotted Wolf and what he might do for the company once they got back to St.

Louis. But Henry Chattilion always changed the subject. Finally Mary Catherine let the subject drop completely.

She was now torn between her allegiance to her father and her love for Spotted Wolf. He said very little during the trip out from the Black Hills, except that he was anxious to see his people. He had the Sioux scalps attached to his rifle, and he was looking forward to the honors he would receive from all the Arikara people.

By late afternoon of the third day they arrived at the Arikara villages. Spotted Wolf led the way, fearing trouble if his people did not recognize who it was riding boldly along the river. He was not sure what to expect, but when the scouts from the village saw him they waved and whooped and called the villagers out to greet them.

Michaella watched Jean Patrick, who was concerned. He knew that Spotted Wolf was still not sure how he would be welcomed here with a lot of strangers accompanying him.

"We'll just stay back with your father and Sorrel," he told Michaella. "Spotted Wolf will manage this on his own."

Michaella tried to reassure Mary Catherine. But she remained fearful, keeping her position near Spotted Wolf.

"What's going to happen?" she asked him.

"My people are glad to see I have returned safely," he answered. "But they are concerned that I have brought all of you with me." He pointed to a brightly dressed warrior coming out toward them. "That is Man of Thunder, the chief of the village. I can tell he is not happy."

"Maybe we should leave and let you talk to your people alone," Mary Catherine suggested.

"No, I do not want that," Spotted Wolf said. "I want them to know that these are all my dear friends, and that you are to be my wife."

Mary Catherine sat on her horse with her head held high as Man of Thunder and the entire village came out. Women and children followed warriors on horseback, and all stared in curiosity.

As Spotted Wolf had anticipated, Man of Thunder greeted him first. Man of Thunder was the oldest of Spotted Wolf's uncles, brother to his now deceased mother. Mary Catherine listened closely while the two conversed in Arikara. She had learned a great deal of the language, but Spotted Wolf and the chief were speaking rapidly.

"You have been gone many moons," Man of Thunder began. "We did not expect you to return. We thought you had died in your quest for power."

"But I have returned," Spotted Wolf said with pride. He held up his rifle, lined with the Sioux scalps. "And I have returned with honor."

Man of Thunder grunted. Then he looked past Spotted Wolf with a noticeable frown, wondering what the whites were doing in his company. Spotted Wolf put his arm around Mary Catherine and held her close to him.

"This is Mary Catherine," he told Man of Thunder. "She is to be my wife. I would be happy if you welcome her to the village, and I hope she may become one of our people."

Mary Catherine was stunned. She and Spotted Wolf had not discussed anything about staying with the Arikara. What Spotted Wolf was telling his uncle now was all new to her, and she wasn't sure if she wanted to go along with it. If she said nothing and the village accepted them, it would look bad if she decided later to leave with her father and sister.

Spotted Wolf and Man of Thunder continued speaking. Spotted Wolf told the chief that he hoped to become the kind of chief the people wanted as he grew older. He also said that all the people with him were his friends and that they had saved his life. He hoped Man of Thunder and the other villagers would welcome them.

"Spotted Wolf," Mary Catherine said in a low voice, "before you say anything else to your uncle about our staying here, we have to talk."

"We can talk shortly," Spotted Wolf said. "My uncle wants to learn some more from me first."

Man of Thunder asked Spotted Wolf if he and Mary Catherine really intended to stay among the Arikara people.

"I want to please you, Man of Thunder," Spotted Wolf said. "This is why I am telling you these things. I have gone far away to gain medicine, as you have told me to do, and now I have returned. I hope this pleases you. Now I desire to be the chief that I am supposed to be."

Mary Catherine could detect a slight frown on Man of Thunder's face. He had turned aside from Spotted Wolf to confer with some of the other warriors near him. Mary Catherine suddenly realized that Spotted Wolf regarded Man of Thunder as a

father. She wanted to know for herself what Ma
of Thunder really thought of her.

"Would it make you happy if I was to becom
Spotted Wolf's wife and live here with you
people?" Mary Catherine asked him.

Man of Thunder was taken aback. He hadn'
expected Mary Catherine to know the Arikar
tongue, and he certainly hadn't expected her t
speak to him and ask such a point-blank question

"Why is this woman asking these questions?'
Man of Thunder asked Spotted Wolf.

"She is a good and brave woman," Spotted Wol
answered. "She wants you to be happy as well.'

"Then tell the woman that she is to listen whil
we speak," Man of Thunder told Spotted Wolf
"Tell her that she must know how hard it will be t
live here if you are a chief. Tell her how you wi
have certain duties to perform and that she mus
understand this and live with it. You must tell he
that in the future you will take other wives as suit
your position and that she will not be your first an
most special wife."

"Please ask Man of Thunder if he does not allow
women to speak to him directly," Mary Catherin
said to Spotted Wolf indignantly.

Man of Thunder turned to Mary Catherine. Hi
face was stern, but she didn't feel intimidated i
the least. She didn't care that he had been chief o
the village for a long time and had obviously kep
things going his way. And she wasn't going t
make it easy for him to take over Spotted Wolf'
will and tell him what things had to be like if he
wanted to stay in the village.

"Is there something that Man of Thunder would like to tell me about how Spotted Wolf's life will be lived?" Mary Catherine asked in a low voice. "I, too, would like to hear what you will be expecting of him, for I am to be his wife . . . his *only* wife. If that suits Spotted Wolf, I am certain his esteemed uncle should be suited as well."

Man of Thunder grunted. "It is good that you are a strong woman," he said. "But your strength will gain you only praise from me and nothing else. You are not part of this village, and since you hold no position here, I will not discuss with you the matters that are between myself and Spotted Wolf. No amount of talk from you will change that."

"Now I must speak with her," Spotted Wolf told Man of Thunder. Spotted Wolf walked a distance away and Mary Catherine went with him, her blue eyes filled with tears.

"Why didn't you tell me that you were thinking of staying here with your people?" Mary Catherine asked miserably. "When did you decide this?"

"I am aware of the way your father dislikes me," Spotted Wolf answered unhappily. "But that cannot be helped now. I am a man, Mary Catherine. I would not be happy being thought of as less than that. In my world, at least I would be a man."

Standing close to him, she said softly, "But Man of Thunder hates me! He would do his best to break us apart, and I am afraid, Spotted Wolf!"

Pulling her into his arms, Spotted Wolf said gently, "I will allow no man to insult my wife, including my esteemed uncle. Give him time, and as he comes to know you, he will realize how special you are."

"But what if I don't realize how special he is?" Mary Catherine inquired in a disgruntled voice, and Spotted Wolf chuckled.

"I will speak with him," he promised. "Go and wait with your sister, my flower. I will join you soon."

Sniffing, Mary Catherine took a reluctant leave from him and went to stand beside Michaella and the others. Her sister did not miss Mary Catherine's clouded expression.

"What's the matter?" Michaella asked.

Mary Catherine shrugged and gave her a brief explanation.

"Did you know this? I thought you said he was considering going back to St. Louis with us."

"He was," Mary Catherine said mournfully. "I don't know what made him change his mind. I think he wants to please his uncle."

Michaella put a sympathetic arm around her sister's shoulders. "I'm certain it will work out," she murmured, but Mary Catherine was too miserable to be comforted.

Chapter Twenty-Six

MARY CATHERINE WAS shaken because Spotted Wolf wanted her to stay with him among the Arikara. She knew she would have to tell him no, but she also knew she could never get over this man, and the disappointment would ruin her life.

"Maybe you should consider staying here with Spotted Wolf," Michaella suggested. "You love him very much. Maybe it would make you both happy."

"No," Mary Catherine said quickly, drying her eyes. "I know that the chief, Man of Thunder, would make it very hard for us. He has already made it hard for Spotted Wolf—I can see that clearly. But Spotted Wolf feels he has to prove his worth to his people."

"Are you sure Spotted Wolf doesn't want to go back to St. Louis with you?" Michaella wondered.

"Spotted Wolf does not feel welcome," Mary Catherine confessed. "He realizes that Father does not like him. Therefore, he is not at all eager to live near him. This is so hard . . . I don't know how to resolve it."

"Perhaps it will resolve itself," Michaella commented. "Jean Patrick and my problem worked itself out. You will see . . . your troubles will be over soon."

Spotted Wolf returned from talking with Man of Thunder and announced that they were to be guests of the Arikara for as long as they wished.

He led them all to a lodge reserved for visitors, and they arranged their belongings.

Michaella saw that Jean Patrick appeared uneasy. "What's the matter?" she asked him.

"I've been talking with Sorrel and your father," Jean Patrick said. "They feel most uncomfortable here. They remember all too well the night they were almost killed here over twenty-five years ago."

Then Jean Patrick told her briefly about the expedition that her father and Sorrel were both on led by William H. Ashley, which met with a disastrous fate at the hands of the Arikara. Many of the men were killed.

"But we aren't a bunch of eager men looking for furs," Michaella pointed out. "We aren't here to go into their lands and take advantage of them. In fact, we're traveling in the opposite direction. That should account for something."

"You're right," Jean Patrick said. "I'll try to encourage your father and Sorrel to stop worrying and have a little more faith in Spotted Wolf."

Michaella walked out of the lodge and let the men talk. Mary Catherine was gone, talking with Spotted Wolf, and Michaella took the opportunity to look around the village with interest. As in all Indian villages, there were numerous dogs and naked children laughing and playing, filling the camp with noise and excitement. The warriors proudly exhibited their war trophies and implements on their own persons and in front of their lodges.

She was most impressed with the artistry and ingenuity exhibited by these formerly nomadic Indians. There was a great deal of fine pottery to be seen near cookfires and in storage areas. Many of the women were just outside the village, tending huge gardens along the river. Michaella was amazed at the size and variety of the various squash and pumpkins and gourds, as well as the corn plants with the ears growing near the ground.

And she had never before seen living quarters such as those of the Arikara, like the lodge they had been given to stay in. All the people lived in large, round-domed earthen structures that remained a fairly constant temperature inside, though the weather outside could fluctuate between extreme heat and cold. She remembered Jean Patrick telling her that another tribe just upriver, the Mandan, lived in similar fashion.

Though the village was intriguing, Michaella realized that she would not want to stay here permanently. She was also quite certain that Mary Catherine would not. She could only hope her sister and Spotted Wolf came to some satisfactory resolution.

Late in the evening Mary Catherine returned to the lodge and sat down to talk with Michaella. She was still very perplexed about her future with Spotted Wolf.

"Spotted Wolf is talking with Man of Thunder again," she told Michaella. "I am very worried now."

"What's the matter?"

"There is to be a feast and dance tonight. Spotted Wolf told me that he and I are to be the principle guests . . . that we are to be seated next to Man of Thunder and honored in a special way."

"It sounds to me as if you and Spotted Wolf are to be welcomed into the community," Michaella observed, her voice now filled with concern.

"That is exactly how I see it," Mary Catherine said. "But that is not the way I want it."

Just then Spotted Wolf came into the lodge. He told everyone that they were to be welcomed at a feast very soon. Mary Catherine got up from her seat next to Michaella.

"Let's go for a walk," she pleaded. "I need to talk with you."

"We don't have time," Spotted Wolf said. "The ceremony is to begin very soon."

"Please?" Mary Catherine urged unhappily.

Relenting, Spotted Wolf put an arm around her waist. They walked along the river, beside the fields of corn and squash and pumpkins that flourished in the rich soil. Mary Catherine again expressed her dismay at what she had heard earlier. Spotted Wolf knew she did not want to stay in the village after her sister and father left for St. Louis. It was hard for her to understand why Spotted Wolf would ask that of her, especially when he knew how much her family meant to her.

"You know how much I love you," she told Spotted Wolf, "but I can't stay here. I should stay with my father and my sister." Her face was downcast and miserable.

"I believe it would be very difficult for me to live with you in St. Louis," Spotted Wolf said. "When I told you I thought I might like it, I'm afraid I was just wishing. You live in a very different world from mine. Out here in the wilderness we can live together. But back where there are big buildings and many white people, I would not be accepted. Your father has shown me that."

"But you would be with me," Mary Catherine argued. "And you know my father wants me to be happy."

"Why would that make any difference?" Spotted Wolf wanted to know. "You were somebody special until I joined you on the wagon train. Then all the people turned their backs on you because I am Indian. I saw it and you saw it also. They would turn their backs on you again. It would only be worse in a large city like St. Louis."

"You were there for a time," Mary Catherine said. "When you told me your father held a position in the American Fur Company similar to my father's, I thought surely you had grown accustomed to life in the city."

Spotted Wolf shook his head. He had been in St. Louis long enough to know that he did not fit, and he explained it to Mary Catherine.

"True, I learned to speak English there and I learned the white man's ways, but I was taught in an Indian school, not with the whites. They kept us away from the white children because they thought we were not as good as they were. So we learned the ways of the white man by ourselves and were never able to talk to white people."

Mary Catherine could see the reasons for Spotted Wolf's anger. But he should have told her the whole story in the beginning, before she had grown to love him so deeply. She knew he had remained silent because he didn't want to think about losing her. If they had discussed all this before, the chances that they would have stayed together would have been slight.

"What shall we do now?" Mary Catherine asked. "You know how much I love you. I couldn't bear to be without you."

"And I love you equally as much," Spotted Wolf said. "I don't know what we are going to do."

"Hold me," Mary Catherine said. "Just hold me for a while."

Spotted Wolf took her in his arms and they embraced. She began to tremble, fighting back tears. Spotted Wolf told her that he would always love her, no matter what happened. He could understand why she did not want to live with the Arikara, and he hoped she could see why he couldn't live with her people.

"But you have the blood of my people in you," Mary Catherine argued. "You could live with my people as easily as with yours. In fact, it seems to me that you are having to struggle to be accepted by your people. Your uncle, Man of Thunder, didn't really expect you to come back alive. And it seems he really didn't *want* you to come back alive. Isn't that true?"

Spotted Wolf knew: Man of Thunder had never wanted him around. He had been trying to please his uncle ever since returning to the Arikara as a young man. He realized he had never been able to make his uncle happy, no matter what he did. Even now, after he had come back with honors, his uncle was still not pleased.

"No, he didn't expect me to come back alive," Spotted Wolf said. "You are right, he does not really want me here in the village. I do not know why. It can't be because I have white blood in me. There are others with white blood as well."

"I think he is jealous of you," Mary Catherine said. "He is worried that as you grow older you will become a very good chief among the Arikara, and he does not want that. He wants to be the best chief the Arikara have ever had."

Spotted Wolf sat staring out over the river, realizing what Mary Catherine had just said was true. Then he heard a voice behind him. He and Mary Catherine turned to see a small boy standing nervously a short distance away on the trail.

"The chief says you and the woman are to come now," the boy said in Arikara. "The ceremony is beginning."

The boy turned and ran back down the trail. When Spotted Wolf looked at Mary Catherine, she could see anger in his eyes.

"He sends a small boy to tell us the ceremony is beginning," Spotted Wolf said. "He has no respect for me at all. Not even after coming back with honors."

Spotted Wolf took Mary Catherine by the hand and they walked back through the evening breeze. Under different circumstances it would have been a night to enjoy, but she knew that Spotted Wolf was now deep in thought.

In the center of the village a large assembly was gathering. Man of Thunder was seated in the center, surrounded by a number of honored men from various societies. Mary Catherine could see Michaella and Jean Patrick, together with her father and Sorrel, seated far behind most of the other villagers. She pointed this out to Spotted Wolf and he nodded. He had also noticed. Then he indicated to Mary Catherine a young woman seated just to the right of Man of Thunder, obviously a new wife he was taking.

"What does that mean?" Mary Catherine asked.

"That means he called a ceremony, and now he wants to be the most honored," Spotted Wolf answered.

"Where are we going to sit?" Mary Catherine asked. But she could see that Spotted Wolf had no intention of sitting down at all. He was staring hard at Man of Thunder.

"This will not take long," Spotted Wolf said. "Please wait with your father and the others."

Mary Catherine walked back out of the way, while all the villagers watched Spotted Wolf march toward the middle of the circle.

"You are late," Man of Thunder told him. "Why do you want to hold up your own ceremony?"

"Are you sure the ceremony was to be for myself and the woman I want to marry?" Spotted Wolf asked. "I see a young woman seated to your right, and I see that the important positions at the ceremony are for her relatives. In fact, I see that you have seated those who came with me far in the back. I do not call that a ceremony on behalf of myself or the woman I want to marry. I call this a ceremony on your behalf. Do you deny that?"

Man of Thunder rose to his feet, visibly angered. Now all eyes were on the two men in the center. The chief wanted to say something, but he knew better than to challenge Spotted Wolf. Instead, he tried to appease the young warrior.

"You are right. We will have a place prepared for your woman and yourself . . . and for the white people with you."

"It is too late for that," Spotted Wolf replied. "I will leave with those I came here with. I can see that I am not honored here. I will go to a place that honors warriors."

There was a growl from some of the warriors sitting in the crowd. Man of Thunder glared, but Spotted Wolf did not back down. He simply made his point even stronger.

"I came with the scalps of seven Sioux warriors," he said. "But there was no scalp dance. Now a ceremony that is to honor me and the woman I bring with me has no honor for either of us. I say that I have more honor than any of you here! And I can prove that I am a far better warrior than any of you here! Is there any among you who wish to show me that is not true?"

Mary Catherine held her breath. Spotted Wolf was challenging the entire village. She watched as Spotted Wolf looked around the circle of people, waiting for a warrior to stand to his challenge. There was none.

Spotted Wolf walked away from Man of Thunder and the circle, to where Mary Catherine stood waiting with the others. Jean Patrick looked at Spotted Wolf with admiration. Sorrel smiled and clapped him on the back. Michaella and Mary Catherine could both see that their father had suddenly changed his mind about this man. He had seen how much Spotted Wolf loved and respected Mary Catherine or he never would have challenged the entire Arikara village as he just had.

"I want to apologize for the way I've acted toward you," Henry Chattilion said, extending his hand to Spotted Wolf. "You're as fine a man as Mary Catherine could ever find. What's mine is yours."

Jean Patrick shook Spotted Wolf's hand as well as did Sorrel. Mary Catherine hugged him. The party gathered its belongings and packed the mules and horses. It was dark and the moon was nearly full, giving the land an open and silhouetted appearance. Mary Catherine began to feel the beauty of it deep inside her. Riding on a night such as this with Spotted Wolf riding beside her, was like a dream come true.

The Arikara all stood and watched as they got ready to leave. The small boy who had run out to tell Mary Catherine and Spotted Wolf about the ceremony came out from the village and brought Spotted Wolf a small bow with three arrows.

"Will you bring them back to me someday?" the boy asked Spotted Wolf. "And make them strong with your medicine." Then the small boy turned and ran back to the village.

"Let's go," Spotted Wolf said. "We have a long ride back to St. Louis."

The days passed quickly and the nights were warm and wonderful. The mountains were behind them now, with their high peaks that looked down on the wagon road, and that special circle of power called the Medicine Wheel. Now the quaking aspens, among whose white trunks they had made love and hidden from danger, were behind them as well.

Michaella reminisced about the trees with Mary Catherine. In her mind she could still see the dainty leaves moving gently in the breeze, as the trees flourished in the wet draws of the foothills and along the mountain slopes in the high country.

And she would never forget the tiny chickadees that flitted down from the pines to bounce along the ground, searching for seeds and bread crumbs. She thought of all these things and made plans with Mary Catherine that someday they would come back to see it all again and visit Meg at Fort Laramie. The mountains would always be with them.

But for now they all looked forward to the joys of being together and prospering with the soon to be newly managed Intermountain Fur Company. With the evidence in Ketchman's letter, Henry Chattilion would likely become sole owner of the company. He would see to it that things were run differently in the future, and he intended to make Jean Patrick and Spotted Wolf his full partners.

Old Sorrel just wanted to get back to his own shop in Independence. Michaella accused him of missing Fran, the wonderful seamstress who had first showed them how to divide skirts for riding.

One evening as they traveled through Kansas, Michaella walked with Jean Patrick along the banks of the Missouri River. She held his hand tightly and watched the sky turn the familiar deep crimson she had so often seen. On the crest of a hill, Mary Catherine and Spotted Wolf stood watching the sky, too. Michaella knew she would never forget the memories of all they had shared in the wilderness. And she would always have this man beside her, knowing how he made her feel free as the wind. She turned to him and smiled. Their love was forever.

Out of the pages of history, the stories of the women who shaped our nation...

Eastern heiress Lorena Makenzie is determined to make her own life in the West, yet is unprepared for the hazardous journey that awaits her. Her capture by the Cheyenne, and her encounter with the rough-hewn yet intriguing Ben Thorne, who seeks to rescue her, make this a radiant tale of passion and adventure!

0-517-00807-6 $3.95

ON SALE NOW!

A HISTORICAL ROMANCE